THE CRIMES OF ORPHANS

OBIE WILLIAMS

ISBN: 0692929681
ISBN-13: 978-0692929681

To my father, Larry
Who taught me to say what I have to say
and let the chips fall where they may

My mother, Becky
Who gave me her love of the written word
and showed me how to find sunshine
when the skies are grey

And my stepmother, Sue
Who told me that reaching for the stars takes work
and pushed me to raise up my ladder into the sky

ACKNOWLEDGMENTS

I am indescribably grateful
to Karen'Ann, Airyana, and Adison.
None of this could have been possible without their endless
wells of patience and understanding.

Also to Ilana
for all the dangling modifiers and everything in between.

To Mike
for being my first big fan.

To Victoria
for all of her encouragement and advice.

To everyone in LCdlR
for answering so very many odd questions.

To Annie and Lin
for guiding me in directions I never would have thought of on
my own.

And to A
for handing me the keys.

ONE

I

One of life's greatest blessings, Lita had once realized, goes completely unnoticed until it's gone. It is forgetting. Forgetting a terrible memory so completely that you forget there was anything to forget in the first place. It's just gone. Vanished. That is, until it comes back. And the memories always come back, one way or another, but most especially in dreams.

Her fitful slumber interrupted, Lita now sat up in the small bed and rubbed her temples gingerly. Though fragments of the dream still clung to her senses like phantoms—torn sundress; Bible on a wood floor; flames all around—she knew they would fade shortly. The pounding headache, however, wasn't going away any time soon. But perhaps one last drink would take the edge off, and then she could try to get some more sl—

A click touched Lita's ear and her left hand shot like a flash under the pillow, slim fingers immediately finding the grip of her subcompact nine-millimeter handgun. An instant later, its lone eye matched her gaze toward the bedroom door. As the knob finished turning and the door started to creep open, she moved her finger to the trigger.

But when a very large man stuck his bald head in the door, Lita released an annoyed sigh and lowered her weapon. "Fucking Christ, Cutter, don't you knock?"

Tyson Cutter was a force to be reckoned with. He could barely walk through a doorway without having to stoop, his chest was as broad as a whiskey barrel, and his arms looked like they had been carved from pillars of black marble. But despite the fact that he was a full foot taller than her and roughly twice her weight, he was afraid of Lita.

"Sorry to bother you, Lita, but Mr. Grant wants you back downstairs. Bar's gettin' busy again."

"What? It was dead when I came up here. What the hell time is it?"

"'Bout three hours 'til sunup."

She had been out less than two hours. The headache suddenly made a great deal more sense. "You tell that pile of shit to hold his fucking horses. I'll be down in five."

Cutter nodded, and then his eyes trailed down over Lita's body. The bedsheet had pooled at her waist, and she was wearing only a black sports bra.

Quirking a brow, Lita tapped her forefinger on the side of her firearm which, while lowered, still resided firmly in her grip. "Is there anything else, Cutter?" she asked flatly.

He shook his head and quickly closed the door.

Lita tossed the sheet away and stood, wincing at the stabbing pains in her feet that marked the first few steps of every day. She hadn't bothered undressing below the waist before passing out earlier. Her well-worn green camouflage pants were still tucked into her weathered combat boots. Crossing the room, she snatched up a black tank top that lay crumpled on the floor and pulled it on as she approached the old vanity that resided against the wall opposite the foot of the bed.

This tiny room above the tavern that Grant had set her

up with was simply furnished, but it suited Lita's needs. She had a real place, of course, back in Maple City. But since that was forty miles away, staying in this shithole most days had to do until she could earn enough cash to get a car. Besides, crashing here was better than hitching a ride home each morning with some drunk asshole who'd leered at her all night and only tipped a silverpiece.

At the vanity, she swapped her handgun for a hairbrush which she yanked through her wavy, straw-colored hair a half-dozen times—just enough to make it look less slept on. Then the brush was replaced with a bottle of vodka from which she took three strong gulps. Shuddering slightly, she set down the bottle and sighed, forcing the fire from her lungs. Her hands moved to the vanity's faded pine surface and she leaned forward until her nose nearly touched the mirror.

She stood for but a moment staring at emerald green eyes set into a face that looked a full decade older than her actual age of twenty-three. But as soon as her mind started drifting back towards her dreams, she shook her head and stood up straight.

"Time to work," she muttered, then took up her handgun, shoved it into the back of her belt, and headed towards the door.

An overwhelming combination of noise and light swarmed around her the moment she stepped out of her room. She squinted and groaned, her headache surging forth once again in the face of all the added stimuli. The tavern was only lit by oil lamps, but there were enough of them to keep it bright, even up here at the top of the twenty stairs leading to her lovely little loft. As she descended those stairs, she fished into her pocket and pulled out a hair tie.

"It's about goddamn time, Lita!" Grant hollered at her as she reached the hardwood ground floor of the Red Mare Tavern.

"Yeah, yeah," Lita muttered as she pulled her hair up into a ponytail and headed towards the bar.

II

Two hours later, a sleek black classic sedan slid to an abrupt halt on the edge of the clearing outside the Red Mare. Alex sighed and released his death grip on the leather sides of the front passenger seat. "You know, for being so protective of this car, you sure drive like you want to crash it."

"You'll live," Rain replied. He killed the engine and dropped the keys in his coat pocket.

Alex rolled his eyes and climbed out of the car. He stood by his open door for a moment, surveying their surroundings. Fifty yards to the left of the car stood the tavern. Although there were only two other vehicles out front, it was obvious from the noise inside that the place was busy. Folks traveled by foot a lot these days, and though they were miles from any established town, there was a sizeable logging community not far down the road.

To the right of the car, twenty feet away, the ground dropped off sharply in a forty-foot fall to a small lake below. Alex approached the edge of the cliff and peered down at the black water, which reflected the pale light of the nearly full moon above.

"One of these days, you're going to have to teach me how to swim," Alex said. He brushed a stray lock of blond hair from his dark blue eyes and looked over his shoulder to Rain, who had just stepped out of the car. Alex was only fourteen, but he was acutely aware that he should know how to swim by now.

"I'll get right on that," Rain said, then gestured towards the tavern and began heading that way. As he walked, he reached into the inside breast pocket of his long black coat and retrieved a cigarette. He produced a lighter next, and the flash of flint reflected in his eyes before the flame drew up, writhing around the tip of the cigarette. He snapped the lighter closed and took a deep drag, a soft orange glow illuminating his ashen features as he turned his gaze up towards the stars. Though the cities of Ayenee paled in comparison to those the world once held, their light still dulled the stars above. Out here in the woods, the whole universe appeared to be within sight.

Hurrying to catch up, Alex came to Rain's side and had to look up to speak to him. At just north of five feet tall, his head only came to Rain's shoulder. "How long are we going to be staying here?"

"I just need to get something to eat. We've got to make some miles before dawn." Reaching the large wooden double doors of the tavern, Rain shot a brief glance toward four men congregated near the corner of the building, but they didn't pay him any notice as he stepped inside the establishment with Alex following close behind.

Alex jumped a little as the door slammed behind him, then he looked to Rain. "I'll be over here," he said, gesturing to an empty table near the doors. He knew how quickly a situation could erupt around Rain, and he had learned to keep an exit nearby whenever possible.

Rain heard Alex but did not respond. He was busy scanning his eyes over the entire room, unconsciously taking a head count of the patrons. Five at the bar, twelve at various tables, seven others randomly milling about. Three employees as well: one female and two males, one of them very large.

Leaving Alex to his table, Rain approached the bar. He took a final drag from his cigarette and jetted smoke from his nostrils as he snuffed it out in a ceramic ashtray that sat upon the bar's smooth wooden surface. Pushing back the tail of his coat, he took up an empty stool and looked down the bar towards one of the tenders who had just finished serving a young woman.

He was a weathered-looking man, perhaps in his mid-sixties, with white hair and a sizeable gut. As Rain watched him, the man took notice of Rain, looked him over, and then nudged the large man that stood nearby. After the two had a brief hushed conversation, the older man finally made his way over.

"What can I get you, friend?"

"A glass of pig's blood," Rain replied.

The man took a slow, shaky breath. "We, uhh, we don't really serve that kind of stuff around here."

His gaze remaining locked with the man's, Rain slowly slipped a hand inside his coat. The man tensed and took a step back, then sighed when Rain retrieved a cigarette. Rain looked down as he lit it, then let his eyes draw back up to meet the man's once more.

"What's your name, Tender?" Rain asked.

"G-Grant, sir."

Rain took a long drag and allowed it to escape his nostrils, momentarily obscuring his face in a dense cloud of white smoke. "Look, Grant, don't lie to me," he said. His tone was perfectly calm as the smoke parted on the breath of his words. "If you didn't keep blood stocked, any vampire gang that roamed through here would tear this place apart." He drew two goldpieces from his pocket and dropped them on the counter. "That's three times what it's worth. Now just pour the drink."

Grant stared at him for a long moment, then asked, "Is deer okay?" Rain nodded, and Grant dropped out of sight to fish around in the small ice chest below the bar. He returned shortly with a glass in one hand and a crystal bottle full of red liquid in the other. He poured the drink, as ordered, and placed it in front of Rain. "There you go, friend. Just don't cause any trouble, okay?" Grant said warily as he took the goldpieces and put away the bottle.

Rain said nothing, only took up the glass and began to drink, taking drags off his cigarette between sips. As he watched Grant retreat to the far end of the bar, he idly wondered how old this blood was. He could taste cheap anticoagulant, and it had to have been thawed and refrozen at least half a dozen times. Rain shooed the thought away as his ears picked up a fragment of Grant and Cutter's conversation. When he heard Grant say, "that scar," Rain absently touched his fingertip to the deep, eight-inch-long mark that vertically intersected his left eye, fiery red against his otherwise pale skin. Most days he forgot it was even there. Preferred to, anyhow.

Across the tavern, Alex sat feeling relief as he watched the situation play out from afar. In the last tavern they had stopped at, the tender had made things significantly more difficult. Rain had reacted, well, as Rain would. However, Alex's concern surfaced once more as his eyes shifted to a man standing at the bar four stools down from Rain. That man had also observed the interaction and now watched with visible disgust pouring across his face as Rain sipped his meal. Alex groaned to himself as the man slammed his drink down on the bar and made his way towards Rain.

Approaching Rain's right side, the man smacked him on the shoulder with the back of his hand and said, "Hey, pal. We don't want your kind around here. This is a good tavern, and we don't need shit like you stinkin' it up." The smell of whiskey came off him in waves, both from his breath and the large wet stain on the red shirt that hugged his stocky frame.

Rain butted out his cigarette, turned his eyes to Red Shirt for a brief moment, and then disregarded him just as quickly, looking back towards the rack of bottles behind the bar. "Walk away," he said flatly.

Alex, watching the scene, drew a small silver switchblade from his pocket and depressed the button on its face. It snapped open with a quiet click and he held it close to his thigh under the table.

Red scoffed at the warning and reached out once more, this time grabbing Rain's sleeve. "I don't think you heard me, Vampire. I said I want you out of my goddamn tavern!"

Rain moved with such speed that Red never saw it coming. His right hand whipped out, fingers curling tightly around the man's thick neck. In one fell swoop, Rain lifted him off the ground and slammed him down on his back atop the bar. The ashtray fell to the floor, losing a chip and rolling away to hide beneath a stool. Leaning in close, Rain glared into Red's wide, disbelieving eyes. "I said walk away," he repeated, ominously enunciating each word.

Then, a huge paw of a hand landed on Rain's free forearm. Immediately releasing Red, Rain spun towards Cutter and thrust a single open palm into the man's huge chest, knocking him flat on his ass.

But when Rain turned back around to continue addressing Red, he instead found himself staring into the fierce green eyes of a woman who had stepped between them. Before he could blink, Lita shot her hands out and took up two fistfuls of his coat.

"Take it the fuck out of my tavern, or I'll take it out for you!" she yelled, then shoved him away. He took a step back, but did not break his gaze from hers. He didn't say a word, only stood and stared in surprise at the young woman. Alex even blinked twice in disbelief from his vantage point across the room.

Then Red slid off the bar to his feet and shoved Lita's shoulder from behind. "Hey, little girl, why don't you get back to work and let the big boys handle this?"

Lita's lips turned up into a snarl before she spun around and jutted the palm of her hand up into Red's nose. He stumbled back against the bar, but barely had time to reach up to his face before Lita grabbed a fistful of the messy brown hair on the back of his head and shoved him to the floor near where Cutter now stood. "I'm no fucking little girl," she spat. "Cutter, get this tub of shit out of here."

Cutter nodded and dragged Red to the door, then unceremoniously shoved him outside. Returning to the bar, he eyed Rain cautiously, then looked to Lita. "What about this guy?"

Rain looked to Lita as well, as if asking the same question.

"He didn't start the fight. He can stay as long as he doesn't stir up any more shit," Lita said. As Cutter headed back to the end of the bar, Lita gave Rain a questioning look. "You going to?"

"It wasn't my intention in the first place."

"Then take a seat; I'll pour you a drink," she said, motioning to the bar. "Grant is too chicken shit to come back over here." With that, she headed back around to the other side of the counter.

Alex sighed as he watched the scene play out rather uneventfully by Rain's standards. He folded up and pocketed his blade, looking back up just in time to see Grant approach.

"Can I get you anything?" Grant asked.

"Water would be fine, thank you."

Glancing over to the bar, then back to Alex, Grant asked, "Is your friend going to cause any more problems in my bar?"

"Not unless he's provoked," Alex said.

"Great, and he's talkin' to Lita? That'll go real fuckin' well," Grant muttered, then hurried off back to the bar.

Alex chuckled and looked back towards Rain and Lita, trying to get a feel for their conversation.

As Rain reclaimed his stool, Lita grabbed the empty glass that had held his meal. "What can I get you? More of this shit?"

"No," Rain replied. "Whiskey. Neat." He studied her curiously, finding her interesting. Abrasive, but interesting.

"The man knows how to drink, especially for an Ivy," Lita said, making a crack at Rain's slight southern English accent. Much of England had been left uninhabitable after the Last War, but St. Ives Bay was the primary port of departure for those emigrating to Ayenee, hence the slightly pejorative nickname.

She grabbed a clean glass and filled it halfway with golden liquid from a nondescript bottle. Brand names were hard to find these days, especially in a tavern this far from any major town. It was best not to think about where the alcohol came from and just be happy if it didn't cause any ulcers. She set the glass in front of Rain. "That'll be a gold and a silver."

Rain dropped two goldpieces on the counter before taking up his glass and gazing at her over the top of it. "You're not afraid of me." It wasn't really a question.

Lita raised her eyebrows, amused. "Should I be?"

"Most people are," he said.

Lita chuckled. "I'm not most people." Snatching up a rag, she began wiping down the bar. "You got a name, Vampire?"

"Rain Moonshadow," he replied. He had been raised to always introduce himself by his full name, and the lesson had stuck with him even after all his years.

Lita ceased her wiping abruptly, giving him an odd look. Goosebumps rose up on her arms.

Rain quirked a brow. "Problem?"

She shook off the daze and scoffed. "No, I'm just trying to figure out what the fuck kind of name 'Moonshadow' is. Sounds like some sort of bathtub gin."

Rain narrowed his eyes, quaffed the rest of his drink, and slid the glass back across the bar to her. "Well, while I'm alarmed that some tender in the middle of nowhere disapproves of my name, why don't you do your job and pour me another drink?"

Lita clenched her jaw, grabbed his glass, and did as such.

Rain paid, but this time did not tip.

"You're a real prick, you know that?" she said hotly.

"And you've got a foul mouth for such a little…" Lita leaned forward and Rain caught himself, "…woman." He immediately asked himself why he did that.

Lita ground her teeth together and turned away for a moment, tossing the rag onto the counter at the back of the bar. Spinning back around, she glared at him. "You know, you—" she paused, her eyes shifting past Rain towards the front door. A wide grin spread across her lips as she looked back to him. "Your friend is back, and it seems he brought a few of his own."

Before Rain had a chance to stand, a pair of hands landed on each of his shoulders. He moved to pull away, but they quickly yanked him off his barstool. He kicked his feet up, knocking the stool over, but two more pairs of arms took hold of his legs. He struggled, trying to free himself from the four men's grips, but was unsuccessful. The last thing he saw before being carried out of the tavern was Lita smiling and waving at him from behind the bar. "Tootles!" she called blithely.

Grant was just delivering Alex's water when the boy watched in alarm as Rain was carted off. Shoving past Grant, he ran over to the bar and yelled at Lita, "Aren't you going to help him?"

Lita shrugged. "Sorry, kid. As long as it's not in my tavern, it's not my problem."

"Dammit!" Alex yelled. He spun around and nearly tripped over a chair as he sprinted outside.

Lita leaned against the back counter and crossed her arms, watching the young man go. Grant approached her, interested in the scene as well.

"That's just weird," he mused. "I've never seen a human so concerned with a vampire. Never seen no vampire pal around with a human, either."

"I think they're brothers," Lita replied.

"What makes you say that?" Grant asked, looking to her.

"They have the same eyes."

"Huh. What do you make of it?"

"I don't know. It is curious though," she said thoughtfully, her eyes still not leaving the door.

III

Outside, Rain struggled against his four captors as they carried him across the clearing in front of the tavern. He caught glimpses of each of them as he tried to break free. There was, of course, Red. There was also one with brown hair, one in a green shirt, and one wearing a blue coat. When they reached the cliff on the edge of the clearing, they all suddenly dumped Rain on the ground. Before he had time to rise, Brown and Blue each grabbed one of his arms and yanked him to his knees. Green moved behind him, slipping an arm around his neck and holding him in a headlock. Rain glared up at Red furiously. "I gave you a chance to walk away."

Red issued a bark of laughter. His nose was already bruising, and his neck bore a blotchy impression of Rain's hand. "Oh yeah?" he said, "Well now I'm going to show you what happens when you start shit in my tavern." Reaching behind his back, he retrieved from his belt a two-foot-long sharp piece of branch that he must have snapped off a nearby tree. Holding it tightly in his fist, he advanced on Rain.

A nearly inaudible metallic click joined the conversation then, and Alex seized a handful of Red's hair, pulling his head back as he brought his knife's shiny silver blade up to the man's throat. "Let my brother go before I teach your friend here how to smile out of his neck." It sounded like something Rain would say, and Alex didn't particularly like it, but he knew he had to sound tough to make up for his size and age. He tried to keep his voice from wavering as he uttered the threat.

The three men holding Rain looked to Red questioningly, but his grin only widened. "Nice try, kid," he said before thrusting an elbow back, brutally connecting with Alex's ribcage, causing him to cough and stumble backwards. Red spun around and moved towards him. Alex swung his blade at Red's chest, but Red leaned back, dodging it before lunging forward and grabbing Alex's shirt with both hands. Throwing his significantly greater weight into the slender boy, Red turned and vaulted him straight off the cliff.

"Alex!" Rain yelled, moving to jerk away from the men in attempt to jump off the cliff after his brother. He managed to yank his arm free from Brown, but Green redoubled his efforts, holding Rain's throat tightly.

Alex heard Rain's cry, but it already seemed far away by the time it touched his ear. He was suddenly aware of how cool the night air was as it whistled by, bidding him farewell as he dropped towards the blackness below. He didn't realize he was doing it, but he screamed the entire way down, emptying his lungs and releasing the buoyancy from his body. When he hit the water with a violent and painful splash, he started to sink immediately. Icy pinpricks danced over his skin as the frigid water swirled around him, drawing him deeper into its swallowing darkness. He opened his mouth to scream, but nothing would come out. Instead, that coldness rushed in, filling his mouth and pushing at his throat, eager to fill his lungs and send him to an even deeper dark than this. As he thrashed wildly, struggling to make his way upwards, his hand fell open and his switchblade sank away, shimmering down into the forever below. He thought he was done for. Looking towards the surface, it seemed so far away now. He could see the light of the moon up there, peaceful and inviting. He wished he could grab hold of it and let it carry him out of this cold, dim place.

As he stared up at that picture of a moon getting further and further away from him, its image was shattered when something new hit the water. The last thing he was aware of as dizziness encircled his head were slim fingers curling around his wrist.

On the ridge, Rain glared at Red, fury growing in his eyes. Red only laughed. "Oh, did I hurt the vampire's feelings? Can't your poor little brother swim? Well you're next, asshole." He approached Rain, raising his wooden weapon high above his head, but then something made him stop in his tracks. Suddenly, the eyes Red was looking at were no longer blue, though they had been a moment before. No, those eyes had begun to glow a deep, turbulent violet. Red blinked. "I thought vampires' eyes were yello—" but he never finished his sentence.

Rain hollered with rage as he threw his head back, slamming it into Green's nose with a satisfyingly wet crunch. His neck freed with Green stumbling back screaming, Rain yanked his hand away from Blue and, in one fluid movement, punched Brown in the throat and shot his elbow back to collide with Blue's mouth. As all three men scrambled away from him, Rain vaulted to his feet, headed straight for Red.

Red tried miserably to swing at Rain with his sharp branch. Rain blocked the attempt with his left hand and swung his right fist in a blurred hook that shattered Red's cheekbone and most of his teeth on that side, knocking him out cold.

Looking down at Red's unconscious form and hearing his friends scatter, Rain forced himself to breathe slowly and suppress the rage that was urging him to keep pummeling the man, or worse. Finally, his eyes faded back to their normal blue and a brief wave of dizziness washed over him as he came back to his senses. He shook it off and dashed to the cliff, where he scanned the surface of the water for any sign of Alex. His gaze was drawn by movement on the shore below, and he saw someone kneeling over what appeared to be a lifeless heap. His senses were still too dulled by ebbing fury to make out if that heap was breathing. He took off in a dead sprint down the hill and towards the lakeshore.

IV

"Come on, kid, wake up," Lita said. Her wet hair hung in front of her face as she vigorously shook Alex's shoulders. He was breathing, so it looked like he had just passed out, probably from the shock of the fall. It was a good thing. If she'd had to breathe into his mouth she'd have been pissed. It was bad enough that she was wet.

Responding to her shaking, Alex awoke with a start, his eyes snapping open wide as his body jerked and he looked around frantically. He thrashed for a moment, but Lita held his shoulders firmly. "Whoa, take it easy. You took a big fall there, kid, but you're alright."

Rain reached them just as Alex was sitting up shakily, aided by Lita's hand on his back. "Are you alright?" he asked worriedly, dropping to one knee by his brother.

"Yeah," Alex croaked, then coughed wetly. "She saved me," he added.

Rain's eyes shifted to Lita and they locked gazes for a moment before both looked back to Alex.

"Thank you," Alex said after clearing his throat. "My name's Alex, by the way, and this is—"

"Yeah, we've met," Lita interjected. "Name's Lita." Rain gave her a nod and returned his attention to Alex.

"Can you walk?" he asked.

"I think so," Alex said. Rain took one of his arms, Lita the other, and together they helped him stand. He was a bit shaky at first, but soon found his footing.

"Good," Rain said. "Let's get you inside and dried off. We have to head out soon." He turned away from the two of them and began making his way back towards the tavern. After a few feet he looked down at his hand, noticing a smear of blood across it. He stopped walking and stared at it pensively. Finally, he stooped down to wash it off in the lake, then proceeded once more towards the Red Mare.

"A little thanks might be nice," Lita muttered as she watched Rain walk away.

"He's thankful," Alex said hoarsely. "He's just not good at saying it." Lita looked at the young man for a moment, then nodded. They both headed off after Rain.

When the three of them reentered the tavern, Rain returned to the bar to finish his drink. Grant approached the sopping messes that were Lita and Alex. "You know, Lita, you run out of here every time you want to go for a swim, an' I'm gonna start dockin' your pay."

"Fuck off, Grant," she said flatly and headed towards the stairs.

He chuckled, then looked to Alex. "You still up for that glass of water, kid?"

"I'll pass," Alex said, and headed to join his brother at the bar.

"No one appreciates my humor," Grant said, looking to Cutter.

"I thought it was funny," Cutter replied, smiling.

"I pay you. It doesn't count."

A short time later, Lita descended the stairs once more, rubbing a simple white towel through her hair. She tossed another to Alex as she approached the bar. "Here, kid, dry yourself off." Looking to Rain, she said, "You want one more, or are you driving?"

"Both," Rain replied. Lita raised an eyebrow. "Vampires can't get drunk."

"What the hell is the point then?" she asked.

"I like the taste."

Mouthing an, "Oh," Lita poured him one more drink. He slid five goldpieces across the counter and she snatched them up eagerly.

"Hey, Lita, I almost forgot. This came in for you earlier tonight while you were passed out," Grant said as he approached her with a white envelope in hand. Across its front was written simply, *Lita – Red Mare Tavern.* Taking it from him, Lita looked it over curiously. It was a rare occurrence to receive mail these days. There was no official service to speak of outside the major cities, and it was difficult to find couriers who could be trusted.

She was about to tear open the envelope when she noticed Grant was watching her intently. She opened her mouth to tell him to mind his own damned business when his attention was pulled away by customers approaching the far end of the bar. Returning her own attention to the envelope, she opened it and retrieved a single-page letter. As she read it, the color drained from her face. Once she had finished, she folded it carefully and slipped it into her back pocket, her fingers brushing over her handgun as she did. That had been quickly disassembled, dried off, and its bullets replaced upstairs before she had even touched herself with a towel. Just walking from the lake back to her room with a potentially unusable weapon had been enough to set her teeth on edge. Much like that letter was doing

17

right now. Leaning against the back counter, she crossed her arms and stared down at her feet thoughtfully.

"Are we heading out soon?" Alex asked Rain, who was sipping his drink and halfway through a cigarette.

Rain retrieved a small silver pocket watch from inside his coat. "Dammit," he said quietly. "Yes. We'll have to get moving if we're going to find an inn in Maple City before dawn."

Lita's eyes snapped up and she looked to Rain. "Did you just say you're going to Maple City?"

Rain eyed her. "I did. What of it?"

"Fuck, I can't believe I'm going to ask this…" she muttered, then said louder, "Do you think I could hitch a ride with you?"

Rain scoffed. "What in hell makes you think I'd do that?"

"Well, I did save your brother's life," Lita shot back.

Rain looked to Alex, who shrugged. "It is only fair."

Rain fell silent for a time, thinking. Finally, he sighed and said, "You've got ten minutes."

"I just need five." Lita said before rushing out from behind the bar and bounding up the stairs. Rain shook his head, downed the rest of his drink, and looked to his brother.

"If I end up regretting this, I'm going to bring you back here and toss you off that cliff myself."

Alex laughed, though a bit nervously. Rain didn't often make jokes.

True to her word, Lita descended the stairs again not five minutes later, a large stuffed knapsack slung over her shoulder. Even on the occasions that she stayed at the Red Mare for several days at a time, she never unpacked more than she could pack back up in just a few minutes. Of course, she did that anywhere she stayed.

"We ready?" she asked as she met up with Rain and Alex.

"My car is out front," Rain said, pulling his keys from his pocket. Lita nodded and followed him towards the door. Behind the bar, Grant looked up to see that his employee was heading out looking packed for a trip.

"Hey, Lita! Where the hell are you going? You walk out on your shift, I'm firing your ass!"

Turning around but continuing to walk backwards, Lita grinned. "Fine, fire me then, Grant. You're an asshole anyway!"

Coming out from behind the bar, he said, "I can't fire you, you're my only tender!"

"Then I quit!" she hollered, turning around to head out the door.

"You can't quit! You're fired!" he yelled.

"Fine then!" she yelled back, waving a dismissive hand over her shoulder as she stepped outside.

Rushing after her, Grant stood in the open doorway and called out, "Will you be back by next week?"

Lita didn't answer.

TWO

I

How can I be a leader when I'm barely even a woman?

As Lita was jolting awake from her nightmare, Amelie was asking herself this same question that she had been pondering a lot these days. She found it especially came to her at times like this, when she would look over herself in the vanity mirror that sat in her luxurious bedchamber, examining every inch of a body that seemed trapped in some strange place where it was neither child nor adult. She absently drew a brush through her auburn hair as she stared at that lithe form that felt both completely hers and entirely foreign at this peculiar age of fifteen.

She set her hairbrush down and ran her hands along the bottom of her hair, allowing some of it to fall forward and cascade over her shoulders, down to her small breasts. Normally, she preferred to pull her hair back into a tight braid that would lie straight down between her shoulder blades like a dead snake. It was easy to manage and it kept it out of her face. But she knew her father preferred to see her hair down, and since she was bordering on some of the last memories she would ever have with him, she wanted to look the way he liked her best: hair free, simple dress, and no makeup.

He liked it because it reminded him of a time when her mother was still alive. She disliked it for the same reason.

Pushing away the containers of blush and various beauty creams that cluttered her desk, Amelie laid her head down on folded arms. Her eyes drifted closed for a moment, and she began to think of all the responsibilities she was about to undertake.

II

Chicane was one of the founding cities of Ayenee, and at well over a century old, was still the fastest growing of all. When pilgrimage to the manmade eighth continent began, with it came the last semblances of Old World religion, and Chicane was founded upon predominantly Roman Catholic beliefs. Once heralded as the "Vatican of the New World," much of the city's architecture was modeled after that of the now-crumbling Roman metropolis. Throughout most of the city, a person could barely turn a corner without encountering a nearly smothering religious presence all about. However, this was but a sanctimonious surface thinly covering a much darker underbelly.

Chicane was the place to go if a person needed a gun. It housed the largest groups of weapons manufacturers and dealers in all of Ayenee, only rivaled in the world by the shadowy Black Forest group in Ireland—Ayenee's closest neighbor to the northeast—which provided weapons to the entire Irish Army. Furthermore, Chicane was virtually the only city in Ayenee where one could easily procure almost any drug of choice—from concoctions similar to Old World heroin and cocaine, to the newer, darker substances like Black Sapphire and the Skeleton Herb, which brought about vision-like hallucinations and were even rumored to stir supernatural abilities in humans who were not previously among the subset of society that already possessed them— the Gifted.

The city was not without political dissent as well. Its monarchical government was prone to violent coups led by men who believed they could run things with a holier iron fist than whoever held it last. The present ruler, Lord Richard Lamoureux, was the first leader to come into power by bloodless means since Lord Chicane himself had passed away. Lamoureux's predecessor had been assassinated, but no one moved to take control, so an election was held. Richard—widely revered as the headmaster of the Chicane Academy for Higher Learning—won the election by a considerable margin.

It had proven to be a sound decision on the part of Chicane's citizens as the city seemed to have run more peacefully than ever in the twenty years since Lamoureux took control. However, Richard was less a peacemaker and more a leader skilled at hiding things. He was a loving and stalwart man, but the darkness that crept through his city was too much for him to banish on his own. Thus, he found quiet places to tuck it, keeping his people under the false impression that their home was indeed the holy place they believed it to be.

Unfortunately, even a man such as Richard Lamoureux could only hide the evils of Chicane for so long before they began to gather around not only his city, but himself as well.

III

Amelie jerked her head up from near-slumber as a quick rapping came upon her door.

"Come in," she called.

The door swung partially open, and a rather muscular

man clad in a long-sleeved navy blue shirt—standard attire for High Palace guards—stepped halfway inside.

"Your father will see you when you are ready, Miss Lamoureux."

"Please, Christopher, for the last time, you may call me Amelie," she said with a smile as she stood and crossed the room to him. She had never understood the notion that she should be looked up to simply because of the family into which she was born. The man was nearly twice her age. He shouldn't have to refer to her as "Miss" anything.

Christopher chuckled as he stepped back, holding the door open for her. "Yes, Miss La...Amelie."

"Miss Lamb-a-lee?" she giggled. "Well, it's halfway there, I suppose." She patted him affectionately on the shoulder and he smiled. The two parted in opposite directions, Christopher to go about his rounds and Amelie to visit her father.

Making her way down the hallway towards his bedchamber, Amelie licked her lips, finding her mouth suddenly growing dry. With each visit to her father over the last few weeks she had become increasingly anxious, knowing it was only a matter of time before she would have to say goodbye to him forever. Every time she walked in, she feared he was already gone.

Around the next corner, the hallway ended abruptly at large oak double doors. Next to one of these doors stood Michael Calderwood.

Michael had been married in as Amelie's stepbrother four years before, less than twelve months after the sudden death of her mother. She did not blame her father for this, as she knew he had loved her mother, but his position demanded that he again take a spouse as soon as possible. The proceeding union had been born out of politics rather than passion. The Lord must have a wife; that was the church's firm stance. Amelie never cared much for Marietta, her new stepmother, as she was an overbearing and demanding woman who expected far too much from her father, in the girl's opinion. However, she was nevertheless saddened when the woman passed away from a brief and severe illness less than a year into the marriage. After his second wife had died, Richard refused to remarry once more, despite the church's most vehement urging.

Michael was thirty months his stepsister's senior, and had just turned eighteen the month before. He was a slim, wan young man, so much so that he often looked quite ill. The fact that he all but exclusively wore neatly pressed black suits did not serve to improve his almost ghastly appearance. He was nonetheless a reasonably handsome boy, always well-kept and clean-shaven no matter the occasion.

He looked a little startled when Amelie came around the corner, as though he had been lost in thought. "Oh," he said. "Hello, Amelie. How are you this evening?" He offered her a tight smile.

Amelie returned his smile. "I'm well enough, given the circumstances." For a moment, the second half of her sentence seemed to linger in the air. Between close family and friends, such a statement would have spurred conversation about the circumstances that had brought them both to this door. But despite having lived with Michael for nearly a third of her life, Amelie still felt as uncomfortable speaking to him as she would an acquaintance, and she suspected he felt similarly. Finally, after the awkward silence drew out longer than she could stand, she added, "And you? Are you well this evening?"

"I suppose so," Michael said with a sigh. He often responded to such questions that way, and Amelie had never quite figured out what he meant by it. "Shall we?" he asked, reaching for the door, and when Amelie nodded he opened it for her, motioning for her to go first.

At the age of sixty-three, Richard Lamoureux was not an old man by any means. Amelie's birth had been a gift to him and her mother late in life, long after they'd given up on the possibility of children when many attempts had ended in failure. Richard had always told his daughter that God was waiting for the right moment to place her in his arms, and that she had certainly been worth the wait.

Looking at him now, Amelie found it difficult to recall the energetic, life-loving father who had raised her. Lying there under his blankets, Richard was nothing more than a pale, emaciated ghost of the man he had been. His once regal, reddish beard now hung from sunken cheeks and his hair was matted from the sweat of near-constant fever. The leukemia had come on quickly, ravaging his body in only a few months. Staring at the man she had always adored so much, Amelie felt her stomach turn at the thought that his end was nearer than ever.

All of that seemed to disappear for a moment, however, as Richard's crystal blue eyes slipped open and briefly revealed the younger man he once was. "Well hello, you two," he said in a hoarse but cheerful voice. "Come closer, please. Don't look so frightened."

They both approached the bed and Amelie moved to the left side, closer to her father, whereas Michael lingered to the right. Pulling up a chair that had been placed nearby, Amelie sat down and slipped her hand into her father's. She squeezed it lovingly and gave him a gentle smile. Michael remained off to the side, his hands clasped tightly behind his back.

"All of your affairs are in order and taken care of, sir. You can rest easy knowing Chicane will be in good hands," Michael reported, and while Richard looked up to him with a thankful smile and a nod, Amelie frowned, wishing he was more tactful.

"That's a good boy, Michael," Richard replied. "I'm glad

your mother left me with such a dutiful son. Between your drive and Amelie's compassion, I know you two will take good care of my city."

Amelie felt her heart sink a little. Though she had never questioned her father's love for her, she knew that he had always secretly wanted a son as well. But her birth had been miracle enough, one not destined to repeat itself. Because of this, Richard seemed sure that Michael was the perfect son he had always wished for. And while Amelie had no real reason to doubt that, she was nonetheless nervous about sharing such enormous responsibility with a person she could barely even hold casual conversation with.

"And how is my lovely daughter this evening?" Richard asked, looking to Amelie.

"I'm well, Father. It's nice to be able to visit you before bed."

"It's nice to see you as well, darling. You know I've never spent a single night in the same house as you without giving you a goodnight kiss."

Blushing in a way that only a parent can bring out in a teenage daughter, Amelie smiled and looked down. "I know, Daddy."

A silence fell over the room, and Amelie could find nothing else to do but gaze upon her father, wondering how many more moments of this she would get before he finally passed out of her life. He returned her look for some time, a sad sort of smile on his face as he himself wondered how much time he had left with his beloved daughter. Michael shifted his weight, visibly uncomfortable. Noticing this, Amelie opened her mouth to break the silence for his sake, but instead all three turned their attention towards the sound of the bedchamber door opening.

A lovely woman in her mid-thirties entered, sweeping her curly black hair back behind her shoulders as she strode across the room carrying a small cup of pills and a glass of water. Reaching the end of the bed, she nodded to everyone and then smiled to Richard. "Sorry to interrupt the family gathering, sir, but it's time to take your medication."

"That's just fine, Norah," Richard replied. "How is Charles doing?"

"He's doing very well, sir. He wanted me to apologize that he hasn't visited in a while. The new semester is starting and he's got a lot on his plate. He does send his best wishes though." As Norah spoke, she made her way around the bed to Richard's side, slipping past Amelie as she did. "Excuse me, honey." Amelie nodded courteously and stood, pushing her chair back so she wasn't in Norah's way.

"Isn't that just like Charles?" Richard said, his eyes taking on a reflective gaze. "If he wasn't teaching someone something, I don't think he'd know what to do with himself." The nostalgic look was quickly replaced with one of marked strain, however, as he tried to force himself into an upright position. He couldn't even make it halfway.

"That's good enough, sir. Here," Norah said as she pushed up his pillows behind his head. She handed Richard the pills, and he tossed them into his mouth before graciously accepting the water. He swallowed just enough to chase the pills, but then suddenly fell into a terrible coughing fit.

By the time it finally receded, Richard's ghostly face had turned deep red. He slipped back down in the bed, looking even more tired and haggard than before. Norah took his wrist gingerly into her hand, checking his vital signs. His flesh looked almost translucent contrasted against her dark brown skin. She sighed, offering a less-than-hopeful gaze to both Amelie and Michael, to which they both nodded solemnly.

Then the silence of the room was abruptly broken once more, but this time with far greater vigor as the bedchamber door flew open. "Mommy Mommy Mommy!" the little girl yelled as she bolted across the room and crashed into Norah's leg, wrapping her small arms around it tightly. She was between three and four years of age, a cute girl with soft, simple features. Chestnut eyes matching her father's and dark hair that mirrored her mother's, only braided into two short pigtails.

Reaching down and picking up her daughter with an "Oof," Norah hoisted the child's buttock onto her hip and wrapped an arm around her waist. The little one reached up and circled her own arms around the back of her mother's neck.

The arrival of the child brought instant smiles to Amelie and Richard, and some of the gleam even returned to Richard's eyes. Michael, however, suddenly appeared very uncomfortable. He shifted his weight back and forth and wrung his hands behind his back.

"Charlotte, I asked you to stay in the parlor," Norah scolded. "I said I would be back in just a moment, didn't I?" Charlotte dropped her eyes.

Letting out a low chuckle that was rounded out by a slight cough, Richard said, "Oh, it's quite alright, Norah. It's nice to see her again." Then, to Charlotte, "You're getting big, child. How old are you now?"

"Three and three fourths!" Charlotte replied proudly.

"She's a bright one, Norah," Richard said admiringly. "Looks as though you may have another teacher in the family."

"Just what we need," Norah said sarcastically.

"Nuh-uh!" Charlotte cried. "I'm gonna be a doctor!"

"You should be a nurse sweetie. They're the ones who really know everything," Norah said, giving Richard a wink.

Michael stepped forward then and cleared his throat. "Nurse Winters, may I speak with you out in the hallway, please?"

"Of course, sir," Norah replied. "Come on, Char. Let's

get you back where you belong." With that, she headed towards the door. Glancing over her shoulder, she said, "I'll be back to check on you in a short while, sir." She then nodded to Amelie. "Ma'am." Richard and Amelie both smiled and nodded in return.

"And I will leave you two for the night," Michael said, giving Amelie and Richard a nod as well. "I hope you both sleep well; especially you, sir." He then departed after Norah, closing the door behind him.

IV

Out in the hallway, Norah set Charlotte down and turned to Michael. "What can I do for you, sir?"

"I believe we have spoken in the past about bringing your daughter here with you, haven't we?" His voice low but noticeably tense.

"Yes, sir, I know we have. But my nanny didn't show up today, and I thought since Lord Lamoureux doesn't seem bothered by her that—"

"Ms. Winters," Michael interjected, "if we are to ease transition once my stepfather passes, it is imperative that I can count on staff members to follow orders under new leadership. Is that understood?"

"Sir..." Norah began.

"I said is that understood?" Michael repeated.

"Sir, you're hurting me," Norah said, alarmed.

Michael blinked and looked down to find that he had taken hold of Norah's upper arm and was squeezing tightly. He immediately jerked his hand away and took a startled step back. "I-I apologize, Ms. Winters. I don't know what I was thinking. It's been a very strenuous few weeks and I am very tired. Are you alright?"

Norah took a deep breath and nodded, rubbing her arm. "Yes, I'll be fine, sir. I understand your tension. Lord

Lamoureux's illness has hit us all very hard. I apologize again for Charlotte. I'll make sure it doesn't hap—"

Michael held up a hand. "Your presence here is important enough for Richard's care that we cannot risk your absence. If you absolutely must bring your daughter with you, I can have one of the maids watch her so she is not wandering the palace unattended." Michael then looked down as he felt a tap on his leg.

"I get grumpy when I'm tired too. It's okay," Charlotte said, looking up at him. He responded with a thin smile.

"It's true," Norah said with a nervous laugh, "she really does. But anyway, thank you, sir. I'll do my best to get in touch with my nanny, and will come see you right away if I can't."

Michael nodded. "Thank you. That will be all, Ms. Winters." He watched as mother and daughter departed down the hall. As soon as they were out of sight, he closed his eyes and balled his hands into tight fists, then took three deep, shuddering breaths. When he opened his eyes again, they were glassy with tears. He wiped at them quickly, then straightened his suit, cleared his throat, and started making his own way down the hall.

He walked briskly, but in a dignified sort of way that was almost prissy. His shiny shoes made rapid, soft whispers on the plush hall carpet. As he rounded the corner to proceed the opposite way that Norah had gone, he retrieved a small gold watch from his pocket, paid it a quick glance, and then made it disappear again, never breaking his stride.

A short time and several nods to various guards and staff later, Michael was walking along the footpath that crossed the east garden and led to the front door of a small, private chapel reserved solely for the Lord and his family. Though the ruler did make occasional appearances at Sunday mass in the various large churches scattered throughout the city, most of his worship was done in this much more secure location.

Along the path, on alternating sides every dozen feet or so, small oil lamps burned atop slender metal poles. The palace itself had electric lights in every room, but walkways and outbuildings were all lit by flame. On either side of the chapel's double doors, there was a smaller, handheld lamp sitting on a round metal shelf. Michael took up one of these and entered the house of worship.

The lamplight barely cut through the darkness inside, and Michael had to squint to find the pillar candle mounted on a pole at the end of the back right pew. Once that was lit, it was much easier to find each successive one down all six rows. There were matching candles on the opposite side of the aisle, but he didn't bother with those. No other worshippers would be joining him at this time of night, and the palace priest had retired to his quarters hours ago.

Finding a seat at the far-right end of the second pew, Michael snuffed his lamp and bowed his head. He wasn't there long before a large figure emerged from the shadows near the altar and took his own seat in the front row, his back to Michael.

"How are things progressing?" Michael asked quietly, his head still bowed.

"Behind schedule," the man replied in a deep, gravelly voice. "The workers seem to think they won't be able to complete the Construct in time."

"You know that will not stand," Michael said, raising his eyes. In the scant light, he could only make out a silhouette of the man's broad shoulders and wide-brimmed hat.

"Agreed," the man replied. "How would you like me to proceed?"

Michael felt his hand wanting to curl into fist, but he took a slow breath and instead forced that hand to reach for the small medal that hung from a thin chain around his neck. He rubbed it between his thumb and forefinger, focusing on the feeling of the bumps and grooves that made up the words "Pray For Us" on the back and the image of Saint Monica on the front. Finally, maintaining a flat calm in his voice, he said, "I want you to motivate them. However one motivates a vampire, I'll leave to you. I don't care to even think about the fact that such a holy place is being built with their hands."

"Yes, well, they're stronger than humans and easy to keep captive under the right conditions. They won't be a concern once the job is done," the man said.

"Good. And what of your..." Michael cleared his throat, "...creature? Has it had any further luck?"

"The *Visgaer* is getting closer with each passing hour. *He* knows the Catalyst has been moved about Ayenee for the last week or so, but he senses it drawing closer to Chicane now. It shouldn't be more than a day—day and a half at the most—before we're able to locate it." The man emphasized the creature's species and gender with more than a touch of annoyance in his voice. He may not have chosen a proper name for his pet, but that didn't excuse referring to him as some kind of thing.

Michael either ignored the emphasis or missed it altogether. "That cuts it nearly as close as the Construct, but I suppose it will have to suffice. As for your employee?"

"Procuring a specialist as we speak. Scheduled to arrive tomorrow night."

"And you are sure we can trust his judgment? His kind are—"

"*His kind* have no bearing on my faith in him," the man snapped. "He is the only person I trust to recruit in my stead. I would happily do it myself, but the additional layer of ignorance will strengthen your deniability. Believe me, you'll want that after a job like this."

"There are no jobs like this," Michael sighed. "I only

pray I am strong enough to shoulder the burden."

"You're not having second thoughts, are you?" the man asked, turning to look back at Michael for the first time.

"No, of course not. At times I just wonder what...what God saw in me that made Him decide I was the man for this duty."

"You'll have to take that up with someone holier than me," the man said, rising to his feet. "I'm no priest."

"You do see the irony in you saying that, right?" Michael asked, amused.

"It's not lost on me," the man said. He took a step to leave, then stopped again. "Whatever the reason this thing fell to you—holy or otherwise—I feel I should point out once more that going through with it will throw away countless resources of almost limitless potential. Resources that could be very useful to you as Lord of Chicane."

Michael dropped his gaze and was silent for a moment. When he finally looked back up, candlelight reflected in the glassy tears that had filled his eyes. "I have no choice," he said, barely above a whisper.

The man just shrugged. "Your money, your call." And just before disappearing into the shadows towards the rear exit of the chapel, he added, "I won't contact you again until after the specialist's job is complete."

When Michael was sure the man was gone, he stood and went to his usual spot on the long prayer kneeler that sat facing the pulpit. There, he carefully removed his suit jacket, tie, and shirt, meticulously folding each and stacking them neatly on the cushion next him. Then, from the narrow recess under the kneeler, he retrieved a long willow switch. Though he would receive absolution from Father Francis come morning, he must still carry out his own penance in the manner his mother had taught him. So ingrained were her teachings that he had calculated his punishment within seconds of committing his transgressions. One lash for his loss of patience with a mother and her child, two for neglecting the virtue of charity by not immediately offering care for the child in the mother's time of need, and five for laying his hand on a woman in anger.

As Michael carried out his punishment, each sharp smack of the switch across his back was followed almost immediately by the appearance of a reddening weal. But though he had engaged in this form of contrition since before he could remember, he had only a few very faint scars to show for it. On many occasions, he had chided himself for lacking the strength of will to more permanently mark his flesh with proof of his devotion to the Lord.

Maybe soon, he thought to himself as he put away the switch and gingerly put his clothes back on over his stinging wounds. *My will is about to be tested more than it ever has before, so maybe after it will be strong enough.*

He relit his lamp and blew out candles on his way towards the front of the chapel. Pausing at the door, he looked back up towards the altar, its large crucifix nearly imperceptible in the darkness. A brief prayer asking for strength passed noiselessly over his lips, and then he slipped outside into the night.

V

Back in Richard's bedchamber, Amelie laid her head softly on the bed by her father's side and looked up at him with mournful eyes.

"What am I going to do without you, Daddy?" she asked, trying to keep herself from crying as she spoke. That was certainly no way for the first-ever Lady of Chicane to act.

Offering her a reassuring smile, Richard reached over and ran his fingers through her hair. "You are going to do wonderfully, my dear. Don't you worry."

"Are you sure you don't want to hold an election? Perhaps Charles could run. Surely he would—"

"No, no child. This is the way it should be. There is too much risk of corruption with an election. I was fortunate to win, but such luck may not happen again. It's only right for the role to be taken by those who were raised to do it. I believe the time has come for the position to be held by two instead of one, and a woman's touch would certainly do this city some good."

"But I'm still so young, Father," Amelie said, her voice almost pleading.

"I see the woman you're turning into, and she's going to do great things," he said tiredly. "You remind me so much of your mother, you know that?" His reminiscence had taken on a melancholy tone, the mark of a man not long for the world.

She smiled in a sad sort of way at the compliment and looked down at her hands. "But what of Michael? You seem so certain he is right to lead by my side, but sometimes I feel like I barely—"

"You needn't worry, my dear. I know that you and Michael have yet to form a bond, but you no doubt will when working so closely together. You are very different people, and I'm not such a fool to think you won't conflict on a great many things. But with your combined effort, I'm certain you will turn Chicane into the holy land that it was meant to be."

"But Father, I—" Amelie began, her eyes starting to glimmer with tears.

"You will make me proud. Both of you," Richard whispered as his eyes slowly drifted closed.

Sighing deeply, Amelie blinked back the tears and once more laid her head by her father's side. Her hand found his and squeezed it firmly. She wished that if she held on tight enough he might just never leave her. As her own eyes grew heavy, a single thought danced tauntingly across her mind just before slumber dragged her down as well.

How can I be a leader when I'm barely even a woman?

THREE

I

Lita let out a low whistle as the three approached Rain's vehicle outside the Red Mare Tavern. "This is one helluva car, Vampire. How'd you two manage to get your hands on it?"

"Bought it in 1963, the year it was built. Stored it a couple of decades later. Got it out a few years ago," Rain replied. He unlocked his door and then paused, looking to the two as they went around to the passenger side.

Lita furrowed her brow as she glanced at Rain's very human adolescent brother. If he wasn't lying, then her theory that he had recently become a vampire was out. "You're saying you stored this thing for almost two centuries and it still looks this good?"

"We had to do some work on it, but it runs really well now," Alex said. "Would you like the front or back seat, Lita?"

"She sits in the back," Rain said sharply, shooting his brother a look before slipping into the driver's seat.

"Back it is," Lita muttered. She opened the back door

and took a seat, plopping her bag down next to her. Alex sighed and found his own spot up front with Rain.

Lita looked around the interior, marveling over the pristine condition of the black leather seats. "Is everything in this beast original?"

"Everything but the engine," Rain replied with a touch of pride in his voice as he brought the car to life. It idled quietly but vibrated enough that it seemed to have some real power under the hood.

Alex slipped his harness on as the car warmed up, then turned halfway around, craning his neck so he could look at Lita. "You may want to put your seatbelt on."

She looked around, then back to him. "There aren't any back here."

"Oh, right," Alex said and pursed his lips. "Well, I'm sure you'll be fine. Don't worry about it." He turned back around and slipped down in his seat, glancing up at his brother. Rain was staring at the windshield where light droplets of water were beginning to land.

Suddenly, Rain dropped the car into gear and took off without warning, kicking up chunks of dirt and grass behind the vehicle. Lita felt her neck tense as her back slammed into the seat. She dug her nails into the leather at her sides.

"Christ, Vampire. We're not all immortal you know."

Rain glanced contemptibly at her in the rearview mirror, but she didn't see it. She saw nothing, in fact, but an empty driver's seat in its limited oblong view. She pondered on this, an aspect of their kind she never quite understood. It was on the tip of her tongue to ask, but she fell silent, turning her gaze out the window as rain started slipping down it in rivulets.

II

They soon made their way onto a dirt road that passed

through the large expanse of woods that blanketed this part of Ayenee. Following their present path forty miles northeast would land them in Maple City. Another thirty miles past that, the road would turn to cobblestone, and Chicane lay five miles further on, its huge expanse coming up flush with the Atlantic on Ayenee's eastern coast.

South of The Red Mare wasn't much to behold. A few small towns and communities here and there, the most notable being Bartle, but even it was barely half the size of Maple City, which was the third largest in Ayenee after Silver City and, of course, Chicane.

West Ayenee was mostly mountainous, and towns were sparse. There were rumors, though, of a sizeable community on the west slope of Primrose Mountain. It was supposedly a place of peace and kindness, the type that Chicane only pretended to be. The people were said to be solemn, introspective folk. Lita had heard it compared to a place once known as Tibet, and she thought it sounded nice, but also painfully dull.

The far southeast of the young continent was known only as the Blacklands. It was a place still charred and barren from the bombs of the Last War. Nothing lived there, and no sane soul would ever think to venture that far.

III

Lita snapped out of her daze as the sudden sound of rushing wind filled the car. Rain had cracked his window and lit a cigarette.

"Those things are bad for you, you know," Lita said.

Rain glanced over his shoulder briefly, giving her a narrow look.

"Alright, I suppose not," she murmured, then tugged her bag over and reached inside. "Well, two vices for one I guess." She pulled out her bottle of vodka and took a strong chug. Alex looked back as she did, and she held up the bottle to offer some, but he silently declined.

"So where are you from, Lita?" Alex asked pleasantly, trying to lighten the mood in the car a bit. "What do you do besides tend bar?"

Lita sneered, "Well, I come from a little shithole tavern where I serve drinks and break up fights. Occasionally I jump into freezing cold lakes to save stupid little boys' asses. But my favorite thing to do is throw nosey blonds from moving vehicles."

Alex frowned and turned back around. Obviously conversation was out of the question. He looked up to see a small smirk on Rain's face, and he shot him a dirty look.

After a moment, however, Lita sighed and leaned forward. "Look, I'm not here to make friends. You people were just a matter of convenience. But if we're trying to kill time, then let's stay away from the personal and see if I can't maybe learn something here." Looking to Rain, she smacked him on the arm. "You. Why don't you reflect?"

Rain looked to his arm, then to Lita. "What?"

Sitting back, she said, "Well, I figure this might be the only time I run into a mildly personable vampire. You know, the kind that doesn't try to bite you, if there is such a thing. Figure I should learn a bit about them. Give me a leg up next time I have to kill one."

"Hmmm," was all Rain said.

"So? What's with the lack of reflection?"

Rain kept his eyes on the road, not answering her. Alex stared at him for a long moment before finally speaking up himself. "I believe it's about cosmic balancing of advantages."

"What are you talking about, kid?" Lita asked, then took another tug off her bottle.

Alex turned around to face her better. "Well, vampires have an advantage in that they can look human, disguising themselves to trick their prey. So the universe said, 'Okay, you can have that, but you don't get to show up in mirrors. That way humans have a way of figuring you out.'"

"I suppose that's as good of an explanation as any. But what's with the dust thing? Why do they break apart when you take their heads off or put a wooden stake in their heart? And why a *wooden* stake?"

"Well, really, any sharp weapon will work if you do enough damage. Wood just works best. Vampires are unnatural creatures, so they can't handle the natural properties of wood."

Lita pondered this a moment, then nodded. "Alright, what about turning into dust?"

"As I said, vampires are unnatural. The body is just a vessel. It resembles the person it was, even has their memories, but it's just a creature inside, and a mystical one at that. No conscience. It's a so...so..." he paused, looking to his brother.

"Sociopath," Rain said.

"Right. A sociopath. Anyway, like most mystical entities, the creature is made of energy. The stake, fire, sunlight, or decapitation releases that energy from the vessel, and the release is so powerful it destroys the body."

Lita blinked. She wasn't easily shocked, but was genuinely surprised at how intelligently Alex spoke for someone his age. If he really was only fourteen, then whoever raised him must have kept him very focused on studies. She glanced over to Rain. "So then what's your deal? You don't seem like a sociopath. An asshole, maybe, but not a sociopath."

Alex opened his mouth, then looked to Rain.

"I thought you wanted to keep this non-personal," Rain said flatly. He paid his brother a glance, and Alex turned back around and slipped down in his seat.

Lita looked back and forth between the two, then sat

back herself. "Fair enough," she said. She took one last gulp off her bottle before capping it and shoving it back in her bag, then folded her arms over her chest and turned her gaze out the window once more.

IV

As they entered the outskirts of Maple City, Lita looked up to see that the rain had stopped and the sky was growing brighter blue with each passing second.

"You might want to pick up the pace a bit. While the sight of you bursting into flames would be interesting to say the least, I'm not a big fan of fire, and it would be a damn shame to see this car ruined."

Rain frowned. "How far from here do you live?"

"Not far. Another half mile. Take your next right up here."

Rain sped up a bit. "We'll drop you off and find the nearest inn."

Lita shook her head. "No good, Vampire."

"Stop calling me that."

"Well I'll be inclined to change it to 'pile of ashes' if you try to get to an inn. The nearest one is five miles away. You won't make it before daybreak."

"I could put you in the trunk again," Alex said sympathetically. Rain sighed.

Lita groaned and pinched the bridge of her nose. "No, no. You two can come up to my place, crash until dusk, dammit." She honestly wasn't sure why she was being this charitable. It generally wasn't in her nature.

Alex looked over his shoulder at her, surprised. "Are you sure?"

Lita sighed. "Yeah, it's fine."

Rain reached up and adjusted the rearview mirror so he could see her. "Thank you," he said. Lita nodded in return.

Moments later, they pulled up in front of a five-story red brick building. Some parts of Maple City were actually quite nice, reminiscent of late-1950's Old World construction. This neighborhood was not one of them. A burnt out car sat across the street, and a man was either passed out or dead just up the sidewalk.

"Pull into that alley on the right up there," Lita said, pointing past Alex. "There's an inlet on the left-hand side halfway up. This car should fit, and it'll keep it out of sight. That is, if you fancy ever seeing it again."

Rain followed her directions and parked the car where she said. Getting out quickly, he followed Lita into the alley, holding up a hand and squinting as he looked out towards the street. The sun was creeping their way.

"Come on," Lita said, "there's a back door over here. It's in the shade." As they followed her, Alex stayed close to Rain, who looked weakened by this low morning light.

Slipping through the back door, they entered what appeared to be the rear part of a lobby, hidden in darkness behind a winding staircase. Rain sighed and leaned against a wall.

"You alright?" Alex asked.

Rain nodded. "Fine. Just need rest."

"This way," Lita said as she approached a doorway under the staircase. It had a large metal grating over it and she slid this open, then stepped into the cramped metal box inside. Rain followed, but Alex hung back, eyeing the device warily.

Seeing his hesitation, Rain said, "Alex, it's alright. It's just an elevator. I've told you about them before."

"How sheltered *is* he?" Lita whispered, but Rain ignored her.

Alex took a couple of steps forward, looking over the box curiously. "It works on pulleys, with counterweights, right?"

Rain looked to the large lever that stuck up from the

floor, on which Lita's hand was resting. "Yes. This one's a very old design. It doesn't run on electricity." Alex finally nodded his approval and stepped inside. Shrugging off the interaction, Lita slammed the gate shut and pulled the lever. The car shuddered as they began their ascent.

"It only gets stuck sometimes," she said with a wry smile. Alex swallowed hard.

A single chime of a bell announced their arrival to each floor. On the third such chime, denoting the fourth floor, Lita pushed the lever forward, bringing the elevator to a halt. She snatched up her bag and pulled the gate open. Alex was the first one out. Though the mechanics of the device intrigued him greatly, he didn't like putting his faith in any machine whose inner-workings he hadn't seen with his own eyes. Lita motioned to Rain and he exited next, with her taking up the rear.

They made their way down the hallway, which was dimly lit by small oil lamps attached to the wall between each door. At the second door on the left, a red one marked 406, Lita paused to fish a key from her bag. Rain sighed tiredly and leaned against the wall next to the door.

Finally seizing upon her key, Lita jammed it into the lock. The deadbolt groaned as it turned, then the door creaked in its own way, crying out their arrival as she opened it.

"Home sweet home," she muttered as she stepped into the complete darkness inside the apartment. "Come on in. It's not much, but there's a spare bed. You two will just have to cuddl—" Lita froze two steps into the apartment. With impressive speed, she drew her handgun and pointed it at the nearly imperceptible figure of a person sitting on the couch that faced the front door. "Show yourself!" she commanded.

Rain pushed himself off the wall and looked in the door. He could see the person sitting there just fine. He was a lean, athletic-looking man with close-cropped brown hair and round hazel eyes. To Rain, he looked like a soldier. As he watched, the man leaned forward and reached out over the coffee table in front of him. There was a round candle sitting there, and the man hovered his hand about an inch above its three wicks. Rain quirked a brow as he saw the air under the man's palm begin to ripple with heat, and then all three wicks came alight as if on their own.

Withdrawing his hand, the man blew on it briefly, then looked to them with a smirk. "Hello, Lita."

Lita's eyes narrowed into a glare. "Jonas."

FIRST INTERLUDE

O! Child, the setting sun it nears
Didst this day spring joy or tears?
Do not to-night your sadness sow
Morrow brings new seeds to grow

Church had always unsettled her.

It wasn't the structure of the cathedral itself. Much the opposite, in fact. She loved coming into this place when there was no one else around. It made her feel so small compared to its immense size shooting up all around her. Very much a traditional Catholic church, it had been moved here brick-by-brick from England many years ago, and still looked as beautiful as it must have standing upon its original grounds. Twenty rows of large wooden pews led up to a magnificent altar where the priest now stood, a larger-than-life crucifix looming over them all just behind him. Lining the long walls on either side of her were intricate stained-glass windows depicting various stories from the very Bible that sat in her lap, matching that in the lap of every other person here.

The crucifix had frightened her some when she was younger, but now at the age of ten the little girl looked up to it with her emerald gaze and felt a sort of awe wash over her. It was an amazing story, this man who had died for all their sins so many years ago. Her eyes shifted briefly to her uncle seated next to her, and she found herself wondering—not directly, but in the abstract way a child's mind works—if one man's death was enough to pay for the sins some in this world committed.

No, nothing about the church itself bothered her, per se. Rather, it was the people who filled it each Sunday evening. Families, they all were. Husbands and wives with their sons and daughters and their happy little joined lives. She had no concept of what that was, no idea of how it felt to have a mother or father. Something as simple as a car accident had robbed her of those joys too long ago to remember, so instead she was placed in the care of the man she called Uncle and found herself becoming more frightened of with each passing day.

Brushing a wavy lock of straw-colored hair from her face, she looked around the cathedral, taking in the various faces and sighing at all the content families she saw. It wasn't until she looked over her shoulder at the seat across the aisle and two pews back that her face suddenly lit up.

He was sitting there. The new boy, here again for the fourth week in a row. He was maybe three years her senior, but he seemed much older to her. She didn't yet fully understand the tingling feeling she got in her fingers and toes when she looked at him, but she was completely enamored with him. And as she stared at him, his big, round hazel eyes suddenly shifted to meet her gaze, and a soft smile turned up on his face. She felt her cheeks grow hot as she returned the smile sweetly.

The sharp pain of a pinch on her thigh tore her out of her dreamy fixation, and she whipped her head around to meet the glaring green eyes of her uncle.

"If you don't pay attention this instant, you will sorely regret it when we get home," he said in a low, forceful whisper. She obediently folded her hands across her lap and looked down at them, not wanting to be caught in his gaze a moment longer.

As she kept her head bowed, she looked over the light blue fabric of the pretty little sundress she was wearing. It was her favorite, and she tried very hard to always save it for Sunday service. She had a strange dream from time to time that if she looked pretty enough coming here, one of the nice, loving families would offer to take her home. Of course, her uncle would be glad to get rid of her, and readily agree. Then the family would take her to a big, fancy house and make her dinner and give her hugs and kisses and tell her how much she was loved.

She knew it was stupid, but some nights it was the only thing that helped her stop crying long enough to find sleep.

Looking back up towards the altar, she tried to resist the urge to fidget, knowing that mass was almost over. Communion had come and gone, and the priest was wrapping up the concluding rite.

Communion was equally her most hated and favorite part of the evening. The wafer they were fed was the worst; it had a dry consistency that always reminded her of swallowing paper. However, the wine brought with it an odd comfort. Some Sundays it would still be quite full when it reached her, and she would take a greedy gulp from it if no one was watching closely, then enjoy the dizzying feeling that it brought to her head for the rest of the service. Unfortunately, it was nearly empty when her turn came today.

Then, just like that, they were all freed for another seven days. Jumping up from her spot, the young girl went sprinting down the aisle and headlong into the fading sunlight. It was something she did every Sunday, a burst of rambunctiousness that her uncle uncharacteristically allowed. She believed he only let it pass because he was too busy making a good impression on the other members of the church to make a move to stop her. If he didn't allow the child in his care to run frolicking free with all the other kids, they might stop and wonder if he really was the good Catholic man that he presented himself to be.

Of course, he wasn't really fooling anyone. Every single person in the church looked to that little girl the moment she walked in each week, wondering what new injury would have befallen her in the last seven days. A black eye one Sunday, a fat lip another, a limp here, a bruised nose there. They all waited for the week when she just wouldn't arrive, and he would show up with feigned sadness, saying she had died of some mysterious illness in the night. They all knew, but no one said a word. Minding one's own business was an art form.

The sunlight exploded all around her as she went bolting through the large doors. Every week she'd come running out here and across the grass, past the rows of gravestones, and all the way to the white picket fence that separated the church property from the large field just past it and the dense forest land beyond that. Each time she would try to find the courage to keep going, to just run away into those woods and hide forever, but she always stopped short right at that fence. She supposed she always would, at least until she was old enough to fend for herself or her uncle died, whichever miracle occurred first.

But today was different. The girl hadn't made it more than ten feet out the door when she heard a sharp whistle behind her. Spinning around, her eyes lit up once again at the sight of the boy standing by the corner of the chapel.

Cocking his head, he motioned to a dense growth of laurel bushes off to the side of the church, and then disappeared into them. After a quick glance inside to make sure her uncle was still occupied, she tucked her Bible under her arm and followed after him, her stomach suddenly alive with butterflies of curiosity.

"Hi!" she said cheerily as she found him waiting for her in a hidden little area surrounded by the bushes.

"Shhh. Stay quiet, okay?" the boy whispered.

She nodded and glanced cautiously over her shoulder. "What is it?"

The boy sighed and was silent for a moment, just staring at her. It wasn't a long moment, but long enough that she felt her face grow hot again under his gaze. Finally, he gestured to her upper arm where she bore a dark bruise in the shape of a large handprint. "He shouldn't do that to you, you know."

She rubbed her arm and dropped her eyes, only nodding in response as she stared at her small toes in the summertime grass. She noticed he was wearing heavy black boots, the kind a man would wear. Her toes tingled and her face burned on.

"I told my boss about you," the boy said then.

She looked back up at him, confused. "I didn't know you had a job. What do you d—"

He held up a hand. "There's no time for that now. All I can tell you is that my boss agreed to let me help you. He said if you can get away from your uncle, you can come live with us."

She furrowed her brow. "What do you mean? I can't run away. He'll find me."

The boy pulled his Bible from under his arm and offered it to her. "Trade me."

She blinked. "But...they're the same."

"Mine's better," he said with a smirk.

She shrugged and handed her Bible off to him, but when she took his she nearly dropped it. "Huh? Why is it so heav…?" She trailed off as she opened the cover. The pages had been cut out in the perfect shape to hold the black subcompact nine-millimeter handgun hidden inside. The girl felt her stomach drop and she tried to hand it back. "N-No…I can't take this…I don't even know how it works."

The boy closed the cover and pushed it back to her. "It's the easiest thing in the world. Just point, pull the trigger, and people go away."

She felt her legs start to shake and her vision began to swim with tears. She couldn't tell if they were born out of fear or gratitude. "I…I don't think I can…" she whispered.

"I know you can," he said. "Just do what has to be done, and I'll take care of the rest. I promise."

She opened her mouth to protest further, but when he reached out and touched her cheek, the words stopped in her throat. Then he leaned forward and planted a gentle kiss on her lips. Her eyes widened, but then closed, and her head was suddenly filled with a warm dizziness stronger than any communion wine had to offer. She felt like she might faint or die at any moment, and either would have been just fine with her.

Then the bushes rustled, and the sweet moment was yanked away from her as she looked over and let out a small cry at the sight of her uncle glaring at them.

Her eyes immediately dropped to the ground, but as her uncle looked to the boy, he stared straight back, unwavering.

"Get in the truck, young lady. Now!" her uncle barked. She flinched and scurried away. As she disappeared back out front of the church, her uncle kept his eyes locked firmly on the boy. "You stay away from her, you little bastard."

The boy stepped forward until he was inches from the girl's uncle and stared up at him, but not by much. His oddly mature height nearly matched his elder's. "Fuck you, old man," he said, and actually chuckled. "I'm not afraid of you." With that, the boy moved past him, but not before socking his shoulder hard against the man's upper arm.

Spinning around, the man balled up a fist, but then only raised it halfway before he stopped himself and just watched the boy make his way through the crowd outside the church. He walked with his head high and shoulders square, and he never looked back once. The man could feel his blood boiling over the little shit's arrogance.

When the boy reached the picket fence at the far side of the church, he hopped over and moved around to the passenger side of a large grey sedan that sat there idling.

"It's done," the boy said solemnly as he climbed into the car.

"Good," the driver said in a low, gravelly voice before adjusting his wide-brimmed hat and pulling away from the church.

"Just what the hell do you think you were doing in those bushes, you little whore?" her uncle yelled the moment they walked into their small house. He punctuated his words with a kick to her backside that sent her sprawling to the living room floor. She managed to keep from dropping her Bible, though the matter was in doubt for a moment.

She pulled herself to her knees and winced at her freshly scraped elbow. She looked over her shoulder at him and was about to say something, but was immediately met with the stinging blow of a backhand to her cheek, dropping her once more to her stomach on the floor. The taste of blood filled her mouth, robbing her of the sense memory of the boy's lips upon hers.

"Shut up, you little shit. I don't want to hear one word from that slutty little mouth that I saw kissing that fucking bastard kid back there. Not one fucking word!"

She hitched in a breath, trying not to cry. He always

seemed to whale on her worse when she cried. She also made no move to get up this time, knowing he would only strike her down again. She just lay there, waiting for him to do whatever horrible thing he planned to do next.

Sure enough, he took up a fistful of her hair and yanked her back up to her knees. She cried out and reached up with one hand to clutch at his fist while her other still held her Bible firmly against her chest. Suddenly, she felt the hot wash of his breath over her ear. "Looks like I have to teach you the difference between a little boy and a man, don't I?" With that, he headed towards her bedroom, her hair still firmly in his grasp. Her heels slid across the floor as he dragged her along with him.

As they entered her room, she finally gave up the weight of the Bible, and when she saw it hit the floor she briefly thanked whatever god she'd spent the last two hours praying to that it hadn't opened up on impact. Her gratitude was short-lived, however, as she was greeted with the new pain of her shins slamming against her bedframe when her uncle forcefully bent her over the mattress.

"Stay still," he said as he finally released his hold on her hair. She didn't move, didn't make a sound. Even as she heard fabric tearing and felt cool air on her exposed backside. Or as she heard his belt jingling and then the sound of him spitting, followed by a slick stroking noise as he applied that spit to himself. No matter how much she wanted to scream, to thrash, to fight…she didn't dare. Even as she felt his large, heavy gut on her lower back and then the pressure as he pushed against her. That pressure growing, growing, and finally the tearing, burning agony as he forced his way in and began to have his way with her. For some amount of time that followed—a period that was usually very brief by the clock but seemed infinitely long to her—she buried her face into her mattress and tried her damnedest to be anywhere else in the world.

After he had gone, she curled up on her bed for some time. There was no telling how long, but by the time she willed herself to move, darkness had enveloped the house. She sat on the edge of the bed first, then slowly, shakily rose to her feet. She stumbled, nearly fell, but caught herself on the little four-drawer dresser that stood against the wall.

She was dimly aware that her trembling thighs were sticky. No doubt a mixture of blood and the disgusting substance her uncle always left behind. She couldn't stand the thought of it touching her and always scrubbed it away first, even before tending to her wounds. But when she looked down to take stock of the mess, she froze. Her favorite blue sundress. He had torn it open from its hem to the small of her back, and the sky-colored fabric was now marred with a dark storm cloud of red. Suddenly, a strange sensation that she had never experienced before started to form inside her.

It began as a flicker in her mind. Just a glint in a place still ruled by childish thoughts and fantasies. Yet that single spark ignited something, and the ensuing flame rushed forth with such speed and intensity that she was momentarily frightened it would swallow her whole. But there was no fighting it. It indeed devoured her, as well as everything else in its path. In the brief passage of an instant, the young girl's tiny form was filled to the brim with brilliant, searing, blinding rage.

Yanking off her ruined dress, she threw it aside, leaving her nude in the near-darkness illuminated only by pale moonlight slipping in through her bedroom window. Opening her dresser drawers, she began to rifle through them, and felt her anger steadily increasing as she found only variations of what she had just discarded. Yellow sundress, red skirt, green nightgown. "A good little girl dresses pretty for the man that takes care of her," her uncle was fond of saying, and those words echoed through her head as she began grabbing handfuls of clothes and throwing them behind her, blindly searching for something new, something different. Emptying the drawers one at a time, she finally came upon what she sought, hidden away in the back of the bottom drawer. She had all but forgotten it was there.

A few months earlier, the church had put on a clothing drive for the less fortunate children in town, and she had found an old pair of black pants and a simple long-sleeved shirt in one of the crates. The pants were well-worn, shredded clean open at the knees. The shirt was cute in a childlike way, plain white save for a tiny yellow embroidered flower in the middle of the chest. She hadn't been sure why she'd done it at the time, but she had stolen the outfit and hidden it here, where it had remained until this very moment.

Clothed once again, she spun around and darted her eyes over the floor, seeking her next item of interest. Finally, she spied its corner peeking out from beneath a tangerine jumper. Kicking that away, she knelt down and flipped open the cover of the Bible. She pried the small handgun from its desecrated home, briefly marveled at its surprising weight, and then slowly closed her little hand around its grip.

Raising her eyes from the weapon, she turned them toward the half-open bedroom door. She crept to it and peered out into the hall. Seeing nothing, she continued on, pressing her back against the wall as she snuck down the hallway. At the corner, she peered around to find exactly what she expected to see in the living room. Her uncle was sitting in his favorite chair with his head back, mouth splayed open and meaty hands folded across his gut. A half-empty rum bottle sat on the table next to him.

Her bare feet whispered across the floor as she approached him with the sort of stealth that only small children and trained killers possess. Coming around in front of him, she raised the gun, glaring over it resolutely. Her hands didn't tremble at all as she aimed straight for his snoring face. She took a breath, held it deep, and pulled the trigger.

Click.

The girl blinked and looked down at the gun, wondering what went wrong. She had virtually no working knowledge of firearms, but she had done just what the boy had told her to do. After looking over the weapon for a moment, she discovered that the top could be slid back and she remembered the bolt action on her uncle's hunting rifle. Grabbing the slide firmly, she was surprised how much effort it took to actually pull it back. But she knew it had worked when she heard the gun click loudly and the slide snapped back into place.

Unfortunately, she was not the only one who heard it.

"Huh? Wuzzat?" her uncle slurred as he lifted his head and opened his bloodshot eyes.

She gasped and snapped her arm back up, taking aim once more. However, she was all at once unsure if she could pull the trigger again. She felt like she'd used up all of her bravery the first time and now her hands were beginning to shake.

At first, he didn't even notice the gun. "What the fuck are you wearing, you…" he trailed off once he realized what she was holding. "Hey! Where the fuck did you get that?"

She didn't respond, and though she expected him to come at her, he only sat up straight in his chair and stared.

"You hand that over right now, you hear me?"

She still didn't answer, but her hands began to tremble more.

"I mean it, young lady. You put that thing down before you hurt somebody!"

She didn't make a sound, but her vision was beginning to

swim and her hands slowly started to lower.

"That's right. Just give your old man the gun…we don't need to have any more problems tonight."

With a single blink, her eyes cleared and the shaking vanished from her hands. She raised the gun once more as her eyes turned down into a furious glare.

"Wait…" he said. "What are you…no! Don't—" But he got no further.

The sound of that first shot left a ringing in the girl's ears, but she did not notice. The kick of the weapon slammed her elbows against her ribcage, but she did not notice that either. What she did notice was the blood coursing from between her uncle's fingers where he clutched at his crotch.

Though his screams of agony were loud, they were dwarfed by the series of explosions that came next. One bullet entered his right kneecap. Another went into his hip. Two rocketed through his gut, tearing through God only knew what organs. Two more went into his chest. A final one decided to rest deep in his clavicle. Only one remained, and the girl seemed to somehow know this as she approached him. He stared up at her with wide eyes, his body trembling. His screams had stopped after the fifth bullet, but he was still very much alive, and she had come close enough to see the tears streaming down his cheeks, turning pink as they mixed with spatters of blood.

Then—as she stared into the dying eyes of the man who had tortured and terrorized her since before she could remember—she slipped the barrel of the gun into his mouth and pushed it past his front teeth, pushed it so it went over his tongue and scraped across his molars, pushed it until she could hear him gagging on it. Gagging the way he had forced her to gag more times than she could recall. Then, leaning in close, she opened her mouth to say some final words. She had thought so many times of what she would say to him if she had the freedom to say anything; she had dreamt up so many variations. But in their final moment, all that came out was a nearly inhuman snarl.

And she pulled the trigger one last time, gladly sending her uncle to the hell she was sure awaited him.

She stumbled backwards, quickly looking away from the gore. All that rage fell from her at once, leaving behind only a trembling numbness. Less walking, more wandering, she made her way towards the front door, the gun still clenched tightly in her left hand. A glossy sheen had slipped over her eyes, and she felt as though she was moving through water when she reached out to open the door. But when she swung it open, the sight of a person standing there snapped her back to reality. Moving on instinct, she raised the gun and screamed as she blindly pulled the trigger.

Click. Click. Click.

"Whoa, hey! It's okay, it's just me!" It was the boy from the church, standing there holding his hands out and thanking God that she'd already emptied the clip. Her eyes filling with tears, the girl stumbled out of the house and into his waiting arms. She buried her face into his chest and began to sob.

Feeling her slipping down to her knees, he went with her, holding her tightly as she cried against him. "Shhh…" he said and stroked her wavy hair. "Shhh. It's okay now. It's over. You did it, okay?"

Her sobs lessened after a time, but then she suddenly pulled back and looked up at him with wide, frightened eyes. "B-But I'm gonna get in t-trouble! Th-They'll kill me when they f-find out what I d-d-did!"

The boy, however, was perfectly calm. "No one is getting in trouble. Just sit here a moment. I'll take care of it."

The girl watched as he stood and turned around to face the front door. He pulled it closed, then took a moment to look over the front of the house. Finally, glancing over his shoulder to where she sat on the grass, he gave her a smirk and a wink. "Watch this."

Turning back around, he placed his palms on the sides of the doorframe. The girl's tears began to subside, fear replaced with curiosity about what he could possibly be doing. And as she watched, an event the likes of which she'd never seen began to take place.

First, the very air around the boy began to…ripple. She blinked, initially sure it must be more tears in her eyes. But the rippling grew stronger, and it wasn't until she started feeling heat coming from him that she thought of the air above a campfire. Then, from beneath the boy's hands, the wood around the door started to glow. First dull orange, which quickly escalated into bright red. When that wood suddenly burst into flames, the girl gasped and shielded her eyes. And though she lowered her arms again only a few seconds later, the flames had already almost covered the front of the small house.

Stepping back, the boy blew on his hands as he gazed up at what he had created. But before long he turned to face the girl, who was still staring at the flames in disbelief.

"Come on, we need to go before the fire attracts attention," he said as he offered her a hand.

Numbly accepting it, she rose to her feet. Her eyes still not moving from the flames, she said in a weak, nearly inaudible voice, "How did you…" and then she fell forward, collapsing into the boy's arms and finally dropping her firearm to the ground.

He held her against him with one arm as he knelt to pick up the handgun, which he tucked into his belt. Then he scooped her into his arms, cradled her close, and carried her away from where his flames were devouring her past.

The boy never looked back. Instead, he gazed down at the girl in his arms. Her wavy blonde hair cascading over his forearm. Her lovely, almost angelic features. Her white shirt all spattered with blood. In a flash of young teenage knowledge that hinted at the mind of the man he would someday become, the boy came to the sudden realization that she would grow to be both unbelievably beautiful and undeniably deadly.

In that brief moment he wondered if he had done something right...or horribly wrong.

FOUR

I

"A little melodramatic, don't you think?" Lita said, eyeing Jonas as she slipped her handgun back into her belt.

"What can I say?" Jonas replied, folding his arms across his chest and throwing her a sheepish grin as he sat back on the couch. "I like to make an entrance."

"As I recall, you're better at exits," Lita said, giving him a sidelong glance before turning towards Rain and Alex. "At ease, gentlemen. I know this guy, unfortunately." Rain gave her a short nod and leaned against the wall just inside the door. Alex shifted his stance nervously, waiting for some sort of introduction.

At first, nothing came but silence as Lita went to a tiny desk under a window at the back of the living room. She dug a box of matches out of one of the drawers and started making her way around the room, lighting candles here and there.

"Sorry for the darkness," she said offhandedly. "This place doesn't have electricity. Normally I'd just open the curtains." She glanced at Rain. "Anyway,—Alex, Rain—

Jonas." She breezed through the introduction, not looking away from her illuminating work as she moved into the kitchen, which was barely a room of its own. It was just an open C shape of three counters to the left of the front door. A long hallway extended past it to two bedrooms and a bathroom. The kitchen itself contained a small wood stove and a sink, but no other appliances.

The place barely looked lived in.

Alex approached Jonas and extended a hand, which the man received and shook vigorously with a courteous smile. Jonas then looked to Rain, but was only greeted with a turned-away gaze as Rain lit a cigarette and maintained his position against the wall.

Lita slapped the box of matches down on the kitchen counter. "Did I say you could smoke in my apartment?"

"No," Rain said matter-of-factly as he flicked some ash into a nearby candle.

Jonas smirked, waiting for a reaction from Lita, but she only rolled her eyes and leaned against the counter, crossing her arms.

Standing by the end of the couch now, Alex frowned and placed a hand over his stomach, and everyone heard the growling noise that emanated from it. Lita actually chuckled a bit.

"Christ, kid, you sound like you're about ready to take someone's arm off," she said in a lighthearted tone. It was the first time she had spoken to him in such a way, and it made Alex smile.

"I skipped dinner," he said, his cheeks flushing.

"Well, I can't say I have much around here. Usually I just eat at the diner down the road. But let's see…" Reaching up to one of the cabinets, Lita rustled around the near-nothingness inside for a moment before finally pulling down a glass jar stuffed with chunks of jerky and a wooden box half-full of plain crackers. "There you go, kid. Have at it."

Alex thanked her quietly and tried to attack the food as politely as possible.

Lita freed her hair from its ponytail and ran her hand through it with a relieved sigh. "The spare room is the first door on the left, bathroom at the end of the hall."

Rain nodded and continued smoking as he looked Jonas over, sizing him up. Jonas did the same in return.

"You don't look familiar, Rain," he said, tilting his head. "You got a last name?"

"Moonshadow," Rain said and flicked off more ash into the candle.

"What the hell kind of name is that?" Jonas asked with a chuckle.

"What kind of name is Jonas?" Rain retorted, annoyed.

Jonas' smile disappeared. "I was named for my father. He was a colonel in the Chicane Militia." He leaned forward then, resting his elbows on his knees and interlacing his fingers. "I believe a man's father can tell you a lot about what kind of man he is. What was your father like, Rain?"

Alex's eyes dropped to the floor, but Rain's remained locked with Jonas' in a silent stare. Lita glanced back and forth between them a couple of times, then finally said, "So should I leave while you two have it out? You could piss all over the walls while you're at it."

Rain dropped his cigarette into the melted pool of wax around the candle's wick, then turned away and headed down the hall, where he slipped into the bedroom and closed the door behind him.

Alex sighed. "I should probably turn in too. It's been a long night."

Lita nodded, and Alex turned away. However, before leaving the kitchen, he paused at the end of the counter and turned back slowly. First glancing to Jonas, then looking to Lita, he said, "Thank you for being nice to us, and for letting us stay here, Lita. Nobody ever helps us. And Rain, well, he doesn't like people. But I try to, and since you saved my life and all, that kind of makes you my friend." He paused, glanced once more to Jonas, then looked down to the floor. "My only friend," he added quietly.

Lita furrowed her brow, not really sure how to receive that. "Don't sweat it, kid," she said in a standoffish tone. "Go get some rest. Take the grub with you."

Alex smiled, grabbed the food, then nodded to Jonas. "It was nice meeting you." Jonas nodded in return, and Alex headed down to the room himself and disappeared behind the closed door.

II

Lita pushed her hands up into her hair briefly, then dropped them down and shook them out with a heavy sigh, as if washing herself of that last bit of conversation. She then looked to Jonas and her face suddenly dropped all emotion, becoming purely business.

"Drink?" she asked.

"Sure," he replied.

"Vodka okay?" She headed to another cabinet and pulled down a full bottle, as well as a couple of glasses.

"Fine by me. You got any ice?"

"Fuck off."

Jonas chuckled, then stood and stretched with a groan. "Jesus, take long enough to get home? I've been sitting here almost all night."

"Stopped for a swim," Lita said dryly. She poured each of them a full glass.

"Sorry?"

"Forget it." She brought the glasses over and handed him one before plopping down on the end of the ragged brown sofa.

"Okay…well anyway, what's the story with those two?"

Jonas asked. He tipped his head toward the hallway and sipped his drink. "When did you start taking in strays?"

"They gave me a ride home and needed a place to crash. Seemed like the decent thing to do," she said, then put away a third of her drink in one gulp.

Jonas curled his mouth to one side and gave her an incredulous look. "You never do 'the decent thing.' Anyway, I wasn't aware you made a habit of slumming with vampires."

"He's…" Lita began, her eyes drifting off somewhere, not really focusing on anything.

"Attractive? Yeah, maybe in a 'look at my manly scar' kind of way, but the cuddling afterwards might really leave you regretting it in the morning."

"…different," she finished, her eyes snapping back to meet his. "But I didn't drag my ass all the way back here to discuss who I do and don't let stay in my spare room, so you wanna sit down and tell me what this is all about?"

"I figured it was obvious," Jonas said as he sat down at the other end of the couch. He took another sip of his drink and set it on the coffee table.

"Not really," Lita replied, "All your letter said was to meet you here."

"I have a job for you."

Lita took another chug off her drink, slammed it down on the table, and stood. She went to the front door and opened it, then stood out of the way as she held it and stared at Jonas.

"Oh come on, you don't even want to hear what it is?" he asked, not moving from the couch.

"Not really, no."

"So that's it, huh? Just like that?"

"Just like that."

Jonas sighed and looked around the room. "Do you actually like living like this? Holed up in some shitty apartment you barely make it home to three times a week? Working for scraps so far out of town that nobody will recognize you?" He shook his head. "You could make so much money."

Lita glared at him. "One job isn't going to put me in the lap of luxury. It'll just be money spent in a couple of months."

"What if one job could? Enough money that you could retire—for real this time—and do whatever you wanted?"

"No job pays that well."

"This one does," Jonas said. He reached down to where a brown messenger bag sat on the floor, leaning against his end of the couch. From it he retrieved a file folder which he dropped onto the coffee table. "Come take a look. If you're still uninterested, I'll be on my way."

Lita stood there with the door ajar for some time, thinking. She started absentmindedly chewing on the inside of her cheek, but caught herself and stopped. Finally, with a sigh, she tipped her head towards the door. "Come with me. Grab my drink."

Jonas stood, picking up both their glasses and the folder. "Where we going?"

"Away from prying ears." She ushered him out into the hallway and closed the door.

III

"You're not worried they might take off with your stuff?" Jonas asked as Lita led him through a door at the end of the hall and into an empty stairwell.

"Nothing worth stealing. Besides, the elevator's right out there, and they're sure as shit not going out the window." She paid a quick glance up the stairs and down over the railing, then lowered her voice as she looked back to Jonas. "So what's the score?"

Jonas flipped open the file folder and held it out to Lita, who set her glass on the flat wooden banister and took it from him. "The job's in Chicane. A teenage girl. That going to be a problem?"

"Are we talking thirteen or nineteen?"

"Fifteen, I believe. Pushing sixteen."

"Fifteen…" Lita murmured as she thumbed through the folder. It contained mostly op data, including the floor plan to a very large building that seemed familiar but she couldn't quite place. "What are the details?"

"Her name is Amelie, and she's the daughter of Richard Lamoureux, Lord of Chicane."

Lita paused and turned incredulous eyes to Jonas. "You've got to be fucking me."

His face was firm, even. "I'm not." Then, reaching for the folder, "But hey, if this is too heavy for you, I can—"

Lita swatted his hand away. "Don't try to pull that reverse psychology mindfuck bullshit on me, Jonas. I'm just saying that I've seen the High Palace. That place is like a goddamn fortress."

Jonas sipped his drink and nodded. "That's why my employer needs someone of your particular…infiltration expertise."

Lita looked down to the folder for a moment. "Your employer…" Her head shot back up, eyes narrow. "Cleric isn't involved in this, is he?"

Jonas shook his head. "No. Private contract. I branched out a bit after you left."

Lita squinted at him, trying to discern whether he was lying. She didn't enjoy the fact that he probably was. Looking back down, she flipped through the last couple of pages. Most of them were scrawled notes detailing Amelie's physical description, various habits, and usual whereabouts at any given time of day. "You riding shotgun on this?"

"Not this time around. Strictly solo mission, no cleanup

necessary. My employer wants it to be publicly known that this was a hit, just not discovered by whom. Get in, do the job, get out. No traces."

Lita nodded and closed the folder, then looked past Jonas, staring off into space. "Timeline?"

"Soon. For the next three days, you'll have a four-hour window of entry every night between 10 pm and 2 am. The sooner you do it, the better the pay. If you can do it tonight, I'm authorized to accept virtually any price you can name."

Lita's jaw tensed and her eyes shot back to him. "A job like this requires two weeks' prep, minimum. You *know* that."

"Sure, for gathering intel—which you have—and securing entry and exit—which you also have. This is giftwrapped for you, Lita. All we need is someone to pull the trigger."

"If it's so easy, why don't you do it? Or anyone else on the usual roster, huh?" She shoved the folder at him and snatched up her drink, throwing back a large gulp. She was getting tired of this. Her gut wasn't feeling it and her head was starting to ache.

Jonas took the folder and sighed, leaning against the banister. "A lot's changed in the last few years. It's not like it used to be. The major city uniforms have started cracking down hard on contract jobs. Nearly every hitter worth a damn has an enforcer or two in his pocket now, but it's just some piggy who'd squeal to anyone with a bigger sack of gold. This job needs anonymity. We need a ghost, someone who can just disappear after the payout. No strings, no connections. That's why I came to you. It's in your wheelhome and nobody will question you dropping off the continent without any notice."

"It's 'wheelhouse', you dumb shit," Lita said absently as she rolled her glass between her palms, taking a moment to think things over. "Five-hundred thousand," she said finally, "in Ayenee Marks, no bullshit Chicane Credits. Plus safe passage to England." She paused for a beat, then added, "And a car. A decent one. And you know I want half up front, especially if you expect me to do this tonight."

Jonas reached into his coat pocket and pulled out a very small notebook. He flipped it open and scanned over a couple of pages, then nodded to himself and pocketed it once more. "I can do two-hundred thousand and probably trade ship papers by this afternoon, but if you want a decent car you'll have to pick it up at the finish line with the rest of the cash."

Lita quirked a brow. "And how am I supposed to get to the job, huh? Skip merrily the whole way?"

Jonas scoffed. "Like you've never stolen a car before. You can borrow my toolkit if you misplaced yours." She glared at him, but when a moment passed and she hadn't thrown any more arguments at him, he pressed further. "So does this mean you're in?"

Taking a slow, deep breath, Lita looked down at her glass. After staring into the clear liquid's reflective surface for another long moment, she finally replied, "You get me the cash by 5 o'clock, and I'm in," then quaffed the rest of her drink.

IV

"I don't like him," Rain said flatly as Alex slipped into the bedroom. He looked up from where he had just finished lighting three candles on a small nightstand, illuminating the room in soft, flickering shades of orange. There wasn't much to it. Four walls and a curtain-shrouded window. By the nightstand was a simple twin bed with a yellow quilt, and a nondescript wooden chair sat against the wall to the left of the door, next to a small closet. Alex found it odd that someone like Lita would even own a spare bed, though he supposed it was possible that the apartment had come furnished.

"You don't like anyone," Alex teased as he crossed the room. He put his food on the nightstand and sat down on the bed, then bounced his rear on it twice, feeling its comfort level before reaching down to untie his shoes.

"I don't mind *you*," Rain said. He pulled off his long coat and draped it over the back of the chair.

"Of course you don't, I'm your brother. It's inherent." Alex stretched out on the bed with a groan followed by a satisfied sigh as he folded his hands behind his head. He had fully intended on eating more before doing that, but he was finding himself far more tired than hungry.

"Not necessarily..." Rain said absently. He went to the side of the window and pulled the curtain away just enough to carefully peek outside. This side of the building faced west and was still heavily shadowed in the low morning light. "...look at Cain and Abel."

"You don't believe in God," Alex said, staring up at the ceiling as he spoke.

"He doesn't believe in me either. The disdain is mutual," Rain said in a low tone. Down below, a pair of children was running across the road towards a small grassy park. Two young boys, one blond and one dark-haired. They appeared to be playing tag. Rain closed his eyes with a sigh and let the curtain fall closed.

"You going to rest?" Alex asked.

Rain shrugged. "If I do, I'll take the floor. You need to get some sleep." He could tell the boy was exhausted. They'd been travelling around Ayenee and hadn't been home in the better part of a week. Rain insisted on educating his brother to the best of his ability, and sometimes that involved taking him on long trips across the continent. It also allowed them to look for places to stock up on various supplies. Good days were spent on lumpy inn beds, and bad ones camped out in the car which, while beautiful, was considerably less than comfortable to sleep in.

When Alex didn't respond, Rain looked over to see that his eyes had slipped closed, so he left him be and went to the closet to glance around inside. There was no clothing, just a couple of small wooden packing crates stacked on top of one another and an old hunting rifle leaning against them. Turning his eyes up to the closet's single shelf, he quirked a brow at the sight of multiple small boxes of ammunition in sizes ranging from nine millimeter to forty-four caliber. He wondered what a tender who seemed to rarely make it home would need with such munitions.

Rain hated guns, always had. He had never fired one himself, though he was quite adept with a crossbow and would probably be a very good shot if he had any interest in such things. Still, he loathed the devices. Found no purpose in their existence other than to kill.

He considered them the vampires of technology.

Next to the boxes of ammunition were a couple of empty mason jars. Rain grabbed one and closed the closet door. Digging his cigarettes and lighter out of his coat, he then went and found a seat on the floor against the corner opposite the bed. He placed the jar in front of him and was just about to light a cigarette when he heard something slam back in the living room, followed by the creak of the front door opening.

He could hear them talking out there, and were he to concentrate, he could easily make out everything being said. Hell, he could likely hear interaction two apartments down, were the speakers discoursing loudly enough. Without intending to, he picked up the words "shitty apartment" and "lap of luxury," but then Alex began to stir and Rain's attention was drawn to him.

"Mmmm," Alex said sleepily. "What about her?" He turned his head, half opening his eyes to look at his brother.

"What are you talking about?" Rain asked, then lit his cigarette.

"You said you don't like him, but what about her?"

He jetted smoke from his nostrils. "She's abrasive and off-putting."

Alex laughed a little. "And you're not?"

Rain sighed. "There's something about her." He looked to the door, his mind skimming over the few short hours they had known the young woman. "It seems like there's more to her than just some bartender."

"I think you like her," Alex said with a chuckle.

Rain snorted in response.

"Well, either way, being around her might do you some good," Alex said, then yawned.

"What do you mean?"

"You know, interacting with a human. Maybe making a friend."

"You're the only friend I need." He took a deep drag and let the smoke out slow.

"Maybe...but maybe you need more than just a teenage boy to talk with. Did you ever think that involving yourself with people might make you feel more human?"

"But I'm not human," Rain said, looking to his brother.

"You were once," Alex replied, then offered him a warm smile before rolling over to face the wall. He was asleep within moments.

Rain finished off his cigarette, snuffing it out on the inner side of the jar and dropping it to the bottom. Folding his arms across his chest, he leaned his head back against the corner and closed his eyes. He began taking slow, even breaths, gradually falling into a state of meditative relaxation.

The breathing wasn't necessary. He had encountered a number of vampires in his time, but never saw one that shared his own personal urge to continue the autonomic chore of the humans. If anything, the process was actually somewhat painful. The air caused a slight burning sensation as it ran through his dry trachea and pushed open his withered lungs, only to escape back out just as pure as it went in, completely unfiltered by his dead body.

He sometimes wondered why he did it. He hadn't for so many years, but then just seemed to pick it up again out of the blue. It wasn't even automatic. Alex once told him that he stopped if he was concentrating very hard on a task, sometimes for hours at a time. His brother believed it was a subconscious wish to be human again, but Rain dismissed this with a wave of his hand. It was a fool's errand to dream of such things, and it betrayed the naïveté of his brother's youth to suggest it.

Still, he sometimes wished he could remember a time when taking a deep breath felt good. A time when it didn't come with pain. The closest he could come were the first cool inhalations after a cigarette. Smoking hurt worse than breathing, so for a scant few seconds after he took that last drag, breathing felt almost refreshing. Almost.

"Restin', eh?"

Rain's eyes snapped wide open, then narrowed at the sight of the old man standing in front of him. He was clad in garb circa mid-1800's, but its white button-down shirt was stained red from where his throat had been torn wide open, revealing all the cords of his neck beneath.

"Go away," Rain said in a low tone, finding a cigarette as he did. It was always the old man first.

"I know a thing or two about rest, young man. Not the peaceful variety, mind you, but rest nonetheless." The man's lips turned up into a leer, baring crooked yellow teeth.

"Young?" Rain scoffed. "I'm older than you."

"I suppose you are, boyo," the old man said with a laugh. In the exposed meat of his throat, little red bubbles birthed themselves and popped, dropping specks here and there on the floor. "But you an' me, we're not agin' a day, are we? Not now, not ever, aye?"

Rain pinched the bridge of his nose and closed his eyes. "Look, would you just—" when he looked up again, the man was gone. He sighed, took a slow drag off his cigarette, and said unenthusiastically, "Who's next?"

No sooner had he asked than a little girl, about six, stepped out of the shadows across the room. Her curly red hair matched the smears of blood streaking her otherwise white nightgown where it was torn from the center of her chest down to the hem just past her knees. Her right eye was missing, and thick fluid dripped down her cheek like morbid tears.

"Where's Dad and Mum?" she asked in a squeaky voice.

"They're dead, love," Rain said flatly and took another pull from his cigarette. He had seen this show too many times to be shocked by most of its acts anymore. "But you outlived them by a couple of weeks, if memory serves."

"My pretty night dress is all ruined," she whimpered.

"So it is," Rain said absently. He looked up toward the ceiling and shot a jet of smoke from his nose. But when he brought his eyes back down, every muscle in his body tensed. "No," he whispered. "Not you."

A young boy of about eleven had taken the girl's place. "I only wanted help." He was a brown-skinned boy with black hair and dark eyes. Not mutilated like the others, he bore only a single deep bite on the side of his neck. His blood had been much too precious to waste.

Rain shook his head and pushed himself back further against the wall as if trying to shrink away into it. "No. Pick someone else. Anyone else, just not you."

"But I trusted you," the boy said, taking a step closer. "I trusted you and then I was your last. Your very last." His hands moved to the wound on his throat. "Can you still taste it? Is it still sweet like before, or has it turned to ashes in your mouth?"

"No. No, no, no, no…" Rain turned his head to the side until his cheek pressed against the wall and he shut his eyes as tightly as he could. His breathing stopped and he held still, waiting for whatever the boy would say next.

But there was only silence.

Letting out a slow, shuddering breath, Rain slowly turned his head back. He was just about to open his eyes when a hiss came from right next to his ear, close enough that he could smell sour, decrepit breath. "I trusted you!"

"No!" Rain gasped, sitting bolt upright, his breath fast and frightened. He looked frantically around the dim room, but there was nothing. Nothing but his coat on a chair and his brother in a bed.

Had he passed out? Had he been dreaming? At first it seemed to make perfect sense, until he looked down to see a burnt-out cigarette butt between his fingers. That, and the room was filled with the overpowering smell of death.

Rain knew that scent quite well.

He dropped the butt into the jar and pulled himself to his feet. Running a hand through his hair, he sighed and looked over the sleeping form of his brother. Dreaming or not, he must not have made much noise. The boy was a light sleeper.

Turning to the window, he leaned against the wall and pulled the curtain back just a hair again. Time certainly had passed. It was late afternoon now, and the sun would be falling to a safe level in just over an hour. Rain pushed himself off the wall and went about the task of waking up Alex.

It was time to get heading home.

FIVE

I

While Alex slept, Rain spoke to ghosts, and Lita stared at her bedroom ceiling, Amelie was on a small stone bench in the apple orchard past the palace's west wing.

It was a particularly beautiful late summer day. The rain from the previous night had brought out a wonderful smell in the grassy orchard, and the whole world seemed to be at play in the brilliant sunlight. From her vantage point atop the hill, Amelie could see out across the vineyard, past the high stone wall, all the way to the citizens of Chicane as they made their way about town, enjoying the delightfully warm weather as they lived their daily lives.

But Amelie was not gleefully taking in the day. She felt a dim level of relaxation wash over her at the feeling of the sunshine on her bare shoulders, but the sensation was superficial at best. Inside, she was filled with unease. Though she had eventually made her way back to her own bedchamber last night, she had returned early in the morning to visit her father once more and had found him in a much different state than she left him. He was incoherent with pain, and Nurse Winters had to usher her out of the room so she could focus on caring for him. The encounter had startled her badly, and after that had faded she was left with the realization that she and Michael could be taking control of this city in a matter of days, if not only hours.

With that realization came even greater concern over her impending partnership. These were the times that she and her stepbrother should be coming together, beginning to form plans for transitioning Chicane into a new era of leadership. But it seemed as though Amelie had seen less of Michael than ever the past couple of days. She was sure he was probably very busy making arrangements for everything that was to come, but if that was true then why wasn't he involving her? Was he intentionally excluding her, or might he be sitting somewhere right now wondering all these things about her? There was an intangible wall between them, but she couldn't be sure if it was one of intentional design or if it was simply born out of mutual hesitance about getting to know one another. And whichever it may be, Amelie had no idea what to do about it.

Lying back on the bench with a sigh, she looked up at the treetops as her hand fiddled with the end of her long braid. It was a nervous habit she'd had since childhood, one her father always admired while still admonishing her for tying up her hair into knots.

As she watched the leaves sway above her, two monarch butterflies made their way out of the tree. They flitted around one another, dancing through the air in their own private ballet. Amelie smiled, wondering if they might be in love. She pondered whether she would ever find love, whether she would be allowed to. Her father had found his before taking the throne, but was forced into a new union once the first had ended. Would she, too, be pushed into marriage for the sake of image as leader of this city? She wasn't even sure there were statutes to govern such a thing.

A ruler of her age and sex was completely unprecedented.

"Hello, Ms. Lamoureux," Christopher said with a smile as he passed by, jolting her out of her daydream and into an upright position.

"Christopher!" Amelie called out as he continued on his path through the orchard. "Wait a moment."

He paused and turned. "I know, I know. You want me to call you Amelie."

She waved a hand and shook her head. "No, n—I mean, yes, please do—but I thought perhaps you could take a break from your rounds for a short while. Come talk with me?"

Christopher looked out over the expanse of the orchard, then smiled brightly at her. "I can certainly do that." He returned to the bench and stood by its side, folding his large arms across his chest.

Amelie beamed. "Thank you. And how are you doing today, Christopher?"

Turning his face skyward, Christopher closed his eyes and took in the feeling of the sun on his skin. "I must say, quite well. Now that the weather is improving, I don't mind grounds detail even the littlest bit." He looked back to her. "And you? How are you today, Amelie?"

She tilted her head, giving him a thankful look for finally using her first name. However, the cheeriness on her face faded just as quickly as it had come, and her hands moved to her stomach. "Honestly? I'm quite nervous."

Christopher nodded sympathetically. "I can imagine. 'Tis weight enough to be losing a parent, but to take on so much as soon as it happens? Forgive me for saying so, but I don't envy you, young miss."

"Yes, there is all that…" Amelie said, "…but I'm more worried about Michael. I can't help feeling like I'm about to share this city with a complete stranger. I imagine it feels a bit like arranged marriages I've read about, only without the marriage part."

Christopher nodded again, seeming to understand immediately. He looked down at his feet for a long moment, mulling over how to respond. Finally, he raised his head once more, gave her a wry smile, and reached up to pluck a particularly ripe red apple from the nearest tree.

"You know, there's a lot to be learned from these," he said.

"Apples?" Amelie asked, blinking.

"Absolutely. You remember Genesis, don't you?"

"Of course I do," she said. "The original sin. Though, I've read it may have been a pomegranate, whatever that was."

"Either way, it's just a fruit, right?" Christopher said as he began tossing the apple back and forth between his hands. "How could a simple fruit be sinful?"

"Well, it wasn't the fruit itself that was the sin," Amelie replied. "It was the temptation, the knowledge that came with it that brought sin to mankind."

"Very good. But why would God make something as important as knowledge a sin?" Christopher began walking around the bench in slow circles, continuing to volley the apple to and fro.

Amelie furrowed her brow and began fiddling with her braid again as she thought over the question. After a moment, her eyes shot back up. "Well, knowledge is power, and power corrupts, right?" She was thoroughly enjoying this. She had always believed Christopher to be far too intelligent to simply be a guard in the palace. His own father had been one of her father's teaching colleagues, but Christopher had elected to spend some years serving the royal family before pursuing his own higher education. This interaction was reminiscent of her father's various lessons to her over the years.

"That is absolutely right," Christopher said, turning to

her with a smile. "But is that equation universal? Does knowledge equals power equals evil always win out?"

Amelie thought about that only briefly before she shook her head. "No, it doesn't, really. It's about what one does with the knowledge, with the power. Some can do good."

"True, but most cannot. Perhaps that is why God hid away that knowledge at first. He knew the odds were against humans doing the right thing, what with free will and all. History has taught us he was not wrong. The majority of human beings get a taste of power and then cannot be satiated. Only a select few, people like your father and yourself..." He tossed her the apple and she caught it, looking first down at it, then back to him. "...those are the ones who can take power and make it do good for the world."

Amelie nodded thoughtfully, then looked to the apple once more. "And someone like Michael?"

"The only way to answer that is to learn more about him," Christopher said.

Amelie chuckled bitterly. "That's exactly my problem, Christopher. I don't know how to do that. He's like a closed book."

"A book..." Christopher said thoughtfully. "*Les Liaisons dangereuses.* Do you know it?"

"No...I mean I've heard of it, but never read it."

"Michael has a copy on the bookshelf in his bedchamber. You should take a look at it. It may help you learn what you need to know." Then, with a smile and a dutiful nod, he added, "I should be back about my rounds now, if I may."

"Of course, Christopher, if you must go, you are excused. But I don't understand what you're saying about that book," Amelie said.

"Go look at it. Trust me, it will tell you far more than I can." He then gave her a small bow and started back on his way through the orchard.

II

Amelie made her way down the long hallway that lead to Michael's bedchamber, repeatedly looking over her shoulder to make sure she wasn't being followed, though she didn't know why. She had every right to be here, and no one aside from Michael himself would question her for entering his private quarters, but he was presently out for his fencing lesson, according to a servant she had asked.

Regardless, as she reached Michael's door, Amelie leaned in and placed her ear against it, listening for any sounds of movement inside. Hearing nothing, she rapped lightly on the wooden surface, then listened again. When there was still nothing, she took a deep breath and grabbed the brass door handle, half expecting it to be locked. It was not, so after one last furtive glance around, Amelie slipped quickly inside and closed the door behind her.

Sunlight poured in from the two large windows to her right, blanketing the bedchamber in afternoon glow. The room was kept immaculately clean, but Amelie could not shake the sudden uneasy feeling that came over her in here. It felt unsettling and cold, like a musty basement or dust-filled attic, neither of which she'd ever stepped foot into in her life.

In front of the mullioned windows sat an imposing maple desk stained a very dark shade of brown. Amelie approached it and ran her finger lightly along its edge, looking over its tidy surface that held only an inkwell, a quill standing upright in a holder, and a crystal pitcher of water with a pair of upside-down glasses next to it.

At the other end of the room was a large, luxurious bed. It stood tall on its sled frame, four pillars rising up over it and draped with sheer black fabric. Just past it, against the far wall, stood a sizeable bookshelf containing a number of old hardbound novels.

Going to it, Amelie looked over the various titles, then frowned. She had hoped the selection might give her some insight into Michael's interests, but the books were of such a wide range of subjects that she wasn't sure if he actually studied all these things or if the shelf had simply been filled at random for aesthetic purposes. There were books about biology, cooking, woodworking, and a huge selection of fiction titles, none placed in any particular order whatsoever.

One book among all the others caught her eye for a moment, and out of pure curiosity she pulled it down. There wasn't anything significant or dazzling about it. It was dusty and worn, bound with a dark green cover. Embossed on the front was the title, *The Great Gatsby*. She had never heard of it.

Sliding that one back into its place, Amelie began scanning the shelf once again until she found what she was looking for. Its title was pressed in red against a black binding, the French words seeming to scream at her from its place on the top shelf. Reaching for it with mounting curiosity, she took hold of its top and gave it a pull.

It tilted out halfway, and then she heard a click.

Amelie took a step back, curiosity turning into confusion at the sound of gears beginning to creak and turn behind the bookcase. As she watched, wonderstruck, the entire case slid backwards, receding until it was slightly recessed within the wall. It then glided to her left, disappearing completely from sight.

She knew that there were a great many secret passageways and hidden rooms in the palace, built by previous rulers who were rightfully paranoid about the threat of attack and assassination. This one, however, she was unaware of until now.

The room behind the bookcase was too dark to make out anything inside. All the filtered sunlight offered was a view of the first foot of wall on her left side. There, she saw a metal lever protruding at an upward angle and a smaller switch next to it. She supposed the lever was meant to close the bookcase back up, so she flipped the switch. On the ceiling of the room, a light bulb flickered once, twice, then stayed on, bathing the small area in a soft, yellowish glow.

The room was simple, just four unfinished walls and a hardwood floor. Against the wall across from her sat an old desk, its width barely accommodated by the narrow space. It was much more basic than the fancy desk in the bedchamber, and its surface was not nearly as tidy. Almost every square inch of it was littered with various papers and drawings. Every inch, that is, except the back right corner, where a box that looked like a miniature treasure chest was sitting.

Amelie approached the desk, coming abreast of it and the faded wooden chair that sat in front of it. Her hands fidgeted at her sides as she glanced over the scattered papers. She wanted to pick things up and investigate them, but she feared leaving some trace of her intrusion, so at first she only observed. Those that first caught her eye were so yellow and tattered with age that they looked like they could crumble with a wrong touch. Leaning in close, she stared at one of these for some time. She couldn't read it; it was written in a runic language she didn't recognize.

Continuing to move her eyes across the desk, she saw maps of Ayenee and a calendar marked with what looked like the lunar cycle. The date two nights from now was circled in black ink. Finally, Amelie came upon a thin, leather-bound book peeking out from under the corner of a cartographer's drawing of southeastern Ayenee. Carefully lifting the edge of the paper, she slid the book out to get a better look. It was a journal.

Though she wasn't exceptionally comfortable with prying into what might be Michael's most private thoughts, she was even less comfortable with how little she knew about him, so she set aside her guilt for the moment and opened the journal. As her eyes scanned over the small, neat handwriting, her mouth bowed into a frown. Every word was written in what appeared to be German. She didn't know what any of it meant, but she recognized the unique structure from a lesson her Language and Literature tutor had given on dead languages last year. She remembered Mrs. Brooke laughing at her comment that the words looked long enough to choke on, let alone speak. Now she was wishing she had read up a bit more on the subject, but how could she have known to? Why would anyone have bothered to learn a language that was no longer spoken? Except, Amelie thought, if they wanted to hide something.

She flipped through the pages quickly, looking for any section that might be written in English. Even French or Gaelic would suffice; she was more or less fluent in both. But it was all in German. Tight, improbably neat German, page after page after—

Amelie stopped suddenly as she noticed a change. Not in the language, but in the penmanship. In the middle of the page, it started getting more haphazard. It worsened as it came to the bottom of the left page, then grew even messier as it filled the right. She ran her finger over the page, blinked, and turned it. The rest of the scrawlings were illegible, but one word had been written with so heavy a hand that it nearly tore through the paper: *Begabte*. Amelie stared at it for some time, committing it to memory before moving on.

Only a few more pages were filled, and all back in the same neat hand. Just before reaching the last entry, however, she came upon a sketched drawing. It was some sort of structure that looked like a coliseum. Its outer ring boasted a high wall, and the interior held something that seemed ancient. It reminded her of a place she'd read about called

Stonehenge.

Underneath the drawing were written the only words on this page: *Die Konstrukt.* Amelie was pretty sure she knew what that meant, but she intended to make certain later on anyhow. She'd learned all about false cognates in her French courses when she had tried to bless her instructor after a sneeze and accidentally offered to wound her. The memory brought a smile to Amelie's face, until she remembered just where she was and what she was doing here.

Suddenly feeling very conspicuous, she closed the journal and carefully slipped it back where she had found it. Her eyes fell on the wooden box, and she chewed on her lip thoughtfully. Its edges were cast in riveted iron that was complemented by the heavy padlock keeping it secure. She was just starting to reach for it when she heard a noise and froze.

It wasn't a noise of anything in particular. Maybe a random board in the floor settling, maybe air in a pipe, rushing by along with water heading up to a third floor bathroom. But when one is snooping as she was, it seems all manner of noises that would usually go ignored suddenly seem to turn into warnings far too loud to brush off. After the bottoming out feeling in her stomach subsided, Amelie realized that the noise had been nothing. Still, she decided not to press her luck. There was no way she was going to be able to get into that box anyhow.

Moving quickly back to the entrance of the room, she flicked off the light switch and yanked down on the lever. As she suspected, the bookcase began to slide closed again, the turning gears of its unseen mechanisms seeming much louder inside the room. She slipped out of that small study and its secret entrance closed up tight behind her with a decisive click that made her jump. All at once, she found herself wanting to be out of this room as quickly as possible.

But just as she had made it across the room and was

reaching for the door handle, it began turning by the hand of someone out in the hall. There wasn't any time to think or try to hide, so all she could do was step back as the door opened and Michael stopped in his tracks, blinking at the sight of his stepsister standing in his bedroom.

"Amelie," he said, surprised. "What are you doing in here?"

"I…umm…" she paused and cleared her throat. "One of the housemaids said you were expected to return soon and I had hoped to catch you so we could talk." She smiled nervously as she slipped into the lie. "We've been so busy with everything else, we haven't had a chance to talk about plans."

"Plans?" Michael asked, walking past her and over to his desk. He laid down the long leather sword bag he had slung over his shoulder and then turned, leaning against the corner of the desk and looking back to her. "What plans exactly?"

Amelie laughed a little. "What isn't there to plan? We're going to be running this city together soon and I don't feel like we know much about each other's goals for it…or about each other at all, really."

Michael thought about this for a moment, then nodded. "You're right. I suppose I hadn't looked at it that way until now. I mean, we both know that the Advisors will be near at hand to transition us in the weeks after Richard…that is, your father…after he…" Michael paused and Amelie just nodded. "But regardless, it wouldn't hurt for us to begin discussing things ahead of time. Perhaps over lunch?" He went around his desk to retrieve a small black book from one of the top drawers and flipped it open to a spot marked with a bit of ribbon. "When would you be free?"

Amelie shrugged. "I'm free right now, and I haven't eaten lunch yet."

Michael looked up from the book. "Now? No, no, I'm

afraid that won't do. I'm already almost late for a prior engagement. The soonest I can do is three days from now. Eleven o'clock?"

"O-okay," Amelie said. She felt an odd mixture of disappointment and relief. "I apologize, I was unaware you were so busy."

"I've been working on selling off the properties my mother left me. It didn't seem right to manage them as Lord of Chicane. I'll be donating the money to the church, as per her wishes, of course."

Amelie nodded. "Of course. Well, I'll leave you be." She began to turn, then paused. "But, if I may, one question for us both to think over and discuss at lunch?"

"Mmmm. Yes?" Michael asked, his tone tinged with annoyance.

"I think we should know one another's greatest goal for our city. That way we can be sure our paths—"

"A return to the Old," Michael interjected. Then, "I apologize, that was rude. It's just something I've given a great deal of thought."

"The Old?" Amelie asked, tilting her head.

"Yes, as in the Old World. Not the war or lack of human compassion, of course. But…" he sighed and sat down in his chair, prompting Amelie to approach the other side of the desk, looking to him curiously as he went on. "It's been over twelve decades since the human race nearly destroyed itself. Our foremothers and -fathers rebuilt here, but we've never truly risen from those ashes. I believe the time has come for us to stop looking at the achievements of the past as being a road to more ruin, but rather as promises of a bright future that we can seize while staying mindful of the mistakes of our ancestors."

"That sounds lovely," Amelie said, "but all the history I've been taught has said that most of the Old World technology was either used to kill or distance human beings from one another. How can such things be of help?"

Michael chuckled softly, then motioned to the bookshelf across the room. "That is why I prefer to read texts written by those who lived it rather than those who came after. Yes, there were many technologies that we should never resurrect, but there were also a great many that could make our lives so much better. Manufacturing, infrastructure. Electric lights in every home, a vehicle for every family. Resuming the search for medical cures rather than relying on archaic treatments. Cures for illnesses like leukemia." He eyed her momentarily and she nodded, looking down. "There were other benefits of the Old World as well. Remember that it was a time when creatures like the vampires had faded into legendary obscurity. What if that could be achieved again?"

"What of the Gifted?" Amelie asked, raising her head. "They didn't exist before The Last War either."

Michael cleared his throat. "Well, of course, every plan has its kinks to work through. The Gifted are a special case in and of themselves. I'm sure there will be a great deal of discussion over them." He retrieved his pocket watch and paid it a glance.

"I apologize, I'm keeping you," she said, then added with a smile, "I've enjoyed this talk, Michael." She genuinely meant it.

"I have as well, Amelie," he said, returning the smile and realizing with some surprise that he meant it too. He stood to see her out. "I look forward to continuing this over lunch."

"Three days?" Amelie asked, following him to the door.

"Three days," he said, then opened the door for her and she let herself out.

As Amelie headed towards her own room, she tried to figure out how exactly the things she'd seen and the things

Michael had said fit together, but the bigger picture would not immediately present itself to her. She had really only ascertained one thing for certain: after learning more about her stepbrother, she was more concerned than ever about him leading by her side.

III

Michael returned to his chair where he sat deep in thought for some time. As his mind worked away, he used his thumbnail to dig small bits of dirt out of the thin engraved border that ran around the surface of his desk, half an inch in from the actual edge. The housemaids cleaned in here daily, but grime always managed to collect in this small crevice. He knew he couldn't blame the help. If they went over every nook and cranny of the palace with such fine detail, they'd reach Judgment Day before finishing a first run-through. Besides, it gave his hands something to do while he was thinking.

He had lied about being late for a prior engagement, of course. The solitude that lie afforded him would be worth the single lash it would cost. He supposed he could rationalize that he really *did* have a prior engagement with himself, but as soon as that thought surfaced, so did the curt voice of his mother, admonishing him that "Rationalizations are the whispers of Lucifer!" He actually flinched slightly, as though the voice had come from right behind rather than within. His mother would often stand behind him, watching over everything he did, waiting for the slightest infraction.

And with that voice, Michael felt the tugging begin. A shaky cold feeling shot through his stomach and up his spine, and he could already feel a thin layer of sweat forming on the back of his neck. Without thinking about it, his hand moved to the top drawer of his desk, and from it he retrieved an old, weathered rosary. As that cold feeling continued to creep over him, his fingers moved over the faded wooden beads as if of their own volition.

"I don't need to yet," he said. "In a little while maybe, but I'm doing fine right—"

He flinched, his eyes dropping.

"Please," he whispered, his voice trembling. "Just a while longer. Let me feel for—"

Another flinch, this one accompanied by a small whimper.

"No, I won't," he pleaded quietly. "I swear it. Just an hour more and then I promise I—"

He cried out this time, clutching at his head with his free hand as his other curled into a white-knuckle fist around the rosary.

"Okay! I will! I'm sorry, I will!" he blurted in a whisper-yell. Clambering to his feet, he lurched over to the bookshelf and tugged desperately at the faux French novel. Pushing his way into the little room as soon as the shelf had opened enough to do so, he pawed for the light switch in the dark.

Another cry of pain, and he had to clutch at the wall to stay standing.

"I am! Please, stop! I am!"

Seizing on the switch at last, he flipped it and froze for an instant. In that single second, his mind cleared just enough for him to turn his gaze upward and blink at the lightbulb that had come on immediately without its customary flicker or two. Then the clarity was driven from him as he stumbled to the little desk in another fit of pain, the lightbulb forgotten as he clawed open the top button of his shirt and yanked his own rosary out and over his head. Next to the crucifix hung a small brass key. He pulled the wooden lockbox over to him, knocking papers here and there in his hurry to open it. The padlock removed, Michael opened the box with shaking hands and his breathing became thin, almost asthmatic as he looked down to its contents.

Lying on a bed of white silk was a gauntlet. Right-handed and large, its cuff would cover half the forearm of most adult men. Its surface was a dark, aged silver, and nearly every inch of it was inscribed with blackened runes. Unable to wrench his eyes from it, Michael gripped the edge of the table tightly, the rosary beads in each hand pressing insistently into the flesh of his palms.

"What if…what if we don't have to…" he whispered weakly, tears filling his eyes.

But as one final bolt of pain arced through his skull, the last of his willpower fell away. Dropping the necklaces on the table, he snatched up the gauntlet and plunged his right hand into it. It was impossible to describe the sheer rapture that overcame him the moment he closed that metallic fist and those runes began to radiate white light. It was as if that glow shone inwardly as well, dispelling all pain, all doubt, all resistance. As that eternal light filled his body, he fell to his knees, turned his eyes towards the heavens, and wept.

"Forgive me, my Lord, for faltering in my dedication to you. I opened myself to Lucifer and his temptations. Please, Lord, give me strength to stay true to my path. Impart unto me your blessed wisdom that I may see clearly once more." He fell silent for a moment, trembling eyes focused on nothing but the blank canvas of the ceiling. Then, nodding, "Of course, my Lord. I will not forget again. I will repeat it one thousand times if I must, but I will not forget. Thank you for your eternal compassion, Lord."

Michael lowered his eyes, turning them down to the open palm of the gauntlet, its softly glowing inscriptions casting odd shadow fractals across his face. As he watched that hand slowly close into a tight fist, he began to whisper.

"They brought unto him many that were possessed with devils, and he cast out the spirits with his word, and he healed all that were sick. They brought unto him many that were possessed with devils, and he cast out the spirits with his word, and he healed all that were sick. They brought unto him many…"

SIX

I

Rain pulled his coat on as he made his way down the hallway. Alex followed close behind, rubbing sleep from his eyes. They found Lita leaning against the kitchen counter, sipping a steaming cup of coffee. It was the first time either of them had seen her drinking something other than vodka. She had changed her clothes as well, swapping camouflage and tank top for cargo pants and t-shirt, both black.

"Sleep well, gentlemen?" she asked over the rim of her cup. Steam curled around her breath as if to frame her words. Rain nodded and went to the living room window, pushing open the curtains to gaze out at the last bit of pink on the horizon, past the outskirts of the city.

"The bed was comfortable, thank you," Alex said.

Lita nodded. "Rain didn't hog the covers?"

Alex laughed. "No, he took the floor."

"Hm. Impressively chivalrous for a guy without a heartbeat."

"Your friend is gone," Rain said, still looking out the window.

"Yeah, I don't mind letting two guys stay after a long night, but three's a bit much. I'm not that kind of girl. Anyway, there's more coffee if you want some." Rain held up a hand to decline, then lit a cigarette, so Lita looked to Alex questioningly.

Alex wrinkled his nose a bit. "Do you have any tea?"

"'Fraid not, Ivy, but your roots are showing. How long has it been since you've been back to the mother country?"

Alex glanced at his brother, who finally turned his attention back to them. "A long time," Rain said. "You ready to go, Alex?"

"I am," Alex said, then looked to Lita. "Thank you for giving us a place to stay for the night." She nodded, and Alex looked to Rain expectantly.

Rain cleared his throat. "Yes, thank you. The floor was more comfortable than my trunk."

"No problem, big guy," Lita said with a smirk. "But before you go, I was hoping you might lend one more favor my way. That should about square us up, I think." She had been thinking about this all night. She knew she could steal a car here in Maple City with relative ease—and if this didn't pan out, that was exactly what she would do—but there was no real way for her to tell if it would break down on her halfway through the Maplewood Forest. However, if she could get to Chicane and pick up a car before the job, it would be a cinch to get across town to the docks.

Rain raised an eyebrow. "And what favor would that be?"

"Another ride?" Lita asked, then sipped her coffee as she stared back at him.

Rain looked to Alex, who gave him a small nod and an insistent look too blatant for anyone in the room to miss. The exchange was so lacking in subtly that it nearly made Lita laugh. She could tell the kid liked her.

Rain sighed. "Where are you heading?"

"Chicane," she replied.

He pondered this a moment. "My car doesn't have enough fuel to take us clear out to Chicane and back to our house—"

"But," Alex interjected. "We have more fuel at home. You can come there, have dinner, and then we'll take you to Chicane."

Rain looked like he was about to protest, but Alex gave him another look. Finally, with another resigned sigh he said, "Yes, that would be fine."

"Works for me," Lita said, "Just as long as you can get me to Chicane by 10 o'clock. Not to be demanding of a charity ride or anything, I'm just supposed to meet someone for something important. So if that works, great, but if it doesn't, I can just—"

"Shouldn't be a problem," Rain said, feeling his anxiety eased at the knowledge that she wouldn't be staying long. He didn't like strangers in his home, and Alex happened to be the only person alive who he didn't consider a stranger.

"Perfect," Lita said. "Let me go get my bag and I'll be ready to go." With that, she headed down the hall towards her bedroom.

"I could eat you for this," Rain muttered.

"Promises, promises," Alex said, and nudged his brother playfully.

A short time later, Lita returned with her knapsack slung over her shoulder. "Ready to go when you two are."

"You take that thing everywhere?" Rain asked.

"Hell yes. I can live out of this thing for weeks if I have to. Now let's go, we're burning moonlight."

II

The cramped elevator reached the lobby of the apartment

building with a slight thud that made Alex place a hand on its wall with a startled look on his face.

"I'm glad I don't live here," he said. "This thing makes me nervous."

"Trust me, kid, if you lived in this city, you'd have a lot more things to be nervous about than an elevator," Lita replied. She slid open the door and they headed out to the back way leading into the alley.

Rain and Alex followed her halfway down the narrow road towards the inlet where Rain had parked that morning. As they turned right into the small space there, however, all three of them froze in their tracks.

"Like that," Lita muttered.

The four men standing around Rain's car turned their yellow eyes towards the trio as they came around the corner. The one leaning against Rain's trunk had hair down to his shoulders, and his mouth turned up into a fanged grin. There were two others to the right of the car, one in a grey jacket and one with a blue shirt. The one standing to the left wore a yellow tank top that fit tightly against his lean, muscular frame.

"You're going to want to get away from my car," Rain said in a low growl.

The one with long hair started to laugh, but then Blue Shirt said, "Hey, Shane, take a sniff."

Shane's nostrils flared and he tilted his head, looking at Rain. He suddenly pushed off the trunk and stood up straight. "Oh, sorry, pal. Didn't catch your scent on the car. We'll get out of your way..." his eyes shifted to Alex and Lita, "...but why don't you share some of your breakfast with us first, huh? Least you could do after forgetting to mark such a pretty car and all. You got my hopes up."

"Wrong tree," Rain said.

Shane gave him a confused look. "What are you say—"

Lita let out an annoyed sigh and stepped forward,

drawing her handgun and training it on Shane's head. "He's saying get the fuck out of here, Sally, before we dust you and your playmates."

Shane laughed, taking a step towards her. "What are you gonna do, sweetheart? A bullet won't kill me."

"One, maybe not. You take another step and I'll empty this fucking clip into your face. Won't have much of a head left to argue with then, huh asshole?"

"Oh heavens," Shane taunted, "You've got me trembling, little girl."

Lita didn't even blink before pulling the trigger. Shane's reflexes were fast enough to begin a dodge, but the bullet still managed to turn most of his right ear into a bloody splatter before rocketing into the back wall of the inlet. The boom of the gunshot crashed off the alley walls around them before echoing off into the darkening sky.

"You fucking cunt!" Shane screamed, clutching at the side of his head.

"Last warning," Lita said, but Shane had already lunged forward as she began to speak, his other hand flashing out and wrapping around the wrist of her extended arm.

Without hesitation, Lita pulled that hand towards her as she shot out her other, cracking Shane squarely in the nose with the heel of her palm. He stumbled back, but managed to yank the gun from her hand as he did, and he quickly threw it behind him down the alley. Enraged, Lita stepped forward and delivered a hard kick to his chest, sending him sprawling to the ground.

The other three began moving towards them, but the brothers were ready to go. Rain tapped Alex, pointed to the one in the yellow tank top, then quickly made his own way towards Grey Jacket and Blue Shirt.

Grey swung at Rain's face as he approached, but Rain ducked it, slamming a fist into Grey's gut and throwing out a side kick that sent Blue against the brick wall of the inlet.

As Grey doubled over, Rain rose quickly and drove a knee into his face.

Alex moved in on the offensive before Yellow could attack, swinging a balled fist around to meet his cheekbone. Yellow stumbled back a bit, but as Alex kept advancing on him, he pushed off the alley wall and shoved Alex hard with both hands, sending him reeling back and falling to his rear on the ground.

As soon as Shane had hit the ground, Lita brought a foot up and moved to slam it down into his face. However, Shane caught that foot with one hand and grabbed the back of her knee with the other. Hoisting her up as he rose, he threw her into the wall of the alley opposite the inlet. Her back hit the wall and she let out an "Oof!" as she slid to the ground.

Just as Grey was falling backwards from Rain's knee to his face, Blue leaped onto Rain's back, trying to put him into a headlock. Grinding his teeth, Rain used his foot to push off his car and shove back, slamming Blue against the inlet wall and rocketing his head back at the same time, cracking it into his nose. Blue howled in pain as he released Rain and fell to the ground. Rain deftly dropped to one knee, drew a wooden stake from a sheath sewn into the lining of his coat, and plunged it into Blue's chest. The vampire gasped, and then his skin and clothes turned to ash and he crumbled apart like dry earth onto the hard ground.

After being shoved to the ground, Alex looked up to see Yellow rushing to dive on him, so he rolled back quickly, bringing both feet up to connect with Yellow's chest, then vaulted him back towards the mouth of the inlet. Rolling over, Alex quickly scrambled to his feet and drew a stake of his own from a boot sheath. Yellow rolled over as Alex moved on him, but as the young man brought the stake down, Yellow threw a foot up and kicked it from his hand, slicing open his palm in the process. Alex hissed, drawing his hand instinctively to his chest as his weapon clattered out into the alley.

Pulling herself to her feet as Shane moved on her, Lita ignored the pain in her back as she glanced up towards the fire escape above. Shane came in for a low tackle, but Lita jumped up, grabbed the fire escape, and rocketed both her heels out to connect with Shane's chin. As he stumbled backwards, Lita was already back down on her feet and headed his way. Before Shane could regain his bearings, Lita wrapped her arm around his neck in a headlock, jumped up, ran two steps across the alley wall behind him, and came down on Shane's other side, twisting his head around backwards with a loud crack. He crumbled into bits instantly.

Just as Rain had dispatched Blue, he saw Grey moving towards him. Using his upward momentum as he rose from his kneeling position, Rain grabbed Grey's collar with both hands and vaulted him into the back of the inlet. Grey hit the wall and fell to his rear. Not giving him a chance to rise, Rain dashed forward and stomped Grey's head against the wall, feeling it break into dust under his boot.

Whipping around to see Lita had taken care of her opponent, Rain hollered, "Are you ok?"

"Peachy, but—Alex!" Lita exclaimed as she came around the left side of Rain's car to see Alex pinned on his back near the rear of the inlet. She moved to assist him, but Rain was already there and he grabbed her by the shirt, yanking her back.

"He can handle himself," Rain said calmly. Looking down to see Alex's stake on the ground, he kicked it over to his brother.

Lita watched more anxiously than she cared to express as Alex struggled with Yellow until the stake slid up next to him. Snatching it, he thrust it up into Yellow's chest, and then shielded his face as ashes rained down on him.

Rain and Lita both went to Alex as he sat up, coughing and sputtering. Rain offered a hand, which Alex took with his left as he cradled his bleeding right against his chest.

"You're wounded," Rain said as he pulled his brother to his feet.

"It'll patch," Alex replied.

"Here," Rain said as he pulled a handkerchief from his back pocket. Alex held out his hand and hissed as Rain wrapped it tightly. "That'll do until we get home." Then, looking to Lita. "You fight like you've done this before."

Lita laughed. "Me? I'm not the one who came armed for this specific gig. I mean, Christ, Rain, who the hell are you? You ignore a meal pouring from this kid's hand, you kill your own kind, you—"

Rain's reaction was so swift and fierce, Lita didn't even see it coming. All she knew was that suddenly his hand was around her throat, her back was against a wall, and his nose was inches from hers.

"*They are not my kind.*" His voice was deep, furious, and his eyes, glaring and blue, stared into hers like bullets. And as she stared back in that wide-eyed moment of shock, she watched those eyes change for just an instant. They didn't turn yellow like those others, but rather flashed a deep, turbulent violet. Only for a second, and then it was gone.

Then Alex was next to him, grabbing his arm. "Rain! Let her go!"

Rain hesitated for a moment, then blinked and released his grip. He stumbled back a step and shook his head, wavering slightly on his feet. Lita coughed, putting a hand to her throat and shooting him a hateful glare.

"I...I'm sorry," Rain murmured, then shook his head again.

"Yeah," Lita said shortly and took a step away from him.

Rain sighed and pulled his smokes and lighter from his coat. Startled and angry though she was, Lita couldn't help

100

notice the lighter's flame wavering from shaking hands as he lit his cigarette. Snapping the lighter closed, he said, "We should get going," through a thick cloud of smoke. "If you're still coming, that is. Your call." Not waiting for an answer, he turned away to head towards the driver side door.

Though Lita hardly wanted to get into that car now, she knew she needed this ride. So all three piled into the same seats they had occupied before and, after some careful maneuvering to get out of the tight alley, they were off.

III

They made their way east across town, and then left Maple City behind as they pulled onto the wide highway that extended forty miles to Chicane. The whole time, not a word was spoken in the car. Even once they had passed over the last of the pavement and the wide road had turned to dirt—there wasn't enough cooperation between most cities to pave the roads outside of city limits—the silence persisted.

Alex sat glumly in his seat, his stomach in knots, thinking his brother had dashed any chance he had of keeping his new friend. He kept his eyes locked out his window, refusing to look at Rain because he thought he might actually cry if he did, which was the last thing he wanted to do in front of Lita.

Rain sat feeling, on a level, guilty for what he had done to Lita. She had fought side by side with them and he hadn't even offered her an explanation for his anger. But how could he explain it? He opened his mouth a couple of times to speak, but nothing would come out. In the end he decided, as he did with most things, that it was better left unsaid.

Lita, on the other hand, was just trying to think about

nothing at all. She knew if she dwelled too much on what had just transpired, she'd probably end up saying something that would get her dropped off on the side of the road. She also knew that if she let her mind really start digging into the job at hand, it would start digging up the past as well, and that would just complicate things. She didn't need complication. She needed a payday and a way out. So she did what she could to clear her mind and just watched the trees whip by around her at what she considered to be unnecessarily high speeds.

After a while they turned off the main road and onto a nearly nonexistent path that led them deeper into the woods. Not far after that—Lita guessed a mile at the most—the trees suddenly opened up into a large clearing and the car eased to a stop.

"Home sweet home," Alex said.

SEVEN

I

Stepping out of Rain's car, Lita looked up to the brothers' house and felt her jaw drop. It was at least two stories, but by the way its roof came to such a stark peak and its foundation was anchored into a slight hill, she guessed it to have both an attic and basement to boot. Compared to her cracker-box apartment, it may as well have been a mansion. She had seen houses like this in Chicane and Silver City, but never in the outlying areas. No one bothered to build them that far from civilization. Except, apparently, someone like Rain. He seemed like he would prefer seclusion.

Rain led them up three stone steps to the front door, digging his keys out of his pocket as he did. Opening the door and stepping inside, he flipped a light switch to the right of the entrance, but nothing happened. He turned to Alex with an aggravated sigh.

"Did you forget to fuel the generators before we left?"

"No, I…" Alex began, then paused, then looked down. "…maybe."

Rain pitched a thumb over his shoulder. "Go." Alex hopped off the steps and ran around the back of the house.

Leaning against the doorframe, Rain muttered something Lita didn't quite catch and then lit yet another cigarette.

"You ever run out of those?" Lita asked.

"I buy them in crates. Supplier from Italy."

"Nothing like stockpiling," she said, then scanned her eyes over the two-acre clearing that surrounded the house. She guessed that clear-cutting this area likely provided more than enough lumber to build the house itself, as well as the sizeable shop that sat off to the left near the tree line. It had a pair of car-sized doors as well as a regular-sized one next to them.

The two stood in uncomfortable silence for a few minutes, and then a low rumble came from behind the house. A couple seconds later, the light inside came flickering on.

"Come on in," Rain said, stepping inside.

Following him, Lita's awe over the residence only increased at the sight of the massive living room. To the left of the front door was a sitting area. A black leather couch sat next to a matching chair, the two arranged in an L formation around an oak coffee table. All of this sat upon a large red area rug which, in turn, rested upon flawless hardwood floors, all residing in front of an immense stone fireplace.

To the right of the fireplace was a two-way swinging door that probably led to a kitchen and a short hallway past that which looked to have a door or two at the end. A bedroom and a bathroom, perhaps. To the left of the fireplace, near the corner, was a short oak bar stocked with full crystal decanters and glassware. Sitting between that and the fireplace stood a large armoire, seeming oddly out of place in this room. Directly ahead of the front door was a long flight of stairs that went up to the wall, then doubled back on itself, leading to God knew what upstairs.

Lita let out a low whistle. "Where did this place come

from?"

"I built it," Rain replied matter-of-factly.

She gave him an incredulous look. "All by yourself?"

He took off his coat and hung it from a tall wooden rack next to the door. "You'd be surprised what you can accomplish when you're immortal." With that, he headed off towards the kitchen.

"Huh," Lita said, then followed him, tossing her bag on the couch as she passed.

As she came into the kitchen, Rain was standing with the refrigerator door open, looking less than happy. "Alex!"

Lita looked over the kitchen as she walked in. Straight ahead of her was a dining area with a round table surrounded by four chairs. A mullioned door bordered by thick black curtains led out to the side yard past that. To her left was an island with a built-in stove, various pots and pans hanging on hooks above it. The fridge Rain stood at was against the wall to her left, each side of it bordered by black tile countertops that wrapped around the corners of the kitchen in L shapes.

"What is it?" Alex asked as he came in the side door.

Rain slammed the refrigerator closed. "All of this is bad."

"It's been almost a week," Alex replied. "It would have been bad anyway. We should have come back sooner."

"You're lucky we didn't have anything in the freezer," Rain said in a low tone as he passed his brother and went outside. He returned a few minutes later carrying a particularly fat hen by its broken neck, its feet still twitching slightly. "At least your automatic feeder worked," he remarked.

"That's something, I guess," Alex said. He had found a spot at the table and was dressing his wounded hand with gauze.

Lita was leaning against the wall next to the door to the living room, her arms folded across her chest. She watched with mild interest as Rain beheaded the chicken with a cleaver from the countertop knife block, then produced a glass pitcher from a cabinet under the island. For the next minute, the only sound in the kitchen was that of dripping liquid, constant at first, then gradually slowing to a stop once the pitcher was nearly half full.

Rain dropped the chicken on the cutting board and pulled a drinking glass down from a high cabinet near the fridge. He filled it, then put the pitcher away in the refrigerator. Heading towards the door, he nodded to the chicken as he passed Alex. "There's dinner. Clean out the fridge when you're done." He then passed by Lita and out of the kitchen.

Alex made a mock salute and grumbled, "Yes, sir," before rising and going around the island to see about the chicken.

Lita cocked her head towards the door. "Where's he going?"

"Upstairs, probably to write in his journal. Are you hungry?"

She pulled from her pocket a small black wristwatch that had no band. It was still early, and a good meal would definitely help keep her focused. "I could eat."

"Hopefully you like chicken. I make it a lot, so I'm pretty good at it."

"Sure, that's fine. I'll be right back, need something out of my bag." She left the kitchen, but wasn't gone long before she came back with two wooden boxes in hand, one about half the size of a shoebox and the other a bit smaller than that. She sat them both on the table and opened their hinged lids. The larger had various small cleaning tools and rags in it, whereas the smaller was tightly packed near-full with 9mm bullets. Retrieving her handgun from her belt, she sat down and began disassembling it.

"Do you have to clean that thing every time you use it?"

106

Alex asked, keeping one eye on her work as he started in on his own task of cleaning the chicken. He'd never seen a gun up close before and was curious about the mechanics.

"I don't *have* to, but I do," she said as she peered down the removed barrel. "Hasn't failed me yet."

"Do you use it often?"

"When I need to," she replied.

Alex nodded and fell silent as he focused on the chicken, trying to hurry. He hadn't eaten much in the last day.

"So Rain really built this place?" Lita asked, not looking up from her work.

"He did. Took him a few years. He built the shop first and lived out of it until the house was done."

Lita paused, looking up at Alex, debating with herself about her next question for a long moment. Finally, she just decided, *fuck it*, and went for it. "Alright, let's straighten something out here, because there's one thing I just don't get about you and your brother."

"Can't figure out the math, eh?" Alex said, looking up with a smirk. "How can I be so young and human and he be so old and immortal?"

"Yeah, pretty much."

"Well, long story short," he said, looking back to his work, "I was born in 1693, and I died in 1705."

Lita quirked a brow. "What now?"

"Just as I said. I died. Then, three years ago, I came back." Alex said this like it was nothing, as though human resurrection was a perfectly common occurrence.

"What do you mean you 'came back'?" Lita asked, still staring at him, parts of her gun in each hand.

"I mean exactly that. One minute I was lying there dying in 1705, and the next thing I know I'm waking up and over four and a half centuries have passed."

"And how exactly did you accomplish that?"

"No idea. It just happened that way."

"And Rain?"

"He became a vampire some years after I died. In fact, believe it or not, he's actually my younger brother. If you count the time I was gone, I've got almost six years on him."

"No shit?"

"No shit."

Lita chuckled and shook her head. "Christ, the people you meet in taverns." Looking back down at her weapon, she started popping bullets into the magazine. "Okay, miracle boy, how did you manage to die in the first place?"

A long silence followed, and Lita looked up to see Alex just staring down at the chicken in his working hands. The look in his eyes made her immediately wish she could retract the question.

"Do you like your chicken baked or fried?" he asked, his voice a little shaky.

"Baked is fine," she replied. She had just finished reassembling the cleaned and reloaded weapon, and she cocked it with a decisive click before flipping on the safety and tucking it back into her belt as she stood. As Alex continued his work, she wandered into the kitchen, looking things over. She paused at the refrigerator where she opened and closed the door a couple of times, looking at it curiously.

"Never seen a refrigerator before?" Alex asked, smirking.

She shot him a look. "Yeah, smartass, I have. Just never in someone's house, only in taverns and restaurants." Closing the door, she turned her eyes to the thing sitting on the counter next to the fridge. "But what the hell is *that*?" It was an odd little box, about two feet wide and one foot deep. It had a see-through door on the front with a panel of buttons next to it.

"It's a microwave," Alex said with a chuckle.

Lita tilted her head. "What, is that like a small oven?"

Alex couldn't help but laugh. "Yeah, sort of. Didn't you call me sheltered because I'd never ridden in an elevator?"

Lita threw her hands out to the sides. "Hey, we can't all have immortal brothers that collect centuries-old crap, okay pal?"

Alex grinned and shook his head as Lita leaned against the counter and crossed her arms, watching him work.

"He really isn't like other vampires, is he?" she asked after a time.

"He certainly is not," Alex replied.

"Care to share?"

"It's a long story...not the kind that can be shortened." He glanced at her. "And anyway, it's not my story tell. But if you stick around long enough, maybe he'll tell you himself."

Lita nodded and looked down. A sudden feeling of unease settled into her stomach. She tried to ignore it by keeping the conversation going.

"So what's the deal with his eyes?" she asked.

"I'm sorry?"

"In the alley, when he pinned me against that wall, his eyes changed. They turned kinda purple."

"Oh," Alex replied, "that. It's a familial trait. An inherent power, like the Gifted have now. It switches on with rage, increases strength and speed briefly. It's unpredictable though, makes the person irrational."

"So you have it too then?"

Alex shook his head. "No, I've never felt it. I don't exactly have a short temper."

"But you said it was familial. So your father had it?"

Alex nodded, but once more fell silent. Lita let the subject drop, turning her attention to her watch that she had just pulled from her pocket again.

"Don't worry," Alex said. "We'll get you to Chicane when you need to be there. Rain may be—well, Rain—but if he says he'll do something, he won't let you down."

Lita felt something in her stomach turn at this. She suddenly thought she was going to be sick. Trying to keep a calm demeanor, she said, "You got a bathroom I can use?"

"Oh, sure," Alex said. "Left out the door, then the door on the left at the end of the hall."

"Thanks," Lita said, and let herself out of the kitchen. She crossed the living room briefly and snatched up her bag from the couch, then headed down to the bathroom.

II

Just what the hell kind of shitshow are you running here? Lita thought. She was standing in the bathroom, her hands clenched tight on the rim of the white basin sink as she stared at herself in the small rectangular mirror above it.

This wasn't her style at all. At least, it certainly wouldn't have been five years ago. Hitching rides from random bar patrons? Letting them stay over and then stopping in for dinner? Even ignoring the fact that she hadn't entertained or been entertained outside of errant one-night stands in longer than she could remember, she was rolling the dice on a job here. A big fucking job. Assuming she could find a car in Chicane was sloppy as hell. On top of that, she was potentially putting these brothers in danger. Sure, she was going to hop a boat once the job was done, but what if someone traced something back to the two of them? They'd dust Rain on principle alone, and who knew what would happen to Alex. They didn't deserve to be mixed up in any of that. Lita closed her eyes and gritted her teeth as her hands moved to her scalp and took up fistfuls of her hair.

A thought occurred to her then, one that had been lurking just below the surface of her consciousness from the moment Jonas had handed her that file folder. What if she really didn't want this job? What if attempting this convoluted approach to Chicane was because she was hoping something would go awry? It wasn't too late to walk away. She could get the brothers to take her back to Maple City, use some of the front money to get up to Silver City and leave this whole continent behind. But that still created the possibility that someone might trace her back to the two of them, and in this case it would be burned employers, who would do a lot worse to them than any authorities would. So no matter which way she went, she put those two in danger simply because they took her there.

Lita's eyes suddenly snapped open as an idea flashed through her head. It wasn't a great idea, but it would surely turn out better in the end for everyone involved. Really, she didn't have a choice—or, at least, telling herself that made the plan a lot more palatable.

She stooped down to her bag and rifled through it for a minute. Finally seizing on the small item she was looking for, she shoved it in her pants pocket and yanked the bag's drawstring closed.

Back out in the living room, she deposited the bag once again on the couch and followed the wonderful scent of baking chicken back into the kitchen.

III

The next hour was spent waiting for and then eating Alex's meal, which Lita decided was indeed delicious. The conversation remained mostly superficial, including a great deal of Alex relating various interesting stories he'd heard from his brother. Lita stayed silent most of the time, as she could tell Alex liked to talk, and she didn't mind listening. After finishing their food, they cleaned their plates and moved to the living room. Lita sat on the couch while Alex took up a spot on the floor across the coffee table from her, sitting cross-legged and talking more about his brother than she was sure Rain would have cared for.

Presently, Rain descended the staircase smoking a cigarette. Both looked up at him as he entered the living room.

"Rain!" Alex said enthusiastically. "I was just telling Lita that you once rode in an actual airplane!"

"Is that so?" Rain asked. Coming to the end of the couch, he glanced at Lita, then back to his brother. "Been telling a lot of stories?"

"Just little ones," Alex said quietly, dropping his eyes.

"Don't sweat it. He's not spilling any of your dark secrets. Just running at the mouth while I look for his off switch."

"Let me know if you find it," Rain said, then plopped down in his chair and flicked some ash into the coffee table ashtray.

"Will do," Lita said, then glanced to her watch again.

"Itching to get going?" Rain asked.

"Soon probably, but it's definitely time for a drink."

"What a surprise," Rain said, and it looked for a moment like he might actually smirk.

Lita's eyebrows shot up. "Was that a joke? Be careful, it can sting the first time." Standing, she headed over to the bar. "I remember your poison—whiskey neat—but what about you, Alex?"

Alex looked caught off guard. "I don't, I mean I've never..."

"You've never had a drink?" Lita asked, surprised. In Ayenee, legal drinking age meant being able to see over the bar. "Well, no time like the present, unless your brother takes issue with it."

Alex looked to Rain questioningly, and he simply shrugged. "Okay, what should I have?"

"Vodka's never steered me wrong."

"Okay then, vodka it is."

"You got it, kid." With that, Lita began whipping up

their beverages. She brought them over in short order, carefully balancing all three glasses as any tender would. She set down both of their drinks, then sank down onto the couch with her own clutched in two hands.

Rain nodded a thank you as he picked his up and took a strong drink off it. Lita did the same. Alex eyed his hesitantly for a moment before finally taking it up and tipping back, quaffing nearly a third of it in one gulp. He coughed hard, his face quickly turning red as he struggled to set the glass down without spilling it.

"Whoa, calm down there," Lita said with a laugh. "You can't drink it like that right away, you know. You gotta get used to it."

"It burns," Alex wheezed.

"Well, yeah. But trust me, the further down that glass you get, the smoother it'll be."

Alex swallowed hard and nodded, then tried again, this time taking a small sip. He still winced, but said in a hoarse voice, "That's not so bad." Lita chuckled, and even Rain smiled a bit.

The three of them enjoyed their drinks in relaxed silence for a time. Rain and Lita put theirs away quickly while Alex sipped at his in an effort to keep up. With a quarter of it still remaining, he set down his glass and looked to Lita. "How much does it take to get drunk?"

She shrugged. "Depends on how used to it you are. For you, probably not much. For me, more than I'd care to say. And Rain over here, well this poor bastard can't even get there. Why do you ask?"

"'Cause I feel kinda…" Alex began, then fell over on his side, his face hitting the rug as blackness encircled his mind.

"Alex?" Rain bolted from his chair to his brother's side and gave him a good shake. "Alex, wake up." Snatching up the boy's glass, he smelled it, then his gaze shot to Lita. "What did you do?"

113

Lita's face had become stern, cold. "What I needed to."

"You slipped us something?" Rain asked, his voice rising. "What the hell are you trying to pull? Drugs don't work on—" As he moved to stand, he faltered and grabbed the coffee table for support. His vision began to swim.

Lita rose quickly and climbed over the back of the couch, putting some space between her and Rain. "The kind of drugs you get from the right Gifted will do the trick on anyone."

Rain tried once more to stand, but stumbled again, grasping the arm of his chair. "Why...why did you..."

"I'm sorry, Rain. It's nothing personal. I need a car, but this is better than getting you or your brother killed. I'll try to leave it somewhere safe in Chicane...or maybe Maple City, I haven't decided yet. I'm sure you'll find it if you look hard enough."

"You're not taking my c..." Rain began, then toppled over, falling limp to the floor between the coffee table and his chair.

Grabbing her bag, Lita moved in quick strides across the living room and back down the hall to the bathroom. Inside, she dropped her bag and stripped her shirt off, which she replaced with a black turtleneck. She also produced from the bag a silencer, which she screwed onto her firearm before slipping it back into her pants, and a large military knife that she tucked into her boot. Hoisting the bag onto her shoulder, she was about to leave the bathroom when she paused at the mirror.

She stared into it for a moment, sharp green eyes staring back at her as she began tapping into that old cold emptiness she used to be able to conjure on a whim. She took a deep breath, nodded to her wide-eyed reflection, and said, "Time to work."

Back in the living room, she went to Rain's coat by the door and fished through the pockets until she heard the jingling of car keys. Clenching them in her fist, she paused long enough to pay the unconscious brothers one last glance before slipping outside and closing the door behind her.

SECOND INTERLUDE

Dost thou regret thy path this day?

We each sometimes lose our way

To-day the rains of lessons fall

That morrow's seeds may grow tall

Eight years had left a trail of blood behind her that kept gold in her pocket and food on her plate.

The young woman stood atop the hill, near the tree line, gazing out over the clearing below. It was a cool, late summer night, the kind that reminded her autumn was just around the corner, waiting like a harbinger of dead, white snow. The ground still radiated warmth from the sunny day earlier on, but the air carried a gentle, swirling breeze that picked up the ends of her wavy blonde hair, tickling her chin and dancing it in front of her eyes.

Without breaking her stare at the cottage that sat in the middle of that clearing, she gathered her hair into a ponytail and tied it up with a piece of string. "Is it almost time?"

He glanced down at his wristwatch. "Five more minutes."

She suddenly turned to him. "Christ, can't we just go now? I really don't see why we have to stick to such a strict schedule."

The man shrugged. "You know what he taught us. If you plan everything perfectly, down to the last minute and bullet, no job can go wrong."

"Yeah, sure, like there's any difference. They're just as dead whether we wait another five minutes or not." She sighed in exasperation. "I don't even see why we work for him anymore."

"Come again?" he asked.

Double-checking her handgun as she spoke, she said, "You heard me. He doesn't do shit aside from setting up the jobs. We could do that ourselves and save the cut he takes."

"We don't have his connections."

"Pff. Like it's hard to find someone willing to pay for a killing in Ayenee."

"Look, let's just get this job done, and we can talk about it over dinner. My treat."

"You're not getting into my pants."

"Never hurts to try."

"Let's get moving. Take the east side around back, there's fewer windows. Give me five before cleanup."

"See you on the other side, Killer."

"Don't call me that."

As they parted ways, she looked towards him once more, that familiar icy cold settling into her emerald eyes. She watched him move along the tree line, staying low and out of the moonlight while he went around the side of the clearing and headed towards the back of the small house.

It wasn't much of a little dwelling. Just a single-story log cottage with a small door and a square window to each side. A tall stone smokestack rose up from one side of it, presently streaming out a thin billow of grey smoke that curled up towards the night sky. Inside, she knew, were two women, soon to be deceased. Anything beyond that—whom to point her gun at—she had no need to be informed of.

She had seen enough over the years that the setting didn't matter anymore. She'd done it in all sorts of places, to all manner of people. Gun smugglers holed up in rat-infested apartments. Drug runners partying in crowded downtown taverns where electric lights flickered and women danced nude on stages. Even an important chairman on the Silver City council. That one had paid quite well.

She had been doing it so long now, it was all she knew anymore. Pull the trigger, take the gold, and live for a couple of weeks to a couple of months, depending on how good the job was.

In the first years after her departure from her hateful uncle, she spent more of her time training than actually performing jobs. Her employer had all but raised her from that point. No, not raised. That wasn't the right word. He had made her. Made her into what she was.

She would spend hours loading and unloading magazines, disassembling and reassembling weapons, until her fingers shook and bled. She would fire round after round into targets until her hearing disappeared for days at a time. He would send her into crowded stores to steal an item, only to leave her to get beaten as a lesson if she was caught. Within two years she ascended from bait and cleanup to the rank of his most skilled hitter, even better than his protégé who had brought her on in the first place—much to her good friend's chagrin.

But she had never cared for authority, and she was quickly reaching a point where she believed herself to no longer need her employer, teacher though he had been.

She pushed those thoughts away and brought her mind sharply back to the present job as she approached the front door. Sidestepping it, she pulled her firearm close to her chest and listened for sound of movement inside, trying to place the occupants. She heard no voices, but she knew the layout of the house from the file she'd been given for the job. The kitchen was just inside the front door, and one of the residents was in there.

She removed one steady hand from her firearm and wrapped it around the doorknob, turning it slowly, silently. It rotated fully without any effort; the door was unlocked. She took in a deep breath, held it, and swung around, stepping inside before pushing the door shut behind her.

The woman inside was at the oven, back facing the door. She turned around, hearing someone come in, and the two of them locked eyes for a moment. Then the woman's mouth turned into a round shape, beginning to form a word that began with the letter W.

In the years to follow, she would sometimes catch herself wondering what that woman would have said.

"Who are you?" Likely.

"What are you doing here?" Distinct possibility.

"Would you like some fresh-baked bread?" Sure, why not.

Whatever the words were, they were cut short by the eerie hollow sound of a bullet rocketing through a silencer before it dashed across the room and drove straight into the woman's sinus cavity.

Before the target had even hit the floor, the young woman knew that something was wrong.

This was no corrupt politician or weapons smuggler. This wasn't the product of a grieving parent avenging a murdered child or a family feud over inheritance. She appeared to be nothing more than a simple, pretty homemaker. Her blood-spattered brown hair draped down over a white apron; her dead hands lay limp inside a pair of potholders. She was somebody's wife. Somebody's love. Somebody's...

"Mommy?"

The woman's eyes and weapon both shifted their aim across the room, landing upon a little girl who was no older than ten. But the girl was not looking at her. She was staring down at the lifeless form of her mother lying there in front of the oven.

The woman's hands and eyes began to tremble, and as she lowered her weapon, she watched the little girl rush over and fall to her knees. She grabbed her mother's shoulders and began to shake her desperately.

"Mommy? Mommy, wake up! Mommy?"

The woman took a step back and felt her rear hit the wall next to the front door. She was dimly aware that her head was shaking from side to side. This job was wrong, all wrong. Who would contract something like this? Who would bring harm to such a sweet, normal family? The type of family that cared for one another. The type of family that loved one another. The type of family that...

I never had.

The little girl looked up at her then, her small eyes streaming with tears. "Why? Why did you kill my mommy?"

The woman shook her head again, her mouth falling open. All of that icy, remorseless cold had fallen away from her now, and she was left with nothing. No explanation. No reasoning. She was lost. Everything she'd done in the last half of her life had suddenly stopped making sense. She was, in all honesty, as confused and hurt as the little girl was at that very moment.

"*Why?*" the little girl suddenly screamed at her, and in that second the woman saw a bitter hatred in the girl's eyes that she knew all too well. It was the same way she'd looked at her uncle moments before ending his life.

"I...I don't know..." the woman whispered, and for the first time in years she felt the cool wetness of tears streaming down her cheeks. With that sensation, the instinct to run kicked in, and she started fumbling behind her back, feeling for the doorknob, intent on turning around and bolting out of this place.

Then she heard the windows at the back of the house shatter and flames burst across the hallway outside the kitchen.

The girl screamed at the sight of the fire, instinctively covering her face with her arms and huddling against her mother's corpse. When the woman saw that frightened response, her need to run fell away and a wholly new instinct took over. She had never felt it before, and wouldn't be able to exactly place it until many years later. She would think back on this day and realize it was an instinct that the woman she'd just killed had felt every day. Protect the girl. The need was basic, overpowering, motherly.

The woman moved quickly, tucking her gun into the back of her belt and rushing over to the girl, stooping to grab her. "Come on, we have to get out of here!"

The girl screeched and swung her fists at the woman. "No! Get away from me!"

The woman recoiled, but then redoubled her efforts. "No, you need to come with me! We have to get you out of this house!"

"No! You killed her! You killed my mommy!" The girl was hysterical now, flailing wildly.

The woman looked around frantically. The fire was ravenously spreading through the house. It had already slipped along the wall of the kitchen to their left. In moments, it would engulf the front door and they would be trapped. She didn't have time for this.

Looking back to the little girl, the woman suddenly grabbed her shoulders and shook her hard. "Look! Yes, I killed your mother, but I shouldn't have, and if I could take it back, I would! But it's too late for that now! All I can do is save you! Now do you want me to help you, or do you want to burn up in this house?"

Snapping out of her hysteria, the girl looked up at the woman with gleaming wet eyes before taking in her fiery surroundings as if for the first time. She drew a shuddering breath and whispered, "Save me."

"Come on, stay with me and stay low," the woman said. The kitchen was rapidly filling with smoke, so much so that the door only a few feet away was already almost impossible to see. The two moved in a crouching walk towards where the woman believed it to be. Within a few steps, it came into view, but flames were licking dangerously close to both sides of it. The woman reached out and grabbed the doorknob, but took in a hissing breath and yanked her hand back immediately from the searing metal. She glanced down at the girl, who looked back at her unsympathetically. "Back up," the woman warned as she rose to her feet. The girl complied, crawling back a ways.

Squinting through the smoke, the woman stared down the door and squared off her body. She took in a shallow breath and held it, then lunged forward, thrusting a boot out at the door. It connected right above the doorknob, and she heard the frame crack slightly, but the door didn't budge.

She shook her head, let out her breath, and took in another small one. The smoke was getting thick, and her lungs and eyes were burning. Glaring at the door, she pictured it as her partner's face, imagining what she was going to do to him for starting the cleanup early.

She felt the door give with a loud crack under her boot this time, and it swung open fully. But the oxygen had become so thin inside that the sudden rush of it from outdoors ignited, and a large burst of flame slammed into the woman, vaulting her over the girl and halfway across the kitchen.

Suddenly finding herself on her back and staring up at the ceiling, the woman could feel a tingling, burning sensation in her chest and face. She coughed, wheezing for breath that wasn't there to take. Shaking, feeling dizziness threatening to take hold and swallow her down into this fiery place, she pushed herself up into a sitting position and squinted to search for the pale moonlight of the doorway, to catch sight of the little girl.

But she was nowhere to be seen.

With a groan, the woman moved to push herself up further—just in time to hear a loud cracking noise from somewhere above, followed by a sudden crushing pain below her knees.

She cried out, her head hitting the floor with a harsh thud as she fell back once more. She tried to roll over or move her legs, but could do neither. Raising her head, she looked down to see a burning piece of rafter lying across her shins.

She laid her head back and began to sob. This was how it was going to end for her, burning up in a fire of her own design. She was going to die here next to the body of her final victim, charred to ash like her uncle all those years ago.

Then the pain came. It was white and searing, eating into the flesh of her legs like some hungry beast. She could feel her skin start to crack and peel as hot liquid dripped over her from her melting pants. She could hear a sizzling noise, and a scent like cooking rancid pork filled her nostrils.

But just as she thought she was going to black out and that would be the end, the intensity of her agony dropped noticeably. All of a sudden she could move her legs again, though the pain that surged up when she did made her head swim. Before she could really assess what was happening, there was a tugging at the side of her shirt.

The little girl was there. She had pushed the rafter away, and was now trying to get her up. She didn't speak, only looked at the woman insistently with her wide, shimmering eyes.

The woman somehow struggled to her feet with the girl's help. With her first step, she cried out as the pain nearly buckled her knees, but the girl was right there next to her, supporting her, staying with her the whole time.

Once free of the house and a safe distance away, the girl pulled away, allowing the woman to slip down to her rear on the ground. They both were taking in gasping breaths of the cool night air. Looking to the girl, the woman's eyes sprang fresh tears at the sight of her numb, solemn face. It was round and coated with soot, save for two clean streaks descending from her brown eyes. She just stood there, staring down at her. Not angrily. Not accusingly. Just blank.

"Wh-Why?" the woman stammered. "Why did you save me?"

The girl gave a little shrug. "Because you saved me."

The woman's brow furrowed. She watched the girl turn away and take off running towards the tree line. Then she turned her eyes down to her legs, staring at the blistering flesh that peeked out amid the tatters of her pants. She shuddered, suddenly feeling very cold.

He was beside her then, his strong hands on shoulders. "Jesus, Killer, did you get trapped inside there?"

"Uh huh," she replied blankly.

"Are you okay? Can you stand?"

"I think so." Her voice felt small, far away inside her own head.

"Alright, let's get you up then." He pulled on her, and she groaned as he slowly brought her to shaky feet. It hurt like hell, but she was pretty sure she could stay standing, maybe even walk. She turned her sleepy gaze to him as he spoke again. "Come on, we have to go after her before she gets too far."

The woman's eyes suddenly came alive with fury. She pushed him off her with her right hand just as she swung her left fist into his jaw so hard that he went sprawling to his ass. She had her handgun out in a flash, pointed straight at his face.

"You're not going near that girl. You're going to get your ass up and walk the other direction."

He blinked. "But I—"

"Shut up!" she screamed, her finger tightening on the trigger. His mouth snapped closed. "You're going to get up, you're going to walk the other way, and you're going to go back and tell him I'm out."

"You're…out?" He tilted his head.

"That's right. I'm out. And if I so much as sense that either one of you comes looking for me, I won't hesitate to put a bullet in each of your heads. Do you understand me?"

He nodded slowly.

"Good. Now get the fuck out of my sight before I decide to kill you for what you made me do tonight."

He hesitated, staring at her.

"Go!" she screamed, and he flinched, then scrambled to his feet and took off running away from where the girl had headed.

As soon as he disappeared from sight, the woman let out a weak whimper and fell back to her rear in the grass. She sat there for some time, watching the house burn. Sat there and thought about what she had done. Not just tonight, but over all the years that had passed. She thought about what she had become, and what she could possibly do to fix it.

She didn't suppose she could ever atone, but she thought maybe she could go on living. So she forced herself back to her feet and began the long, painful walk home.

EIGHT

I

Lita dropped into the driver's seat of Rain's car and tossed her knapsack into the seat next to her. She felt the key slide effortlessly into the ignition and she gave it a turn. The sound of the engine roaring to life made her jump, and she quickly looked over her shoulder towards the house. A moment passed, and then she sighed a curling fog into the cool night air. That drug was strong enough to put even Rain down for at least two hours. She could drive this car through the living room and it wouldn't wake them.

Turning back around, she adjusted the rearview mirror and put the car in gear. With each step she had to remind herself what she was doing. It had been a long time since she'd driven a car, particularly a stick. As she slipped her hands over the smooth leather of the steering wheel, she shifted her braking foot to the gas and slowly started letting out the clutch.

The car sputtered, lurched, and died.

"Dammit," she muttered, smacking the steering wheel.

Smooth, she thought. *Stalling a car. Trademark of a seasoned assassin.* She let out another sigh and shook her head. *Cut the nerves, cut the bullshit. Start the car and let's get this shit moving.* She nodded to herself and started the car once more.

The second round went more smoothly, and a short time later Lita was leaving the clearing around the brothers' house via the narrow dirt path, headed toward the main road.

Making her way at a reasonable speed, she stared unyieldingly into the illuminated field of view created by the headlamps. Although her eyes were firm, her hands shifted nervously over the steering wheel as if of their own volition. It wasn't until she approached the T intersection of the main road that she realized she was doing it and forced herself to stop.

She halted at the intersection and stayed there for a few minutes, looking back and forth from left to right.

Left would take her back to Maple City. She had a car now, and enough front money to live off of for quite some time. She could just pack up all her things and head out for western Ayenee. It was quiet over there. Maybe find a newer, nicer tavern to work in. Pick up a halfway decent wage and just be left the hell alone.

Right meant complete freedom from this manmade and godforsaken continent. This breeding ground for all things wrong in this world. This bearer of her darkest secrets.

Her hands tightened on the wheel, and in a single moment of unfettered resolve, she turned right onto the main road and began her way towards Chicane. There was no way she could have known how much that one decision would alter the course of her life.

II

Lita picked up speed now that she was out on the open road and getting comfortable with this car. Inside, she began systematically deadening anything that might hold her back once she arrived. She stalked her mind, searching for the exact thing that was attempting to dissuade her so that she could give it a good killing.

It wasn't that the target was a young girl, though she initially thought it might have been. While Lita was aware that there was a time when fifteen was considered childhood, she also knew that such a time had long since passed in their world. In a place like Ayenee, you grew up fast. Even Alex would be considered a man by most people.

She shook her head at that, trying to push away any thought of those two for the time being. In whatever small part of her resided an underdeveloped conscience, she felt bad for what she'd done to them. Alex had been decent to her, far more so than anyone else she'd encountered in a long time. Even Rain had been hospitable in what must have been his own way.

She shook her head again and forced her mind back to the job at hand. So it wasn't the age of the target. Fifteen was a woman in her eyes, especially given that the girl had been born a politician. She'd have been raised to be an adult since birth. This had been a possibility her whole life, it just happened to be coming about tonight.

Was it the fact that the target was of such an important political stature? Lita had never cared much for putting down prominent figures, although there had been only a couple in her tenure. She didn't like the notion that her actions had such a radiating influence on so many lives. Granted, it was just another job, one that would have been done by someone else if not her, but it still meant she played a pivotal role in some alteration of history. It made her feel…noticeable. A sensation she despised.

In the end, she decided the variable in this situation that made her uneasy was Jonas' unnamed employer. He had sworn Cleric wasn't involved, but she didn't believe that. She only *wanted* to believe it. No passage of time would ever, in Lita's opinion, change Jonas' undying loyalty to that son of a bitch. But even if Cleric was in on this, someone still had to hire them, someone who could afford the outrageous price tag she had placed on her services. That's what was putting her on edge. The more powerful the employer, the less they could be trusted, and there was no trusting anyone with pockets that deep.

But it was too late to quibble over such things now. The job was taken, and the best Lita could hope for was to put a bullet in her target and not have to put a few more in anyone who might stand between her and the rest of her pay.

The ground under the tires changed texture and the car's smooth ride took on a low vibration as she hit cobblestone, marking the extreme outskirts of Chicane. As if somehow connected to that very change in the road, she suddenly found herself thrust into a dense fog and she smiled at her good fortune. She couldn't ask for better infiltration weather.

Getting close now, she took a deep breath, and with it she started picturing glaciers. She remembered her schoolteacher explaining them when she was young, and the notion still awed her to this day. Mountains of ice, so powerful that they could cut through solid land. It was magnificent.

But tonight, her reasons for drawing up the imagery were much more useful than nostalgia. In thinking about the bitter cold of those frozen peaks, she could almost feel a thick layer of ice forming around her heart. Her skin tightened, muscles tensing. She was shut off emotionally and primed physically. She could do this.

III

Lita squinted as a bright light pierced through the fog.

Realizing as she got closer that it was a checkpoint, she quickly snatched her handgun from where it rested on the seat next to her and tucked it under her knapsack. She rarely came to Chicane, so she had nearly forgotten that these guard stations had been erected at every entrance to the city six months ago in attempt to quell the illegal traffic that regularly passed through here. Rolling to a stop outside the booth—its bright red paint penetrating the fog almost as much as its search light—she took a deep, calming breath as the guard approached.

He was a tall, slender man, not much older than her. Lita cranked down the window as he stooped to peer in at her. "Evening, ma'am," he said, his breath casting out a thick fog that mixed with the haze all around and glowed as it passed over the headlights. Lita nodded in return. "It's awfully late to be out for a drive. May I ask your intended business in Chicane?"

"Just looking for an inn to pass out at for the night," she replied.

The guard tilted his head, looking over the vehicle for a moment. "This sure is a nice car," he said. She knew what he was implying. A vehicle like this didn't look like it ought to belong to the thrown-together tomboy behind the wheel, her old knapsack riding shotgun.

"It's my husband's," Lita shot back, off the cuff. "I just found out he's been diddling the maid, so I thought I'd come into town, head to a few taverns, blow off some steam on his pocket." She flashed him a broad grin. "What time are you off, sir? Perhaps you'd like to join me for a drink later."

The guard chuckled and Lita felt her tension dissolve. He'd fallen for it. "Not until dawn, ma'am. Long after your fun will be over, I'm sure. You have a safe night, you hear? And try not to dent up this pretty car in all this fog."

Lita flashed the smile again and topped it off with a

wink. "I might just dent it up on purpose to teach that bastard a lesson." The guard laughed and stood, patting his hand on the roof twice before retreating to his booth. As Lita cranked up the window and dropped the car back into gear, her smile disappeared, her features going cold again.

The remainder of the drive to the High Palace was brief. It stood near the west side of the city, close to the border of the Maplewood Forest, and for a very specific reason. The road Lita had come in on was not considered the main point of entry to the city. That was Gabriel's Passage—the large, well-maintained highway that ran south from Silver City and straight into the heart of Chicane. The High Palace had been built near the forest wall both to keep it far removed from that main thoroughfare and to allow the city's leader quick egress in the event of attack.

Across the street from this side of the palace sat a small cemetery. Lita pulled up on the opposite side of it and killed the engine. Pulling over her knapsack, she retrieved her firearm and then dug out her job file and laid it open on her lap. After spending some time carefully reviewing the contents once more—paying particular attention to the parts detailing the palace's layout—she slapped the folder closed and shoved it back into her knapsack. She then put her hair up into a bun and covered it with a black stocking cap she produced from her bag. Though she despised hats, she knew her light hair would shine like a beacon under the nearly full moon, even in this dense fog. Finally, she loaded her various cargo pockets with a few more supplies from her bag: a small flashlight, a magnesium flare, and a pair of foot-long black metal spikes.

Slipping out of the car and into the cool night, Lita shoved her handgun into her belt, rolled her turtleneck up over her mouth, and headed into the cemetery.

IV

The trip across the graveyard went without incident, save for a near stumble over a low-lying footstone. Lita chastised herself for being so out of practice. Coming to the road at the far side, she crouched behind a gravestone and peered both ways down the street, which was dimly illuminated by the shrouded moon. Seeing no signs of life, she sprinted across the way and ducked into the well-maintained laurel bushes just outside the palace wall. It never ceased to amaze her how often people planted this convenient sort of cover just to hide the presence of a wall. Aesthetics and proper security did not go hand-in-hand.

Rising slowly, Lita traced her finger over the mortar between the wall's bricks, looking for a weak place. Finally seizing on a small crevice, she fished one of the metal spikes from her pocket and, with a single grunting thrust, buried it a few inches into the crumbled spot and shook it to confirm its hold. After paying a quick glance about to make sure she was still alone, she hopped up, planted one foot on the spike, and used it to vault over the wall.

She landed on the other side with a light thud in the grass, immediately dropping to a crouch and peering ahead up a small hill leading to an orchard. The trees would offer her good cover, but there was a nearly thirty-foot gap between her and them where the ground dipped enough that she would be completely visible beneath the fog. She would have to make a dead sprint for the tree line, lest some perimeter guard catch sight of her.

She gazed down the wall in both directions and, seeing no one, took off across the small clearing, staying as low as possible. Reaching the orchard, she proceeded past the first row of trees and ducked into the second one, sliding down to a crouch with her back to a trunk, facing back the way she came.

And not just in time. No sooner had she secured her position than a bright beam of light cut through the fog from down the row to her left. Lowering her eyes, Lita concentrated on keeping her breathing light and shallow as she slipped her hand silently back to draw her gun and bring it down to her side.

As she remained crouched, motionless, she saw the light begin bobbing up and down in time with the sound of approaching footsteps. A moment later, a slightly heavyset guard passed right by her, only to stop less than five feet away. He was close enough that she could reach out and grab the back of his calf, should she feel so inclined.

Lita raised her weapon slowly, holding her breath as she aimed it at the small of the man's back. But he took no notice of her, instead aiming his flashlight down the hill towards the wall, trying to decide if he had heard something from there.

A long moment of tense silence followed before a noise cut through the night from far to the right, nearly causing Lita to jump and definitely making the guard hop a few inches. It was the snarl of two entangled felines, screaming at each other from somewhere on the far side of the orchard.

"Goddamn cats," the guard muttered, sighing as he headed off in that direction to investigate. Once he departed, Lita let out all the burning air from her lungs as slowly as she could, trying to fight off the enormous knot that had just tied itself up in her stomach.

But now was not the time to dwell on the close call. Having brushed passed one guard making his rounds, there was a good chance she didn't risk seeing another before getting inside. Rounding the tree to the left, she held her gun out in front of her and moved in a crouched run down the row towards the palace. Only about a hundred feet to go.

There was another small strip clearing outside the far end of the orchard, but beyond it were more bushes beneath the dining hall windows. Lita considered that a break. After paying all directions a cautious glance, she bolted across that clearing and into those bushes, barely making a rustle. She was quickly slipping back into her old ways.

Rising, she placed a hand on one of the intricate mullioned windows and gave it a push. She frowned when it would not budge. The file had said one of these would be left unlocked. If Jonas had misinformed her, she was going to bloody his face. Sidestepping, she moved to the next one over and tried it. Still nothing. This was fucked. There was no way she could break one of these without attracting guards.

Shaking her head, she stepped over to the third and last window, biting the inside of her cheek worriedly as she pushed on it. It swung open freely and she breathed a sigh of relief. Jonas was lucky.

After silently entering the dining room, she closed the window and crept to the left side of a long oak banquet table. As she pulled her turtleneck down and banished her stocking cap to a pocket, she idly wondered how spending a good number of her younger years crouched down had not left her with a bad back.

Taking in her surroundings, she developed an immediate distaste for this room and wished to exit it as quickly as possible. Besides the fact that the arched, vaulted ceilings reminded her of a cathedral, the combination of acoustics and hardwood floor caused even her gentle footfalls to echo. She hurriedly made her way to the small service door near the back of the room and carefully pulled it open, peering inside first with her gun, then with her eyes.

The service kitchen was vacant, and it took her but a moment to traverse its small space to the door on the other side. She opened this one with the same care as the last.

The glow of the moon through the windows illuminated the kitchen well enough, but did nothing to cast light up into the tight, winding staircase behind this door. She fished out her small flashlight and flicked it on, then slipped into the cramped stairwell and closed the door behind her. Handgun in her left hand, flashlight in her right, she crossed her wrists to turn the beam of light into a moving target. Carefully, she crept up the old wooden steps, aiming her gun high up the whole time.

Lita was by no means claustrophobic. She had spent plenty of time hiding in tight spaces, waiting for just the right moment to spring out and end the life of an assigned target. However, she did not like this stairwell one bit. Had she been detected at any time since her arrival, the guards could have waited to trap her in this spot and come in at her from both sides. She wouldn't stand a chance.

As she reached the top of the stairs, she shook the notion out of her head. She told herself that no one had seen her, that no one ever saw her. That helped some.

There was light coming from the under the door atop the stairway, so she shut off her flashlight and pocketed it. Leaning against the doorframe, she opened the door just a crack, grateful for its well-oiled hinges as she peered out to see what lay beyond.

The door opened into a second floor hallway, right at a corner junction. To her left, it ran about fifty feet before turning another sharp corner, and she saw no one down that way. Looking to her right, she narrowed her gaze and lowered into a half-crouch as she saw a guard approaching. As Lita watched, he stopped at a door and gave it a knock. A muffled response came from within and the man opened the door halfway, sticking his head inside.

"Just stopping in to say goodnight, Ms. Lamoureux, and to see if you need anything," the man said.

Lita tightened her grip on her handgun. He was talking

to her target, and if she had been a few minutes earlier he would have walked in on them. She had gotten lucky.

"Just for you to call me Amelie, Christopher," a young voice replied from inside the room.

Christopher chuckled. "Any day now, little miss. You sleep tight."

She wished him the same and Christopher closed the door, then headed back the way he had come.

Lita waited a moment after he was out of sight around the corner, then gave the other direction another cursory glance before slipping into the hallway. She hurried down to Amelie's door, trying to keep her footfalls light but quick, feeling exposed out here. Once there, she turned and rested her back on the doorframe, pulling her gun close to her chest. She stole a brief moment to close her eyes, take one deep breath, and give herself a quick nod. When her eyes snapped back open, that familiar cold had settled into her sharp green gaze. She spun around, turned the door handle silently, and crept into the room.

Amelie was sitting at her vanity, her back to the door. She hadn't heard Lita come in, and her mirror was angled such that it didn't reflect the door from her vantage point. She just sat there, brushing her shimmering auburn hair, lost in countless thoughts that had nothing to do with her impending assassination.

As Lita fully entered the room, she raised her weapon and narrowed her eyes, aiming both at the back of Amelie's head. As her finger began to tighten on the trigger, her free hand moved to close the door behind her.

However, some slight error in calculation made her misjudge how hard to push the door, causing it to slam shut with a small bang.

Amelie jumped and spun around, her hand freezing mid-brushstroke. As her eyes landed upon her assigned killer, her mouth fell open.

But she was not the only one. Staring across the room at that young woman, Lita felt her own limbs seize up. Her heart began sprinting in her chest and her gun-wielding hand started to tremble, then lower inch by inch. She took a shuddering breath, and then spoke in the tiniest of whispers.

"…no."

Amelie lowered her hairbrush to her lap as her shaking lips formed a single word of their own.

"You…" she said, her eyes quivering at the sight of the woman who had murdered her mother.

NINE

I

"If this is a joke, it's not fucking funny," Lita said at last.

"I agree," Amelie said shakily. But what her would-be assassin had just said put her slightly at ease. Had she been intent on following through with the murder, she'd have done it already. She shifted in her seat, turning to better face Lita.

"Stay still," Lita snapped, raising her gun and taking aim once more.

Amelie did as she was told, but asked, "What are you doing here?"

"I should be asking you the same question," Lita replied.

Amelie cocked her head questioningly. "I…live here."

"No. *No no.* You live in some little cottage a hundred miles from here. You're some little farm girl with a—"

"Dead mother?"

Lita shot her a look. "Don't fuck around with me, kid."

Amelie sighed. "I *used to* live in a cottage, years ago. My father sent my mother and me there after he'd received threats against our lives. He thought we'd be safe there. When you ki—" she paused, eyeing Lita. "When she died,

138

he brought me back here."

Lita lowered her weapon. The girl wasn't going anywhere. Even so, she went to the door and locked it, then leaned her back against it and looked down thoughtfully. Her eyes darted back and forth as she went over things in her head. Why? Why would Jonas contract her for this job? Why would he think she'd actually do it?

"You didn't answer my question," Amelie said after a while.

"The person without the gun usually isn't allowed to ask any," Lita said sourly.

"Even if it's pertinent?" Amelie shot back.

"What is it?"

"Why are you here? Why would—"

The door handle suddenly rattled violently, followed by a loud pound on the door. Lita jumped and spun around.

"Amelie? Amelie, open up!" a voice boomed from outside.

"Christopher!" Amelie gasped and covered her mouth.

Lita took aim at Amelie again. "You say a word and you're both dead," she hissed, then backed against the wall next to the door. Just as she did, she heard the sound of a key being slid into the handle and watched the latch turn. Christopher barged in right after, a large-caliber revolver in hand. His eyes went to Amelie before he scanned the room. *Idiot move*, Lita thought.

"Amelie, is everything alr—" He stopped short when a boot to the back of his knee dropped him to a kneel. The next thing he knew, a gun barrel was pressed against his temple and his own weapon was being yanked from his grasp.

"Get over by her. Stay on the floor. Move slowly," Lita said as she took a step back and closed the door with her foot. Guns in both hands now, she aimed one at each of them.

"Who the hell are you?" Christopher demanded as he moved to rise. Amalie started from her chair towards him as well.

A startling *pop* and the splintering sound of a bullet lodging into the front of Amelie's vanity just six inches to her left silenced them both.

"Does nobody fucking listen in this house?" Lita barked. "You, big guy, stay on the fucking floor and go sit by her. You, little shit, stay in your goddamn seat. And both of you shut the fuck up for a minute."

They both did as they were told, Christopher rubbing Amelie's arm and giving her a reassuring nod. Lita stuffed Christopher's revolver into her belt but kept her own weapon trained on them as she went back to leaning against the door.

"Okay," Lita said after a time, "I think everyone in this room can agree that this situation is fucked. So let's try to straighten some shit out. How much you two help with that will determine whether or not you walk away from this, understood?" Amelie nodded, but Christopher gave no response. He only stared at Lita, and she knew he was waiting for his chance to act.

Lita looked to Amelie. "Five years ago, I killed your mother." Christopher blinked, looking up to the young woman as well, but she just nodded solemnly. "It wasn't anything personal. I was just doing my job. I didn't know a damn thing about you two. Hell, I didn't even know your age, let alone that you were the Daughter of Chicane."

"Alright," Amelie said, "I get you. That's why you took this job. You didn't know I was the same girl."

"Right, but it doesn't make any fucking sense. Why would someone hire a hitter to do a job they had already botched?"

"Maybe your employer didn't know," Amelie suggested.

Lita shook her head. "If my employer is who I think it is,

he knew damn well."

Amelie quirked a brow. "You don't know who hired you?"

"Didn't ask," Lita said matter-of-factly.

"Assassins don't ask questions," Christopher said with a scowl. "All they care about is the money. The rest is just details."

Lita turned her gun on him. "I don't remember saying a goddamn thing to you."

Amelie was fiddling with a lock of her hair as she stared thoughtfully at the floor. Suddenly, her eyes snapped up. "What if you were set up?"

Lita glanced to her, then back to Christopher. "That's an excellent point. One that brings me to you. What exactly made you come barging in here?"

"I'm not telling you anything," Christopher said. "And why are you helping her, Amelie? This woman murdered your mother, and she was sent here to kill you."

Amelie touched Christopher's arm. "Yes, but if you haven't noticed, she hasn't yet. Nor did she years ago when she had the chance."

"And that makes it okay to help her?" he whispered forcefully.

"'Judge not lest ye be judged', Christopher. Jesus himself said to forgive those who know not what they are doing. This woman is clearly lost and our guidance may help her find her way."

They both looked to Lita, who was staring at them incredulously. "Is the prayer circle over, or did you two want to sing a few hymns? I need an answer to my question. Now."

Christopher stared at Lita for a long moment, then finally said, "A guard came to me and said he had seen an intruder entering the east dining hall window. I came to secure Amelie while he went to guard her stepbrother.

Hardly conspiratorial."

"Oh?" Lita said doubtfully. "So is that your standard procedure for guards who see someone breaking into the place? Don't try to stop them, don't sound any alarms, just come looking for you to report personally?"

Christopher cleared his throat. "No. They are trained to engage the threat and make as much noise as possible."

"Uh huh," Lita went on. "And this guard, was he assigned to watch that particular area of the palace tonight?"

"No, actually," Christopher said, his brow furrowing. "He's the head of Michael's entourage."

"Henrik?" Amelie asked. Christopher nodded.

"Who's Michael?" Lita pressed.

"Sorry, Michael Calderwood. Amelie's stepbrother." Christopher said.

"Right," Lita went on. "So this Henrik guy comes to you out of the blue to warn you that I'm here and you come running straight here without wondering why it went down that way. I'm gonna go ahead and guess that was probably a pretty predictable move on your part, right? You see where I'm going with this, big guy?"

Christopher nodded gravely. "And there's no way Henrik is behind this. He's a good guard, but not very bright. Which mean only one thing."

"Fuck," Lita whispered, rubbing her temple with her free hand.

"What? What does it mean?" Amelie asked.

"It means Michael is the one who put a price on your head. Only he could have ordered Henrik to watch that window knowing that she'd be coming through it," Christopher explained. "Then Henrik sent me to kill the assassin before she got out. No loose ends, no investigation, and no one to pay."

Lita, pacing now, kicked the bedpost. "God dammit!"

"You'd do well to keep it down," Christopher warned, "I

didn't alert any other guards, but there are some posted nearby."

Lita sighed and began to chew on the inside of her cheek. Her weapon was lowered now.

Christopher turned his attention to Amelie, who was staring down at her hands, her eyes trembling. He placed a comforting hand on her knee. "I know this is frightening," he said softly, "but now is not the time to be afraid. You're not safe here. We have to get you away, then work things out from there."

"B-But, there's no telling how many guards are loyal to Michael. How can I get away without…" Amelie suddenly looked to Lita. "You! You can take me with you!"

"What?" Lita and Christopher said in unison.

"You got in here without anyone noticing, right? You can get me out just the same." Amelie's eyes pleaded with Lita, but she was unmoved.

"Fuck that. I'm the hell out of here." She turned toward the door.

"You leave that way, you'll hit guards. The rounds are due to come by here any minute." Christopher said. Lita stopped, sighing as she looked back their way. Christopher turned to Amelie. "What are you talking about? What makes you think you can trust this woman?"

"Christopher, who I can and can't trust has just been completely turned upside down. The two things I know about her are that she's deadly and that she won't kill me. I'd say that works out in my favor, wouldn't you?"

He considered this for a moment, then they both turned their eyes to Lita.

"It's not fucking happening," she said.

"Then I suppose you have another way to get out of here?" Christopher asked.

"I could just shoot you and hold her hostage."

"You really think you'd get very far?"

"Farther than having a scrawny little girl holding me back."

"I could pay you," Amelie chimed in.

Lita scoffed. "Oh? Should I send Daddy a bill?"

Amelie narrowed her eyes and suddenly rose to her feet. Lita raised her gun defensively, but the young woman stood her ground. "Now you listen to me. My father is in poor health and will pass any day. Who do you think the power of this city goes to when that happens? Would you rather the Lady of Chicane owe you a favor or be enraged that you left her for dead?" Christopher blinked in surprise and looked to Lita, trying to suppress the grin that wanted to turn up on his face.

Lita chewed the inside of her cheek thoughtfully as she stared at Amelie, teetering on the verge of decisive action.

"I remember saving your life," Amelie added quietly.

Lita sighed heavily. "I can take you as far as a couple of people who might be more interested in helping you. That's it. Now put on some dark clothes and move your ass."

Without hesitation, Amelie bolted for her closet.

"Un-fucking-believable," Lita muttered, then looked to Christopher. "So are you going to do anything to facilitate this or just sit there on your ass?"

Christopher pushed himself to his feet. "I'm not sure which way you came into town, but we need to get you out of here without any checkpoint guards seeing you."

"And how am I supposed to do that?" Lita asked.

"Head west from the palace until you reach Stonewall Road, about a quarter of a mile from the checkpoint. Turn left. As you go along, the road will get closer to the tree line. Once you reach a bridge, take a left off the road and it'll loop around and underneath, then lead you onto a path into the woods. It's almost impossible to see from the road, but it's there. That path will let you out about a mile up Maple City Highway. Just keep your headlights off in the forest until you're well clear of the city."

"Sounds reasonable," Lita said, nodding, "but that assumes I can get the two of us out of the palace."

"I can send the guards in the wrong direction, buy you some time and a clear path."

"What about the ones loyal to her brother? Will they go for that?"

Christopher sighed. "They will if it looks like you attacked me and took off with her. I'll need you to—"

He didn't have a chance to finish before Lita drew his own revolver and cracked him across the cheek with it, knocking him back to the floor. She then dropped it and kicked it under the bed.

Christopher brought his knuckles up to his cheek and glared at her. "Thanks."

"No problem," she said with a smirk. Getting to hit someone had lightened her mood. "Are you ready yet, kid?"

Amelie emerged from the closet a moment later, clad in a black, long-sleeved shirt and slacks. "How's this?"

"Great," Lita said unenthusiastically. "Alright, big guy, how we getting out of here?"

Christopher rose once more and went to a large oak armoire that stood against the wall facing the end of Amelie's bed. He threw his weight against the side of it and slid it over to reveal a square door in the wall. It was the opening to an old dumbwaiter.

Amelie blinked. "I didn't know that was there."

Christopher chuckled. "You get the blueprints to this place when you become head guard. I know all of its secrets." With that, he opened the dumbwaiter door and started pulling the rope inside, bringing it up to their level. "This will take you down to the basement. Adjacent to that is the wine cellar. In the back, past the last row of shelves, there's an old cellar door. It might take some prying to get it open, but it'll lead you right up into the orchard." He glanced over his shoulder at Lita. "Will that do for you?"

"Perfectly, actually," she said, holstering her weapon and crossing her arms.

"Good. Wait five minutes after you get down there so I have time to redirect all the guards, then get the hell out of here." Christopher finished hoisting up the dumbwaiter and stepped aside. "Now listen, about eight or nine miles outside of Maple City, there's a little road that leads to a big old cemetery in the forest, do you know it?" Lita nodded. "Alright, at noon tomorrow either I or someone I send will meet you there and tell you what to do next. If it's not me, they'll have to give you a password so you know I sent them. The password is ladybug." Lita coughed suddenly, trying to contain a laugh. "Problem?" Christopher asked.

She cleared her throat. "No, no. Nothing at all. Ladybug. It's...adorable." Even Amelie had to cover her mouth to hide a smirk.

Christopher sighed and shook his head. "You be safe now, you understand young miss?"

Amelie suddenly ran to him and threw her arms around his midsection tightly. "Thank you," she whispered. Christopher, after a moment of shock, hugged her back gently. Lita rolled her eyes at the exchange, but allowed it a moment to take place. When Amelie pulled back and looked up at Christopher, her eyes glimmered with a thin veil of tears. "Christopher, please tell my father I love him and..." She paused, unable to think of anything else to say as she realized she might very well never see him again. She tried to fight back the sudden urge to stay. "Just that I love him."

"I will, Amelie. I promise." He gave her another quick hug and whispered, "Just be careful," before motioning for her to get in the dumbwaiter. She nodded, then rose up on her tip-toes and gave him a quick kiss on the cheek before climbing into the small, square space.

Lita went next, lifting one foot into the box before

pausing to look at Christopher. "Make sure you keep your boys good and off our backs, big guy. I'll have her out of here in no time."

Christopher extended a hand. "The name's Christopher."

Lita eyed it, then him. "Good for you." She climbed into the dumbwaiter.

Letting out a snort, Christopher leaned down and peered in at Lita one last time. "You get her killed, I will find you."

"Yeah, good fucking luck," Lita said with a laugh and closed the door. Christopher gritted his teeth angrily as he slid the armoire back into place, then waited for the squeaking of the dumbwaiter's pulley to stop before recovering his lost weapon from under the bed and heading into the hall.

II

They made the return trip to Rain's car with relative ease. They encountered no guards; Christopher had kept his word. Amelie did well for a little rich girl, in Lita's opinion. She had stayed low and silent the whole time. She only encountered some trouble at the outer wall, but Lita was able to climb to the top and then pull her up and over. At last they found themselves crouched behind a gravestone at the edge of the cemetery, Rain's car within sight only thirty feet away.

"I'll go get it started, then you come and get in," Lita said.

"You won't leave me?" Amelie asked.

"Tempting, but no," Lita replied, then hurried out, staying low as she advanced on the vehicle. She quickly rounded it, hopped inside, and brought it to life before gesturing Amelie over. She followed Lita's example, climbing into the passenger seat just as quickly.

Christopher's way out of the city was brilliant. Lita didn't see a single soul and she'd have never believed there could be a road under that bridge if she hadn't seen it for herself. It was almost unsettling how easy it was for them to leave town and get back onto the highway towards the brothers' house.

"This is a nice car," Amelie said, cutting through the silence once they were far enough from the city that Lita felt comfortable turning on more than just the car's running lights.

"Count yourself lucky. I'm really sticking my neck out returning this to the asshole I borrowed it from," Lita replied.

"You don't seem the type to borrow things," Amelie ventured.

"Yeah, well, he's not the type to loan things out," Lita replied.

Another long silence ensued.

"My name's Amelie," she said finally.

"I know," Lita replied dryly, staring at the road.

"What's yours?" she asked meekly.

There was a lengthy pause before she finally replied, "Lita."

"That's pretty," Amelie said, but was again only greeted by silence. She turned her eyes out the window, watching as rain began to drizzle against her youthful reflection.

"Lita?"

"What?"

"When we first met, why didn't you kill me?"

"You reminded me of someone I used to know."

"Who?"

"It's time to be quiet now."

TEN

I

Lita was concerned.

Not because she had backed out of her job and taken flight with the target. She was damned good at hiding if the situation called for it. And not because she was returning a stolen car to a likely furious and possibly homicidal vampire. Were she really that afraid of him, she'd just keep on driving. No, Lita was concerned because there was a young girl in the seat next to her that she was on a mission to protect, and she had no idea why.

The person she knew herself to be had never acted this way and, in her defense, she'd never had any reason to help anyone but herself. No one had ever done her any charity. Even the freedom Cleric had handed her—a gift of death in a wrapping of gospel—had turned out to be a debt she was forced to repay in conscience, innocence, and blood. So to do something selfless—to make an attempt at saving another human being, putting herself in real danger in the process—that wasn't like her at all. And she did not particularly enjoy it.

Bringing the car to a stop outside the Moonshadow

house, Lita sighed and killed the engine. "You ready to see some fireworks, kid?" she asked, glancing at Amelie. The young lady nodded, though she didn't know what she was agreeing to. Lita chuckled. "I should send you in first." She was only half joking.

Lita climbed out of the car, grabbing her bag in the process, and headed for the house. Amelie followed close behind. Pausing briefly at the front door, she reached back and brushed her fingers over her firearm. She didn't figure on having to use it, but she compulsively double-checked its availability before walking into any tense situation. She nodded to herself and went inside.

Rain's head shot up as soon as they walked in, but Lita could only see his face over the back of the couch. He was kneeling in front of the armchair, tending to a very groggy-looking Alex, who must have only come around moments earlier. The boy leaned against the arm of the chair, his face pallid, head propped up in one hand.

Rain, however, held no visible lasting effects of the drug in his eyes. All they reflected were rage as soon as he caught sight of Lita. He rose to his feet and rounded the couch with startling agility as he advanced towards her. "You have exactly three seconds to explain just what the hell you think you were—" he stopped, both in his tracks and his speech, as Lita held up a hushing hand and Amelie stepped out from behind her, looking spooked.

Rain blinked. "Who is this?" he asked, his tone unchanged. Alex raised his head, squinting at the three of them.

"Her name is Amelie," Lita said in a calm, quiet tone. Her eyes didn't flinch from Rain's. "She's the Daughter of Chicane."

Rain's right eyebrow rose slightly and his hands found his hips. "And what is she doing here?"

"Her brother—" Lita began.

"Step," Amelie interjected.

"Her *step*brother," Lita continued, shooting the girl a look, "is trying to have her killed. She needs a place to hide out for a few days."

Rain glanced back and forth between the two. "And how do you figure into all of this?"

Lita's eyes dropped then and she bit the inside of her cheek. "I was supposed to kill her." Amelie looked away as well and Alex sat up, piqued interest clearing the last of his mind's fog.

Rain's jaw clenched, the tendons in his neck flexing. "So let me get this straight," he said, the volume of his voice not rising, but anger rising within it. "First you neglect to mention that you're an assassin. You then proceed to steal my car in order to go on a job. Then you snatch up your target and bring her back to my home, where she may very well be followed by further—and likely more competent— killers?"

"We weren't followed," Lita said quietly, but her gaze remained lowered. She hadn't felt much shame since childhood, but the tightness in her chest was bringing back unpleasant memories.

Rain's hands fell to his sides and balled into tight fists. He opened his mouth to say more, but stopped when Amelie suddenly took it upon herself to step forward.

"Sir," she said cautiously, "Please don't be angry with Lita. I asked her to bring me somewhere I could be safe. She felt sure this place could offer me that. But I don't wish to put you or anyone else in danger. I'd rather go and find somewhere myself to—"

"Wait a minute," Alex said as he pushed himself out of the chair. Rain gave him a look, but Alex shot one right back as he approached the group. "We can at least treat you, our guest, to something warm to drink. Right, Rain?"

Rain bristled, but then sighed and released the tension

from his fists. "Fine. Take the young lady in and make some tea, Alex. I'm going to have a conversation with Lita."

Alex motioned for Amelie to follow him. She whispered a quiet "Thank you" to Rain before heading along. Lita raised her eyes finally, looking to Alex first, but all he returned was a mistrustful glare before escorting Amelie to the kitchen. She sighed and turned her gaze to Rain.

He pointed towards the stairs, as though sentencing a small child to time in her bedroom. "Upstairs," he said firmly.

Lita, feeling too emotionally drained to put up any of her usual stubbornness, only nodded and headed that way with Rain following behind.

At the top of the staircase there was a long hallway with three doors on each side and one at the end. Rain moved in front of Lita and led her to the second door on the left, opening it and ushering her into a moderately sized bedroom. It was simply furnished, not personalized in any way. Lita supposed it was a guest room.

"Sit," Rain said, pointing to the bed. Lita dropped her heavy bag on the floor and sat on the edge of the bed. She stared down at her hands in silence.

II

Downstairs in the kitchen, Alex had gone to the stove and motioned Amelie to sit at the table. She took up a chair and looked around the kitchen.

"You have a lovely home," she said.

"Thank you," Alex replied as he pulled a teapot down from one of the hooks above the stove and carried it over to the sink. "My brother built it himself. I wish I could say I helped, but I was...away for several years. When I came back it was already done."

"It's just you and him living here?" Amelie asked.

"It is. In fact, you and Lita are the only other people who've ever stepped foot inside this house. That I know of, anyway." The teapot full, Alex shut off the sink and carried it to the stove.

"It seems like a lot of space for only two people," she said.

Alex chuckled. "Not compared to the High Palace, it isn't."

"No, I suppose not," Amelie said with a smile.

"I'm not sure I could live in a place that big. I feel like I'd get lost." As the teapot heated up, Alex started retrieving mugs and other things from various cabinets.

"I do feel a little lost in there sometimes," Amelie replied distantly, her eyes drifting towards the bay windows and the moonlit landscape that lay outside. Alex said something then that she didn't catch. "I'm sorry, what was that?" she asked, returning her attention to him.

"I asked how you take your tea," he said. "We have no cream, but we do have sugar and honey."

Amelie's face lit up. "I haven't had honey in months! I was told there had been a shortage this year!"

Alex smiled. "My brother has a way of getting things that aren't always easy to find. So honey it is then?"

"Yes, please," she said, returning his smile and feeling a warm blush creep up on her cheeks. Alex pretended not to notice, but he soon felt his own face start to burn as well.

III

Upstairs, a long silence had passed between the two of them. Rain had found a spot leaning against the closed door and was smoking a cigarette in a slow, thoughtful way he sometimes did, listening to the almost imperceptible hisses and crackles of burning tobacco and paper with each drag he took. Lita, however, had hardly moved at all. She still sat just staring down at her hands, feeling numb.

"You've got to be the worst assassin I've ever heard of," Rain finally said. "I can't say I condone humans killing one another, but what in God's name would possess you to try to rescue your..."

For the second time since they met, Rain felt words fail him because of a single look in Lita's eyes. This time, it wasn't her rage that stopped him cold. It was something he hadn't seen in her before. As she looked up at him, her green eyes glistened with tears.

"The last person I killed was five years ago," she said shakily, "and it was that girl's mother."

Rain's brow knitted. "What?"

Lita opened her mouth, and before she knew it was happening, it all began spilling out. She barely touched on the matter of her uncle, but Rain read between the lines there. She told him about being raised to be an assassin. Then the assignment gone wrong that opened her eyes to what she was doing. Finally, her acceptance of this last job out of pure desperation to be free of this place that haunted her so.

By the time she was finished, the strong-willed, brash woman was nearly sobbing and Rain, displaying a level of patience that can only be learned through immortality, stood silently listening.

"When I saw that girl again, I couldn't do it," she whispered. "And when she asked me to help her, I couldn't say no. I took from her the one thing I've always wished I'd had." Her eyes were set on Rain, tears trickling down her cheeks. "Can you imagine what that did to me? What it's like to lose your mother so young you can't even remember her face, and then to be raised by a hateful, abusive bastard?"

Rain's jaw clenched reflexively. "I think you and I have

more in common than you know."

Lita dropped her gaze once more and shook her head. "I just don't get it."

"What don't you get?" Rain asked.

"Why I took her. Why I agreed. I mean, I get why I couldn't kill her, but this...this isn't me. I don't help people. I do what needs to get done to help me, and I get the fuck out. So why? Why did I take her?"

Rain suddenly chuckled and Lita looked up quickly, hurt, thinking he was laughing at her. He raised a hand, assuring her that he was not.

"Redemption is a funny thing," he said in a gentle tone. "Even if we don't ask for it—even if we don't think we want it—sometimes we seek it out. In our words and our actions. Because something drives us to make right the things that we did. It's what allows us to keep living with ourselves."

Lita nodded, then sniffled and wiped her nose. "I guess," she said wearily. "Well, anyway, I brought her this far. I should get the hell out of here before I cause any more trouble. Just promise you won't turn her away. She's innocent in all of this." She started to stand, but Rain stepped forward, gesturing for her to sit.

"Nobody's going anywhere," he said. "There's plenty of room in this house. Alex and I will help you look after her. Anyone who comes looking for either of you will have to answer to us."

Lita shook her head in disbelief and new tears sprang into her eyes. "Why? Why are you helping me after everything I did?"

"We're all looking for forgiveness from someone," he said softly. "Even if it can't come from those we hurt."

Lita sniffled again and wiped her eyes with her forearm. "Thank you," she whispered. Rain nodded.

"Take a few minutes to collect yourself, then come

downstairs and we'll all talk things over." He turned to leave.

"I don't get you," Lita said, almost inaudibly.

Rain paused, looking back at her. "How do you mean?"

She laughed briefly, a short, bitter sound. "All my life I've watched people do the most awful things imaginable to one another out of nothing more than greed and lust and anger." She looked up at him, her eyes wide and naked. "But you're a fucking *vampire*, yet you're the first person who's ever offered me anything without expecting something in return. You're..." she paused, looking for the right word. "...unique. I can't be the only one to see that about you, right?"

The corners of Rain's mouth turned up into a slight smile, but his eyes showed sadness so profound it nearly made Lita want to turn away. "When you're a monster, no one sees what kind of man you are."

With that, he pulled the door closed, leaving Lita alone to think things over.

THIRD INTERLUDE

Didst thou watch a flower die?
Did thy tears bid it good-bye?
Tremble not, for 'tis not gone
In morrow's blooms it carries on

Laughter was a thing not often heard in this house.

The two brothers giggled as they ran across the living room of a three-story abode in rural England. The younger of the two laughed cheerfully as his bare feet danced around a corner and he took off running down a hallway. He was a small child, barely six years old. His shaggy black hair fell in a mess upon his forehead, threatening to obscure his dark blue eyes and possibly prevent foresight of dangers that might lie in his giddy path.

The boy giving chase was five years his senior. He moved with the spry but awkward gait of a prepubescent lad, quickly gaining on the child he pursued. His own blond locks were unruly as well, but he had the presence of mind to keep them brushed away from his line of sight.

"You're it!" the older brother said as he tapped the

younger lightly on the shoulder. However, the little one didn't appear to notice. In fact, he had stopped running altogether and was now staring at something more interesting than their game. The older brother followed his gaze up toward the long, dark flight of stairs that led to the third floor.

"You know we're not allowed to go up there," the older brother said. He placed a hand on the younger brother's shoulder and tried to turn him away from his fixation, but to no avail.

The younger brother pulled away, still staring intently up the stairs. His gaze was piercing, the keen fascination of a child who has stumbled across something he knows he's not supposed to do, but will end up doing anyway.

The older brother knelt in front of him. "If we go up there and Father finds out, he'll be angry. You know we should not make him angry." His gaze trailed down to his younger brother's lower lip, which had a three-day-old split still healing in it. The little boy's own eyes went to his elder's right wrist, which bore a yellowing bruise in the distinctive shape of a large handprint.

"But Father is not to be home for a long while, and I very much wish to see what's up there." His eyes went back to the stairs. "Do you not?"

The older brother chewed his lower lip thoughtfully and glanced towards the stairs himself.

"Could we not go up and straight back down?" the younger brother implored. "He would never know. Please?"

Sighing resignedly, the older brother finally nodded. "Very well. Only to the top to see what's there, then straight back down. We mustn't tarry long." The younger brother grinned and nodded eagerly. "Stay behind me," the elder said. Leading the way, he went to the stairs, took a deep breath, and began the ascent towards whatever mysteries lie ahead.

There were fifteen steps, the older brother knew. He had counted them on several occasions, but had never been brave enough to attempt the defiant voyage. What a wonder that a child nearly half his age had finally talked him into it.

Halfway up, the older brother stepped on the eighth wooden stair and it screeched loudly, seeming to call out their crime to whomever might be listening. Both boys tensed, and the younger even started to turn to run screaming from whatever horrible beast had made that noise.

As soon as they realized what the sound had been, they both sighed and exchanged glances and nervous laughter before resuming their voyage. Though neither would admit it to the other, they both felt the same fear crawling up their spines. They worried that the moment they reached the top step, some hairy beast that had clawed its way free from their nightmares would lurch out of the darkness and steal them away. Some scaly creature from a black place between worlds that had breath like decay and a special taste for curious little blue-eyed boys. Something worse than they could ever imagine. Something worse than their father.

But as the older brother's line of sight finally crested the top step, he realized there was no evil here. In fact, there was nearly nothing at all, save for a long hallway that came to an end at a lonely door. Somehow that was more disconcerting. For all their bravery, they had merely replaced one mystery with another.

"Now, let us return downstairs and find a new game to play," the older brother said.

"No!" the younger brother cried. "We must see what's behind that door. We cannot turn around now!"

The older brother glanced back down the stairs. He didn't like this at all. But as he looked back to his brother, he was once more met with that pleading face he could not bear to deny. "Straight to the door, look inside, and then back down. We cannot stay up here much longer." The younger brother nodded emphatically, but didn't budge. He was waiting for his big brother to lead the way, as he always did, though the older brother didn't know why. He wasn't anything special. He couldn't even protect his little brother from their own father. He wished he could; seeing the younger boy take the brunt of Father's rage was far more painful than any bruise laid upon his own flesh, but he was still too afraid to stop it. Maybe in a year or two. Maybe when he was bigger, stronger. Maybe...

With a deep breath and a nod, the older brother began leading the way down the hall. There wasn't much to the narrow expanse, he realized. Low-burning sconce oil lamps cast their glow from near each of the four corners. A pair of floral paintings hung opposite one another at the middle point of the two long walls. Under the painting to their right was a standalone oak sideboard with three cabinets, one large between two small. Its top was bare save for a thin layer of dust and a very large, very expensive-looking vase. The decorative piece, which was big enough to be an urn, was dark blue with a black inlay of elaborate swirling patterns. The younger brother regarded this with some interest as they hurried by.

Finally reaching the door, the older brother paused to once more glance over his shoulder, wondering how they had possibly trekked this far. He looked to his brother, who nodded slowly, encouragingly. Then his gaze shifted back to the door in front of them. In his mind, he suddenly conjured up the frightening image of opening this door only to find another long hallway with another door at the end. This would lead to another, and another after that. An endless linear maze of curiosity designed by their father for the sole purpose of catching them trespassing where they didn't belong.

The older brother bit his tongue forcefully, hoping the

flash of pain would deter him from his wild and frightening imagination. It worked long enough for him to will his palm to the dingy brass doorknob and his fingers to encircle it. But as he moved to turn it, it protested, uttering a soft click and refusing to budge more than a fraction of an inch.

"It's locked," the older brother muttered, but when he looked to the younger, he saw that the boy's gaze was fixated just below the doorknob.

"The keyhole," the younger boy whispered, his eyes bright with wonder. The older brother looked down and noticed it too. From somewhere past that tiny opening, a light was flickering, casting an orange glow at them. The brothers exchanged a glance and a nod, and the elder knelt down to peer inside.

His pupil strained with the change of light and depth. It was surprisingly bright inside, and as his eye adjusted he saw that it was due to a fiercely blazing fire inside a grey stone fireplace across the room. He felt great surprise at the revelation that there was a fireplace up here he'd never known of, but even greater was his curiosity as to how it could be burning with such passion. Father had been away for hours.

A long minute crept by as the older brother gazed onward. The younger brother tugged at his sleeve insistently a couple of times, wanting his own turn to look, but the elder refused to budge. He was just about to give up and pull away when a cold sound of rattling metal touched his ear and something moved into his line of sight, blackening the orange keyhole shape that had been casting over his eye. As the younger boy watched, all the color drained from his elder's face. He jerked backwards, falling onto his rear, but continued to stare wide-eyed at the keyhole from a distance.

"What is it?" the younger brother asked. When he received no answer, the boy moved to take a closer look for himself.

"No!" the older brother cried out, lunging with such force that his little brother jumped.

"But I want to see what's in there!"

"No, we must go back. We must go back downstairs before—"

Both children suddenly froze in unimaginable terror as they heard the front door slam two floors below.

"Boys! Come!" a deep, booming voice echoed, causing both of them to break out in gooseflesh immediately.

"Go! Run!" the older brother whispered sharply as he scrambled to his own feet. The younger did not protest this time, not for a second. He immediately broke into a dead sprint towards the stairs. The elder moved to follow him, but suddenly called out, "Wait!" to warn him not to pound down the stairs.

The younger boy looked over his shoulder at his brother's cry, but in his panic he forgot to stop running first, and his feet became intertwined, sending him flying forward. With a crashing pain, his shoulder collided with the sideboard and he landed flat on his stomach, all the air rushing from him in a sharp gasp. The pair looked up simultaneously and watched in hopeless horror as the large vase began rocking atop the cabinet. It tottered forward, then back, and for a moment looked like it might right itself, seeming to move in sickeningly slow motion. But despite the mental pleas of both children, it finally fell forward and shattered on the hardwood floor.

Not a second later, the boys could hear their father's heavy footsteps echo across the ground floor, and then come pounding up the first flight of stairs. Fear gripped the older brother's insides, but something instinctual kicked in and then he was moving. He rushed to his little brother, pulled open the sideboard's large center cabinet, and quickly thanked God it was completely empty inside.

"Get inside, now!" he whispered urgently to his little

brother.

"But you—"

"I'll be fine. Just get in there, and no matter what happens, don't you make a sound."

Tears welling in the little brother's eyes, he nodded and scrambled to squeeze into the confined space. Once he was inside, the elder closed the door, then was on his feet headed towards the stairs, intent on putting some distance between himself and his brother's hiding place. He made it just four paces before the looming form of his father came into view at the end of the hall.

To a small boy, Father looked like the embodiment of a force of nature. A blacksmith by trade, his body had been hardened through years of work. Thick ropes of muscles lined arms that led to large, calloused hands. Even after he had attained notable success and wealth when his renowned work was commissioned by the King himself two years before, he had never eased in his tireless work ethic. He might as well have been cast from the very silver and steel he pounded down every day.

But swords and blacksmithing were the furthest things from their minds right now. Father had reached the hallway, and was no more than five paces from the older brother. The man glared down at his son contemptuously, his hands balling into fists that appeared to the child to be the size of boulders.

"Explain yourself, boy." His voice was not raised, but that was somehow more frightening than if it were. It was even, flat, and nearly overpowering in its booming depth.

"I…uh…that is, I was…" the boy stammered, trying to force something, anything, to come out.

"Out with it, boy, and don't dare lie. You'll only worsen matters for yourself." That chilling evenness remained in his voice. Like the calm before a storm.

The boy dropped his eyes. "We were p-playing a hhiding game. I c-came up h-here to m-make s-sure he did not hide h-here. I know w-we're n-not allowed t-to—"

"Look at me when you speak!" Father suddenly yelled. The boy flinched, then cautiously raised his eyes to meet the man's furious gaze. "Good," he said, that flatness returning. "Now stop stuttering and explain how you broke this vase."

The boy swallowed hard. "When I heard you c-c-" he paused for a deep breath, then went on, "When I heard you come in I was frightened and I bumped it and it fell, sir." Though he controlled the stutter, his voice began to crack and he could feel his eyes starting to burn.

"It seems the time has come for a lesson about trespassing. Do you agree, boy?"

"Yes, Father," the boy replied obediently. He had learned long ago that this was the required response to such a question. Failing to provide it would only double the punishment about to be doled out. His gaze fell once more to his feet. Handcrafted leather shoes, brown and soft. He was due for a new pair soon. As he watched, a salty drop of wetness fell upon one of them.

Father's hand moved to his belt, but not to remove it. He was reaching for the arsenal he kept there. His three favorite weapons.

First, there was the switch. He had stripped and soaked in water three slender, foot-long pieces of willow tree branch. Once they were pliable, he had braided them and tanned them in the sun. It had created a fierce beating tool as flexible as it was stinging. It had not cracked once in nearly a decade of use.

Next was the bullwhip. There was nothing particularly special in its design—just six feet of brown leather—but Father was good with this. Though he could remove a great deal of flesh with its crack, he always kept his blows shallow enough that the boys could still do chores the following day. God forbid their punishment turn into some sort of holiday.

Finally, there was the dagger. As with the switch, Father had made it himself. Were it detached from its frightening owner, it would have been lovely to behold. Small but razor-sharp, its solid silver blade was six inches long, stemming from a black oak handle with spiraling silver inlay.

On good days, he reached for the switch. On bad days, he reached for the whip. Never had a day been so horrible that he had reached for the dagger.

Today, he took up the whip.

The boy sighed as Father yanked the small leather tie that held the coiled whip to his belt, and his heart started quickening at the sound of the loose end falling to the floor. Knowing what he was expected to do, he unbuttoned his shirt with trembling hands, then let it slip off his slender frame and fall to the side. As he turned around and placed his hands on top of his head, he dimly wondered how many lashes he would receive. Father never divulged such information, only doled out the punishment. The most he had ever gotten was five, for not chopping enough firewood before a long snowstorm.

He closed his eyes upon hearing the tip of the leather slide across the floor, then clenched his teeth and tensed at the hiss of the whip cutting through the air, and finally cried out as it sliced decisively from his right shoulder blade down left to his lower back. There was a brief moment of fleeting hope after each strike until he heard the leather slide across the floor again as it was drawn back for another lash. The second came, drawing another cry, but not as bad as the first. Then a third, the moans growing quieter each time. On came the fourth, not so bad now; his back was getting hot and numb. After the fifth, he breathed a heavy sigh of relief.

But the whip dragged back once more. He screamed at the sixth, as he wasn't expecting it at all. Seventh and eighth brought more terrible cries. The numbness had disappeared, and his nerves felt like they were on fire. Ninth now, and it nearly drove him to his knees. His breath came in short, shallow sobs. The tenth, however, was the worst by far. The sharp tip slipped around the back of his neck and licked him just below the ear. For a moment, his vision faded out, and when it came back the crotch of his pants was warm and wet. His face flushed with hot shame.

Finally, as he heard Father begin coiling up his hateful tool, the boy collapsed to his hands and knees. Wetness coursed down his sides and soaked into the back of his pants. Beneath his hitching sobs, he could hear the faint sound of small droplets falling on the floor.

"Did you learn your lesson?" Father asked sternly.

"Y-Yes, Father," the boy replied. He slowly raised his head, and as his gaze fell on the sideboard, his eyes widened.

The large cabinet door was open just a sliver, and from within a single eye stared at him, shimmering slightly in the hallway's dim light. As the older brother watched, that eye turned upward to look past him, and then there was a small gasp before the door clicked shut once more. Rising to his knees, the older brother looked up in horror at the realization that his father had seen this as well, and was starting towards the sideboard.

Then something happened. Perhaps it was the ten lashings that finally pushed him over the edge. Perhaps he could not bear the thought of watching his little brother receive the same punishment. Perhaps it was that horrible thing he had seen behind the door at the end of this hall. Whatever the cause, for the first time in his eleven years, the boy did the one thing he'd always dreamed of. He made a move to fight back.

Scrambling to his feet, he lunged for the dagger on Father's belt. For a fraction of a second, he thought he had it, and then Father's massive hand clasped around his wrist. His head whipped around, his eyes locking with his eldest son's. Those eyes grew wide with momentary surprise, and then the rage took over.

What happened next was as new to the boy as his own defiance was to his father. In an instant, the eyes staring down at him shifted hue from deep blue to a dark violet that almost seemed to glow with fury.

His free hand moving with speed the child had never seen, Father took the boy by the throat and lifted him effortlessly off the ground. Then, drawing the dagger with his other hand, Father brought its tip to within an inch of his son's eye as that glow in his own gaze grew more intense.

"Is this what you wanted?" Father boomed. "Is this what you were trying to snatch away from me, you little whelp? Well why don't you take it now?"

The boy could not answer. Between the hand holding his throat so tightly he could hardly breathe and the debilitating fear gripping his entire being, he was completely paralyzed. From inside the cabinet, the younger brother dared to peek out once more, and now looked on in frozen terror.

"Well, boy? Answer me! Is this what you wanted? Why don't you take it?" Father's rage was growing with each syllable. "Why don't you *take it!*" With those last two words, he drew back the dagger and plunged it to the hilt in his son's right side, just below his ribcage. The boy's mouth fell open as a mixture of shock and unprecedented pain invaded his small body. His little brother had to clasp both hands over his mouth to hold back his screams.

Then, as quickly as it pierced him, the dagger was withdrawn. Father dropped the boy on the floor and stumbled backwards, crushing pieces of broken glass beneath his heels. He blinked a couple of times, and the violet glow in his eyes dissipated, returning them to their normal shade of blue. He looked down at his son, but he seemed suddenly dazed, disoriented.

"Clean yourself up," he said absently, as if talking to

himself. "Find your brother and get this mess cleaned up." With that, he stepped over his son and headed downstairs. Father had virtually no working knowledge of human anatomy, especially in his perplexed state. He had no idea that his son was already starting to bleed out.

As soon as Father was gone, the younger boy burst form his hiding place and crawled over to his brother. The older boy cried out weakly as the younger tried to pull him into his lap, but only managed to place his head there.

"He stabbed you! I can't believe he stabbed you! Can you move?"

The older brother was beginning to sweat profusely, but he felt terribly cold. "I'm tired," he said, barely above a whisper.

"But I have to help you first," the younger brother said. "I have to patch your hurts, like you always do for me. Then we can nap. Father always lets us nap after lessons, right? We just have to get you to bed and you'll be better later, right?" His voice was cracking.

"I don't think I can get up," the older brother said, and his eyes began to drift closed.

The younger boy shook him violently, and his eyes snapped back open. "You can't go to sleep here. You have to get up so we can fix you. Please, get up!" Tears were flowing freely down his cheeks now, and he was quivering terribly.

The older brother, however, was no longer crying. "You have to do something for me," he said hoarsely.

"Anything. You're my big brother. I have to do what you say."

"You have to be strong. Be strong, but don't be afraid to hide. Hide until you can grow up big and run far away. Promise me you'll do that." His eyelids were very heavy now, and the oil lamps seemed to have faded. All he could see was his little brother's frightened face.

"But I need you so I can be strong!" the younger boy wailed. "You have to teach me how! You teach me how to do everything!"

"I can't teach you…you have to…yourself…know you can…"

"Please stay awake…" the younger boy pleaded.

"…I'm tired…" the older murmured.

"…Please…" the younger whimpered.

With the last of his strength, the older rubbed the younger's forearm softly. "I love you, baby brother," he whispered. Then his eyes slipped closed and his hand fell away as blackness enveloped him completely.

ELEVEN

I

"The Enforcers in the Crimson Hollow district aren't turning up a thing, sir."

Christopher was standing at a window on the top floor of the palace's north tower, which offered a beautiful view of the glowing city spread out across the night's hushed landscape. But down in the streets, it wasn't hushed in the least. Every Enforcer in Chicane was on patrol tonight, working elbow-to-elbow with nearly all the palace guards. They were digging through every inch of this city looking for young Amelie and her unidentified abductor. And the one man who knew that they would not be found here was the same man who had been orchestrating the search for the last three hours.

His mind drifted just left of nowhere as a young lead guard named Nikolai was trying to speak to him.

"Christopher, sir? Did you hear me?" He reached out timidly to touch his commander's shoulder, but withdrew his hand as Christopher turned to him.

"I did, Nik. I apologize. I'm just...preoccupied," Christopher said. He appeared weary but alert.

Nikolai nodded. "I'm sorry, sir. I know this must be a difficult position for you to be in. Everyone here knows that you are quite fond of Ms. Lamoureux."

"Amelie," Christopher whispered. He rubbed his cheek thoughtfully.

"I'm sorry, sir?"

Christopher shook his head. "Nothing, Nik. Yes, I am fond of Amelie, as we all are, which is why we're not going to stop working until she's found."

"No one plans to, sir," Nikolai said adamantly.

"Good. Now I know the Enforcers aren't pleased about cooperating with the palace guards. How is that working down there?"

"Well enough. They are doing what they need to be doing without enough argument to cause any hindrance."

"Glad to hear it. Now head back out and tell all the unit leaders to look harder. Start turning over inn rooms if necessary. I want this city picked through by dawn.

"And if she's not in the city anymore, sir?"

"We've sent word to Maple City Patrol, but it won't be safe to comb the woods until sunup. We all care about Amelie, but I'll not needlessly risk lives." Christopher noticed a look of concern on Nikolai's face. "We'll get her back, Nik. I promise."

Nikolai nodded, seeming somewhat comforted by his leader's words. "I'll get back out there then, sir." He turned to head back down the tower's stone steps.

"One more thing, Nik."

He paused and looked back. "Sir?"

Christopher touched his ear and nodded towards the doorway.

Nikolai leaned back and glanced down the stairwell, then nodded to Christopher and stepped closer to him.

"Omicron, monarch, two, centigrade," Christopher whispered.

Nikolai's eyes widened and he was momentarily speechless. He shook it off quickly though. "Team?"

"Thomas, Jasmine, and Morris, but only if you absolutely must tell them. No one else. Henrik is compromised, and others may be as well."

Nik nodded. "Delivery?"

"Hopewell, twelve-hundred, ladybug."

"Yes, sir," Nik said dutifully, and turned back towards the door.

"If I'm absent come dawn…" Christopher said.

Nik paused in his tracks, and nodded once. "Understood, sir."

"Good. Dismissed. And be safe."

"You too, Christopher."

As Nikolai's footsteps echoed down the stone stairway, Christopher returned to the window, looking out over the city once more. The code system was something he had hoped would never be necessary, but now he was feeling a wash of relief that he had devised it in the first place. Only Nik and the other guards Christopher had named knew the code. Besides being the highest-ranking guards under him, they were also friends to Christopher, people he trusted implicitly. They were his go-to team in an event like this.

The code was made up of four values: a Greek letter, denoting a specific hostile situation; a species of butterfly, indicating the status of one or more royal family member; a number or numbers, indicating which member or members of the family the status applied to; and a unit of measurement, which gave immediate orders to be carried out. The combinations were too numerous to list, but the sequence Christopher had just relayed to Nik translated as follows: centigrade meant increase security and hold positions; monarch two meant Amelie was in a safe place with a rendezvous plan; and omicron—the one Christopher's team had always called him paranoid for—

meant that a Calderwood had betrayed the house of Lamoureux.

It never sat well with Christopher how transactional the marriage of Richard Lamoureux and Marietta Calderwood had been. Though he had seen no evidence to make him directly suspicious of the woman or her son, he strongly believed in being prepared for any contingency. He couldn't say he was particularly happy about being right.

Christopher glanced at his watch, then paid the cityscape one last look before heading downstairs. He was due to brief Michael himself in thirty minutes, a meeting he had been greatly apprehensive of until he was able to speak with Nikolai. At least now he could be somewhat at ease knowing that Nik had been given the details of the rendezvous at Hopewell Cemetery. Should anything happen to him, someone would still be there for Amelie. But Christopher was going to do everything in his power to make sure he could greet young Ms. Lamoureux himself...even if that meant getting Michael Calderwood's blood on his own two hands.

II

"Your failures are trying my patience, Cleric."

Michael sat at the head of the long cherry wood table in the palace's second-floor conference room. His hands were resting on the tabletop, and between his right thumb and forefinger was his medal of Saint Monica, which he rubbed incessantly. His disappointed gaze was set across the room where Cleric was leaning against the far corner of the table, slowly drawing a small knife through a large red apple.

"Failures?" Cleric scoffed. "I haven't failed once, let alone repeatedly. This situation with your stepsister is a setback, but one that will be rectified in short order. And the Construct is back on schedule, set to be completed before daybreak." He popped a sliver of apple into his mouth.

"Perhaps," Michael said, "but it will all be for nothing if your pet doesn't find the Catalyst in time, and now we're forced to split its attention to help us find Amelie so you can finish the job your specialist failed to."

Cleric took his time chewing, enjoying the fact that Michael's grip on his religious trinket grew tighter with each passing second. Finally, he swallowed, cleared his throat, and said, "I don't know how I can explain this again in a way you will finally understand. The Visgaer doesn't find things by deducing where they are; it helps keep us on the right course of events such that we will find the Catalyst on our own. Even with this unexpected development, the Visgaer assures me that we will have the Catalyst in our possession by midday tomorrow."

"Yes, well, forgive me if I don't share your confidence," Michael said. "You gave me similar assurance that your employee would select a suitable specialist, and we see where that has gotten us. I trust that he has been dealt with firmly?"

Cleric touched the tabletop with the tip of his knife and eyed Michael. "How I handle my employees is none of your concern. He exercised poor judgment, but he will more than make up for it when he assists me in finishing the job you hired me to do, as well as taking care of the failed specialist."

"For your sake, I certainly hope so," Michael said.

Cleric chuckled and resumed slicing his apple. "That almost sounded like a threat. I hope you don't think this changes my fee any. I will finish the job, so I expect you to come through with payment, otherwise you and I will—"

Michael held up a hand. "Spare me the menacing speech. I am a man of my word. If you smooth this bump in the road and our efforts continue as planned, you will be provided with all the men and weaponry you need to deal with this General you so desperately seek."

Cleric opened his mouth to speak, but Michael cut him off once more.

"I'm not finished!" For a moment, his fingers shook from squeezing the medal so hard. Then, he abruptly pocketed it, cleared his throat, and rested his hands with interlaced fingers on the table. When he spoke again, his calm demeanor had returned. "You underestimate me, Cleric. Though I may be young and inexperienced with the matters in which you specialize, I am not a fool, and you don't intimidate me. Would you like to know why?"

"Enlighten me," Cleric said, his voice taut.

"Because you're operating under the assumption that if this job goes awry, you can cut your losses—perhaps kill me in the process—and just continue hiding from the General while you figure out a new way to deal with him. But there is the troublesome matter of the envelope."

Cleric knew Michael was waiting for him to ask 'what envelope', but he refused to indulge the child. He simply popped another sliver of apple into his mouth and began chewing, waiting for Michael to continue.

Michael sighed and went on. "This envelope is packed full of all the information about you I've been able to gather since we started our dealings. If you fail in the duties I have hired you for, or if any harm comes to me, that envelope will be hand-delivered to the General himself within a day's time. So you see, Cleric, if you live up to the reputation that made me decide to hire you in the first place, you will get everything we agreed upon. But if you do not, there won't be a place in Ayenee you can hide from your enemy. Do I make myself clear?"

"Unmistakably," Cleric muttered.

"Good," Michael said, then pulled his pocket watch from inside his suit coat. "The guard Christopher is due here any moment." He rose from his seat and put the watch away.

"Last chance to decide. Are you completely certain in your belief that he was involved in helping Amelie and your specialist escape?"

"Without a doubt," Cleric said. "If he hadn't been helping her, she would have killed him."

"She?" Michael asked incredulously.

"You know, I can only imagine how many people expressed that same sort of disbelief right before she put a bullet in them," Cleric mused.

Then there was a knock at the door.

III

"Come!" Michael called.

Christopher opened one of the conference room's double doors and stepped inside. He paid Michael little more than a passing glance before giving Cleric a much more thorough sizing up. The mere imposing presence of the man caused Christopher to unconsciously hook his thumb into his belt next to the holstered revolver there, a movement that did not go unnoticed by Cleric. "You wanted to see me, Mr. Calderwood?"

"I did, Christopher," Michael said. He made his way around the long table, buttoning his suit jacket as he walked. "I wanted to introduce you to Cleric here. He's a private investigator who has done some work for me in the past, and I've brought him in to help with the search for Amelie."

Christopher couldn't help noticing that Michael stopped his approach just out of arm's reach. It took nearly all of the guard's self-control to keep from lunging for the little shit and throttling him right then and there. "If you don't mind me asking, sir, in what capacity will Mr. Cleric be helping exactly?"

"Well, he will begin by taking your account of events again. We want to see if you might be able to recall anything you may have overlooked the first time through."

Christopher glanced at Cleric, who held his position across the room, still working on his apple. He was chewing thoughtfully, regarding the two of them with almost passive indifference. "With all due respect, sir," Christopher said, looking back to Michael, "I don't have time for that, and you don't have the authority to order it of me."

"I beg your pardon?" Michael asked, quirking a brow.

"No one informed you?" Christopher asked. "Upon hearing the news of Amelie's abduction, Lord Lamoureux immediately declared a state of guardianship authority, which means I presently command everyone under this roof…even you, sir. Now, if you'd like to take that up with the Lord, then—"

"Apparently you are the one who is uninformed," Michael interjected. "Richard slipped into unconsciousness less than an hour ago. The nurses tell me his vital signs are so weak that they expect him to pass before daybreak."

Christopher felt like he'd taken a blow to the stomach. "I…I just spoke with him. He was awake and completely alert."

Michael sighed and gave a small shrug. "Sometimes these things happen quickly. Henrik was there to see it and he said it all happened very fast."

"Henrik…" Christopher whispered.

"Yes. But with Richard incapacitated and Amelie absent, control of Chicane has fallen to me, and I am immediately rescinding guardianship author—"

Before he even knew what was happening, Michael found the side of his face pressed against the tabletop, Christopher's hand squeezing the back of his neck tightly, and the barrel of a revolver digging into his right temple. "Cleric!" he croaked.

"Don't look at me," Cleric said nonchalantly, not moving a muscle except to draw his knife once more through his apple. "I'm surprised he let you prattle on as long as he did."

"Keep your hands where I can see them," Christopher warned Cleric, whose only response was to pop the apple piece into his mouth. Yanking Michael back up straight, Christopher said, "You're going to back up with me towards the door, and you'd do well not to move much. This pistol has a very sensitive trigger."

"Cleric, do something!" Michael blurted, prompting a gruff shake from Christopher.

"Keep your mouth shut," he warned. They began backing towards the double doors.

"I don't know what you expect me to do," Cleric said with apple in his cheek. "You got yourself into this."

"Just keep doing what you're doing, Cleric. Stay right there," Christopher said. Then, to Michael, "And you, we're going to turn to our left and you're going to open the door on the right. Slowly."

They did as such, and as Michael opened the door, Christopher kept one eye on Cleric over his shoulder. He still hadn't budged as the two began stepping out into the hallway. But before Christopher could lead Michael all the way out of the room, he was ambushed.

It happened so fast that it took Christopher a couple of seconds to piece it together. First Michael was being pulled out of his grasp and into the hallway. Then somebody was shoving him back into the conference room, pinning him against the wall with one hand on his shoulder and the other on the wrist of his gun-wielding hand. His ears caught Henrik's voice out in the hall telling Michael to get to safety, and then his eyes settled on the man holding him. It was Thomas, one of the members of his trusted inner-circle.

"You son of a bitch!" Christopher growled.

"Sorry, Chief," Thomas said, holding him tight against the wall. "Sometimes the tides gotta ch—" his words twisted into a howl of pain as Christopher rammed a knee into his groin. Thomas released him and fell to his knees, but before Christopher could make use of his gun, Henrik barreled into him from the side, shoving him against the end of the table. Christopher felt an explosion of pain in his left hip, but it didn't prevent him from rocketing his elbow back and connecting it with Henrik's mouth, sending him stumbling backwards. Turning, Christopher raised his revolver to aim at Henrik, and that's when he felt a sharp pain just below his left ear.

Confused, Christopher pawed at his neck and, with a wince, yanked out a small black dart that was embedded in his flesh. Turning his eyes towards Cleric, his vision already seemed to be coming in slow and delayed. For some reason, he noticed the apple and knife on the table first, and then the pistol in Cleric's hand. Suddenly, Christopher's own revolver felt much heavier in his grasp. He looked down at it, thinking someone was trying to pull it from his hand, and that was the last cogent thought to go through his mind before he collapsed.

"Fucking prick," Henrik muttered, and spat a mouthful of blood on Christopher's back.

"You couldn't have done that before he busted my balls?" Thomas asked in a strained voice as he pulled himself back to his feet, one hand on the wall and the other still clutching his groin.

"The tranquilizer works faster when the heart rate is elevated," Cleric said coolly. "Besides, you should count yourself lucky. You deserve much worse for betraying him."

Henrik and Thomas exchanged confused glances as Cleric went to the back corner of the room. There, he pressed on one of the large wooden panels that lined the walls and it popped open, revealing a tightly spiraling metal staircase that descended down into darkness below.

"Now," Cleric went on, "do you two think you can manage taking him down to the basement and securing him on your own, or do you need my help with that as well?"

"We got it just fine," Thomas muttered, to which Henrik nodded in agreement.

"Good," Cleric said. "Make it fast. You have ten minutes." He proceeded past them, heading for the hallway.

"Where you going?" Henrik asked.

"To get a friend," Cleric said, and left the two to their work.

TWELVE

I

Rain rubbed his cheek, idly thinking that he was due for a shave. The concept never ceased to be interesting to him. His heart didn't beat and his respiration was superfluous, but his hair and fingernails continued to grow, just at a much slower pace than humans'. He grew a five o'clock shadow over the course of two weeks, and only required a haircut twice a year. The need for both was usually pointed out by Alex, unless Rain happened to notice himself by touching his face or having to brush his hair from his eyes. The latter would have to be remedied in the next couple of weeks too. Shaving was still difficult without a reflection, even after centuries of practice.

They had all made the silent, collective decision that important conversation would not begin until Lita joined them in the sitting room. Rain had taken up residence in his favorite chair, a cigarette perched languidly between his fingers on the edge of the armrest. His gaze fell blankly somewhere between the bar and the armoire, near the corner of the room. He had settled into this thoughtful position moments before when he realized interaction in the room was devolving into small talk, a pastime he detested with notable ferocity. So rather than force himself to engage in it, he ran through a checklist in his mind of the hidden weapons throughout the house, the best defensive positions for points of ingress and egress on the property, and all the other preparatory thoughts that become second nature to anyone who manages to survive even a sixth of the time he had spent in this world.

Alex sat reclined against the corner of the couch furthest from Rain, his legs curled up under him in the odd, birdlike position he often favored. He watched Amelie curiously as she walked around the sitting room, surveying her surroundings. When she walked around behind the couch, he actually craned his neck to follow her to his end and then over past the bar and towards the armoire. Rain scoffed inwardly, thinking his brother might have a crush.

Or maybe he's just enjoying the company of the living.

Rain banished the thought to the part of his mind where dead things lurked just as his eyes slipped back into focus, landing on the young woman when she crossed his line of sight. He quirked a brow as she reached towards the armoire, but then relaxed when her hand hovered an inch away, her fingertips tracing through the air. She was only admiring the craftsmanship, not snooping around.

Amelie's eyes moved up towards the ceiling from there, and then suddenly came down to meet Rain's gaze with such quickness it made him blink. She smiled at him. "You have a lovely home here, Mr. Moonshadow."

Rain snorted and Alex gave a short bark of laughter. "Rain, and thank you," he said.

Amelie blushed a little at their laughter, but a glance to Alex and his reassuring smile put her at ease. "Rain," she said, looking back to him. "I like that. It fits your last name well. Very creative of your parents."

"My parents gave me neither, actually" he replied, and

tapped his cigarette over the ashtray sitting on his chair's armrest.

Amelie found that statement curious, but didn't take Rain for the type to enjoy prying, so she let it rest. Anyway, her attention had been drawn to his cigarette. She eased herself onto the couch a cushion's space away from Alex and watched Rain smoke with rapt interest.

"I take it smoking isn't common in proper social circles these days?" Rain asked. In the brief time since Amelie's arrival, he had already developed a casual indifference to her presence. By his standards, that meant he liked her.

"I've never seen anyone do it up close before. It smells funny." She sat back and crinkled her nose. "No offense."

"It's better you think that way," Rain said. "They're bad for you."

"Then why do you do it?"

"I said they're bad for *you*." He took a final long drag and snuffed it out in the ashtray. Alex gave him a look that asked him to be nice, but Rain either didn't notice or didn't care. Amelie looked back and forth between the brothers, confused. Rain waved a hand dismissively. "Alex can explain in the kitchen. The teapot is ready."

Alex jumped up immediately and headed that way, but Amelie just looked more perplexed. "How do you know? I didn't hear it whi—" before she could finish, the high-pitched whistle drifted into the living room. Rain smirked, touched his ear, and pointed towards the kitchen door where Alex was waiting.

"Come on, Amelie," Alex said, "I'll fill you in so Rain can stop confusing you." She nodded and stood, skirting by Rain and his oddness.

"Summarize, Alexander. Not a whole life story," Rain said.

"Yes, yes," he muttered as he ushered his new friend through the door. A moment later, the whistling stopped and Rain's eyes landed upon the empty space in the corner once more.

They rested there for a series of moments as he thought about angles and memories and the various other things that an immortal mind tends to ponder when idle. His eyes shifted towards the front door, though, when he sensed something too subtle for human ears. His mouth pulled to the side as he considered it, debating whether it was worth investigating. He paid a brief glance to the stairwell and decided it might be a while before Lita showed herself. So he rose and headed to the door, stopping long enough to grab his coat off the rack on his way out.

II

Outside, Rain began walking the perimeter of the house, his keen eyes scanning the night for anything on the move. Somewhere in the distance a bird called, but that was not the noise he had heard. Nearing the side of the house, he briefly regarded the rosebush planted there. He preferred roses to any other plant. They were durable, guarded, and required very little maintenance.

Rounding the corner on the west side of the house, opposite the side with the kitchen door, he stopped and sighed. There was a tall maple tree that stood just a few feet from the house and Lita was leaning against it, her arms crossed, gazing out towards the tree line.

"This tree is a security risk," she said, not looking at him.

"Oh?" Rain replied, shoving his hands into his coat pockets.

"It provides easy access to the window of the room I'm staying in."

"That's why the windows have locks."

"An intruder could break the glass."

"I would hear it."

"You should cut it down."

"No. I like that tree."

There was a long pause. Had the maple been capable of complex thought, it probably would have wanted to uproot itself and slink away. Rain broke the silence when he walked into Lita's line of sight, forcing her to look at him.

"Is that why you came down here? To assess the safety of my lawn?"

She glared at him. "No. I just wanted some fresh air."

"That's just as accessible out the front door," Rain retorted. "You weren't taking off on us, were you?"

"Do you see my fucking bag?" Lita snapped.

"No...I suppose not." He looked up at the leaves of the tree, observing the subtle beginnings of color change in them. Fall was on its way.

Lita sighed in a way that seemed to contain a hint of apology, and said in a calmer tone, "I'm just not sure how ready I am to face that girl in there. I mean, what I did..."

"What you did isn't a pressing issue right now," Rain said. "It's what you are going to do that's important, because it could save her life, and probably yours as well. Worry about atonement later."

"And if I can't?" she asked. "Atone, that is."

"Won't know unless you try, and the best place to start is with 'that girl in there'."

Lita nodded and sniffled once, then looked up towards the tree herself, taking in all the intertwining branches and mostly green leaves. She thought that in a month or so she'd be able to see the sky from this spot, and then the snow would set in. She wondered if she'd live that long, or if she even wanted to.

"You know," she said thoughtfully, "if you ever have kids, you shouldn't put them in that room. They turn thirteen and they'll be sneaking down this tree to do God knows wh..." she trailed off when she looked back to him and saw that he was staring down at his feet. "Oh," she whispered. "I'm sorry, I didn't even think…"

Rain waved a hand. "Honest mistake. But what about you? Do you plan on having any children?"

Lita suddenly looked as if she'd been struck. "What…what the fuck kind of question is that?"

Rain blinked. "Uh, a pretty straightforward one, I thought. You're obviously no longer an assassin, so I just assumed you might eventually like to settle down and—"

"And what? Become some little housewife to an asshole husband so I can squeeze out a litter of screaming brats? No fucking thank you."

"I was only asking."

"Well *don't* fucking ask." She pushed herself off the tree and shot him a glare. "Don't you have enough knowledge from however many centuries, Vampire? Do you really have to pry into my brain? Fuck, come on, let's get this tea and cookies horseshit over with." She brushed past him, heading around the corner and back to the front of the house, not waiting for a response.

Rain stood dumbfounded for several seconds, wondering what had just happened. Finally, he just shook his head and sighed heavily as he fished a cigarette from his pocket. "I'm going to kill her," he grumbled as he retrieved his lighter. He paused just before lighting up, however, and pulled the cigarette from between his lips. Raising his head, he closed his eyes and took a deep breath through his nose.

Her scent was there, swirling all around him. It was feminine, but not elegant. Not like flowers or the spring air, but rather like an autumn breeze, weaving its way through branches well on their way to winter slumber. It was the scent of a fall evening casting its glow over a serene lake. It was the smell of sunset, something he hadn't seen in so long.

"Stars, hide your fires," he whispered, and then it was

gone, replaced by the smell of burning tobacco as he made his way back towards the front door.

III

Inside, Rain found Alex setting teacups and a pot on the coffee table, and Lita standing at the bar, examining the various decanters there.

"Amelie's in the lavatory. She'll be right out," Alex said, taking back his previous seat on the couch and looking at Lita. Rain approached her and leaned against the side of the small bar as she picked up a glass and reached for the vodka.

"Do you think now is the best time for that?" he asked quietly.

Lita did not look at him as she considered this, but said, "I guess not." She set the glass back down, trying to hide the shaking in her hands.

Rain sighed and said, "Water it down," before slipping past her and going to his chair.

Lita obliged, then moved to the couch with her drink in hand. She eased herself down onto the cushion closest to Rain's chair and furthest from where Alex sat, avoiding eye contact with the young man. He was a good kid, even regarded her as a friend, and upsetting him was upsetting her more than she cared to admit.

"Do you want some?" Alex asked, and Lita looked over to find his soft, forgiving smile and his hand offering her a plate with several little squares of bread. She couldn't help smiling back, and she took a piece with a thankful nod. She had barely known him a full day, but she was sure that Alex had to be one of the most genuinely good-hearted people she had ever met.

Moments later, Amelie found her way back into the living room and over to where they all sat. She had removed her hair from its braid and it now cascaded over her shoulders in waves. As she moved to sit down on the floor across the coffee table from the couch, Alex started to get up to offer his seat, but Amelie waved a hand at him. "It's alright. I like sitting on the floor," she said with a smile.

"Alright, young lady, let's hear your story," Rain said. He snuffed out his cigarette and immediately lit another.

"Are you fully intent on killing us all tonight?" Lita asked, waving a hand in front of her face.

"Well, that depends. Are you planning on drinking all of my booze?" he shot back, smoke jetting out of his nose.

"Would you like me to wait until you two are finished circling and snarling, or should I begin?" Amelie asked impatiently.

"Yeah, settle down you two. How are we to sort all this out with your constant lovemaking?" Alex added.

Lita nearly choked on her drink. "*Excuse* me?"

Rain stifled a laugh. "It's called flirting now, Alex. Lovemaking means having sex."

"Oh," Alex said, his face suddenly burning. "Well, then stop that."

Lita rolled her eyes and sank back into the couch, putting a boot up on the coffee table. Rain cleared his throat at this, but she ignored him. He let it go for the time being, turning his attention to Amelie and gesturing for her to continue. "You have our full attention."

Amelie, a slight blush on her own cheeks as well, took a deep breath to compose herself before beginning. "As you know, my stepbrother, Michael Calderwood, is attempting to have me killed. My father is nearing his final days and when he passes, control of Chicane falls to Michael and me evenly. It seems obvious that he's trying to take the entire city for himself."

"Doubtless," Rain said. "So what do you plan to do about it?"

"Find a way to expose him, to bring him to justice. But

I'll need help. I have no way of knowing who I can trust and who may be loyal to Michael. I need people who I can be certain have no allegiance to him." She looked to Rain expectantly.

"It's not my concern," he said flatly. "I can offer you sanctuary for a few days, but that's the extent of my involvement. Who has power in the city of Chicane is of no consequence to me or my brother." He glanced at Alex, who reluctantly nodded. He, too, knew it was not their fight.

"What if it is?" Amelie asked.

"What do you mean?" Alex asked.

Amelie sighed. "I...I don't know. I haven't quite put it all together yet. Yesterday I snuck into his room, trying to find out more about him, and I found some strange things in his hidden study there. His journal, for starters. It was written in German, and of course, I don't speak a word of German. But there was an entry—a recent one—and it looked like it was written with such *rage*. It kept repeating this one word, and the pages were almost torn, it was written so angrily. Beg...erm...be-gab-tee..."

"*Begabte?*" Rain asked.

"Yes, that," she replied.

"It means gifted," he said.

Amelie nodded. "Yes, I looked it up after."

"Gifted?" Lita said over her drink. "As in *the* Gifted? People with special abilities?"

"I think so," Amelie said. "It would fit. Later, he and I were discussing plans for the future of Chicane and he went on about how he wanted to return it to the Old World ways. He was very adamant about it, especially about it being a time before monsters were among us." Her eyes flicked towards Rain as she said this, and it did not go unnoticed by him. Amelie went on. "But when I pointed out that would also mean a time before the Gifted, he became evasive and put me off to a lunch at a later date. One he conveniently penciled in *after* my intended demise."

"I lived in the Old World, and it wasn't any better than this one," Rain said. "Did you find anything else in his study?"

"Nothing that made a great deal of sense to me. Drawings of a strange building. It looked old, maybe religious. Also a calendar diagramming the moon in—" Rain suddenly held up a hand to halt her and his face took on a thoughtful composure for a brief moment.

"There's a lunar eclipse at dawn day after tomorrow," he said at last.

"Oh," Amelie said, "Does that mean something?"

"I don't know yet. Continue."

"Well, there wasn't much else. Some very old papers covered in odd runes was about the last of it."

"What sort of runes?" Rain asked.

"I don't know. I didn't recognize them."

"Could you draw them?"

"I...I think so. Maybe a couple of them."

Rain looked at Alex and nodded towards the coat rack. Alex hopped off the couch and went to Rain's coat to fish a small notepad and pencil from one of its pockets. He flipped the pad to a blank page and brought it over to Amelie. She smiled a thank you and he returned to his seat.

Amelie chewed on the corner of her lip nervously. "What if I draw them wrong?"

"It's alright," Rain said. He put out his cigarette and leaned forward, resting his elbows on his knees and interlacing his fingers. "Just close your eyes and try to visualize the pages. Draw what you see." Amelie nodded, took a deep breath, and closed her eyes. Everyone fell silent.

A couple of moments passed, and then Amelie opened her eyes and leaned forward, carefully drawing six different symbols on the paper. They weren't exceptionally complex, which helped her to draw them from memory, but she still thought it was a longshot that any might be correct. With a nervous sigh, she handed the notepad to Rain, who sat back and began studying it carefully.

"Do you recognize them?" Lita asked. She had leaned over at one point to look for herself, but didn't see anything more than a few haphazard scribbles. Foreign languages weren't her forte.

"Maybe," Rain said quietly. "It looks like *Piyasu*." Everyone stared at him blankly.

"Rain, how about filling in those of us who don't have almost five centuries of photographic memory in our heads?" Alex said, waving a hand to get his attention.

Rain blinked. "Sorry. The Piyasu were a small religious sect that existed in the Ottoman Empire around the fourteenth century. They were very noble, like knights or monks. They believed themselves destined to banish evil from the world."

"So what do the symbols mean?" Amelie asked.

"I'm not definitely sure," Rain said, rubbing his temple. "I only read one book about them, and it was a long time ago. Their writings weren't exactly an established language, more of a conglomeration of symbols from multiple cultures. This one here..." he tapped the paper, "...I believe it equates to 'the striking hand' or, more commonly, 'weapon'. But this one..." he leaned forward, pointing at it to show Amelie. "Are you sure you have that one right?"

She nodded adamantly. "That one, definitely. It was repeated at least a dozen times on the page I looked at. It's the only one I'm completely sure of."

Rain sat back, clenching his jaw tightly. His eyes were storm clouds of concern.

"What is it, Rain?" Alex asked. "What does it mean?"

"It's a verb. It means 'to cleanse'," he said gravely.

"And that's bad?" Amelie asked.

Rain stood and began pacing behind his chair. "Not if

you're referring to a toilet bowl, but it is if you're talking about a group of people. Have any of you ever heard the name Adolf Hitler?" He paused long enough to regard them, but got only blank looks. "He led an army that killed over ten million people trying to create a pure human race." Rain glanced at Amelie. "Your brother sounds charming."

"Step," she corrected. "Do you see now why I need help? If he plans to hurt the Gifted of Chicane or anywhere else, he must be stopped. People with those special abilities are blessed by God, and a great many of them use their powers to help the community around them. We cannot allow them to be harmed by some insane vendetta!" She took a shuddering breath, fighting back tears.

Alex and Lita looked away, but Rain stared her down, his gaze narrowing. "What's your ability?"

She looked up and blinked. "What? I…I don't have…"

"Stop," Rain said flatly. "You clearly have far too much vested interest in the Gifted not to have your own stock in the matter. No human is that selfless or understanding."

"Rain!" Alex said sharply, "Stop it, she's just—"

"Shut up, Alex," Rain said, not looking at him. He took a step forward, towering over Amelie now. "What is it? What can you do?"

"N-Nothing," Amelie stammered. "I can't do anything, I s-swear."

Rain reached down and pulled her to her feet by her arm. "To God? Do you swear to God?"

"You're hurting me," Amelie whimpered.

"Rain, let her go!" Alex demanded, standing.

Lita kept her seat, sipping her drink and watching the whole scene coolly.

Rain kept his eyes locked on Amelie's and when she still said nothing, he shoved her away, sending her stumbling into Alex's arms. "If you can't trust us, you're on your own. Get out of my house."

Alex was fuming. "Rain, you—" but Amelie put a hand to his lips.

"Shhh," she said, sniffling as she lifted his bandaged hand. Alex blinked, but didn't pull away as she carefully unwrapped the dressing to reveal the deep, reddened cut in his palm. She then touched the center of the wound with her fingertip. Just as Alex took in a hissing breath to indicate pain, a soothing, warm white glow began flowing from Amelie's finger and into the cut. Right before everyone's eyes, the jagged edges of sliced skin began to smooth and return to their normal color. They pulled together, closed up, and sealed, leaving not a trace or scar behind.

Amelie took a step back, leaving Alex to open and close his fist, marveling at the complete regeneration of his palm. Lita let out a low whistle, then finished off her drink and set the glass on the coffee table before looking to Rain for his reaction. Amelie wiped her eyes and looked to him as well. He gave her a nod.

"It's a useful gift," he said gently. "Why do you hide it?"

She gave a small shrug. "I don't know. It's just never come up, I guess."

Lita scoffed. "Because it's never had to. Pretty easy to avoid the broken and bleeding when you live in a palace."

"Is that helpful?" Rain asked, giving Lita a look.

"I'm just saying that she might want to get to know the darker parts of Chicane before she tries to run it," Lita said, then sank back into the couch.

"It's okay," Amelie said, "she's not wrong. The ability's not as useful as it seems anyway. I can only mend small wounds. Nothing severe, and not sickness. Were that the case I could have helped my father." Her voice trembled with this last sentence, and Alex placed a comforting hand on her shoulder from behind.

"With practice, it could grow stronger," Rain said. "Most gifts do."

Amelie sniffled and nodded. She then looked to Rain and stepped towards him, raising a hand. "I can heal scars though." She motioned towards his eye.

Rain took a step back, holding up his own hand. "Mine are fine where they are, thank you." He sat back down in his chair.

Amelie looked to Lita then, hesitantly, but the woman waved her off. "I've earned all of mine." Amelie nodded, then sighed and slipped back down to her position on the floor.

Clearing his throat, Alex said, "Well, now that it's cold, does anyone else want some tea?"

"I don't mind cold tea," Amelie said, smiling at him wearily. It had been a long night, and the strain was finally starting to set in.

"I need another drink," Lita said, pushing herself off the couch and returning to the bar.

"Make me one too," Rain said. Then, after a beat, "No mixer this time."

Lita chuckled.

"So what now?" Alex asked as he poured himself and Amelie each a cup of tea. He added honey to hers and a little sugar to his own.

"We are to meet with Christopher, the palace head guard, tomorrow at noon so he can inform us of what to do next," Amelie explained.

Rain quirked a brow at Lita as she handed him his drink. "So while devising a plan to bring Amelie here for safety, you scheduled a rendezvous for the middle of the day?"

Lita pulled her mouth to the side sheepishly as she reclaimed her seat on the couch. "I guess I didn't really think that one through. We were a bit preoccupied with getting out of there alive."

"We'll work around it. But how can we be sure this Christopher can be trusted?" Rain asked.

Amelie bristled. "I have nothing but the utmost faith that he would do anything to protect me. I've known him for four years, and he's never shown anything but complete loyalty. Besides, why would he have helped us escape if he was conspiring with Michael?"

"He did seem pretty gung-ho about it," Lita added.

"And that's reason enough for you to trust him?" Rain asked, staring at Lita.

She considered this briefly. "No. And even if he is loyal, but someone else finds out about the meeting, we'd be walking into a trap. Either way, we'll want to come prepared."

Rain nodded. "Then we should start discussing strategy." Looking back to Amelie, however, he only then realized how exhausted she appeared. "But Lita and I can handle that. Alex, why don't you go get Amelie set up in a bedroom upstairs. Lita's in the one next to you, so put her on the end."

Alex looked taken aback. "Don't you want me here to help with the strategizing?"

"I know where to find you if I need you. You should go get some rest yourself."

Alex stared at his brother in disbelief, but Rain was unmoved. "Fine," he said finally, rising. "Come on, Amelie. I'll get you all settled in."

She stood and followed him. As she passed Rain's chair, however, she suddenly leaned over, threw her arms around his shoulders, and squeezed him tightly.

"Hrm!" Rain said, tensing.

"Thank you," she whispered, then released him and quickly followed Alex.

"You're a brave soul," Alex said as he led her up the stairs. Rain watched them go, obviously disturbed by the interaction. When he looked to Lita after they'd gone, she had a smirk on her face.

"Hey, they say you catch more flies with sugar," she said.

"I'm going to kill you in your sleep," Rain said flatly, then lit a cigarette.

"It'd probably be best if you did," Lita replied. She suddenly leaned forward, snatched the cigarette out of his hand, and took one deep drag before handing it back. She blew the smoke up towards the ceiling and returned her gaze to him. "Jonas was just playing middleman when he contracted me. If the person calling the shots is who I think it is, we're stepping into messy territory. He's no fuckaround."

"Tell me more about him," Rain said, then took his own drag off the cigarette. He could taste her lips on it.

"Name's Cleric. He's led a group of assassins for at least twenty years, so he knows his shit. No real way of telling how many he's got on his roster—he always made sure we didn't know much of anything about each other. When I was still with him I figured it to be a dozen, fifteen at the most. Could be more now."

"Did he raise them all from children?"

"Nah, the ones I did know anything about were all mercs or ex-military types. Jonas and I were his pet project. Wanted to see what kind of hitters he could make if he got us while we were young. Didn't help keep me loyal, apparently."

"Which begs the question why he would re-contract you for a hit you'd already failed to follow through on."

Lita shrugged. "Your guess is as good as mine. Makes about as little sense as having Jonas play middleman. Cleric always set up jobs personally."

"Then how can you be sure he's involved?"

"I just am. Gut feeling, you know? The same one that told me I shouldn't be taking this job in the first place. But goddamn, the money sounded good."

"Desperation makes us do funny things," Rain said. He

rose to his feet and headed across the room to his coat, but kept speaking. "So I imagine Cleric's unlikely to give up on Amelie just because you made off with her?"

"Not likely at all. He'd go to the ends of the Earth to finish a job." Lita watched him go to his coat, retrieve his keys, and then come back and cross over to the armoire next to the fireplace.

"Then why didn't he get someone to finish the job on Amelie five years ago? And why didn't he kill you, for that matter?" Rain asked as he unlocked the top cabinet of the armoire.

"Well, either she wasn't the primary target in the first place or the client called off the rest of the job. As for me, who knows? He could be surprisingly sentimental about me and Jonas, so maybe that had something to do with it. Whatcha got in there?"

"Weapons," Rain replied.

"Oooh," Lita said with childlike glee, "I love weapons!" She hopped to her feet and went to Rain's side, but when he opened the armoire doors, the excitement dropped from her face. "You've got to be kidding me."

The cabinet was filled with edged weapons. A wide array of daggers, knives, throwing axes, short swords, and sais hung from hooks that lined the inside. "I don't like guns," Rain said.

"Yeah, and I'm sure your enemies will thank you for that when they're laughing over your corpsy dust pile."

"I've made it this long without them," Rain retorted. "I can fight far better with this than I could with any gun." He pulled out the one item that seemed to stand out most among the others: a silvery metal rod about eighteen inches long and an inch and a half in diameter. Taking a step back, he held it up to show Lita.

"It's a stick," she said doubtfully.

Rain took hold of the device with both hands and gave it

a twist near the middle. With a click and a metallic sliding sound, the rod telescoped out, expanding to nearly four feet long.

Lita quirked a brow. "It's a longer stick."

Rain smirked, then moved in a flash. Turning, he slipped one end of the staff behind her and hooked it into the trigger guard of her handgun before bringing the staff around full circle, pulling the gun from her pants and whipping it across the room, where it hit the backrest of the couch and landed on the seat cushion with a dull thud. Completing the circle of the staff as he sidestepped back in front of her, he gave it one last twist and a six-inch, double-sided blade popped out of the end, its tip coming within inches of Lita's throat.

She glanced down at it, then back to him. "So...it's a sharp stick."

Rain couldn't suppress a soft chuckle as he stepped back and went about the task of manually collapsing the staff back down. "Alex designed it. It took him a few months to get the springs just right, but it's rather brilliant."

Lita shrugged. "If you say so. I'll stick with my gut-shredding pieces of flying metal, if it's all the same to you." She went to the couch to retrieve her handgun, checked the chamber to make sure the round in it was still seated properly, and shoved it back in her belt. "Anyway, it's a very shiny collection. But unless you've got something in there that can stop the rotation of the Earth, you're gonna be sitting at home playing with your knives all by yourself during the rendezvous."

Rain knelt down and opened the bottom drawer of the armoire, then looked to Lita. She came back over and, seeing what was inside, threw her head back and laughed hysterically. It was such hearty, genuine laughter that even Rain was smiling broadly by the time it had finally subsided.

Wiping tears from her eyes, Lita said, "Good Christ, I

must be tired. I'm delirious."

"I don't doubt it," Rain said. He closed up the armoire and pocketed his keys. "You should go get some sleep. We can sort out the rest of the plan in the morning."

"We should set up some sort of watch, just in case," she said.

"Got it covered," Rain replied. "I'll take the whole night. I don't have to sleep."

"Huh. I'm not sure if that's a curse or a blessing."

"Little of both."

"Alright, well if there's trouble, give a shout. Or rattle your knives maybe," she suppressed another round of giggles as she headed for the stairs.

"Hey," he called.

She paused at the banister. "Yeah?"

"I'm going to walk the property outside, make sure everything is quiet. You okay to keep an eye on things in here?"

"I think I can keep from burning the place down, sure."

"I mean you're not going to climb down my tree and take off, right?"

She shrugged a shoulder. "Nah, sounds like too much work."

He chuckled and gave her a nod. "Goodnight then, Lita."

"Night, Rain."

THIRTEEN

Christopher's senses returned to him one at a time, and though it all happened in less than ten seconds, it seemed a great deal slower to him.

Smell was the first thing that pierced the dense fog surrounding his mind, and it made itself forcibly known. There were several intertwining odors in this place, but one in particular snaked its way into his nose so thickly that he could practically feel it dripping down the back of his throat: mustiness. Heavy and smothering like a wet wool blanket, it threatened to take hold of him in his dizzied state and rip out the contents of his stomach.

Taste came shortly after, and it was all heavy metal. That started bringing together fragmented memories of the fight, but he couldn't remember being hit. A quick brush of his tongue found all of his teeth intact, so that was some small relief.

Feeling returned in a tingling wave next, and as sight had yet to arrive on the inbound sensory train, he instinctively moved to feel his surroundings. That's when he realized he was sitting up, and his hands were tied to thin wooden slats like the arms of a dining chair. He attempted to shift his feet, but his ankles were tied as well.

Sound rushed in then, all at once, as though he had stepped out of a tunnel. Somewhere to his right was a tapping noise. It was quick, regular, the sound of water dripping on stone. There was wind outside; the rain must have picked up again. And there was the sound of two people talking quietly some distance away.

However, more frightening than all of the mysterious feelings and smells of this drippy, musty place was what Christopher heard behind him. Something was there, very close, and sensing its presence raised the hairs on the back of his neck. It issued some noise that, though soft and quiet, was altogether horrifying in its subtlety. It was something slithery, though not wet. Something that might have scales. A little at a time, at random intervals, whatever it was writhed just a bit. Just enough to be heard but not clearly identified.

It slid, and then stopped.

Silence.

It squirmed, and then stopped.

Silence.

Then there were three sets of three taps of something hard and sharp against something stony.

Tap tap tap. Silence. *Tap tap tap.* Silence. *Tap tap tap.*

Silence.

Christopher's breathing started to tremble, but he quickly caught himself and forced it to regulate. He was the head guard of the High Palace of Chicane, not a little boy frightened of the dark. It was time to open his eyes and face whatever was waiting for him.

As his vision came into focus and he saw the two figures standing before him down here in the palace's wine cellar, Christopher felt an absolute and undeniable certainty that he was going to die. With this epiphany, however, came not the fear that would be expected, but rather a resolution to inexorably bind any knowledge of Amelie to secrecy, as well as a prayer to God to give him the strength to do so, no matter what befell him.

Ahead of him and slightly to the right, leaning against a dusty wine rack, Cleric stood with his large arms crossed, staring intently back his way. At least, Christopher thought he was staring. Between the wide-brimmed hat that shadowed everything above his nose and the black bandana that was pulled up to his bottom lip, all he could make out was Cleric's mouth, which was presently smirking amusedly at him.

Michael was dead ahead, but there was no guise of passive beguilement on his features. His posture was as stiff and perfect as the crease in his collar, and his face was drawn and severe. He stood with his hands clasped behind his back, looking like an undertaker waiting a bit anxiously for his newest corpse. And Christopher knew that after he was done, this ghoul would set his sights back on Amelie, and then all of Chicane. He knew it was up to him to keep this man's dark intentions from going any further than this very room.

But behind him, something writhed.

"Welcome back," Michael said. "We were worried you'd sleep all night." Oddly, his voice did sound slightly concerned.

"I feel like I could have," Christopher replied, his voice relaxed, almost conversational. "What was in that dart, anyway?"

"Special concoction," Cleric said with a touch of pride. "My own formulation. Even works on vampires."

"Really?" Christopher said. "You made it yourself?"

"Mmmhmm. I like to dabble in chemistry."

"Well, it's good to have a hobby. I like to knit, personally. Scarves mostly. Thinking about making a sweater this winter though."

"I know what you're doing," Michael interjected. "I've

read about counter-interrogation techniques. First trick is to talk too much, not too little. Except this isn't an interrogation."

"Oh?" Christopher said, keeping up his carefree tone. "Well, if it's a dinner party, you really need to work on the…"

Tap tap tap.

"…ambiance."

Michael sighed and approached Christopher. For a moment, it looked as though he might come right up and stand over him, but at the last second his eyes flicked upwards, looked over Christopher's shoulder at something behind him, and he stopped short about five feet away. "This is an offer," he said, and brought his hands around to his front, clasping them together once more as though pleading with his prisoner. "A one-time offer, so I implore you to take it seriously."

Christopher quirked a brow. "And what would that be?"

"If you tell me exactly what I need to know, I will not have to hand you over to Cleric here."

"And I suppose you'll have him torture me?" Christopher asked. "He looks like he might be good at it." He actually heard Cleric chuckle at this.

"Lord, no!" Michael actually looked taken aback. "I would never wish such suffering on a human being!"

Christopher was in disbelief. "Are…are you insane? You tried to have Amelie killed hours ago, and I'm fairly certain you had Henrik assault Lord Lamoureux."

"I am not insane," Michael said curtly. Then, softer, almost regretfully, "Amelie and Richard's deaths are an unfortunate but necessary sacrifice. I tried to arrange them to be as quick and painless as possible. Now, because of your interference, we have been forced into this equally unfortunate but equally necessary situation."

"Necessary?" Christopher blurted. "How the fuck is any

of this necessary?"

"It is God's will," Michael said, as though it was a fact as plain as the rise and fall of the sun.

"Jesus," Christopher breathed. "I just thought this was all a power grab, but you really are insane."

Michael lunged at him, grabbing his bound wrists and moving in so close their noses almost touched. "I am not insane!" he hissed. Christopher felt the right arm of the chair shift slightly with a creak.

"Michael," Cleric said sternly.

Michael stared Christopher down a moment longer, then pushed off the chair—that armrest creaking again—to stand back up straight. He turned and walked a few steps away, retrieving Saint Monica from his pocket as he did. When he turned back around, he had regained his composure, but he rubbed that medal tightly between his fingers.

"I can only offer you mercy one last time," Michael said. "Cooperate, and your passing will be without pain."

"Go fuck yourself," Christopher said.

Michael sighed. "I am sorry you have to become a casualty in all of this, Christopher. I know that we will meet again one day in heaven, and I pray that you will grant me your forgiveness when we do." With that, he gave Cleric a single nod. "I will be in the chapel when you are finished," he said, and headed for the stairs.

"You don't want to stay and watch the next part?" Christopher called, but received no reply, save for Michael's departing footsteps and the sound of the upstairs door opening and closing.

"Would *you* want to?" Cleric asked as he approached Christopher. He towered over him, arms crossed. "To be honest, I don't really want to. I take no pleasure in it. A clean kill is a thing of beauty, but this...this sort of thing gets messy. I'd much rather avoid it altogether." Then, in a move that seemed completely uncharacteristic of a man like him, Cleric lowered himself to one knee, as though he was going to address Christopher like a small child. He tipped back his hat, and Christopher found himself looking into a pair of crystal blue eyes surrounded by deep lines of age and framed by a few long strands of silvery hair. "Look, Christopher," Cleric went on, "I know you're only in this position because you did your job better and more loyally than your fellow guards. Truth be told, I think it's a damn shame."

"That makes two of us," Christopher muttered.

"Which is why I'm going to give you one last shot at making the smart choice," Cleric said. "Now, you think I'm going to put you through some kind of torture that you can resist, but that's not the case at all. You see, you can either give the information I want freely and, in return, I will let you go as gently as if you were falling asleep." He patted Christopher on the knee as if to accentuate this point. "Or," his grip tightened considerably, "I can have the knowledge ripped out of your mind and you will, until your very last moments, suffer incomprehensibly. The decision is yours."

Christopher seemed to genuinely consider this for quite a while. Cleric remained as he was, looking up at him patiently. Finally, Christopher nodded, took a slow, deep breath, then snapped the chair's right armrest off at the support and swung its splintered end around in a tight arc towards the side of Cleric's neck.

But something stopped his arm dead three inches from its target. Christopher felt momentary confusion as he realized Cleric hadn't moved—hadn't even flinched—so it was not him who had halted the attack. Then the confusion gave way to terror as he realized the hand holding his wrist was not Cleric's…and it was not human.

Its skin was grey as steel, but matte and bumpy, irregular like the gnarled limbs of an old tree. Its hand, which had only three fingers and a thumb, was both enormous and as spindly as a bundle of sticks. Its fingers had to be five inches long and at the tip of each was a milky, razor-sharp claw that extended another six. Staring at it, Christopher realized then that, although its fingers were curled in a circle about his wrist, it wasn't actually touching him. There was a two-inch gap between his skin and its palm, yet some unseen force inside the creature's grasp was holding him. Then, as he watched, that invisible grip tightened. Christopher screamed as both the wooden armrest and the bones in his forearm splintered audibly.

"Christopher, since you seem so eager to choose the path of greatest resistance, I'd like you to meet my lovely pet: the Visgaer." Standing, Cleric stepped back to give his monster room to work.

Allowing his eyes to move from the excruciating pain in his arm up to its source, Christopher felt his heart go cold and his stomach contort. Its dusky arms looked emaciated. Long and bony, they connected to a torso that was little more than canvas-like skin pulled taut against protruding ribs. Its only semblance of clothing were randomly intertwined white muslin strips wrapped mummy-like around its chest, abdomen, and shoulders; bound to its wrists and thighs; and covering its pubic area. As Christopher forced his gaze further upward, he found that its eyes, too, were covered in those bandages, but what was visible of its face left him with barely a grip by which to hold on to his sanity.

Its ears and nose appeared to be nothing more than concavities in its skull. It had nearly no hair, save for stringy strands of white that hung limply off various spots on its scalp. But more horrific than every other inch of the creature was its mouth. Its upper jaw was humanlike in structure, but its lower hung down and out nearly half a foot, coming to a bony point below its white, cracked lips. That whole mouth was lined with yellowy, curved fangs that dripped shimmering drool like something straight out of a child's nightmare. Its tongue, black and pointed, wriggled inside, and though its mouth seemed to be a fixed width, Christopher could swear it was grinning at him.

"You see, Christopher, my pet has a few gifts," Cleric explained. "Telekinesis is what's got you by the arm there, but his real specialty is finding out what's in people's minds."

"I won't…tell you…" Christopher wheezed between panicked breaths.

"Oh, I know," Cleric replied. "You've already made that abundantly clear. But the Visgaer here can read your memories. Unfortunately, he can't do it from the outside with someone as resistant as you. He has to touch your mind…literally." With that, he gave the Visgaer a nod, then added, "You can't say I didn't warn you."

The grip on Christopher's wrist tightened further, tearing open the flesh, revealing shattered bones underneath. He opened his mouth to scream, but the Visgaer's other hand was suddenly hovering over his face and his throat sealed itself shut. He felt that unseen force push against him, tilting his head back. He tried to close his eyes, but they were willed open. He had to watch in petrified terror, tears streaming down his temples, as two of those long, sharp claws approached his eyes. They were the last thing he saw before a wet *pop* ushered darkness and indescribable pain into his world.

Christopher's final moments were, as promised, filled with greater agony than he had ever known. In the midst of it, he regretted his loyalty to Amelie, but being only human, this was understandable. Somehow, he had the presence of mind to be glad that those second thoughts did not emerge until it was too late to act upon them. In his last conscious instant, he thought of Amelie in the orchard, bathed in sunlight. He thought maybe he loved her a little that day, and he prayed for that love to somehow keep her safe.

FOURTEEN

I

Atop the stairs that led to the second floor of the residence Alex once affectionately dubbed *Moonshadow Manor*, there was a long hallway with three doors on each side. To the left, the first was Alex's bedroom, and the second and third were guest rooms, taken up by Lita and Amelie, respectively. There was a seventh door at the end of the hallway which opened to stairs leading to an expansive attic. On the right side of the hallway, in order, were Rain's bedroom, his study, and finally a sizeable bathroom in which Alex and Amelie now stood.

Amelie shook her dripping hands off over the white basin of the sink before reaching for a hand towel that hung from a ring on the nearby wall. Looking around the bathroom for the fifth time, she was still impressed by its size and construction. It wasn't the largest bathroom she'd ever been in by any means—there was one in the palace better than twice this size—but it was certainly the grandest she'd ever seen in a private residence. "I still can't believe your brother built this all on his own," she said, looking to Alex, who was lounging with his back against the door frame, staring up with no real focus at the break between hallway and bathroom ceilings.

He shrugged. "Most places are built on a deadline. Rain took his time. Years of it. If there's one thing he has no shortage of, it's time." He looked to her, and couldn't help smiling at the sight of her in the simple white tunic and loose-fitting grey knit pants he had offered her as sleepwear, articles of clothing he had outgrown some time ago. The sight was humorous: a princess, for all intents and purposes, dressed in clothes he had all but discarded himself.

Amelie blushed a touch under his gaze. She also felt funny in these clothes, though not because they were common; she was not nearly that petty. Rather, she felt a strange sort of dizzying tingle at the thought of a young man's clothes touching so intimately against her skin. A young man whose eyes were enrapturing her in steadily increasing measures. She cleared her throat and inquired further about the house, too nervous to speak of anything more daring. "I'm curious though, if he built this house for himself—before you returned, that is—why make it so large? Why put in heating and toilets, this mirror, things he didn't need? He doesn't seem the sort to entertain guests."

Alex blinked, opened his mouth, and then closed it again. His brow furrowed. In three years he had never thought to ask those questions himself. He opened his mouth once more, but jerked his head toward the sound of footsteps cresting the stairs and beginning down the hall.

From the footfalls, Amelie knew who was coming. From the way Alex's face brightened as he looked down the hall— the same way she had been looking at him moments ago— she immediately knew that any affection she felt for him was presently unrequited.

Stopping at the door of the room she had been put up in, Lita looked down the hall towards Alex. "Goodnight, kids," she said, able to see a bit of Amelie's reflection in the bathroom mirror.

Alex glared as his flat "goodnight" and Amelie's polite one interlaced with slight asynchronicity. Even from here, Lita could see his face flush before she slipped inside her room and shut the door behind her.

Alex sighed and returned his attention to Amelie. Her gaze had dropped to her hands, where she was clicking her left thumbnail on that of her right index finger. "I'm sorry, what were you saying?" he asked.

Amelie shook her head. "Nothing important, really." Stifling a genuine yawn, she added, "I'm sleepy though. I think it's time to turn in." She looked back up to him, her eyes betraying a hint of sadness. Alex nodded and took a step back into the hallway, and when she passed she paused just long enough to touch his shoulder softly and give him a strange little sympathetic smile. Then she headed to her door, stopping only to say, "Goodnight, Alex. And thank you again, for everything."

"G'night, Amelie," he said, then puzzled over that smile as she disappeared into her room. For some reason it had reminded him of when the parish priest had come to him and Rain to tell them their mother had been killed. It had been a long time ago, but Alex remembered that gaze as clearly as he recalled the downpour that had been hammering on the living room window and the way he had been bouncing Rain on his knee, the year-old boy oblivious to how much their lives had just been ripped inside out. That look...it had been one of knowing, of predetermined sympathy for events that had yet to transpire. But why, he wondered, would Amelie have regarded him in that way? He filed it away for later and went to his own bedroom, planning to read a little before dawn broke and he allowed sleep to take its inevitable hold.

II

Though he had been sitting for some time, Rain rose spryly from his chair as if he'd only been there a moment. One of the nice physical advantages of being the creature he happened to be was that his muscles never truly reached a state of relaxation. He could sit comfortably in a chair or lie in a bed and feel at ease, but the moment he needed to vault from his position he could always do so on a whim. There were no creaks or groans, no extremities falling asleep. He was always ready *to kill*.

He frowned. No, not to kill. To move or react or fight, but not to kill. Not for a long time. He wasn't that person, that monster anymore. He never would be, not again. He'd die before he became that again.

As he stepped outside to begin his perimeter walk, a biological orchestra of nighttime sounds filled his ears. He gave a small shrug, repositioning his coat on his shoulders, and headed off around the east side of the house. He stopped by the shop, making sure it was still securely locked and nobody was lurking about. It reminded him that he needed to get that old rattletrap truck in better working order by next spring as a birthday present for Alex. It was about time for him to learn how to drive, but Rain wanted the truck in more reliable shape than it was now, good only for occasional sputtering missions to Maple City for supply restocking.

Passing by the chicken coop with its automated feeder that Alex had devised, Rain wondered if his brother might be better off servicing the truck himself. He always seemed to know how everything worked simply by touching it. It had taken Rain six months of scrounging up parts and books, as well as a great deal of hard studying to piece together the large generator that powered the house, fueled only by vegetable oil. When it had nearly exploded the previous winter, Alex had assessed and fixed the problem in less than two hours, using random items from around the house. It had been running strong ever since. So perhaps they would work on it together, as they had his own car. Rain continued to mull this over as he reached the tree line and left the house's clear-cut property behind.

He walked casually along the sinuous path that snaked its way through the dense forest of maple trees. The nearly full moon loomed sleepily close to the horizon, casting an orange glow between the tree trunks. All around him, crickets were beginning to quiet their love cries for the night. He pulled his lighter from his pocket and fiddled with it as he walked, debating having a cigarette. Flicking the lighter open, he sparked the flint once. The act did not create a flame, but he stopped for just a second and glanced up towards the treetops. For reasons unknown to him, he thought, for a brief moment, about butterflies.

He shook his head and continued on, dropping the lighter back into his pocket. Presently, he stepped out of the tree line once again, this time into a small clearing that extended out twenty feet before dropping off over a seventy-foot cliff. It would be a dangerous place to stumble blindly out of the woods, but it offered a beautiful view of eastern Ayenee, which lay before him like a painting on an artist's easel. The glowing outskirts of Chicane to the left, the Vitale River and all its unnamed tributaries snaking off to the right, like a system of veins feeding lifeblood to the massive entity known as Maplewood Forest. Somewhere in the distance, mixing with the blue-black of the horizon, the Atlantic Ocean lapped against the young continent's coast.

III

Lita stretched her arms out and arched her back, groaning as she heard it crack for what seemed like miles. A sharp tilt of her head to either side elicited a few more pops, and then she went to work on her knuckles. Loosened up and a bit more relaxed, she went to the bed where she drew her handgun and set it on the nightstand, then opened up her knapsack, starting to rifle through it in search of a hairbrush. Sometimes it was a real bitch to find something in this thing with everything she had crammed in there. But she needed all of those things. Needed them just in case. So she'd be ready at the drop of a hat *for a job*.

Her jaw clenched. Fuck that. She wasn't that gal anymore. She hadn't been for a long goddamn time. Tonight was just some oversight, some moment of weakness born out of a promised paycheck that was too good to be true. She would never go back to that again. Not for any amount of money.

Hairbrush finally in hand, Lita plopped onto the bed with a sigh and began forcefully brushing through her hair's tangled waves. As she tamed it, she saw it occasionally fall into small ringlets. Seizing these, she attacked them viciously, raking at them until they straightened out to her liking. The last thing she needed was to look like some dollish little girl. She had considered lopping it all off a handful of times, but something always seemed to make her change her mind.

Her nerves were too fried to permit sleep, but she felt too out of place here to wander the house, so after putting away her brush she decided to acquaint herself with this room. Adjacent to the foot of the bed was a closet door, so Lita went to explore further. Looking inside, she found the structure of the closet interesting. It wasn't very deep, and it was filled with shelves, more like a linen closet than one meant for a bedroom. She supposed it made sense for practical storage, and could easily be converted were someone to take up the room permanently. For a moment, she caught herself thinking how nice it would be to live in a house like this permanently, but she quickly forced the notion from her head. People like her didn't deserve a place like this. They deserved little cracker-box apartments with no electricity, peeling paint, and the rhythmic creak-moan of prostitutes hard at work next door. The assassin's retirement home, where the water smells funny and the old ghosts never seem to knock first.

The shelves of the closet were filled with various things: folded blankets, two wooden boxes labeled *light bulbs*, a whole shelf of identical leather-bound books—all blank, she checked a few—and an unlabeled, lidded apple crate. This last item piqued her curiosity, so she pulled it down and found a seat on the floor, placing the box in front of her. After removing the lid and a few of the items inside, however, she grew disappointed at the realization that the box was little more than a catchall. There were candles, a stack of folded handkerchiefs tied together with twine, and a small metal box with the word *fuses* written on it. She was about to put the whole thing away when her fingers touched something coiled and slender, soft and leathery. She jerked her hand away, her first thought being that it was a snake. She immediately scolded herself for the snap reaction and leaned in for a closer inspection.

Retrieving the item from the crate, she turned it over twice in her hand, wondering why someone would keep something like this. It was a piece of brown leather, about eighteen inches long. One end was ragged, torn, but the other tapered down to a sharp point. Lita examined the sharp end closely, because there was something on it. A brown substance, dry and flaky. All at once, she became entirely certain it was blood. Her stomach bottomed out and an icy shot ran up her spine. She suddenly wished it really had been a snake as she shoved it back in the box and brushed her hands off on her pants. Closing the box and standing, she pushed it back into the closet, then shut the door and leaned her back against it with a sigh.

IV

Standing on the perch of the world, Rain was not looking at
the view, although he had many times in the past. Instead,
he was staring at a spot on the ground just a few feet from
the cliff's edge. There, in an oval shape six feet long and
four feet wide, the earth was scorched black. He knelt down
in front of it and ran his hand over the anomaly in the
otherwise immaculate flora. The blades of grass at the outer
edge tickled his palm as his fingertips wandered over the
bumpy texture of the burned ground.

Three years had passed, and he still didn't know what to
make of that night. He had been over it countless times, the
thoughts sometimes keeping him up for days on end. Alex
was no help; he remembered almost nothing of the event.
Rain equated that to being unable to recall one's own birth.
Even if Alex could recall what had happened, Rain didn't
suppose he'd have any explanation for it. All Rain knew was
that one moment he was sitting on the edge of this very cliff
as dawn approached, seriously considering his own demise
as he had many times before, when suddenly there was a
flash of white light and a burst of heat so intense that he
thought the sun had crested the horizon and sent him to
some circle of hell specifically designed for monsters of his
sort. But as soon as it had come, the light and heat vanished,
leaving him momentarily blinded and stunned. Once that
faded, the real confusion set in. Alex was just…there. Gone
so long and then suddenly back: naked, trembling, and
looking just as he had on the day he'd died.

Now, crumbling a bit of dirt between his fingers, Rain
looked out to the horizon once more as he pondered the old
adage: *never question a good thing.* But he knew from experience
that many terrible things arrived under the guise of

something wondrous, and he knew even better that nothing wondrous came free. Though Alex's return had made his life bearable—he hadn't again considered suicide since that night—he couldn't help wondering what price he would someday pay for the universe's generous gift, if it even was a gift. It made him feel both uneasy and guilty to think of his brother as some sort of harbinger, and he hated it. He already had more guilt than he knew what to do with, and unease was not a color that suited him at all.

But it couldn't have been a gift. He hadn't earned a damned thing aside from damnation itself. The only thing he could imagine was that it was meant to be a new form of torture. He'd be allowed to watch his brother grow old and frail and then die in his arms once again. Or perhaps Alex would simply grow to hate him for his introversion and temper and leave him alone all over again. Rain shook his head and lit that cigarette after all, deciding it was time to head back home.

V

Lita chuckled to herself as she pushed off the closet door and went back to sit on the bed. Hoisting one foot up to rest across her knee, she unlaced her boot and tugged it off, setting it aside on the floor. Pausing before moving on to her other boot, she pushed down her threadbare wool sock and looked over the topographic map of burn scars that covered her foot. As she pushed her pant leg up, her fingertips followed the lines of those irregular fractals all the way to where they began to fade midway up her shin.

She found her mind wandering without permission to the Maple City Hospital, five years earlier. She remembered sitting on the edge of a white-sheeted bed, the muscles in her arms drawn taut as she gripped the linen and tried to contain her screams of pain, her teeth feeling like they'd crack from being clenched so hard, watching the seconds slowly drip off the clock. The original burn had been terrible, but she could at least dull it with painkillers and ample amount of booze. The nerve therapy was, in Lita's opinion, far worse than the initial wounds. Sitting for what seemed like hours with her bare feet in buckets of sand, Lita thought she was being tortured for the things she'd done. Worse yet, Nurse Winters refused to do her sessions unless she showed up sober.

Winters had been firm and straightforward, two qualities Lita admired, and thus they had been friendly. Friendly, but not friends. For Lita, that was something of an accomplishment. She spent a year with the woman—one to two hours, twice a week—recovering from what she always obliquely referred to as her "accident". Lita never went into details and Nurse Winters never asked. She didn't seem to care, so long as Lita made a concerted effort towards recovery. On the first visit, Winters had told her flat-out that she didn't seem the type to return for all her sessions, and it was pointless to start if she was only going to waste both their time. Lita, simultaneously enraged and fueled by the assumption, took the words as a dare.

In the wake of walking away from the life she'd known for nearly half her existence, she had promised herself she'd make healthier choices. They hadn't all worked out—she still couldn't part with the bottle—but she never missed a single visit with Nurse Winters, and to this day she was thankful for it. Even as it was, she had ongoing pain and numbness, especially on cold days. She could only imagine how much worse it might have been if she'd blown off the long, torturous regimen. In the end, she had been proud and had made Nurse Winters proud. It was the first thing she had ever followed through on that didn't end in the death of another human being.

At the conclusion of her last session, Nurse Winters told

Lita that she was free to go and that she would be missed. Lita had said she'd try to visit, but knew she never would. Winters, however, said it wouldn't do any good. She would be leaving herself in another two weeks. She was pregnant, and had decided to set aside her career to raise the little one. Lita's response, which Nurse Winters took as congratulatory, had been, "Well, hey, if you like the idea of living with something that shits and screams all day, good for you." They had parted ways, and that night Lita drank so much that she hadn't been able to move from her bathroom for nearly twenty-four hours.

VI

Rain ascended the stone steps of the house just as the slightest glow began to form on Ayenee's eastern horizon. He hung his heavy old coat on the rack as he had many times before, then took the stairs slowly, thoughtfully, one by one. His body might never feel truly tired, but his mind was weary. Recent events had stirred up emotions and memories that he was usually content to leave buried. All he wanted right now was to indulge in the thing he did that resembled sleep. However, reaching the top of the stairs, he found himself looking not at his own bedroom door, but at Lita's.

Lita sat up from the reclined position she'd taken after shedding her boots and instinctively reached for her weapon at the sound of footsteps in the hallway. She was nearly certain they were Rain's, but not quite sure enough to let go of her gun. Her tension dissolved finally and she released her old friend as a few more footfalls confirmed his identity. She recognized his gait even after only a short time around him. She slipped off the bed and approached the door, unsure why even as she did so.

Approaching Lita's door, Rain wasn't sure what he was

doing. Surely she had to be asleep. But even as he thought it, he knew it wasn't true. He could hear her in there. Was she just as close to her side? He could make out her breathing, even her heartbeat, and as he listened they both quickened and grew louder, filling his head like a rising chorus. His own unnecessary respiration sped up as well, and were his heart capable of beating, it would have been booming in his chest. His breath caught in his throat as he raised a fist to knock on the door.

As Lita reached her side of the door, she heard his booted steps come to a stop, and she thought she saw two shadows just under the crack of the door. She suddenly felt warmth form in the pit of her stomach and race out to her limbs and up to her face, followed by a small wave of dizziness. Was he out there? She wasn't sure, but either way, she needed to stick her head out, to see if everything was okay, to see if he needed something. She reached for the doorknob, her hand trembling as it moved towards the brassy fixture.

Rain stopped as he heard a wet gurgle. Lowering his fist, he looked towards the stairs. The young boy was standing there, staring back at Rain with his vacant, black eyes. The gurgling noise had come from the blood bubbling thickly from the tearing bite in his neck, pouring out with heavy splatters on the hardwood floor between his bare feet.

Lita froze as she felt a sharp wave of painful nausea tear into her stomach. Looking over her shoulder at her knapsack, she saw the neck of a bottle protruding from its opening. She withdrew her hand, which began to shake even more as sweat broke out on her palms and neck. It took everything she had to suppress the pained groan that tried to work its way out of her insides.

Rain slipped quietly away and slinked to his room, followed by the *drip, drip, drip* of his haunting apparition's ever-flowing wound. He didn't bother with the light, nor did he even remove his shoes. He yanked back the covers on his bed, slid underneath them, and curled up tightly into a ball. Though his back was turned, Rain could feel the continued presence of the boy standing over him, staring, bleeding, unblinking.

Lita stumbled back to her bed, tugged the bottle free from her bag, and dropped its cap on the floor in her haste. On some level, she could hear it roll under the bed and spin for a while before coming to a rest, but the sound was mostly drowned out by her loud, strong gulps of the fiery nourishment. When she finally tore her lips away, she barely managed to set the bottle on the nightstand before uttering a thin cry and crawling onto the bed. Forgetting the formality of a blanket, she assumed a fetal position and pulled the pillow over her face, blocking the light she'd neglected to turn off, fearing her shaking body would bring her falling to the floor if she tried to rise.

Trembling, alone, they each found sleep next to their respective demons, both wishing in their final waking moments that someone was there to offer them refuge in promises of sweet oblivion.

FIFTEEN

I

Lita glanced at her watch and took in a deep, soothing breath. Ten minutes to go.

While she was enjoying the peace and quiet of spending a late-summer morning in what had turned out to be one of the most expansive and beautiful cemeteries she had ever seen, she had also been out here nearly two hours and was more than ready to get this show on the road. She had spent the first hour meticulously combing through the property, behind enormous headstones and around elaborate mausoleums, checking for anywhere that might hide an enemy waiting to ambush her. She also scouted the best spot to conduct the meet, a place where she had a decent view of the dirt road coming out from the forest, but could also see a good percentage of the cemetery around her, which had to be close to five acres. She still couldn't believe she'd never known the little Hopewell Cemetery turnoff she'd passed countless times led to all this. Amelie said at least three past Lords of Chicane were interred here, as well as many prominent members of politics and clergy. Lita had wondered if she'd sent any of them there herself, but elected not to share that musing with the rest of the group.

That particular conversation had taken place just as breakfast had begun, but was soon replaced with the arguing that would not end until Lita was actually in the car and driving away from the brothers' home. For as much as Amelie and Alex had held themselves together like adults through the madness of the last few days, they couldn't have acted more like teenagers in reaction to the news that they would be staying behind for the rendezvous. It didn't matter how much Lita tried to explain the way these sorts of things worked, they both felt like they were being sidelined on account of their age. By the time had she made it out the door, Alex seemed like he was starting to understand, but Amelie was still fuming. Now, standing in this cemetery waiting for parties unknown to arrive, Lita found herself hoping the two would do something age-appropriate with their time alone together, like get into the liquor and make out for an hour. It would calm their nerves and give them both some much-needed real-life experience.

At least breakfast had been good. No, fucking fantastic. Rain had really dipped into the larder to make sure they were well fed for the day ahead, a home-cooked meal like none she'd ever had waiting for them as they all begrudgingly dragged themselves from sleep. Even Amelie had seemed impressed. Lita's watch just ticked off the 12 o'clock hour and she still wasn't hungry yet. But her head was starting to ache. Resorting to little more than maintenance drinking through the last few days' traumas was wearing on her. She considered herself well past due for a bender.

She was just considering taking the edge off with a swig or two from the bottle in her bag when she heard tires on the road below. She looked mournfully through the back window at her knapsack on the seat, then turned her attention to where a military-grade canvassed truck had just appeared from the woods. It released a low growl and a plume of smoke from its vertical exhaust pipe as it started ambling up the hill and around a bend to where the road through the cemetery passed by about a hundred feet in front of where Lita stood. As the truck came around that way, it pulled off the road to face her and the engine shut off, restoring the pleasant quiet of this secluded place.

Lita drew her handgun and held it at her side. There was no point hiding it. If it was Christopher inside the truck, great, but if he'd sent anyone, they'd be similarly armed. It was just expected at meetings of this sort.

Much as Lita half expected, it was not Christopher who climbed out of the truck, but two other High Palace guards, each carrying a large automatic rifle. The path between them and her ran between two rows of mausoleums until it opened up where the stout buildings ended twenty feet away. When the two men had reached the nearest of these buildings, Lita held up her free hand and they stopped in their tracks.

"There's a word I'm going to need to hear from you before we say anything else," she said.

"Ladybug," the man on the right replied.

She relaxed a little, but not entirely. Something didn't feel quite right here. "Alright, now where's Christopher?"

"He couldn't come without arousing suspicion," the man on the right said. "He sent us to bring Ms. Lamoureux to a safe house."

"Yeah, that's not how this is going to go down," Lita said. "She's plenty safe where she is right now. So what we're going to do is set up another rendezvous, one that Christopher will be attending, and we'll figure out where to go from there."

The two men exchanged a glance and the man on the left finally spoke up. "That's not going to work for us. We're under Christopher's orders to secure Ms. Lamoureux immediately."

Lita shrugged. "Sorry, boys, but I'm just passing along Amelie's orders not to bring anyone to come get her but Christopher or that other guy…"

"What other guy?" the man on the right asked.

"Shit, what was his name?" Lita said, her brow furrowing. She snapped her fingers a couple of times, as though trying to coax the name out of her head. "Harold? No…H-something…Henry?"

"Henrik?" the man on the left asked. "That's me."

"I thought it might be." She was already raising her gun as she spoke, and she punctuated her sentence with a bullet to Henrik's left thigh.

He dropped his rifle as he fell to the ground, clutching at his wound with both hands and hollering in pain. His partner had his rifle aimed at Lita almost as fast as she retrained her own gun on him…but before either of them could pull the trigger, the mausoleum door to the man's left flew open and Rain burst out looking like a homicidal marauder out of some desert wasteland.

He was wearing his coat, of course, but also coveralls, a pair of falconry gloves, and a full welding helmet. When the man looked over and saw that coming for him, he recoiled and issued a surprisingly high-pitched shriek. Rain made quick work of him, grabbing the barrel of his rifle with one hand and clouting him in the temple with the other. As he fell to the ground, Rain ripped the rifle from his hands and took a few steps back.

Lita, who suddenly found herself trying like hell to suppress a case of the giggles after what she'd just witnessed, approached quickly and snatched up Henrik's rifle. While Rain unloaded his and tossed weapon and ammunition away in opposite directions, Lita put away her handgun and aimed her newfound toy at the guard who was not presently writhing and moaning in his own blood.

"So he's Henrik," Lita said, "but I didn't catch your name."

"Thomas," he muttered. He propped himself up on one elbow and held his other hand to his head as he glared up at her.

"Well, Tommy, I figure you've got about ten minutes to start heading towards the hospital with Henrik here before he's liable to bleed out on the way, so what's say you answer a couple of quick questions for me and then everyone can be on—"

A loud *crack* echoed through the cemetery and a cloud of dust burst forth from the ground mere inches from Lita's feet. She leapt backwards, lost her footing, and her free arm pinwheeled as she fell to her rear, though she somehow managed to keep hold of the rifle. Thomas was suddenly clawing at his ankle, probably reaching for a backup revolver. Lita moved to take aim at him, but then *crack crack*, two more dust clouds erupted right next to her, forcing her to roll away and cover her face.

"Lita!" Rain's voice came muffled through his helmet. Thomas had stopped trying for his weapon and was scrambling away for cover, so Rain dashed to Lita's side and started tugging her to her feet. Then, with yet another *crack*, the faceplate on his helmet shattered, losing half its protective black glass. Rain cried out as he threw his arms over his face, and then it was Lita's turn to pull his weight.

"Jesus fuck, Rain, come on!" she screamed as she half-dragged, half-guided him towards the open door of the mausoleum he had been hiding in. *Crack* again, and Lita actually heard the air cut apart inches from her ear. "Fuck, fuck, fuck!" she yelled, still tugging Rain along, only a few yards away now. She shot a quick look over her shoulder and saw that Thomas was just getting back to his feet and he finally had that little ankle shooter in his hand. Lita issued a burst of automatic gunfire in his general direction, almost losing the damned rifle in the process with no second hand or shoulder to keep it steady. She couldn't exactly aim, but she was close enough to send Thomas diving behind some gravestones. It was the last bit of time she needed to thumb the safety on the rifle and throw it inside the mausoleum, then grab Rain with two hands proper and hurl them both headlong into the protective embrace of six-inch-thick concrete walls.

"Stay here!" Lita barked at Rain as she left him on the cold stone floor, drew her handgun, and turned back towards the door. But before she could get there, it slammed shut in front of her, cutting off all but a few meager slants of light filtering in through small, grated moisture vents high up near the ceiling.

Outside, Henrik was sitting on the ground with his back pressed against the door. He had managed to hobble over there and get it shut, but when it started pushing back against him at intervals coinciding with the thud of Lita's boot, he realized he wasn't going to be able to hold it long. After the third such kick, just as Henrik was sure she was going to get out, Thomas was there, butting his shoulder against the door to hold it tight while he closed the hasp. There was no padlock—Rain had broken it when he and Lita had decided to use the mausoleum as a point of ambush—but the hasp had a turning eye mount that would keep it shut for the time being.

"Hey, you alright, man?" Thomas asked, dropping to a crouch next to Henrik.

"No!" Henrik spat. "That psycho bitch shot me! I want to get the fuck out of here!"

"Don't worry," Thomas said, patting Henrik on the shoulder. "We'll get you some help. Cleric's guy up there covered our asses, so we just need to take care of those two and we can get gone."

"But Cleric wants us to—" Henrik began.

"*Fuck* what he wants. He's not here taking a bullet to the leg. I'm gonna go get those blast charges from the Construct work out of the truck and we're gonna bring this whole building down on their fucking heads, get me?"

"Yeah," Henrik said, "sounds good."

"Good," Thomas said, standing. "Stay put. I'll be back in two—"

Crack. Thomas dropped face-first on the ground with all the grace of a bag of rocks.

"Tom?" Henrik said, blinking. "Christ, Thomas?" he said again, and fought against his pain to crawl over to the man. He shook him, trying to roll him over. Then, just as he was coming to the realization that he could see straight through a hole in Thomas' head, there was a final *crack*, and his own lights went out.

II

From a small archway below a spire that topped a nearby mausoleum, Jonas wriggled free and hopped down to the ground, stretching the stiffness out of his muscles with a groan. While Lita had been there for two hours, he had been for nearly five. He took a pretty serious gamble by guessing where Lita would decide to set up for the rendezvous, but it turned out she hadn't changed so much in the last five years. She ended up parking within ten yards of where he'd figured she'd go, and he only had to adjust slightly to get the perfect view through the scope of the sniper rifle he now had slung over his shoulder.

What he hadn't anticipated was that she would bring that bloodrat fellow—Storm? Snow? Some ridiculous name— who she had said was just some guy sleeping the day off in her apartment. Jonas had decided to wait and see how the vampire's presence would make things play out and, as it turned out, his natural vulnerability had helped Jonas get

Lita trapped more perfectly than he'd originally planned. He didn't like not getting the chance to dust the freak, but that could wait for another time.

Making his way across the grass towards the banging sound of Lita ceaselessly trying to escape the mausoleum, Jonas began whistling a tune he'd known too long to recall where he learned it. Some jaunty Old World ditty. An old-timer in a tavern had once told him it was called "Windy Change" or something like that, but Jonas didn't care. He just liked the way it felt on his lips, especially when things were working out according to plan.

Inside the mausoleum, Lita had stopped to catch her breath and rest her leg. That damned door was built solid. She was bent over, hands on her knees, and she glanced towards Rain, having to squint in the near-darkness of their stone prison. He had pulled the welder's helmet off and was sitting up, rubbing the side of his face with one hand.

"You alright?" She asked breathlessly.

"I will be," he said. His face stung like a bad sunburn, but there was no blistering. It would be all but healed by nightfall. "What the hell is happening out there?"

"I'm not sure," Lita replied. "Those two fuckers were holding the door closed, and I could hear them talking, but then…" she trailed off as she tilted her head to the side, listening.

"Then what?" Rain asked.

"Shhh. Hang on," she said.

Outside, Jonas had reached the mausoleum and ceased his whistling as he gave a light rap on the door. "Lita? You awake in there?"

"Jonas, you piece of shit, let me the fuck out of here!"

Jonas laughed. "I don't think that would be in either of our best interests, Killer. No, I think that's probably the best place for you and your boy toy for the time being." Fishing into one of his cargo pants pockets, he retrieved the one thing he always carried with him, and which had come in handy more times than he could count. Unwrapping its protective cover of burlap and twine—which kept it both from poisoning him and knocking against his leg too hard— he retrieved a lead rod, about half an inch thick and five inches long. It slipped perfectly into the eye mount on the door's latch, and he held it there with both hands as he closed his eyes and began to concentrate.

"Jonas? Jonas!" Lita hollered. "Where did that mother fucker go?"

Rain was behind her then, and she could hear him sniffing at the air. "Do you smell that? I think it's melting metal."

"Jonas!" Lita screamed and booted the door again. "What the fuck are you doing?"

Stepping back to survey his work as he blew the heat off of his hands, Jonas nodded to himself at the malformed glob of cooling metal now holding the door shut. It wasn't pretty, but it would hold. "Just keeping you out of trouble until this all blows over," he hollered. "You should be thanking me."

"I'll thank you with a bullet to your skull once I shoot my way out of here!" Lita yelled.

Jonas chuckled. "Not unless you want bullets bouncing around in there with you. Even if you could manage to shoot through the door, you'd just set off the charge I'm putting out here."

"The fuck are you talking about?" Lita asked.

"I told you, I'm just keeping you here until this is all over and done with. I'm not a complete dick. I'll put a construction charge on this lock out here and set it for eight o'clock tonight. By then my employers will be long gone with the girl, and since they'll think you're dead, you'll be free to blow town."

Lita glanced back at Rain worriedly. "And how do you

expect them to find Amelie?"

"Oh, come on, Lita!" Jonas scoffed. "How rusty have you gotten? Isn't it obvious that we had people waiting by the main road for you to pass so they could backtrack to where you came from? They've got a damn good tracker, almost as good as Sti—" He jumped a little when the door rattled harder than before, causing the fresh weld to shift slightly.

"Jonas!" Rain growled, "If I have to break out of here, I'm going to kill you in ways you've never imagined!"

"Jeez, calm down, bloodrat. It's not like this is any skin off your pale ass. Now quit knocking the door before you set this bomb off and blow us all to hell." Jonas returned his attention to the cut of explosive he was wiring to a half-disassembled wristwatch. Apart from hitter and cleanup, another role Jonas occasionally provided for Cleric was demolitions. It wasn't often called for outside of jobs that were meant to send a big message, but Jonas had a knack for it. He figured it went hand-in-hand with his natural abilities. *Everything burns,* he liked to say. *You just gotta know what kind of fire to set.*

"Alright, Killer," Jonas said as he finished up his work. "You two better get comfortable in there. Just be sure you're clear of the door at eight o'clock." He paused for a beat. "Might want to cover your ears, too."

"Jonas, I'm warning you," Lita said.

"Yeah, yeah, I heard you the first fifty times. Tell you what, look me up sometime once you've ditched the neck sucker. Preferably after you've calmed down and gained some perspective on this whole situation."

"Jonas!" Rain yelled.

"Jonas!" Lita echoed. "Tell me you at least halved the charge so you don't liquefy our brains!"

There was no response.

"Jonas?"

But he was already gone.

III

"Did you hear something?" Alex asked, looking towards the front door.

"I...I don't think so," Amelie replied. She furrowed her brow as she followed Alex's gaze across the room. They had spent the last couple of hours sitting in the living room, wending their way through topics of conversation, beginning with their shared frustration over being left behind and moving on from there. The subject at hand was places they had been or would like to go when Alex's head shot up abruptly, his eyes like those of a deer who has sensed a nearby predator. The very look had stopped Amelie in the middle of her description of the Silver City Opera House, and now they were both silently listening to the house around them, waiting for any sign of whatever it was Alex had heard in the first place.

Standing, Alex took up the combat knife that had been residing next to him on the coffee table and quietly made his way towards the window to the right of the front door. Its heavy black curtains were drawn, and Alex moved to the right side of the window to peer out without moving the drape. Outside, the grass in the clearing shifted this way and that at the whim of a light breeze and a few bees were buzzing about here and there, but there was no other movement. Nothing seemed out of the ordinary, but Alex suddenly felt very sure that something was amiss.

"Alex?" Amelie whispered. "Do you see anyth—"

"Shhh," he interjected. Then, a moment later, he looked over his shoulder at her and pointed towards the stairs. "Go," he whispered.

Amelie obeyed without hesitation. It was, after all, second nature for her to unquestioningly heed the orders of her protectors in times of peril. Following the plan that had been discussed before Rain and Lita left that morning, she hurried to the right side of the staircase and through the steel-reinforced basement door. Its weight slammed shut with such force that she jumped, and she had to fumble in the dark for a moment to find the two sizeable locks and slide them into place. A chill ran through her then as she realized just how dark it was in there. She knew there was no light switch up here at the top of the stairs; Alex had said there was a single hanging bulb with a pull chain down past the bottom step. She also knew she should feel her way down there and find a place to hide, but she couldn't will herself to move away from the door. Instead, she pressed her ear against the cold metal and held her breath.

Out in the living room, Alex had crossed the front door and was now peering out the window to the left of it with the same uneasy caution he had with its twin to the right. Still nothing. Had he been hearing things? In fact, what *had* he heard? He didn't have any way to describe it, but it was a sound that was more *felt* than *heard*—the sound of *disturbance*, like the way a settling house tells you someone is moving around upstairs. That sense of disturbance unsettled him greatly, because while it was easy to write off a sound as misheard, it was much more difficult to write off a feeling as misfelt.

As he stood there, Alex resolved to have a serious conversation with Rain about rethinking the gun policy in this house. He understood why his brother didn't like them, but he also knew he'd feel a hell of a lot better right now with a gun in his hand rather than a knife—even though he had never actually fired one before. Glancing down at that knife now, Alex squeezed it tightly and went to the door. He raised the blade in one hand as he grabbed the knob with the other, and he slowly started inching the front door open.

He had gotten it maybe two inches open—just enough

for the midday light to cut a bright, thin line diagonally across the room—when something on the other side slammed it into him, hard. He stumbled back, reeling, but for a brief moment thought he would retain his balance…until a man roughly the size of a small gorilla burst inside and rammed Alex's chest with his shoulder, removing any hope that he might stay on his feet. The next thing he knew, he was on his back on the hardwood floor. Somehow, he had the presence of mind to keep his hold on the knife, but he quickly realized it wasn't going to do him much good when he looked up to see that large man pointing a sawed-off shotgun at him.

"Hi there," Cleric said, peering down at Alex from under his wide-brimmed hat. "I believe you have a house guest who I will be taking off your hands now."

Alex felt his jaw tremble and his lips try to bow downward, the last ghosts of childhood impulse to cry in the face of confrontation. He bit down on the corners of his mouth and took a sharp breath through his nose, taking firm hold of his composure before daring to speak. "You've got the wrong house," he finally said.

"That so?" Cleric asked.

"It is," Alex replied, and propped himself up on his elbows. "So why don't you get the hell out of here before I show you out?" The final word wavered and he had to bite down inside his mouth again.

Cleric smirked approvingly. "You know, young man, most days I'd admire a pair like that on a kid your age." The smirk disappeared. "But I'm in a no-bullshit kind of mood right now. So here's how this is going to work: you have until the count of five to produce the girl, or I'm going to blow off one of your extremities. You ever seen what a twelve-gauge does to a limb at this distance?"

Alex swallowed hard and didn't answer.

"One."

Amelie's eyes widened. Her heart began trip-hammering in her chest.

"Two."

Alex pushed himself up a little further, his free hand flat on the floor now, and one of his feet planted as well.

"Three."

Cleric raised the shotgun, taking aim at the young man's left foot.

"Four."

Alex's muscles went taught, ready to spring at the last moment, to go for the man's thigh with the knife.

"Fi—"

"Stop!" Amelie cried as she burst through the basement door, stumbling and nearly falling in the process.

Cleric's eyes flicked towards her to be sure she was unarmed, and were back on Alex before the boy could take any advantage of the distraction. "Tsk, tsk," he said, "'Wrong house.' You lied to me, young man. But, I suppose I'll let you keep your limbs anyway." He adjusted his aim, pointing the gun at Alex's face.

Suddenly, an eldritch screech ripped through the living room.

Amelie screamed and recoiled in horror at the sight of the Visgaer standing in the kitchen doorway, its long claws gripping the doorframe, head barely clearing the opening. Alex felt his heart lurch in his chest, somehow feeling exponentially more terror than he had been just seconds before.

But Cleric looked surprised in a different sort of way. "Are you sure?"

The Visgaer issued an irregular series of clicks from its throat.

"Well then," Cleric said with a bemused chuckle. He swept back his long duster and slipped his shotgun into a holster strapped to his leg, then returned his attention to

Alex. "So are you gonna come at me with that thing or just lie there all day?"

Alex blinked. "Excuse me?"

"The knife, kid. Now's your chance. Show me what you can do with it."

"Um...okay," Alex said, deeply confused. Moving slowly, he started pushing himself to his feet. Halfway up, he suddenly lunged from a kneeling position, thrusting the knife at Cleric's abdomen.

Cleric sidestepped almost casually and caught hold of Alex's arm. "Gut shot, huh? Damn, kid. You don't fool around." With a twist of his arm, Cleric drew a pained cry from Alex and watched as the knife fell from his hand. He then cracked the young man between the eyes with an elbow to daze him, and finally yanked him into a tight headlock, cutting off his air supply.

"Alex!" Amelie yelled, and started towards them, her eyes set on the knife.

Cleric cleared his throat, looking towards the Visgaer as he tipped his head in Amelie's direction. "You mind?"

The Visgaer started towards her and Amelie screamed, changing directions to back away from it. But it was quick, crossing the room on those long legs in just a few strides. It reached out for her, and Amelie suddenly felt like all the air had been pulled from her lungs by some unseen force. She fell to her knees, clutching at her throat, but there was nothing to pry away. She looked helplessly towards Alex just in time to see him go limp in Cleric's arms, and then her own vision began to swim. A few seconds later, she slumped to the floor and was out.

IV

Michael heard footsteps and looked up from his book. Peering into the rearview mirror of Cleric's car, he furrowed his brow at the sight of the man and his creature approaching with Amelie draped across the monster's arms and some boy thrown over Cleric's shoulder. He stepped out of the passenger side of the car just as Cleric was opening the trunk.

"Who the hell is that?" Michael asked.

Cleric dumped Alex into the trunk. "That's the Catalyst," he said with a smirk, and slammed the lid closed. "Now get back in the car. We've got work to do."

"Huh," Michael said, then looked over the top of the car at the Visgaer as it placed Amelie in the back seat. "While I am impressed that your pet came through as promised, I must ask just what you think you're doing bringing her back here alive."

"Insurance," Cleric said as he came around to the driver's side door and opened it. He stooped into the car momentarily, grabbed something from under the seat, and returned to slide it across the top of the car towards Michael. The young man stopped it and blinked. It was a large envelope, stuffed to the brim with a stack of papers, and it was spattered with blood.

"What have you done?" Michael whispered.

"I'm not sure if you didn't think I'd guess who you left it with or you just thought I wouldn't kill the palace priest, but either way, you grossly underestimated me," Cleric said.

Michael took a shuddering breath and looked to Cleric, his eyes glassy.

"Now listen here, you little shit," Cleric went on, "we are going to finish this job as originally planned. Then you are going to give me what you owe me. Then, and only then, I will take care of the girl. But I swear to God, if you try to fuck with me again, I won't kill you...I'll make sure she takes power in Chicane and then let her decide what to do with you. Is that understood?"

Michael swallowed and nodded.

"Good. Now get in the fucking car."

FOURTH INTERLUDE

Didst thou stand up straight and tall?
Defy the winds to make thee fall?
As night–time draws across thy land
Thou art one day more a man

In seven years, everything and nothing had changed.

Brushing loose locks of ebony hair from his cobalt eyes, the thirteen-year-old boy stared blankly down at two slabs of steak sizzling in the skillet before him. The heat from the stove was pleasant. It was late January, and they were experiencing an unusual cold snap. The woods around the house were blanketed in white on this particular evening.

As he prepared dinner, the boy glanced across the kitchen to the breakfast nook where Father sat. He was just as large and formidable as ever, but the intervening years had bestowed him with a more prominent belly than before. He had taken to drinking a great deal since the death of his firstborn son.

However, he was still no force to be toyed with. Although his abdomen had lost its definition, his arms still rippled with the muscles of a hard-working blacksmith. Those arms that led to those thick wrists that ended in those meaty hands. When the boy stared at those hands, he sometimes thought he could still see blood on them. The same blood he had scrubbed from his hands, the blade, the floor. He had scrubbed and scrubbed and…

With a loud holler, the boy yanked his hand away from the stove as he felt the flame lick his flesh. With the sudden movement, he nearly lost the whole skillet, and one of the steaks fell to the floor with a wet slap.

The boy closed his eyes with a sigh as he slid the pan back onto the stove. Father slammed down the mug he'd been drinking from and stormed over to his son.

"What is wrong with you, boy, wasting perfectly good meat? It seems you will go hungry tonight." Since the incident years before, Father's temperament had become increasingly unpredictable. His rare moments of kindness were more tender than they ever were when his eldest son was still alive, but his rage was also much worse, and far easier to incite.

"It will not go to waste," the boy whispered, "I will eat it dirty." He stooped down to pick up the fallen cut of beef.

The boy's pain was immediate and much more prominent than the burn on his hand when Father reached down and snatched up a handful of his shaggy black hair, yanking him back upright.

"I said you are going hungry. Is there something wrong with your ears, boy?" Father leaned close, glaring. The boy shook his head. "Good. Then finish my meal, and God help you if it's overcooked." With that, he shoved the boy away, forcing his side to slam painfully against the stove.

All of a sudden, the boy's heart began pounding wildly, but not out of fear. It was a new sensation, wild, almost animalistic. He had never felt it before in his life and had no idea where it came from, but the self-assured instinct that came with it was far too powerful for him to second-guess.

Before he even knew it was happening, his hand had wrapped itself around the heavy handle of the cast-iron skillet. Then that skillet was swinging through the air, coming around in a wide arc towards the back of Father's head. It connected with a loud clang, and Father dropped like a sack of grain.

The boy's breathing came in panicked heaves as he stood over Father's motionless form, the skillet still grasped firmly in his hand. He stood there for almost two full minutes, just breathing and staring at the unmoving shape of the man who had tortured him his entire life.

Then Father began to stir.

"Move," the boy whispered to himself, trying to coax his limbs out of entropy, but they refused to budge. He just stood dumbfounded, frozen in place.

Father groaned, moving one hand to the floor and beginning to push himself up.

"Move!" the boy yelled, and the sound of his own voice startled his body into submission. He launched himself forward, headed for the kitchen door on the far side of the breakfast nook. However, he only made it three steps before a firm hand grabbed the hem of his pant leg, causing him to stumble forward, his stomach hitting the table and an "Oof!" forcing itself from his lungs.

When the boy spun around, his eyes widened in horror at the sight of Father scrambling to his feet. He had seen the look in Father's eyes only once before. It was just before he killed his brother. Just before those eyes changed.

What happened next occurred in the span of only seconds, but the boy's mind seemed to somehow be working faster just now. He came to the realization that, although Father was moving incredibly fast, he had injured the man more than he gave himself credit for. Not only had blood already completely wet the hair on the back of

Father's head, it was also trickling from his right ear, all the way down the side of his thick neck. The young man supposed that maybe he had hurt something on the inside, because he certainly hadn't hit him on the ear. Furthermore, although he was advancing at a steady pace, he was wobbling, just like he did after a night of heavy drinking. He was unbalanced, and the boy could use that.

Those realizations must have come hand-in-hand with that animal instinct to act, because there it was flaring up again. Father was only a couple of feet away, arms outstretched, ready to take hold of his throat, or maybe slam his face into the hot stove, or perhaps just stick a knife in his side like his brother's—the blade was right there on his belt, after all. But the boy would allow none of those things, his new instinct was going to make sure of that. So as Father rushed towards him, the boy shot his foot out to the left, hooked the chair next to him by its leg, and slid it directly into Father's path.

A sort of awe fell over the boy as the scene before him seemed to happen in slow motion. Father's eyes widened in a nearly comical manner as he realized his impending fate, just before his shins collided with the chair. Unable to evade it, he stumbled headlong over the chair and his chin slammed directly down on the edge of the table, blood spraying from his nose and mouth as he once again collapsed in a heap on the floor.

The boy did not hesitate this time. He headed straight out of the kitchen and into the front room, making his way towards the front door. However, he stopped suddenly when he realized his feet were bare. Cursing to himself, he bolted for the stairs, taking them two-by-two up to the second floor.

Hurrying out of his bedroom minutes later, he pulled on his winter coat as he headed for the stairs. He had nearly made it to the stairwell when he heard his name bellowed drunkenly from the floor below. His stomach dropped and he froze in his tracks. He felt his chest tightening up and he was gripped with the sudden impulse to hide. It was, after all, exactly what he had done all these years.

But this time was different, he forced himself to realize. This was the day he had been thinking about for the last seven years, it had just come as much more of a surprise than expected. He had already thought about it in so many ways. Sneak out in the middle of the night. Poison Father's dinner, perhaps. Or maybe just light fire to the house, as long as he made sure he had some food packed away first.

But he had only actually tried to escape once, the previous summer. When Father had caught him, and the boy had suffered the horrible, inventive punishment for that particular crime, he had thought he would have to wait at least another year before he tried again. Now, by virtue of the most spontaneous and unplanned of events, he could be free. All he had to do was get out of this house alive.

He could hear Father's footsteps now, approaching the foot of the stairs. The boy's eyes darted about as he tried to come up with a plan. Shooting his gaze to the doorway atop the stairs, he considered the large, full china cabinet next to it. Block it. Yes, block the doorway and go out a second-floor window.

Setting his new idea into motion with decisiveness that surprised even him, the boy dashed to the cabinet and started pushing it with his shoulder. For a moment, it refused to budge. Then, with a squeal of wood against wood, he began to slowly inch it in front of the doorway.

The boy's father momentarily paused his slow ascent of the stairs and looked up in confusion as the light up ahead started to disappear. His head still swimming, he wondered if he might be blacking out. But it didn't take long for him to realize his son's stupidity.

"If you can push that in front of the door, do you really think it will stop me, you little whelp?" the man screamed as he resumed his climb, gripping the stair rail tightly the whole time.

Having just fully obscured the door upon hearing this, the boy pondered it for a moment as he took a step back from the large cabinet. The fear inside him swelled when he realized Father was right. But then instinct stepped in once more and told him just what to do, and that brought a smirk to the boy's lips.

With a great lunge, the boy slammed his shoulder against the front of the cabinet as hard as he could. He thought it would take more than the one try, but the cabinet slid, creaked, and began to tilt. As he watched it there, teetering on the edge, the boy recalled the horror he had felt watching a vase do the same thing seven years before. This time, he begged for gravity to win.

And as though his wish was granted, the china cabinet fell back and went tumbling down the stairs. He heard a panicked scream. He heard a thunderous crash. Then he heard nothing.

The boy's chest was sore and tight. His shoulder already ached terribly. But he was not done. Not bothering to check Father's condition, he headed towards the far end of the hallway. He could go out the window there, hop down onto the woodshed, and jump from there to the ground. Get one of the horses from the stable and get out of here. If he played his cards right, he could reach London in a day. Maybe find an orphanage that would feed him, or a nice family to...

"Come play," a voice whispered.

The boy's blood ran cold as he stopped and turned wide eyes towards the doorway to his right. That long flight of stairs leading up into the darkness of the third floor. Only it wasn't really darkness. There were small lamps. They gave off just a little light. Just enough to see by to spend four hours scrubbing blood off the floor. Oh, and the keyhole flickered, but big brother had said not to go near that. Said he shouldn't see what...

"Come play with me."

The boy covered his eyes and shook his head. "Leave me be!" This was not the first time he had heard such things. Maybe half a dozen times in as many years he had sworn a voice called to him from up there. He had told himself it was just in his mind. His mind missing his brother. But in all this time he had never stepped foot on a single one of those steps again. Not since descending them covered in his brother's blood. Not since the day they buried him out back by the stables.

Father had knocked him around the living room something good that day. After he watched his brother die, after sitting there with him in his lap until he grew cold, he went to the bottom floor and told Father. Told him that he wasn't moving, that he wouldn't get up. It was the only time he had ever seen the man cry. He cried and hit him a few times, then collapsed to his knees and cried some more. To this day the boy wondered if Father even realized that it was he who had done it. It was as though he had chosen to forget it. The boy supposed he would too, if he could.

Dropping his hands from his face, the boy looked back towards the doorway to the first floor, holding his breath as he listened for any sign of movement. When nothing came to his ears, so he slowly turned his gaze up towards the stairway again.

"Only to the top to see what is there, then straight back down," he whispered to himself, and began hurriedly ascending the stairs.

Coming to the top floor, the boy felt his stomach getting cold, his heart sinking at the sight of this long expanse of walls and floorboards again. The most horrible moments of his life had been spent up here, and he immediately questioned why he would step foot in this place again.

But there was that curiosity. That little part of him that remained from years ago. Perhaps the only part of his childish nature that had not died with his brother or been killed by Father in the years since.

It was that curiosity that drove him forward, propelling him down the hall towards the door. His eyes scanned over the top of the sideboard as he passed it by. Its surface was still empty; the vase had never been replaced. He supposed he could never fit in that cabinet now, and that thought made him pause to listen for Father once again.

In that second he nearly turned back. Almost headed back on his way out of this place. But one more glance at the door effectively sealed his fate as that last burst of curiosity pushed him forward.

Coming to the door, he stared down at its knob, but didn't bother reaching for it. He knew it was locked. Father still came up here from time to time, but only when he thought that the boy didn't know any better, especially late at night. The boy had slipped out of his room long after his bedtime one night to get a glass of water. On his way back, he had to duck behind the china cabinet as he watched Father come out of his bedroom and head up those stairs.

But now the hallway was his, the door his. One good kick would reveal its contents and he could be on his way. No more secrets, no more tortured dreams. He could let it all go and be free of this for good.

His eyes slipped closed in that last moment, as if he couldn't do it while looking. Taking in a deep breath, he raised his foot and thrust it out. He felt it connect, heard a crack, then a creak, then a slam. He felt warmth rush over him from beyond the door. It was there, laid out for him to see. All he had to do was open his eyes.

But he couldn't. Much as he wanted to see what the

room had to offer, he couldn't bring himself to look. He felt as though he would be defying his big brother if he looked. He had told him not to peek, told him to get out of there, told him to run. How could he have come this far? How could he have refused his brother's dying wish? How could he…

Then he heard a rattling of metal, and his eyes snapped open.

For a long moment his mind refused to believe what his eyes were seeing. Were she not moving, he would have taken the young woman to be a corpse. Her pallid flesh seemed to cling tightly to nothing but bones, her long arms extending from a simple white dress speckled brown with dried blood. Her slender wrists were tightly bound with heavy metal shackles, long chains running up from them and connecting to a large ring bolted above the roaring fireplace. She was nearly a silhouette, sitting on her knees in that light, but behind her stringy blonde hair and above her emaciated cheekbones, he could see her crystal blue eyes. They were staring straight at him.

Her chains rattled as her hands reached out as far as they could, bony fingers extending to him, imploring him to come closer. Her eyes softened, pleading with him. Her alabaster lips parted, and in a voice that sounded like a sweet melody played through rattling bones, she said, "Is that my son I see?"

"M-Mother?" the boy whimpered. He didn't remember her, at least not in the strictest sense. He had vague recollections of her beautiful voice singing him to sleep and her soft skin and sweet smell as she rocked him in a big wooden chair, but that was all. The rest had been filled in by his brother in the short time they spent together.

Father had been better when Mother had been around, he'd always say. Not perfect, but better. He never saw Father hit her, and they loved each other, and she protected them as best she could.

But around the time the boy was one and his brother was five, Father and Mother had gone out one night and by morning there was only Father left. He told them nothing, but days later the parish priest had come to inform his brother that she'd been killed in some kind of accident, though never said what. She was just…gone.

But not gone. Because here she had been this whole time. Here waiting for him to rescue her, so they could run away together and have a nice home and she could rock him again. Rock him and sing him to sleep. Hold him and make him feel warm with her soft skin, the way she used to. She would make him remember again. She would make him happy again.

He was in a daze now as walked towards her, arms outstretched. Slipping down to his knees, he fell into her arms and laid his head on her shoulder, his eyes falling shut. He felt her gentle touch on the back of his head, caressing his hair as she whispered to him.

"Shhh, Mother's here now. You need not be afraid."

But his stomach suddenly told him something was very wrong. If his brother had seen her in here, why had he run away? If she was alive, why had she been locked up here all these years? If she was holding him, why wasn't he warm?

He opened his eyes and looked up at her, but she was not the same. Her crystal blue eyes had become yellow and wild, like that of an animal bearing down on its next kill. Her lips curled open into a wide grin, and to the boy's horror, he saw her teeth had become sharp, glistening fangs.

"Mother is here now," she hissed, and the boy tried to pull away. Her hand tightened on his hair and she yanked his head to the side. He felt a tearing pain, followed by dizziness, and then blackness.

"My God, what have you done?"

The room was spinning as the boy came to, but his senses immediately sharpened at the sight of Father standing in the open doorway. He was banged up pretty bad, arms all scraped and a deep gouge above his eyebrow. Groaning, the boy turned his head to the other side, looking up at the woman he thought was his mother. She sat in front of the fire staring at Father with a confused look on her face.

"I thought he was meant to be my dinner."

"Why in God's name would you..." Father shook his head, a pained expression on his face. "After everything I have done for you, keeping you here and safe after what you turned into, you repay me by taking our last child?"

The boy didn't understand what was happening. He hadn't been taken anywhere. He did feel strange, though. He was having a hard time making sense of anything. But as the two of them spoke, he slowly pushed himself to his knees.

"I...I wanted someone to play with. I wanted to—" Mother began, but her words were cut off when Father strode across the room and delivered a backhand to her cheek.

"Enough!" he yelled. Turning his eyes to the boy, Father retrieved his whip from his belt and took a few steps back. "It appears I will have to take care of you now."

The boy just sat there on his knees, blankly staring at the floor. Somehow, all the fight had fallen out of him. He wanted to die. In fact, somewhere inside he felt like he was already on his way. He didn't quite know what Father meant about her taking him, but he didn't really care. He just wanted this to end so he could finally be with his brother and be left alone.

The hiss cut through the air and the boy felt searing pain slice into his chest and down to his abdomen. Blood immediately soaked his now-torn shirt, but he didn't even flinch. He just wanted it over. This angered Father, of course, and he quickly drew back and struck again. The second lash cut across the boy the other way, into his chest and stomach again, but he again made no noise, and no tears fell.

"Scream, damn you!" Father cried out, drawing his whip back once more.

But the boy would not scream. He would not cry. He would not beg. He welcomed it. Just as soon as he could have that blackness, all of this would finally be over. And just as he wished it, that prayer began to be answered. The whip lashed out again, this time slinging around the back of his neck and curling tightly about his throat. Father tugged on it, and the leather pulled tight, cinching the boy's windpipe closed. His face grew hot and his chest heaved. His eyes drifted closed, and when he felt that darkness beginning to surround him, he opened his arms, inviting it in.

"I did not want this," Father said. The boy thought he sounded far away now. "You brought this on yourself, just as your brother did."

His eyes snapped open and the sense of defeat was gone. There was no more pain, no more angst. He no longer wished it over or begged for his own death. In the instant that those words filled his ear, something new came over him. It wasn't fear. It wasn't instinct. It was something deeper and far more powerful than any of that. It exploded inside him like a fire, rushing into his veins and fingers and heart. It filled his body with heat, with life, with power.

The boy glared up at his father, and the man froze at the sight of his own son's eyes. Those eyes weren't scared. Those eyes weren't pleading. Those eyes weren't even blue. Glowing with turbulent violet energy, those eyes were murderous.

The boy brought one foot up, rose to one knee, then pushed himself to his feet. Enraged, glowing eyes locked on his father, he balled his fists at his sides and began pulling back against the whip. His own eyes widening, Father tightened his grip on the handle and pulled back himself. The boy could feel the whip tightening around his throat, but he still took a defiant step back, then another, then another. Father could feel his feet sliding forward, so he yanked back harder. Mother sat before the fire silently, grinning and watching the violent tug of war, just waiting for delicious blood to be spilt. She didn't rightly care from whom.

Leaning back now, the boy heard noises coming from the taut leather. First a groan, then a tearing, and then a loud snap. In a flash of white, searing pain, the vision in the boy's left eye disappeared completely for a moment, and he felt warmth begin trickling down his face. Both father and son stumbled backwards when the weapon broke. The boy's back hit a wall and he immediately pushed off it, propelling himself straight for Father in a blind rage. As he moved, he ripped the tattered remnant of the whip from his throat and, without thinking about it, shoved it in his pocket.

Eyes filling with fear mirroring that which he'd created in his sons so many times, Father fumbled for his belt, looking for another weapon. Before he had time, his son's hand encircled his throat and he felt his back slam against the far wall. Even so, he continued to scramble, trying to obtain a means by which to defend himself.

His hand finally found his sheathe, but found it empty.

"Is this what you wanted?" the boy asked, leaning forward and raising the blade of that fine silver dagger to touch the man's cheek. "Is this what you were reaching for, dear Father?" His eyes were more brilliant than ever now, that violet glow surrounding the blackness of his pupils, staring into the trembling eyes of the man who gave him life and took his brother's. "Well why don't you take it?"

The blade went in smoothly, even easily, much to the

boy's surprise. It slipped into Father's lower abdomen, just below the navel. The man gasped, his eyes widening and filling with tears, Adam's apple jumping up and down.

"Do you feel it now, Father? Do you feel what he felt? The pain? The fear? Knowing that you're going to die?" the boy's tone was even and calm, but with an undertone that matched neither that nor the rage in his eyes. It was malice, slithering there just beneath the surface of his words. "Before you do, Father, I want you to know one more thing. Do you know what that is?"

His breath coming in hitching half-gasps, Father strained to look at the boy, his vision already beginning to fade in and out. "Wh-Wha..." he gasped painfully.

The boy leaned in so close his lips brushed Father's ear as he whispered, "I'm not afraid of you anymore." With that, he yanked the knife straight up and out, and felt the warmth of Father's intestines spill over his shoes just before the man's eyes rolled back and he slumped to the floor.

As the boy stepped back, the rage fell away, and his eyes returned to normal. Dizziness set in immediately, and he stumbled against the wall by the door. Breathing heavily, he raised his eyes to look over towards his mother, who was sitting there, smiling at him.

"Now we can be together, love. We can be together forever. Just let me go and we'll be together," she said in a sweet voice. It was seductive, and it might have drawn the boy in, were it not for the fact that it still whistled through that bed of bones.

Taking one step back out into the hallway, the boy looked up to the oil lamp in the corner. Reaching for it, he unscrewed the oil font from the underside of the fixture, then looked back to that animated corpse of a woman.

"I'm sorry, Mother," he said softly.

"Son, what are you—"

The boy drew back with the font, and threw it across the

room. It shattered in the fireplace with a blinding explosion, instantly engulfing the creature that was once his mother, along with half the small room.

Her screams echoed behind him as he slowly moved down the hallway and descended the stairs. By the second flight her cries had ceased, and the boy felt himself growing weak. He wanted to stop, to just lie down and go to sleep. But he knew that if he didn't get out of this house, he would never wake up again.

Crawling over the destroyed remnants of the china cabinet strewn about the bottom half of the stairs, the boy finally found himself in the sitting room once more. Standing still for a moment, he listened to the house. He could already hear the fire crackling upstairs, quickly moving across the walls, devouring this hateful place from the inside out. His eyes scanned over the home where he'd been born and raised, finally coming to rest on an oval mirror that hung on the wall between the sofa and the kitchen door.

Approaching it, he gazed at his reflection for the last time. He almost didn't recognize what he saw. The boy there was pallid and shimmering with sweat that matted his hair to his forehead. His left eye was a horror to behold, a deep bloody gash crossing over it from his forehead to his cheek. The only things he found familiar were his deep blue eyes. When he looked into them, he felt he was looking into the eyes of his big brother. A sense of assurance washed over him from somewhere he didn't know or understand. It told him that no matter what he became, those eyes would never truly change, and so his brother would always be there. Always.

Taking a deep breath, he left that place behind and headed out into the snow. The light was fading out there, the sun just now dropping to the horizon. Woods surrounded most of the residence, but just in front of him was a large clearing that afforded a view of rolling hills below, offering a magnificent look at a dozing sky splashed with wondrous color. His brother once told him that Mother loved to come out here and watch the sunset; she would sing them lullabies while the sky turned dark.

He began to trudge through the snow, but didn't make it far before he collapsed to his knees. As he gazed upon that last sunset of his life, the reds and oranges and pinks seemed more vibrant than he had ever known. They radiated out to him with their brilliance, telling him sweet lies of a life set before him with opportunities like happiness and love.

By this time tomorrow, his body would already be changing. It would age rapidly until it reached the perfect physical form for a predator. He would be a killer, a monster of the most unimaginable sort. But in his last few moments of humanity, he was just a boy. A boy who had taken a stand against everything he feared, and had finally been set free.

SIXTEEN

I

"Well this is fucking fantastic."

Lita was standing in the center of the mausoleum between its two stone coffins. Her hands rested on her hips and she squinted as she peered about, trying to make out the fine details of their prison. Though her eyes were almost fully adjusted now, it was still pretty damn dark in here.

Rain, on the other hand, was making his way meticulously along the walls, examining every stone and crack he could find, looking for a weak spot or anything else that might facilitate their escape. He paused long enough to pay her a glance. "You could probably be doing more than standing around right now."

Lita quirked a brow. "And what do you suggest I do, Rain? Unless you've got a pickaxe hidden in that coat of yours, we're not going a damn place until 8 o'clock."

He turned around to face her. "You're saying there's no way we can get that door open without setting off what he put out there?"

She shrugged. "Maybe, but I'm sure as hell not lining up to try. Look, I'm sorry that I pulled you into this, but there's not a lot either of us can do about that now. So what I'm going to do is try to enjoy the peace and quiet until this evening, and assuming that charge doesn't bring this entire building down on our heads, I'm going to pack up and put all of this in my rearview mirror."

"Sorry?" Rain took a step towards her. "You're sorry? You came into my house, drugged my brother and me, stole my car, asked me for sanctuary, and then led killers back to us—killers who are after my brother and an innocent girl right this moment—and you're *sorry?*"

Lita prickled. "What do you want me to say, Rain? You think I wanted this to happen?" She pushed off from her position leaning against a coffin and threw her hands up. "You think I like the idea that we're stuck here while God knows what is happening to your brother and Amelie? I'm just being realistic. For all we know, they're both already dead."

"He's still alive," Rain said flatly.

"How the fuck do you know?"

"I know."

"Well, that's grand, but you're still on your own. I don't know how I managed to get out of this little situation alive, but I'm not about to tempt fate further once we get out of here. I'm going straight to the road and pitching a thumb until I can get a ride the hell out of here." She turned and started walking away from him.

Rain was right behind her. He took hold of her upper arm and spun her around forcefully. "No. You don't get to walk away from this one. Your demons spilled over into my life, so this time you're just going to have to face them."

"I've been staring at a demon for the last two days. Go to hell," she spat, then shoved his shoulder in attempt to pull away from his grasp.

Rain's reaction was immediate. He balled up his fist and cracked her across the jaw with a sharp right hook.

Lita stumbled a step and brought the back of her hand to her cheek. Her eyes seemed to come ablaze with emerald fury, her lips turning up in a smirk. "Is that it, Vampire? Is that all you have to fucking say to me?" She lunged forward, returning a much harder punch to his chin, punctuated by a fierce right jab to his chest, sending him back a few steps of his own.

Releasing a furious growl, Rain hurled himself at her, taking her by the shoulders and slamming her against the back wall of the mausoleum. She winced, closing her eyes momentarily, and then glared up at him as she stood there pinned. "What's it gonna be, Rain? What the fuck are you gonna do?"

Despite the dim light, from this distance she could see the tendons in his jaw and neck flexing, his eyes roiling with fury, looking like he was on the verge of snapping…and yet, somehow holding back, hesitating.

"Oh, for fuck's sake," Lita said impatiently, then grabbed him by the back of the head and brought their lips colliding together.

Rain couldn't even act surprised. As he pulled her body against his, deepening the kiss, he could feel her heart pounding rapidly in her chest. The sound of it filled his ears like a drum beat, and it seemed to draw his own body into its rhythm. As her warmth began to spread into him, he could feel it quickening him, arousing him, making him feel alive again.

Their hands moved desperately over each other's bodies. Rain slipped his up Lita's sides, bunching her shirt, so she broke the kiss and pulled the tank top the rest of the way off. In turn, she grabbed his coat and yanked it off his shoulders, allowing him to drop it off his arms. The coveralls were next, and as she unzipped them and pushed them down, she yelled in frustration at the sight of a t-shirt and jeans. "Goddammit, are you naked under there anywhere?"

Rain couldn't help laughing as he stepped out of the coveralls, but the mirth was quickly cut off when Lita accidentally cracked him across the jaw with her elbow while yanking his shirt up and off. She didn't offer an apology and he didn't seek one, only took her by the back of the neck and pulled her towards him, the intensity of their movements resuming as though it had never missed a beat.

The last of their clothing discarded at their feet, Lita tugged Rain, guiding him to one of the two coffins where she hopped up to sit on the edge. After an intense shiver at the feeling of cold stone against her skin, she pulled Rain simultaneously back into their kiss and between her parted legs. He moved against her, and though the friction felt nice, he seemed to be having trouble finding the right angle. "Here. Let me," she said at last, and reached down to guide him.

Though Lita had made use of a handful of men in her time, her reasons for doing so amounted to little more than satisfying an itch. She always got what she needed out of the situation and then discarded it by the wayside. For everything she had survived as as a child, it sometimes surprised her that she wasn't completely repulsed by the very idea of another person touching her. Yet somehow, over the years, she had managed to almost completely detach her adult sexuality from the traumas of her youth. The only thing that really held her back from seeking out true intimacy was the heat. Any time another body came that close to her, she felt like she was smothering in the heat it forced onto her and into her. It felt like it was killing her, and she had never been able to get past that frightening sensation enough to find complete pleasure with any partner.

But as Rain finally slipped inside her, she felt at first nothing but cold. It was both startling and exhilarating.

When he moved into her completely and she wrapped her legs around him, she gasped at the chill that filled her entire being. Running her hands over his back as she pulled him against her, she became dimly aware of the familiar texture of damaged, irregular flesh, but further consideration of the matter could wait until later. As he began to move against her, inside and out—as they rocked together in quickening, breathless rhythm—she felt warmth begin to fill them both, but it was not the strangling sensation she had experienced in the past. All at once, she realized his body was warming her by the heat of her own fire, and with that realization came the possibility that she was not the dead thing inside that she had been sure she'd become in her short time on this Earth. She suddenly understood that she was capable not only of having warmth within her, but also of sharing it with another. Her heart was giving his body life for just a little while, and the sensation made her feel truly alive for the first time in a long, long time.

Giving in completely to that shared rhythm, the two slipped to the floor. Lita guided Rain's hands to help her find what she needed, and the sensation of her lost in that pleasure against him brought him to his own conclusion shortly after. In the moments following, they just held one another, savoring the warmth they had created between them, Rain trembling slightly with his lips near her ear, Lita slowly catching her breath with her cheek on his shoulder.

II

"I imagine you could use this," Rain said, handing Lita a leather flask he had retrieved from his coveralls. She was sitting on most of their discarded clothes, though she had put her underpants and tank top back on, and had pulled Rain's coat over her as a makeshift blanket. Taking a sip from the flask, she shuddered at the unfamiliar taste of whiskey, but nodded a simple thank you.

Rain stood and turned around, thoughtfully surveying their enclosure with a renewed sense of calm. Looking up at him, Lita had to contain a small gasp that tried to escape her. He had put his pants back on, but nothing else. She was sure he had done so as a courtesy; he didn't seem ashamed of being naked, and certainly had no reason to. He was all slender muscle, lines of definition cut firmly into his flesh. Lita had never put a great deal of stock into physical appearance, but Rain was undeniably attractive.

However, none of that was what had caught her breath in her throat. It was what she saw on his back, what she had briefly felt during their intimacy. All of his flesh from shoulder to waistline was a crisscrossing latticework of deep, straight scars. On top of all that, seared into his left shoulder was some kind of symbol. It was a crescent moon curved around a circle with a single droplet shape stretching down from the underside of the moon.

"Good God, Rain," Lita whispered. "Your back."

Rain glanced over his shoulder, as though he had forgotten it was there. "Mmmm," he said, then turned back to face her and leaned against the end of the coffin they had recently defiled. It was then she noticed for the first time the two long scars across his chest and abdomen, which formed a faint X in his flesh.

"What does the symbol mean?"

"My father was a blacksmith; it was his trade symbol. He branded me when I tried to run away when I was twelve," Rain said soberly.

"I can't imagine why you'd want to run away," Lita replied. "What about the other scars? On your back and…" she gestured to her left eye.

Rain answered almost nonchalantly as he went about lighting a cigarette. "All from my father's bullwhip. This one on my eye is the last he gave me before I killed him."

Lita grimaced, suddenly thinking of the bloodstained piece of leather she had found in the closet. "How did you get up the courage to kill him?" She knew all about how much mustering that took. It was no small thing.

"I was turning into a vampire, so he was trying to kill me. I killed him first."

"So...you turned right after that?"

"No, first I killed the vampire that made me, then I turned."

"What, just some random vampire attack?"

Rain hesitated for a beat, then said, "It was my mother. She was attacked and turned when Alex and I were very young. We thought she was dead, but my father kept her locked away in a room in our house. One day I got too curious about that room." He took a deep drag from his cigarette.

"Jesus, why would he keep her?"

Rain shrugged. "Maybe he just couldn't let her go." Diverting, he nodded towards her bare feet peeking out from under his coat. "How'd you get yours?"

Lita glanced down and quickly pulled them from sight. "The fire from the first Amelie job. Would've been all over for me if she hadn't pulled me out of there."

Rain was quiet for a stretch before asking his next question. "How many people have you killed?"

Lita swallowed, then said quietly, "Ninety-three."

Rain nodded and brought his cigarette to his lips.

"What about you?" Lita asked cautiously.

"What *about* me?" Rain asked, raising an eyebrow from behind a cloud of smoke.

Lita sighed, took a swig from the flask, and then looked at him earnestly. "Look, Rain, the way Alex talks I know you haven't always been...whatever it is you are. A vampire with a conscience, I guess? Well that means, at some point, you were a standard-issue vampire, so I'm assuming you didn't play nice with the locals. If you want me to help you once we get out of here, I need you to be straight with me. So how many is it?"

Rain stared at her for a moment that seemed to stretch on for miles. When he found her eyes to be utterly unwavering, he said, very slowly, "Twenty-one thousand, seven-hundred forty-two."

Lita coughed involuntarily, then cleared her throat. "How…is that possible?"

"I became a vampire when I was thirteen years old in 1711. From that moment, I killed indiscriminately for nearly three-hundred fifty years." Rain stated this very matter-of-factly, burying any emotion he had about the matter.

Though Lita was no stranger to death, she couldn't even wrap her head around a number of that magnitude. Merely trying brought up goosebumps in her flesh. She rubbed her arm in effort to be rid of them. "So, wait, two things. First, you don't look thirteen. Second, what happened to change things? Why did you stop killing?"

"To the first question, the answer is simple. While it is true that vampires are immortal, the myth that they retain the age they were when they turned is erroneous. Within a year of becoming, every vampire's body changes to peak physical condition, which appears as a mid-twenties age. If they start out young, they grow older. If they're turned when they're old, they actually get younger. It makes them more effective killers."

"So you didn't have to work for that body?"

"No."

"Lucky."

"Hardly."

"And the moral one-eighty?"

Rain cleared his throat and snuffed out his cigarette. "At the end of the Last War, the Great Plague that was nearly wiping out humanity also left me starving. I once heard that the immunity rate was only 0.015 percent, so it was nearly impossible to find someone to feed on who wasn't ill. I was too afraid to drink from the dying; I didn't know what it would do to me. Then, one day, I came upon a perfectly healthy young boy—no older than Alex was when he died— just sitting in a park playing in the middle of a city full of the dead." He paused and reached for another cigarette. Lita could see his hand shaking.

"I didn't attack him right away. I talked to him for a little while, trying to make sure he wasn't sick. Of course, he had no idea what I was. He asked me if I wanted to see a neat trick, and then he touched the ground and made a flower grow right before my eyes."

"He was a Gifted," Lita said.

Rain nodded. "The first one I ever saw. I didn't understand it, but I didn't care. All I could think about was eating. So I took him, and I fed, and he tasted like nothing I'd ever had before. But his blood…it did something to me. It changed me."

"It gave you a conscience," Lita said.

"I think it partially healed me. Made me just a little human again. Since that day, I've had to live with everything I've done…and I have a photographic memory. It was just very sharp when I was human, but once I became a vampire I could recall everything I did or saw."

"You remember all of them then?"

"Every last one."

Lita let out a low whistle. "And you can't even get drunk. Fuck."

"Tell me about it," Rain said, and lit his cigarette.

"So now you just…what?"

He shrugged. "Live. Or as close to it as I can come. It's easier—a little, anyway—with Alex here."

"But you don't know how he got here, or why?" Lita asked, then stifled a yawn.

Rain shook his head.

She sighed and repositioned some of their clothes into a makeshift pillow before lying down. She shivered, pulling the coat tight around her. "And now I might have gotten him killed all over again."

"He's still alive," Rain said with remarkable assurance.

"Okay, say he is. What then?" She yawned again.

"We're going to find the people behind this."

"And do what?"

"Damage." He snuffed out his cigarette. "Get some sleep. You'll need it come nightfall."

"You got a plan?" Lita murmured, already drifting.

"I do," Rain replied. "We check the house, and then we find Jonas."

SEVENTEEN

Alex awoke to darkness. His first instincts pushed him towards panic, and his breath quickened as he tried to sit up. Fortunately, he did so slowly enough that his head touched metal with a soft tap and not a loud thud. His chest tightening, he lay back down and moved his hands to feel the walls around him. Almost right away he realized he was inside a trunk, and he knew this because he had been in one before.

Some months earlier, he had wondered what it must be like for Rain on the occasions they had been caught without safe refuge at the dawn hours. Those had been long days which Alex spent sleeping restlessly in the back seat after they'd found an out-of-the-way place to park Rain's car. He knew it must be infinitely worse for his brother, crammed inside a trunk for hours on end. He was much taller than Alex, and didn't fit particularly well. So one afternoon, bored and alone while Rain rested, Alex had gone out to the car, climbed into the trunk, and closed the lid. He stayed in there for nearly ten minutes before becoming unnerved and releasing himself. At the time, he hadn't had any reason for doing it other than pure curiosity, but today he was thankful he had.

However, that trunk had been easy to escape from. After the first incident that led to Rain spending the day in there, the two of them had decided to retrofit the latch with a release button inside. The mechanics of the job had been simple enough, and Alex had enjoyed working on it with his brother. This trunk, on the other hand, seemed to have been altered for the exact opposite purpose. Whatever upholstery that might have once lined it had been stripped away. There was no spare tire, nor did there seem to be a jack or any other normal trunk tool either. Feeling the lid again, Alex realized it had several outward dents in it. People had been locked in here before, he suddenly realized, and they had tried to kick their way out.

A suffocating feeling surged up inside him and his mind started towards panic once more. What was he doing here? Why had he been taken captive? Taking a slow, deep breath, he did his best to push those questions down and out of the way of rationale thought. They didn't matter right now. All that mattered was escape. He could tell the vehicle was moving, but he had no idea how much time he had before it reached a destination. He couldn't hear anything coming from the cab of the car, so whoever was in there was driving in silence. He remembered going after that big guy and stupidly getting pulled into a chokehold. And then there was some kind of creature he'd never seen before…what the hell was that thing? And Amelie, Christ. He had no idea if she was still alive, but he knew he had to get out of here and find out.

He moved his hands blindly over the locking mechanism of the trunk and furrowed his brow. The setup was different than Rain's car, but not by much, and it didn't seem to have been reinforced in any way. Slipping his fingers down over the large hook that held the trunk closed, he found it to be worn and battered, but still very secure. There was no way he could manipulate it without making enough noise to draw attention. But as he had told Rain when they were working on his car, it wasn't the latch you had to worry about, but the brain that controlled the latch. In this case, that brain was a simple mechanical device inside a small box just above the hook.

Feeling the box, Alex discovered it was held closed by only two small screws. However, two screws might as well be a padlock to someone without any tools. He cursed the loss of his switchblade to the lake outside the Red Mare Tavern, and resolved to find a new one when this was over. Perhaps even some sort of multi-tool. He had seen those peddled at markets in Maple City, but most were rusty or in ill repair. Right now, he would take the rustiest screwdriver in Ayenee over the only tool available to him: his thumbnail.

He slipped his nail into one of the screws and pushed it as hard as he could, trying to get it to budge. It didn't, even as his nail began to bend. He struggled, pushing harder, until suddenly his nail tore off deep into the quick beneath. He pulled back his hand with a hiss and jammed his thumb into his mouth, nursing it for a moment.

Redoubling his efforts, he tried the other screw with his uninjured thumb. Initially, it seemed as stubborn as the first. Then, just as he was sure he'd lose another nail, the screw wrenched free from its initial tightness and began turning bit by bit. After a few rotations, he was able to grab it between his fingers and unscrew it the rest of the way. He pocketed it and went to work prying at the seam of the box. Little by little it pulled back, and after a few fractions of an inch he was able to pivot it on the remaining screw until it was open. His heart pounding excitedly, he felt around inside to find, as he had hoped, the mechanism was nearly identical to that in Rain's trunk. Ignoring the stinging in his thumb, he used it to manipulate the locking mechanism as he pulled up on the linking rod with his other hand. With a soft pop, the latch came free and the trunk opened a fraction of an inch.

Pausing his movements for a moment, Alex held the trunk lid still so that it was barely open and waited. Listening, he searched for any voices or movement inside the car that might indicate they had heard what he was doing. A full minute passed before he finally cracked the lid just enough to peer outside.

At first, he saw only white. The harsh glare of the afternoon sun seemed to bounce off every surface out there, stabbing into eyes that had adjusted to pure blackness. Gradually his vision cleared, and through his slender viewing space he was able to see the road slipping away behind the vehicle, all dirt and smashed vegetation. Their path was only wide enough for one car, bordered on each side by endless trees blurring past them. Wherever they were headed, it was away from any established town. Alex wondered whether he could find shelter by nightfall even if he did escape. He had no idea how far they had travelled. As he pondered this, a puff of black smoke belched up from the car's tailpipe and erupted in his face. He was unable to stifle an involuntary cough that burst forth from his lungs.

From inside the cab came a short, unholy screech, followed by muffled voices.

"Good Lord!" a young, startled voice said. "That thing scared me half to—"

"Be quiet," a second voice commanded. Alex was almost certain it belonged to the big guy from the house. "What did you hear?"

Alex used one hand to hold the trunk as near to closed as he could and the other to cover his mouth. His body went through a series of violent heaves as he tried to contain the coughing fit. But then that became the least of his worries as, all of a sudden, he got the distinct feeling he was not alone inside his own head. It was a strange sensation, like pressure pushing in on his mind from all sides. It felt like he was being smothered in a dense fog, and for a moment all he wanted to do was fall asleep.

Doing the only thing he could immediately think of to combat whatever was happening to him, Alex closed his eyes and tried to think of nothing at all. He pictured huge, swallowing waves of blackness. He pictured nothingness. He pictured being back in that lake, drowning all over again. Down, down, and down.

And just when it seemed he could not win out against that unseen invading force, another scream issued from the cab. This one, however, was not otherworldly at all. It was the terrified cry of a young girl. Alex's eyes popped open. A single thought—*Amelie!*—burst into his mind not a fraction of a second after the vice-like grip released his psyche.

"Put her to sleep," he heard the big guy command.

Amelie's screams tapered off abruptly.

"Thank you," the younger male voice said, exasperated. "Now may we please drive in peace?"

No one said anything further. In the trunk, Alex's mind was racing. There was no way he could slip out of the car now, not if they had Amelie. If he did that, she would surely be killed, and though he might well encounter the same fate by staying, he knew he had no other choice. He couldn't leave her behind to die while he saved himself.

He stayed still for a time, holding the trunk nearly closed while he waited for any further signs of danger from the car or his mind. When he felt confident he could move safely once again, he rolled on his side and retrieved the screw from his pocket. Reaching out to the hand holding onto the trunk lid, he took a deep breath, held it, and slashed the screw deep across the soft flesh of his palm just above the wrist. He let out his breath carefully, trying to block out the pain and the holler that wanted to come with it. Then, switching hands holding the lid, he opened it just enough to reach out as far as he could with the injured palm. Holding it past the bumper, he flexed it over and over, forcing blood to drip generously onto the road behind them as they sped along. He did this for as long as he could—close to a mile—before his bleeding slowed, his palm growing tacky.

He retrieved his hand and shoved it into his pocket, wiping off as much of the blood as he could in there, out of sight. Then he went about reversing his escape procedure, manipulating the hook once more to close the trunk as quietly as he had opened it. He replaced the locking mechanism's box cover and returned the screw, but gave it only one full turn, just in case.

Alex didn't know what had become of Rain, but he did know that his brother would come looking. And if he came down this road, he would know he was on the right track.

A significant amount of time passed; he had no way of telling how much. At one point, he fell into fractured, inconsistent sleep, but was awoken once more when the car came to an abrupt, skidding stop. He heard doors opening and closing, the vehicle's occupants exiting.

"You bring the girl, I'll grab the boy," the big guy said. The only response was a series of irregular vocalized clicks.

"I have preparations to take care of," the young man said.

"No one's stopping you," the big guy said.

Alex could hear hurried footsteps walking away, and then heavier ones approaching the trunk. He immediately went limp and closed his eyes. During the long drive, he considered his options upon being released from this steel prison. His first instinct was to come out fighting hard, but he realized that not knowing where he'd be or how many captors he may have would make that a very bad idea. Besides, if they had intended to kill him outright, they could have done so easily back at the house. Taking him meant they needed him for something, and that gave him time— time he fully intended to bide. So he elected to feign unconsciousness, hoping he might be able to at least observe his surroundings without being noticed.

He heard the trunk pop open and fresh, cool air rushed in as light filtered through his eyelids. Then there was a fingertip tapping him on the forehead. He willed himself to stay perfectly still. But when that hand suddenly grabbed his ear and twisted it hard, Alex's eyes popped open and he cried out.

"I thought so," the big guy said, and then pointed a gun at him. There was a pop and Alex felt a sharp pain in his left breast. The dizziness set in almost immediately, and he had just enough time to gaze up at the man, notice curiously that there were no longer any trees around them, and then his mind spiraled down through the grey and into the black.

EIGHTEEN

I

Rain crouched down and his eyes played over Lita's sleeping form. She had been out for hours, nearly the entire day slipping by around her. For the most part, she had slept peacefully, aside from a couple brief tossing fits. Rain was almost sorry to have to wake her. From the depth of her slumber, he knew she mustn't have had a decent rest in some time.

He gently touched her shoulder and gave her a small shake. "Lita, it's time to—"

Her reaction was as quick and precise as it was fierce. Her eyes snapping open, her hand flashed out and took hold of Rain's wrist, bending it at an angle that would be painful for a human. He looked down at her hand, then to her. For a moment, there was a glint of wild animosity in her green eyes, but it disappeared in the space of a blink and she released him.

"Sorry," she said, sitting up and rubbing her eyes.

"My fault. I should know better than to shake a sleeping assassin. Next time I'll throw pebbles from across the room."

She peered at him with the eye that didn't have a fist in it. "Next time?"

Rain only responded with a coy smile before finding a seat on the floor and lying down on his back, his hands behind his head. He had dressed himself, but only in the t-shirt and jeans, not his daytime attire.

"You've been busy," Lita said. While she was sleeping, he had removed the heavy stone lid of one of the coffins and stood it up against the door. The other coffin had its lid slid halfway open.

"I figured we shouldn't take our chances with the explosion. The lid should dampen some of it, and I emptied out the other coffin for us to take cover in."

Lita chuckled. "Hopefully Mister and Misses Harper don't mind," she said, glancing at the nameplate above the door.

"I actually think it was Misses and Misses," Rain replied.

"Huh," Lita said. She stood up and stretched with a groan as she shifted on her feet, trying to coax the painful tingling from them. Then, with a shiver, realized she was still only wearing underwear and a tank top, so she snatched up her pants and began putting them on. "How much longer until the fireworks?"

Rain checked his pocket watch. "About twenty minutes."

She had just finished pulling up her pants and paused with her thumbs still hooked in the waistband. Then she pushed them back down along with her underwear and stepped out of both.

"What are you doing?" Rain asked, quirking a brow.

"If I might die in twenty minutes, I think I'd like to get laid one more time," she said nonchalantly as she knelt down and started unbuckling his belt.

"Do I get a say in this?" he asked with a chuckle, but made no move to stop her.

"Not really, no," she said, smirking. There was certainly

273

no coaxing necessary. He was ready by the time she had gotten his clothing out of the way, and she wasted no time straddling him and letting out a soft moan at the strangely exciting coolness of him entering her once again. He moved his hands towards her, but she took them and placed them firmly on her hips. "You just relax. I'll take it from here."

And so she did. He finished first this time, but she followed shortly after, rocking with a hand between her legs and enjoying the feeling of him under and inside her. She lost sense of time during, and half expected the place to blow up right in the middle of it all, so she was surprised when she had come down from the last waves of pleasure and he told her they had about eight minutes to spare.

They dressed quickly, stealing glances and stupid grins at one another the whole time. Though they were well aware that the rest of this night could bring terrible things once they escaped, they also needed these few moments of levity so they could keep their heads about them.

Rain pulled the empty coffin lid aside and gestured for Lita. She tried not to picture its most recent occupant as she climbed inside and did her best to make room for him. He was right behind her, and it was a tight fit, but he managed to pull the lid closed and lie down with her, knee-to-knee, face-to-face.

"Would you like to hear something funny?" Rain whispered. His breath was a cold chill against her lips.

"Sure," she whispered back.

"This is my first time in a coffin."

Lita snickered. "Want to hear something funnier?"

"What?"

"It's not mine."

Rain laughed. "What are you talking about?"

"Well, I had this mark—this real shitbag undertaker who was scamming money and jewelry off people. So I hid out in one of the coffins in his showroom..." she suddenly started laughing, "You…you should have seen the look on his face when I—"

The force of the explosion ripping through the building dwarfed whatever startled cries may have come from the two of them. Through the shaking and the sound of falling stone, Lita felt Rain's arms around her, and she clutched close to his chest, holding her breath until it was over, one way or the other.

When silence came, and with it the realization that they had not been killed, Lita released a shuddering cry, followed by a shaky little laugh. Lifting her head, she sought out Rain with her lips, finding first his rough chin and then his mouth. The kiss, though brief, somehow seemed more passionate than any that had come in the hours before.

Reluctantly pulling back, Rain reached up and cautiously slid the coffin lid aside enough for them to get out. Dust and small rocks rained down upon them and Lita coughed, but when they both climbed out to survey the damage, they were surprised at how little there actually was. The coffin lid blocking the door was split into several pieces, and the door itself was hanging half off its hinges, but for the most part it seemed as though Jonas had actually taken some care in his application of the explosives. Needless to say, it didn't serve to reduce either of their desires to see him good and injured before morning.

In seconds, they both had their possessions in hand and were rushing headlong into the cool night, towards Rain's car. They both knew what was at stake. Lita was a bit surprised that Jonas hadn't done any damage to the car. She half expected him to at least have melted the tires. He had expressed some appreciation for fine mechanics in the past, so perhaps he just couldn't bring himself to harm the old girl. No matter the reason, she was just thankful for small favors as they climbed into the car and Rain brought it to life.

As he got the car moving, Rain glanced her way. "Seatbelt."

"Oh don't worry," she said with a grin, "I've seen you drive. I'm all over it."

As they made their way down the hill to the edge of the cemetery, the sun was just disappearing behind the horizon. The sky was still quite blue, but there was no longer any danger of direct exposure. At the bottom of the hill, they pulled onto the dirt road that led out to the highway and Rain gunned it, kicking up rocks and debris behind them as the car fishtailed briefly and then shot like an arrow out of the cemetery and into the woods.

They reached the highway junction in no time, and Rain brought the car to a halt. "Wait here," he said before unbuckling and stepping out. He walked to where the little dirt road merged onto the larger dirt highway. Lita tilted her head and watched from inside the cab as he crouched down, observing the ground, looking first left, then right, then left again. He ran his fingers over the soil, then picked up a pinch and sniffed it. It was like watching an animal on the hunt.

Rain retreated to the car and got back in. "Looks like Jonas headed towards Maple City."

"Good, I know a guy who can help us find him there. But let's get the hell to your house first."

"Yeah," Rain said. He was already on the road, pushing the car as hard as it would go. For once, Lita didn't begrudge him the speed one bit.

II

Bursting into the clearing outside Moonshadow Manor, Rain threw the car into park and left it running as he got out and ran for the house.

Lita was right behind him, but she felt her stomach

bottom out at the sight of the front door standing wide open, and her mind immediately began conjuring up some truly grisly possibilities before she even reached the front steps. Inside, she saw none of the horrors she expected, and Rain was just standing in the middle of the living room, looking around slowly. She passed him on his right, heading to the open basement door and hollering down it. "Alex? Amelie?" The only response was a slight echo. She started towards the kitchen, but stopped in her tracks when Rain held up a hand.

"You don't need to do that. There's nobody in the house." He was staring down at the floor in front of him, his eyes moving side to side as though he was reading a book.

"What is it?" She asked, unable to see anything herself aside from some floorboards and a little dust.

"Somebody came in through the front door. A man, big…bigger than me. He had a gun. Then there was a scuffle right here, and…" he paused, closing his eyes. His nostrils flared and he flinched, grimacing. "Something not human came in through the kitchen, then…" he trailed off, thoughtfully retreating towards to the front door. Lita followed him curiously. Outside, he knelt in the grass just off the front steps. He sniffed the air, made another sour face, and this time actually spit on the ground. "They both left carrying something heavy, the big man and the creature." He stood and walked fast towards the road entrance to the clearing. Just past the tree line, he looked about for a moment, then nodded. "They came here and got into a car, not big but not small, maybe a sedan, and then they headed back to the highway." He turned and looked back to Lita, who appeared concerned. "Nobody was killed in the house or out here. I believe they took both Alex and Amelie alive. What do you think?"

"What do I think? Well, first off, I think that was both

very impressive and incredibly creepy." Rain didn't look amused, so she went on. "The big guy could be Cleric. Probably is, given everything else we know. A not-human creature though? I assume you don't mean a vampire."

"No. Something much worse." He started back towards the house, lighting a cigarette as he walked.

"Then I got nothing on that one. I've known Cleric to press-gang vampires into his service, but never anything else."

"Well, we'll just have to see what Jonas knows then." Reaching the house, he said, "Wait here," and headed inside, a stream of smoke trailing over his shoulder as he walked. He returned shortly and tossed a canvas sack to Lita, which she caught, and then he turned to lock the front door.

Peering inside, Lita blinked at the sight of an apple and what appeared to be a sandwich wrapped in butcher paper. "Did...did you just pack me dinner?"

"Can't have you fainting while we're interrogating your old partner," Rain said as he passed her, headed to the car. Lita followed suit and then they were back on their way.

III

"Tell me again, why aren't we just tracking the car that Alex and Amelie were taken in?" Lita asked as they pulled left onto the highway, headed for Maple City.

"I can't reliably track a car over long distances like that."

"Seriously? After you just painted a whole picture from a little sniffing and squinting back there?"

"People are messy. They leave footprints and scuffs and distinct smells. A car on a well-traveled road is a different thing entirely. Besides, even if we could follow them directly, we'd have no idea what sort of forces might be waiting for us wherever they went. If we want to have any chance of getting the two of them out alive, we can't go in blind. We need to know what Jonas knows."

Lita nodded in agreement, but then said, "It may not be as easy as you think to get him to talk. He's an idiot, but he's loyal to Cleric. He'd die for him."

"You said Jonas was Cleric's cleanup man, right?" Rain asked.

"Yeah."

"So Cleric's orders would have been to kill us back in that cemetery?"

Lita paused. "Probably."

"Then why are we still alive?"

She said nothing, only furrowed her brow and stared out the windshield.

"I think Jonas has feelings for you. We can use that to our advantage when we question him."

She ignored the comment about Jonas' interest. "Cleric trained us to resist interrogation. Jonas won't be an easy crack."

"I have my ways," Rain said, then took a drag from his cigarette.

Lita looked at him, her eyes suddenly firm. "You are not to kill him. If that has to happen, it will be left to me. Do you understand?"

Rain looked back at her, but seeing the resolve on her face, made no move to argue. "Fair enough," he said, returning his eyes to the road.

Sighing, Lita turned around and reached into the back seat to grab the food Rain had brought her, and ended up grabbing her bottle of vodka from her pack as well. There was only about a quarter of it left. She took a strong pull off it before returning it to its home.

"Try to stay focused," Rain said.

"I am," she replied, "Just a little maintenance."

He glanced at her, then said cautiously, "After this is through, I can help you with that if you'd like. I know something about addiction."

Lita looked at him and his cigarette askance. "Is that so?"

"I mean the drink," Rain replied. "The craving for it, the need. It can be overwhelming, but I've learned ways to get past it." He looked to her once more. "You can too."

Lita scoffed, but only halfheartedly. "Let's not go planning the wedding just yet there, pal."

Rain left it at that. Her response hadn't been a no, and now was not the time to push the issue. "So you said you know someone in Maple City who can help us find Jonas?"

"Yeah, a guy that used to work for Cleric. Goes by the name of Stitch." She had unwrapped her sandwich, finding it to be ham steak left over from breakfast in between two thick slices of bread. She took a greedy bite.

Rain paid her a skeptical glance. "You're joking."

Lita shook her head and tongued the wad of sandwich into her cheek. "We nicknamed him that because of the way he sees reality." She paused, chewed, swallowed. "For him, it barely holds together at the seams."

"Doesn't sound like a very reliable source."

"He is, trust me. He senses things that normal humans can't. It's like how we can only see colors from red to violet. He sees things outside that visual spectrum."

Rain blinked and gave her a surprised look.

"Hey, I'm not stupid, okay?" she said sharply. "I just choose to learn things that are actually of use to me instead of filling the brain space I've got with silly books."

Rain waved his hand like a white flag. "Alright, go on."

"*Anyway*, that sight of his lets him find things without having any way of knowing where they are. He's great to have around when you're trying to find a mark or your car keys, but he's also crazy as shit. It's like he doesn't have a filter for all that stuff that's coming in, and over the years it's driven him mad."

"Is that why he's no longer in Cleric's employ?"

"Sort of. One day Stitch just got something in his head that didn't sit right with him, and he went after Cleric like a rabid dog. He came close to killing him, but Jonas stepped in and lit the poor bastard up like a torch. He left Stitch with half his skin charred off, but Cleric let him live. I don't know if it was as a warning to others or out of some sick pity, but now he just lives in alleys in downtown Maple City, scrounging for food and freaking out the locals."

"And you're sure we can track him down?"

"Won't be a problem. He stays in about a four-block radius. I take him food sometimes, talk to him a little."

"Those must be interesting conversations."

"Like you read about." She sighed and slipped down to a more comfortable position in her seat as she worked on her sandwich.

They drove in silence for a while, each of them mulling over a flurry of different thoughts. Concern over the wellbeing of Alex and Amelie, wonderment over one another, questions about themselves regarding feeling such curiosity. Before long, they were entering the outskirts of Maple City. Lita finished her meal and sat back up, looking around with no particular fondness at her hometown.

"So where are we headed?" Rain asked.

Lita nodded ahead and pointed. "Take a right up here."

Rain obliged, following her directions towards the heart of Maple City.

NINETEEN

Alex groaned as he came around to blurry surroundings that seemed to take their sweet time coming into focus. His head was swimming, just as it had when Lita had drugged him last night, though that seemed a lot longer ago now.

As his full range of senses returned to him, he found that he was sitting on bare earth. He tried to stand, but realized he was bound. His legs were straight out in front of him with his ankles tied together and his hands were behind his back, wrists crossed and similarly bound. He was leaning against something that felt like a post. Moving his hands a little, he winced at the feeling of coarse rope rubbing against his skin. He shifted against the post and could tell that it was made of wood and only about six inches in diameter, but a quick tug and its refusal to budge told him it was anchored firmly in the ground.

"Alex? Are you awake?" a hushed voice inquired from directly behind him.

"Amelie?" Alex blurted in surprise. He craned his neck in effort to look over his shoulder. He couldn't see her, but he felt her hair brush against his cheek.

"Shhh, stay quiet," she whispered. "I'm right behind you, tied up as well. We're back to back, see?" Slender fingertips tickled his palms and Alex felt a modicum of ease knowing he was at least in close proximity to his new friend and fellow captive.

Looking around, he tried to get a feel for his location. Nightfall was approaching, the light pouring away past the world's horizon in a gradually darkening cascade. Ahead of him and to his left, about fifty feet away, there was some sort of structure unlike anything he had ever seen. It was an arrangement of enormous rough stone pillars that had been erected at seemingly random intervals, some in pairs with a third lying horizontally across them. Squinting, he could see what looked like runes carved into the closest pillar to him. When Alex was younger, a tutor had once explained Stonehenge to him, and though he had only been able to produce a rudimentary and mostly inaccurate drawing of the ancient landmark, it immediately came to mind as Alex looked over this odd structure. The comparison was more or less astute.

Unlike Stonehenge, however, this construct had a coliseum-like wall completely surrounding it, placing the structure itself in the center of a large arena. The wall wasn't terribly tall—twenty feet at the most—but it blocked Alex's view of the outside world, keeping their exact location a complete mystery to him.

"Where are we?" Alex whispered, turning his eyes up towards the dimming sky.

"I'm not sure," Amelie replied, her voice uneasy. "I woke up here too, not long before you. I remember being at your house when that man came with that…God, that horrible creature. And then I saw it again, right next to me in a car. And then I was here. Please tell me I dreamed that awful thing."

"It wasn't a dream. That thing is very real, and we may have to fight it if we're going to get out of this."

Amelie took a deep breath. "Lord, help us. What *was* it?"

"A demon, I think," Alex said offhandedly.

"Are you serious?"

"Is it really that hard to believe? Last night you had tea with a vampire and a boy who came back from the dead. But honestly, I'm more worried about the people controlling that thing. There was the big guy, I think that might have been the Cleric fellow Lita was talking about. Also, when I was in the trunk of that car—"

"You were in the trunk? Are you okay?"

"I'm fine. Focus, Amelie." Alex snapped, then winced with immediate regret. He heard Rain in his own voice.

"Sorry," Amelie whispered.

"No, I am. I guess waking up tied to a post makes me cross."

"I think you'd need another piece of wood for a cross."

"I'd n...wha? No, I mean it makes m—"

"I *know* what you meant, Alex. I was trying to be funny. To lift your spirits."

"Oh..." he paused, then chuckled in spite of himself. "Sorry, I'm sure I would have laughed if—"

"It's fine." She laughed a little herself. "You were saying? About being in the trunk?"

"Right. When I was in there I could hear Cleric talking to someone. Someone younger. I think it might have been—"

"Michael."

"Right. He's got to be the one who—"

"No, Alex, Michael!" Amelie whispered fiercely. "To your left!"

He looked that way and his gaze fell upon two men approaching from a doorway at the far side of the coliseum. One was Cleric, so he figured the other to be Michael.

Coming upon the two, Michael stood so they both could see him. His dress and manner were sober as always, and he held a large, leather-bound book clasped in his hands over his belt buckle.

Alex thought he looked more like a church pastor than a scheming heir to any throne.

"I'm glad to see you two awake," Michael said. "Though I'm sure it will mean little to you, I feel I should apologize for your poor accommodations. We were not expecting to hold anyone captive here. Amelie, you were meant to be laid to rest hours ago…" he paused and glanced ruefully over his shoulder at Cleric, who was standing a few paces back.

Alex followed that gaze and noticed the man was carrying two lengths of heavy chain over his shoulder. Catching Alex looking at him, Cleric smirked eerily, which sent a chill up Alex's spine and his eyes quickly darting back to Michael.

"…and you, young man," Michael went on, "Alex, correct? That's what Cleric said she called you. Or do you prefer Alexander?"

There was a moment of silence and then Alex blinked, looked around, and finally quirked a brow at Michael. "You…you're actually asking my name preference after taking me from my home, putting me in the trunk of a car, and tying me to a post? Are you arsing about?"

"I don't know what that means, but I don't think I'm doing it," Michael replied. "I am simply saying that, had we known you were going to be a *person*, we would have been better prepared. We're having to make a few adjustments to our initial plans."

Behind him, Cleric rattled the chains.

"How did you find me?" Amelie suddenly spoke up.

Michael sighed. "I'm afraid that we were forced to gather that information from the guard Christopher at the expense of his life. It was a shame it had to come to that. He had always been a loyal and valuable asset. He will be remembered for his sacrifice to our cause."

Amelie felt like she had been kicked in the stomach. "What *cause*?" she cried, her eyes filling with tears.

Michael glanced at his watch. "I haven't time to explain at the moment, though hopefully I will soon. I have several matters to attend to, but I'm afraid I must impart one more piece of bad news. It pains me to even say it aloud, but in the interest of—"

"Oh, for God's sake, *what?*" Amelie screamed bitterly. "You tried to have me killed, abducted me, and now I'm your prisoner! For once in your life, stop flitting about like a nervous bird and just say whatever it is you want to say and leave us be!"

Michael's jaw clenched and behind him he heard Cleric chuckle. "Your father is dead," he spat, and huffily walked away, searching for Saint Monica in his pocket as he went.

Alex heard Amelie issue a thin, strangled cry, and then felt her shaking behind him. She was sobbing. He let out a heavy sigh and looked mournfully down at his lap. After a moment, he heard indistinct murmurs intermixed with her shuddering breaths. He thought she might be trying to pray. He left her be for a few minutes, then finally whispered, "Amelie, I am so very sorry about your father and your friend, but we need to pull together and find a way out of here, or we will end up the same. Maybe worse."

"My f-father...he's...I d-didn't even get t-to say..." she trailed off, sniffling.

"I know, Amelie, but I need you to be strong. I want you to try to use what you're feeling right now. Get angry and use that to help us get free. If you can do that, maybe they didn't die for nothing." Alex's words felt hollow on his own lips, but Amelie's sobs started to subside.

"I..." she began, then swallowed, and started once more. "I don't know h-how to be b-brave like you."

Alex laughed a little. "Me? What makes you think I'm brave?"

Amelie took in a long, moist sniff, swallowed once more, and spoke. "When I heal s-someone, I get a g-glimpse inside them. It's…It's like I c-can see their soul for a m-moment, and it t-tells me things. Yours told me t-two things, and one was that you are very brave."

"What was the other thing?"

"You've been someplace wonderful," she said quietly. Alex furrowed his brow and tilted his head back, giving her a quizzical look she couldn't see. "Someplace none of us have ever dreamt of," she went on. "I only felt a shimmer of it, but it was perfect." She closed her eyes, and as she recalled the memory, her moist cheeks actually curved up around a tiny smile. "What was that place, Alex?"

"I…" he paused. "I don't remember."

"I hope my father is there."

"Me too."

TWENTY

"Pull up over here," Lita said, pointing to an expanse of curb on their right. "It's still a couple of blocks up, but the car's less likely to get stolen here."

Rain obliged, pulling over and killing the engine. He tugged on a lever under the dash and the trunk popped open. "Put your bag in the back. The car's tempting enough as it is," he said, then stepped out of the vehicle.

Lita pulled her knapsack from the back seat and exited as well. She rounded the back of the car, tossing her bag into the trunk and shoving it closed. When she looked back to Rain, she paused and blinked at what she saw. After locking the car, he rubbed his hand vigorously on the back of his neck and then wiped it around the top of the driver's side door, as well as over the handle.

"What in hell are you doing?"

"The only high-end car thieves in Maple City are the vampire gangs," Rain explained. "They're so powerful that humans don't dare even try for something this nice. If they smell another vampire on a car, they won't touch it, no matter how shiny it is. I'd have done it when we parked at your apartment, but I was a bit preoccupied with not bursting into flames."

"How do you…" Lita began, then shook her head. "You know what? Never mind." She waved a dismissive hand and stepped onto the curb. "I'm just going to add it to the 'creepy people smelling' file and pretend I never saw it."

"Probably best," he said, joining her. She pointed in the direction they were already facing and they began walking.

Coming to an intersection, Lita paused long enough to glance both ways before continuing. "When we find Stitch, you should probably keep your distance and let me do the talking. He's twitchy enough as it is, but a vampire might really set him off."

"Is it that obvious?" Rain asked around the cigarette he'd just put between his lips, then proceeded to light it. He took a long drag and blew the smoke away from Lita, allowing it to trail out behind him.

"To Stitch? Yeah. He probably already knows we're on our way. Besides, even without crazy psychic powers, anyone can see you're not exactly a well-sunned person."

He regarded the flesh color on the back of his hand. "Hmmm. I always thought it was the scar that scared people away."

"It is pretty startling."

"I wouldn't know."

She glanced at him. "No, I guess not, huh? That's gotta be strange. I'm not what you'd call vain or anything, but I'd go nuts if I couldn't see what I looked like for that long."

"You get used to it."

"I guess you'd have to. But the scar's not so bad. Hell, some girls think they're sexy."

"Oh?" He paid her a look.

"Yeah. Usually the fucked up ones."

Rain smirked and flicked his half-finished cigarette away as they crossed another street. Up ahead, a man was walking towards them with a pair of young boys, perhaps three and seven years old, one on each side of him. When they got closer, Lita and Rain moved to the far right of the sidewalk, allowing them room to go by.

But the sidewalk was only so wide, and as the two parties passed each other, Rain felt the toddler's arm brush against his leg. Without thinking, he abruptly stopped and turned halfway around to look down at the young boy, his brow furrowing. At the same moment, the child stopped as well and turned back to look up at Rain with an identical mix of curiosity and concern. For a moment their eyes locked, and Rain noticed that the boy's were so light that they appeared to be grey, and were staring out from under a neatly cropped head of the fieriest red hair he had ever seen.

In that odd moment of connection, Rain formed one very clear thought that he neither understood nor would recall later, despite his uncanny memory. Water. A vast wall of water swallowing everything in its path. Then it was gone as the boy's father, who had advanced another ten feet before noticing his son's absence, turned and barked, "Aiden!" punctuated with a commanding point of his finger at his unoccupied side.

The boy jumped and wheeled around, running to stand where his father pointed. When he arrived, his older brother reached around behind their father and smacked him upside the head. The younger boy began to whimper, but was silenced by a single snap of his father's finger. However, the father wasn't looking at the boy. He was staring at Rain in much the way a dog might stare down another dog who has trespassed in his territory.

Upon their initial approach, Rain hadn't taken much notice of the man, disregarding him as a threat when he saw the children in his company. Now he realized the man was clad in full Irish Army fatigues. But though it was combat attire that any IA soldier would wear, Rain knew their rank insignias, and this man's indicated he was a Lieutenant-General. Rain also took particular note of a strange patch on the man's left arm, near the shoulder. It was a dark green circle, inside of which was embroidered a complex interweaving tangle of black lines. It was some kind of symbol, one Rain had never seen before.

And as Rain stood there taking stock of the man, the man moved his hand to his sidearm with the stealth of a trained killer.

"Rain," Lita said. He looked back at her and she beckoned with her hand. "Come on."

Rain nodded, paid one last glance back, and then went to catch up with her.

"Everything okay?" she asked.

"Just fine," he replied. Behind him, he could hear the trio walking away, the father chiding the younger boy for falling out of line.

"Alright…" Lita said, eyeing him. "Well, anyway, there are a bunch of alleys on both sides of the road up here. Stitch usually hangs out in one of them. You keep an eye to the left, I'll check out the right."

Rain did so, peering down each alley from across the road as they passed. He saw a number of vagrants—some children—but nobody that matched Stitch's description.

They crossed another road, and just after the next building they passed, Lita stopped. "There," she said. Rain turned and followed her gaze, seeing Stitch immediately. He was a gaunt man dressed in rags. Crouched near a wall halfway down the dead-end alley, he rocked back and forth on the balls of feet clad in leather shoes that were all but falling off. His coat was in tatters, his knitted cap full of holes, and he wore several winter scarves around his neck, their frayed ends dangling down near where his two hands played with the air between his bent knees.

"Wait here," Lita whispered, and headed into the darkness of the alley. Rain nodded. Though he could see every inch of the area she was entering, he was sure she would have to squint to find her way. He produced a cigarette and turned away from the mouth of the alley as he lit it, mindful of what she had said about Stitch startling easily.

Approaching Stitch with the same caution she always used, Lita came within five feet of him before slowly dropping to a crouch. She looked over his haunted, battered form and felt a wash of sadness just as she had many times before. Though she hadn't thought much of Stitch when they worked for Cleric, seeing any man reduced to such a hollow shell was enough to pull at the strings of even the most seasoned of cold hearts.

"Hey, Stitch," Lita said gently. "Still keeping in style, I see." It was an ongoing joke she offered him, and though he never responded to it directly, its familiarity eased her tension.

"Already ate today," Stitch said, his voice dry and raspy, his eyes not leaving those nervously fiddling hands. His fingers wiggled and flicked against one another. "Don't ask the rats, though; shhhh, they lie. Gamey this fall. Pick 'em through my teeth. They'll plump winter days though. Christmastime feast." He giggled.

"Yeah, I hear those winter rats are the best," Lita said, crinkling her nose. "But I didn't bring any food this time. I was hoping maybe you could help me."

"Help, hehe. No help. They want to, tying you up with chains and locks and soft walls. Tell you it's help. But they don't have the rats to keep you company. Just pills. White and blue and red-green. Seventy-three times seven is five-hundred eleven pills. Colorful stars, but they make you swim. No, no, no, no! No! Pills! On! Holiday!" His voice began to rise, and he punctuated each of the last four words by slapping his hand down on the cobblestone ground. But then he lifted his eyes to meet Lita and he seemed to calm immediately. His hands went back to fiddling with one another. "Not you. You bring company for the belly and the ears. Give the rats their own bloody holiday. You need help?"

Rain quirked a brow, watching the scene curiously from a distance.

"Yeah, Stitch, I need some help," Lita said. "Help finding someone. Like the old days, you know? You think you can do that?"

"No one's lost. Not ever, really. Someone knows, just maybe not you. And they're not lost for someone, but for you they are, but not really. Because someone tells, tickle tickle on the ear, and then you know, and they're not lost. Found like a hound." Stitch giggled again.

"Can you be that someone?" Lita asked calmly. Rain was impressed by her patience, and at a loss as to where she drew it from. "Someone's lost for me," she went on, "can you be the someone who tells me? The someone who knows?"

"I'm always the someone who knows," Stitch said dejectedly. "But I play, and I'll whisper, psst psst psst, into your..." he trailed off, and suddenly his eyes shot past Lita and landed on Rain. "No! Too pale! He sees me, but I'm not his rat!" He began waving his hands in a ward-off gesture. "You've had your fill! Chick-chick-chickens! My rats here, and I'm not your rat!"

Rain blinked, unsure of what to make of that. Lita looked over her shoulder and made a shooing motion with her arm. He nodded, pointing across the street to indicate where he'd be. She nodded back and shooed him once more, so he left them to it.

"There," Lita said, "he's gone now. But he wouldn't have hurt you, Stitch. He's different."

"Not me," Stitch whispered, "my rats. I have seven, but two make six and then it's thirteen, and Sunday is brunch."

"I'll make sure he doesn't hurt your rats either," Lita

reassured him.

"Make sure you stay inside the white fence, too. The woods are out there. You can't escape that way."

Lita frowned. Though Stitch's rants were usually indecipherable, they sometimes touched random places inside her where she'd rather not go.

"No, no. Not random. Mathematical lie!" He reached back and gave the brick wall a quartet of loud smacks. "One, two, three, four. Walls all around. But I can hear you whispering. Better tell it right, and mind your modifiers!"

"Stitch," Lita said, and snapped her fingers. His glassy brown eyes jerked to her and he leaned forward. With her own eyes finally adjusted to the dark, Lita could see the nearly inhuman semblance of a face Jonas had left him. His lips were peeled back into a perpetual snarl, his nose mostly gone, his cheeks and forehead a mottled roadmap of burned flesh. A thought surfaced that she could have looked the same had Amelie not rescued her from that fire, but she pushed it away. "I need you to focus."

Stitch mimicked the noise of a camera shutter, but Lita didn't get the reference. He seemed to be listening though, so she went on. "I need you to tell me where I can find Jonas." Stitch hissed and pulled away.

"Come on, Stitch, I need this. He'll never know it was you."

"Hot, too hot. It burns. Not again, no no." Stitched murmured.

"I promise it'll be okay. We're gunning for Jonas right now. By the time we're done with him, you'll be the last thing he's worried about. Please, Stitch." She loathed the taste of any plea on her lips, but she meant what she said. She needed this.

Stitch sighed and resumed his rocking back and forth. He was silent for a while, but then finally said rather poetically, "Thirteen of fifty-two; death above kings and below twins too."

Lita regarded him quizzically. "Thirteen out of…wait, The Spade? The Spade Tavern over on Witch Hazel?"

"Mmmm."

"Thank you, Stitch," Lita said, and reached out to lightly touch his shoulder. When she did, his head snapped up and he looked first at her, then at Rain, who had just reappeared in the mouth of the alley to check up on things.

"You and you. One plus one is four. The road started already, but you don't have your maps. You'll get lost but you're on your way, the road, the miles, the years. Midway is half-score, but first there's one into two…" He was speaking to both of them at once now, looking frantically back and forth. Then he reached out suddenly, his hand going for Lita's midsection. She smacked it away.

"Hey, watch it," she warned.

"Watch the road," he shot back. "There's four going this way and that, but they're tied together tight. One will fight and one will die and one will see and one will dig, then one will go so far, shimmering lights all around, and two will return and four will go on…on to something…something more…something…" As he repeated the word "something" he broke his gaze from both of them, looking up in the air and reaching out for something there that neither Rain nor Lita could see. It was as though he was trying to grab hold of a drifting bit of fluff floating before his eyes. Then, as soon as he closed his fingers on whatever it was he saw there, he let loose with a terrified scream.

They both shot to their feet, Stitch pushing himself back against the wall, Lita taking two steps away from him. Rain hurried to Lita's side. But Stitch wasn't making a move to do any harm. Quite the opposite. He looked petrified.

"Children!" he shrieked. "Warring hearts of light and dark!"

"What is he talking about?" Rain asked.

"I don't know. He was fine a second ago and then he snapped," Lita replied. Her hand moved to her firearm.

"Light and dark!" he screamed again. "Warring hearts of light and dark!" As he repeated this over and over, he inched away from them along the alley wall. "Light and dark! Light and dark!" Presently, he came to a service ladder near the back of the alley. It led up to a wrought iron balcony beneath a window one story up. "Light and dark! Light and dark!" He began to climb the ladder.

"What is he doing?" Rain asked, mildly alarmed. Lita didn't respond.

Near the top of the ladder, Stitch stopped and hooked his foot into one of the rungs to steady himself as tied his scarves into a knot around his neck. He then went to work tying the other end of them around the rung directly above him.

Rain started towards the ladder, but Lita put a hand on his arm to stop him. When he looked to her, she simply shook her head, her eyes never leaving Stitch.

"Light and dark! Light and dark!" he kept screaming over and over the whole time. Then, finally, once his scarves were tied firmly at both ends, he seemed to break free of his stupor as he looked down at both of them. In a small, sad voice, he said, "She's coming. God help you all." Then he stepped off the ladder.

At last breaking her gaze as she heard his neck snap, Lita looked down to avoid seeing the life twitch out of his body. She stared at her feet for some time before she said quietly, "Goodbye, Stitch," and then turned to leave the alley. Rain followed close behind.

Stepping back out into the glow of the streetlights, Lita started back towards the car. Rain stopped her half a block up. He took her forearm gently and turned her towards him.

"Why didn't you let me stop him?"

When their eyes met, Rain saw sadness in hers, but also a

strange wash of relief. In a very rational, collected voice, she said, "Sometimes a person can be so lost that death is a sweet alternative. Stitch didn't deserve to live the way he did. We did him a kindness by letting him go."

Rain nodded, and not without a sharp pang in his still heart. He knew that feeling of displacement more than he cared to admit. He released Lita's arm, and though he very badly wanted to kiss her right then, he hesitated too long and the moment passed. They both turned together and continued back to the car, walking in silence the whole way.

Pulling out his keys as they approached the vehicle, thankful to find it as they had left it, Rain said, "So you found out where Jonas is?"

"The Spade Tavern," Lita replied.

"And you know where that is?"

"I do. And even better, I have a plan."

TWENTY-ONE

Alex had been sitting in silence for some time, trying to think what they might do to get themselves out of their present predicament. A few incomplete ideas had come to mind, but nothing that seemed like it would really work. He was actually contemplating a faked a heart attack when he felt Amelie's fingers wiggling around near his hands.

"What are you doing?" he asked.

"I can feel one of the knots in your rope. I think I might be able to loosen it some," Amelie whispered.

"Do it," Alex replied. "But don't move around too much." As he felt her go to work, he watched Michael, who was halfway across the arena examining one of the stone pillars, comparing its inscriptions to a book in his hand. Cleric had disappeared a few minutes earlier, heading through a second door in the coliseum opposite the one he and Michael had entered from.

"Okay, that's the best I can do," Amelie said after a time. Alex's face scrunched up as he began wiggling his hands, finding his left to be just a little more mobile than before. His right, however, was still firmly secured. After a while of twisting and turning his arm, trying all the while to avoid Michael's detection and to ignore the burning pain the rope created in his wrist, Alex finally managed to wrestle his hand free of its bond.

He quickly went to work on his other hand, but as soon as his first had come loose, he realized that his hands hadn't only been tied together, but also to the post and to Amelie's as well. He tried prying at the various knots he found back there, but they all refused to budge. Furthermore, with his right hand still tied, there was no way he could reach his ankles to release them.

"I can only get one hand free," Alex whispered.

"What are you going to do?" Amelie asked.

"Make the best of it. Michael's Catholic, right?"

"Yes, we both are. Why?"

"What's his last name?"

"Calderwood. Why does any of this matter?"

"Just stay quiet. I have an idea." Alex cleared his throat, and when he spoke again, his voice was shaky and timid. "L-Lord Calderwood? Sir?" Michael's head shot up from his work and his wide eyes made Alex think of a puppy looking for a treat. He had to clear his throat in order to suppress a nearly irresistible impulse to laugh. "May I have a moment of your time, sir?"

Michael glanced towards the coliseum door where Cleric had departed, then placed a marker in his book and closed it as he approached Alex. "What is it, young man?" He asked, warily keeping his distance. There was a long rapier sheathed on his left side, and a short dagger on his right. He rested his hand on the hilt of the rapier.

"Well first, sir, I'd like to apologize for the way I spoke to you earlier. I-I was very distraught and I didn't know who you were." Alex bowed his head sorrowfully.

"Well then, I forgive you, of course," Michael said.

Alex raised his head slowly. "Y-You do?"

Michael smiled gingerly and nodded. "Yes, of course I do. I'd be just as angry and confused in your position. I had no idea you would be a human being, let alone one so young. I wish it weren't so, but it is clear to me now that your age and innocence is a test of faith, and I must proceed no matter how much I'd like it to be different."

"I don't understand," Alex said. "Proceed with what? What do you need me for?"

"All will be made clear soon, but do take solace in the knowledge that your sacrifice will usher our world into a time of untold faith and prosperity. Your story will be cherished for generations."

"S-So, you intend to kill me then?" Alex asked shakily.

Michael's eyes softened, but he nodded slowly. "I am terribly sorry, but it is necessary. I do not wish it, but it is what I must do in the service of God."

Alex took a deep breath and nodded. Then, looking around, "You have a priest then? To read me my last rites?"

Michael blinked and his brow knitted. "No...no, I'm afraid not. As I said, we weren't expecting..."

"You can do it," Amelie said quietly.

"Pardon?" Michael asked, walking over to where they could both see him. "Did you say something, Amelie?"

She refused to look at him, but she sniffled and spoke a bit louder. "I said you can do it. The Lord of Chicane is granted certain powers by the church. Performing last rites is one of them."

"Oh," Michael said. "But I've never done it before. I don't know that I—"

"Please," Alex said. "I cannot die without absolution. Whatever you can do, I'm sure God will understand."

"A-Alright," Michael said with a nod. "I think I remember how it goes." He approached Alex and lowered himself to his knees by his side. "Now, close your eyes and bow your head."

Alex nodded and did as he was told.

Michael, too, lowered his head. "God, the Father of

mercies, through the de—"

Alex suddenly shot his free hand out, grabbed a fistful of hair on the back of Michael's head, and brought his knee up to collide with his captor's face. The speed and strength of the act surprised even Alex, who felt he had just tapped into something he hadn't known was inside him. He didn't let it cause him a moment's hesitation, though, as he yanked Michael back up by his hair, loosened his grasp long enough to snatch the dagger from his belt, and then wrapped his arm around the young man's throat, pulling him into a headlock on his lap with the tip of the blade touching his ear.

"Now you listen to me, you son of a bitch. You're going to unbuckle your belt, slowly, and toss away that sword. Then you're going to reach down and untie my ankles. If you try anything, I swear, I will jam this thing straight through your throat."

"Let me go!" Michael cried, then coughed on the blood that was streaming from his nose.

Alex shook him once, and the tip of the dagger nicked the flesh just below his ear. "Don't push me, Michael. I swear to God, you've got three seconds to—"

A white flash erupted in the right side of Alex's head and he lurched to the side as far as his bonds would allow. His body flailed once involuntarily. It was just enough for Michael to slip free and scramble to his feet. He backed away from Alex as he wiped a hand across his nose.

Cleric stepped in front of Alex, grabbing his wrist tightly with one hand and wrenching the dagger from his grasp with the other. He tossed the weapon to Michael, who just watched it fall to the ground before reaching down to pick it up. "You deserve what you got," Cleric chided. "Mind your distance next time." He turned back to Alex and began re-securing his wrist.

Looking at Cleric in his momentary daze, Alex asked in

an oddly polite tone, "Will you please stop hitting me in the head?"

Chuckling, Cleric finished tying his hand, making sure it was painfully tight this time, before he brought a hard punch down just above Alex's left kneecap. The boy screamed in agony. "Better?" Cleric asked.

The pain, though intense, cleared Alex's head. "Much," he said flatly, then spat out a mouthful of blood. One of his teeth felt loose. He glared at Michael. "I should have just killed you, you lunatic." He was getting used to this rage. It felt empowering.

Michael's face suddenly went a deep shade of red, his knuckles white around the hilt of his dagger. It took every drop of control in his being not to leap on Alex and cut him wide open. Only the knowledge that it would ruin everything he had worked for kept his rage in check, but it still needed some outlet, so, with a petulant scream, he lunged at Amelie and slashed the dagger deep across the meat of her shoulder. She screamed and threw her head back so hard Alex felt it shake the post they were tied to.

"You son of a bitch!" Alex yelled.

"Hey!" Cleric boomed. He rushed Michael and took him by the back of his collar, yanked the dagger from his grasp, and threw him to his rear in the dust like he was nothing. Turning on him, he pointed that dagger down at the young man menacingly. "You keep the hell away from her, you little shit."

But Michael wasn't even looking at Cleric. His eyes were transfixed on Amelie. Following his gaze, Cleric looked to her as well and his own eyes went wide.

Seconds after it was cut open, the wound in Amelie's shoulder began to emanate a soft white glow. Its red edges smoothed and came back together, sealing up seamlessly, leaving behind only the blood the wound had spilled in its short existence. Amelie burst into tears, not only at the pain, which would still linger like a phantom for some time, but at the realization that her gift had been discovered by the person she most feared finding out.

Awestruck, Cleric stepped forward and carefully sliced a small cut in Amelie's cheek with the dagger. It wasn't nearly as painful as the first wound, but she cried out again. Both Cleric and Michael watched in amazement as this too healed itself almost instantly. The entire time, Alex was thrashing violently at his bonds, so much so that his wrists started to bleed, but no one else seemed to notice.

"Fascinating," Cleric said.

"I think you mean terrifying," Michael said, rising. Cleric looked back at him quizzically. "One of the very possessed souls we are trying to cleanse from this world nearly took control of our most powerful city. I struggled with my decision to sacrifice her, but now I understand it was truly God's will working through me, showing me the evil I could not see for myself."

"You know, a smart man would put a power like that to use, not let it go to waste," Cleric said.

Michael narrowed his eyes, dropping a hand to the hilt of his sword. "And a righteous man knows notions like that are Lucifer whispering in his ear. It's already bad enough that you forced me to give your hellfire boy and demon hound sanctuary. Don't try to tempt me to share your damnable tolerance."

Cleric stepped closer, pointing Michael's own dagger at him. "Don't forget who you're talking to here. It wouldn't take me five minutes to kill all of you and walk out of here, wash my hands of this whole thing." With little more than a flick of his wrist, he sent the dagger down to stick in the ground at Michael's feet. "You have work to do. Why don't you stop letting these two get under your skin and try getting it done before we run out of time and botch this whole job? I'll even make it easy for you and find something to gag them with." With that, Cleric turned and walked away, headed back towards the coliseum door from which he came.

Michael picked up his dagger and put it away, then walked around so he was in front of Amelie. Crossing his arms, he shook his head, looking at her with a strange sadness in his eyes. "I truly wish the demon inside you didn't keep you from understanding why this is what I must do. My mother understood when she started me on this path, but then she began to falter when she called Cleric off finishing the job he had begun with your mother. She thought you escaping that fate had been a sign from God that you were meant to live. Then, after marrying your father, she lost her way completely, trying to tell me the Gifted were some sort of blessing. I had thought she must have been persuaded by Richard's delicate sensibilities, and I was left with no choice but to send her to heaven. Now I see the truth. Those infective thoughts came not from your father, but from you...from the thing inside you that makes you unclean."

"You're out of your mind," Amelie whispered. "You can't just kill all these people."

Michael's jaw clenched. "The world must be purged of infection so it may return to the glorious path it was once on. Before the Last War, Lucifer led us astray with bombs and guns and we nearly destroyed ourselves. So God, in his infinite wisdom, sought to cleanse us with his Great Plague, but now Lucifer tries once more by giving humans power that no being but God should possess. Once I cast out that sickness, those of us who remain will be truly worthy of our Lord's providence. I am deeply sorry that you will not be counted among us." Looking down, Michael shook his head and headed back towards the pillars he had been examining before.

"Are you alright?" Alex asked over his shoulder.

"Yes, I'll be okay," Amelie replied. "I just can't believe I never saw this madness in him before."

"If we do get out of here, and you become Lady of Chicane, may I make a suggestion?"

"What's that?"

"You should probably require some sort of evaluation of sanity before a person can become an heir. That seems like it would be helpful."

Amelie actually laughed a little. "I'll take it under advisement."

"Good choice." Alex looked around and sighed. "Well, that escape attempt didn't go as well as I'd hoped."

"No...though we did learn that Cleric and Michael don't seem to like each other much. My father once told me that discovering dissent can be as powerful as any weapon."

"Maybe," Alex said, "but it doesn't cut us loose from these ropes."

"True. So what do you suggest we do now?"

"Wait for our next chance."

TWENTY-TWO

I

"I'm not entirely sure how comfortable I am with this," Rain said, and punctuated the sentence with a jet of smoke from his nostrils. He dropped his hand from the steering wheel long enough to shift gears, then flicked some ash out his open window.

They were making their way into a shadier part of Maple City now, towards the end of town where Lita lived. The stretch of road they drove down was littered with trash of all sorts, sloshing up against the ankles of dilapidated buildings that seemed to groan under the weight of their own feeble structures. There were no streetlights in this area. Around the center of town there was a ten-block radius with electrical lighting along the sidewalks. Another five blocks out from that contained torch lamps—some lit, some neglected. Here, there was only a torch still standing every three blocks or so, and all were black.

"You know, for someone who built a whole house by hand, you're kind of a sissy," Lita said, paying him a smirking glance.

"I'm not saying the plan doesn't have merit," he replied,

"only that I'm very flammable."

Lita chuckled inwardly at the thought of a big red warning sign attached to his chest, like the one that hung from the boiler in the basement of her apartment building. She felt a sudden certainty that she would never see it again. For a variety of reasons, the thought failed to upset her.

"I told you, all you have to do is stay away from his hands. Get the jump on him and get him knocked out, and we can tie him up before he wakes."

"And you're sure about binding his hands?"

"Positive. He told me all about it when he was drunk after a job one night. If his palms are flat together, he can't make fire. The asshole even had the gall to say it was God's way of offering him a 'peaceful repose.'" The pitch of her voice dropped into a mockingly low, self-important tone on the last two words.

"I'll give him a peaceful repose," Rain said flatly, then took a hard pull off his cigarette, his eyes fixed intently on the road ahead.

"Just remember, you can't kill him."

He glanced at her briefly, then nodded. "So long as he tells me what I need to know. Anyway, he wouldn't talk much if he were dead."

"You seem to do alright with it," Lita said. Before Rain had time to retort, she pointed down the road. "It's right around this next corner."

Rain took the corner, and sure enough, the second building on the right-hand side was a modest single-story tavern. Its unassuming doorway was lorded over by a hand-painted picture of a large black playing card—a spade. Paying a cursory glance about the street as they approached, Rain noted two vehicles, one in disrepair and the other not far off. "I don't see the truck from the cemetery anywhere."

Lita shook her head. "He'd have parked it at an inn and walked here." Rain paid her a glance, so she elaborated,

"Jonas doesn't exactly have a place of his own. When he's not rooming at Cleric's warehouse between jobs, Cleric sets him up with an inn near the work. It's easier to disappear if things go wrong when you don't have anything worth packing."

"That's a hard way to live."

Lita nearly made a sarcastic comment about Rain's oddly sentimental nature—building a house from scratch and setting up shop there for decades—but something stopped her short. She got the sudden notion that he knew all too well what that sort of life was like and that maybe he had built the house because he was tired of constantly being on the move. Hadn't she dreamt of doing the same, and more often with each passing year? This insight both startled and dismayed her, so she replied simply, "It has its pros and cons," and then diverted his attention to directions once more. "Pull into that alley there and kill it by the back door. I'll double back and head in the front."

"You sure there *is* a back door?"

"I've been in here a couple of times. Besides, when was the last time you were in a tavern that didn't have more than one door? Even the Red Mare has a back exit leading to the outhouse." She grimaced at the thought of that thing, but felt a sort of exaltation at the idea that she might never have to deal with it again.

As they approached the alley, Rain brought the car to a halt. A large delivery truck was parked inside, and next to it a man with a clipboard stood in conversation with a man in an apron.

"Pull over up the road," Lita said. "We'll wait it out." Rain did so. Once there, they both rolled down their windows, Rain to continue smoking and Lita to adjust her mirror for a better view of the alley behind them. "Shouldn't take too long," she said.

Rain nodded and silence fell between them for a little

while. Then something occurred to him. "What's your last name?"

She blinked at the question. "What makes you ask?"

He shrugged. "It seems like something I ought to know."

"Do you always wait until after you sleep with a girl to find out her whole name?"

His eyes dropped suddenly. "I've never…I mean, you're the only…"

Lita's eyes widened and she felt immediately compelled to answer him before he could finish what he was about to reveal. "I don't have one. I mean, I probably did, when I was a kid, but Cleric didn't see the need for them."

"Ah," Rain said. Silence came once more, during which he expected her to ask the obvious question and she expected him to offer the explanation on his own. Neither of them did.

"What about yours?" Lita asked finally, veering in the other conversational direction. "Was Moonshadow a common name in the 1600s?"

Rain stifled a small laugh. "Not at all. It's not the name Alex and I were born with." He looked to her, and she just stared back at him, waiting for him to elaborate. "For a long time, I didn't use any last name. Not until Alex came back. He said we needed one to show that we're brothers. Neither of us wanted to carry our father's name, so he suggested Moonshadow. It's from a poem our mother wrote and used to recite to us as a lullaby."

Lita nodded and smiled. "I like it."

He smiled back. "Thank you."

"And your first name? Rain?"

Amusement disappeared from his face. "It was raining the day I was born."

Lita's brow knitted. "Why would—"

"Alex knows the story better than I do. Maybe he can tell you someday."

"Okay…" Lita said. She felt a small pang in her chest. She wasn't sure if it was because she wished he'd tell her or because she was sorry she'd asked. She looked down at her hands while Rain finished his cigarette, and as he rolled up his window, she finally decided to go for it. "Was I really your first?"

Rain swallowed and nodded.

"How…how is that possible?"

"Well, vampires—normal vampires—have no sex drive. It's not their means of procreation. When I changed, it came back, but it just never ended up happening."

"Oh," Lita said and then, after a pause, added, "Well you were very good."

"Thank you."

"I mean, really. That thing you did with my leg up was…wow."

"I've read a lot of books."

"I see," she looked at him and smirked. "Those must have been some damned good books."

Rain only smiled in return. But the joking didn't distract Lita from her burning question.

"Why did you wait so long?"

Rain thought about this for a long moment before answering. "I guess I just never found anyone who I could…" he trailed off, unable to find the right word.

"Trust?" Lita offered.

"I suppose that would be a good way of putting it," he looked at her cautiously.

"Are you saying you trust me?" she asked warily.

He shrugged a little. "I'm not sure. I guess I've never really thought about what it means to me." He ran his hands over the steering wheel nervously. "What does it mean to you?"

"Trust?" Lita asked. "Like, in a guy?"

"Sure."

She sighed. "I don't know. Well, maybe I do, but it's stupid."

"Say it anyway."

She chuckled self-consciously and shook her head. "I guess…I've always thought I'd know I could trust a guy if I felt like I could dance with him."

Rain's eyebrows rose. "You dance?"

"Maybe."

"Well maybe we'll have a chance to explore that one day."

"Maybe we will." The two exchanged coy smiles that lasted until headlights cut across the car and the delivery truck drove past them. "Time to work," Lita said.

Rain pulled the car around and shifted into neutral as he entered the alley, then killed the engine and coasted up abreast of the tavern's steel service entrance door. As the car came to a halt, Lita asked, "How loud again?"

"As loud as you're talking right now, so long as you're facing this way." She gave him a skeptical look, but he nodded reassuringly.

"Alright then, if you say so," she said, and climbed out of the car.

Rain ducked his head down so he could see her as she stood. "Be careful."

She stooped to peer in at him. "I'll be fine, you just watch your ass. You're not too hard on the eyes for a dead guy, so no sense wasting that getting turned into a big pile of ashes."

Suddenly, the odd tension of their last bit of conversation dissolved, and the smile that passed between them was as natural as their progression from snide to affectionate teasing over only three nights. Inside its brief silence, they both knew exactly where they wanted to be. Then Lita closed her door, and Rain craned his neck to watch her walk up the alley.

II

Lita stepped out onto the sidewalk in front of The Spade, but before heading towards the front door, she paused to look about her surroundings. The street was improbably empty, even for this time of night. There were none of the usual people shuffling to and from night jobs, their heads down, shoulders protectively slumped as they tried to make their way unmolested to their destinations. No vagabonds of the city scrounging for food or making the mistake of propositioning her for sex. The stretch of road seemed ubiquitously dead, and Lita shuddered as a chill crept through her body. She found herself longing for the unexpected comfort that she had so quickly found at Moonshadow Manor, and she couldn't tell if that made her feel less uneasy or more.

Grateful to turn away from the gaping maw of that decaying street, she went to the door of The Spade and slipped inside.

As Lita had told Rain, she'd been in here twice before, but the place had changed in the last six years. The bar remained where it had been, but everything else was different, right down to the shoddy paintjob—a bad shade of brown covering what had been a bad shade of yellow adorning the patched, pitted walls. There were six tables, all round but otherwise dissimilar, arranged in two rough triangles pointing at one another with an aisle up the middle to the bar.

Things seemed nearly as dead in here as on the street outside. At the table nearest Lita's left sat three men in coveralls with rolled-up sleeves, their grimy hands gripping ale-filled steins. All three looked her way when she walked in, but just as quickly disregarded her in the space of the disapproving glance she gave them. It was a look she had mastered in her years as a tender, an automatic "no" that kept her unbothered under most circumstances.

At the center table to her right was a young couple, no older than she. They were huddled together over a book, reading by the light of a small candle that floated in a jar half-filled with water—a common centerpiece made with safety in mind, fire departments being little more than fairytales in most parts of Ayenee. As Lita passed the couple, they burst into simultaneous hushed giggles, never once looking up at her. They were completely enraptured in whatever hilarity it was they were sharing. Normally such a sight would have Lita rolling her eyes, but tonight it made her smile in spite of herself.

Up ahead, the wraparound bar held two occupants. At the far end to Lita's right, a withered old man was perched on one of the mismatching barstools, looming over a whiskey double. To her left, where the bar ended near a hallway leading to the service door, Jonas sat hunched slightly, his elbows resting on the bar top.

Lita approached without bothering to feign stealth. He had known she was there from the moment she stepped inside. She figured the odds to be about even between him bolting straight away or staying in his seat. When she didn't hear the clamor of an overturned barstool and fleeing boots, she was no more surprised than she would have been if he had taken off. A good plan meant being flexible to all possible outcomes.

As she took up the second stool to Jonas' right—leaving a buffer between them—Lita drew her firearm and placed it to her right on the bar. It was a mark of trust between her and Jonas, but it also served to put tenders at ease. Better for them to know where your weapon is than to be surprised by it should you get rowdy. To Jonas' left rested his large-caliber revolver. Lita crinkled her nose at the sight of it, as she had many times before. It was a clunky thing, and only worsened Jonas' already terrible aim. Though he was a crack shot with a rifle, small arms were not his forte.

"Didn't figure you to be in for an early round," Jonas said coolly. Lita noticed two things immediately: he was fidgeting with something in his hands and he was drinking water.

After a job, Jonas could go on a bender that almost put Lita to shame. Even back at her apartment, sharing a drink, he had been trying his hand at management, not gunning for anyone himself. But when he was assigned a mark, whether the job lasted a day or a month, he was sober as a judge. And he was drinking water.

Then there was the fidgeting. Jonas never fidgeted. He had a placid, collected manner about him that had complemented her short fuse, something Cleric no doubt liked in their partnership. She was a loose cannon that needed proper aiming, and Jonas had had a way of keeping her steady. But he hadn't even looked at her. His eyes were locked on his hands, hovering just above the bar, flipping something over and over in his fingers.

It was a business card, the sort only hospitals and high-end entrepreneurships used anymore. While various military still used radio technology, telephones were a thing of the past, so there wasn't much use in the cards. Hospitals used them for appointment reminders, and a few morbidly successful enterprises used them as flashy ways to give out their addresses. But the card Jonas was fiddling with was different than either. One side held a single symbol: a dark green circle, the inside filled with an interweaving tangle of black lines. On the other side, two sentences had been scrawled in black ink, but Lita was unable to make them out before Jonas held up the card in his thumb and forefinger and it burst into flames. He dropped it into a nearby ashtray and looked to her at last, his hands returning to the bar, fingers interlaced.

"You've got some explaining to do," Lita said. The tender approached, looking for a drink order. "Vodka double," she said, reaching for her pocket without looking his way. Jonas beat her to it, setting two goldpieces on the bar.

"At least you're getting something other than water," the man said. When neither of them responded, he served Lita's drink and departed to the far end of the bar. Tenders who wanted to live through their career choice learned quickly when to leave well enough alone.

"You were saying?" Jonas asked and took a sip of his water.

"Don't make me repeat myself," Lita warned, then snatched up her drink and quaffed a quarter of it.

"What do you want to know?"

"For starters, final yes or no: is Cleric running this job? And don't waste my t—"

"Yes, he is," Jonas interrupted.

"I thought so, you shit. Now why in hell would he contract me for a job that I had already botched once before?"

"He didn't. I did. Cleric assigned me to set up the contract. I came to you. I didn't know that Amelie was the same girl from your last job."

"That's bullshit. Cleric hates middlemen and he doesn't subcontract."

Jonas shrugged. "He did this time. He needed the job to be double-blind. He said he couldn't risk anything being traced back to him and Michael, so he sent me to hire someone outside of the usual roster. Said it was my big break."

Lita's brow furrowed. "That doesn't make any sense. Cleric's not that paranoid."

"Things have changed. He doesn't know that I know, but he's getting desperate. Running scared."

"What the hell would Cleric have to be scared of?"

Jonas took another sip of his water, returned it to the bar, and said quietly, "IASOFT. They're gunning for him."

Lita tensed and goosebumps appeared on her arms. "They're supposed to be a myth."

"Cleric probably wishes they were."

Lita shook her head in disbelief. "Holy fuck." She took up her drink, then said over the top of it, "Michael must be clueless if he's working with someone who's got that kind of mark on his head." Jonas nodded. Lita pondered on this for a moment, then tipped back more of her drink. "Okay," she sighed, breathing the fire out of her lungs, "say I believe you. Why in hell would you contract me?"

Jonas reached out to a candle in front of him and began waving his fingertip side to side through its flame, watching the fire lick up around his knuckle with each pass. "Maybe I thought if you picked up where you left off it would put you back in Cleric's good graces."

Lita's eyes narrowed. "Even if I'd gone through with it, I told you this was a one-time shot."

He shrugged. "Guess I hoped a fresh taste would change your mind. And even if it didn't, the payout would have set you up good. I was doing you a favor." He folded his hands once more, looking to Lita calmly. His gaze infuriated her.

"A favor? How is marching me into a setup a fucking favor?" It was becoming increasingly difficult to control the volume of her voice.

"I didn't know it was a setup," Jonas replied, "and I figured even if it was, you'd be able to handle yourself. Which you did just fine, except for taking the girl. I never thought there'd be a chance in hell you'd offer a mark sanctuary."

Lita's eyes wavered and dropped to her glass. "I owed it to her."

"And what did it get you?" Jonas asked. "They left you

and the vampire for dead and went after the girl anyway. You're damned lucky I put my ass on the line by not finishing the job like Cleric wanted me to." He paused long enough to quickly survey the tavern. "Where is your bloodrat friend anyway?"

Lita regained her focus in a flash and leaned in closer to him. "Never you fucking mind about him, Jonas. I'm right here in front of you and you're going to tell me everything you know, even if I have to dangle you from the Winter River Bridge to get it. Because I swear to fucking Christ, if you—" she broke off her threat mid-sentence and shot her gaze to the end of the bar where the old man had stumbled trying to get off his stool, dropping his drink in the process.

"Goddammit, Emory, I told you that's the last time!" the tender hollered as he stomped off in that direction.

When Lita looked back, Jonas and his revolver were gone. The service entrance door was already swinging closed.

Smirking as she picked up her glass, Lita said calmly, "You're on," and put away the rest of her drink.

III

Out in the alley, Jonas found himself unexpectedly thrust into darkness as the metal door—which did not open from the outside without a key—slammed shut behind him. He had frequented this place enough to know that the tender always kept a torch burning in this alley and if it wasn't lit, something was amiss. The full moon was still low in the sky, casting thick shadows that enveloped the entirety of this dead-end strip of road.

Taking slow, cautious steps, he held his revolver out with one hand while he used the other to grope around blindly for something, anything, to set ablaze. Having spent over half his life able to create light out of nearly nothing, he was very uncomfortable in any darkness he could not readily dispel.

He moved three more steps and then, behind him, he thought he heard something shift in the darkness. Whipping around, he aimed his weapon blindly. The thought occurred to him to set the wooden butt of his gun on fire, but he worried the heat might set off the ammunition inside.

Of course, he had immediately surmised who was stalking him in this darkness. Lita had accused him of planning her setup, and here she had marched him right into one. "Show yourself, you fucking corpse!" he hollered. "Fight me like the man you wish you were! I'll light up this whole town with your body!"

"Jonas." The whisper was quiet, but seemed so near his ear that he thought he felt the cold breath on which it was delivered. Uttering a thin cry, he spun around and squeezed off a single shot, the muzzle flash briefly splashing the alley walls with white light cut at odd angles by stark black shadows. There was no one to be seen. He heard the bullet splinter a wooden fence at the back of the alley, and then nothing but silence.

His hands began shaking as he moved in a slow circle, trying to listen for any sound, any change in the atmosphere around him. But all he could hear was his own breathing and the booming of his heart in his chest. *Thud thud thud; in; thud thud thud; out; thud thud thud; in; thud thud thud...*

"Jonas," the voice whispered again from somewhere to his right. This time, he did not scream—he pivoted on his heel and fired three quick, booming rounds. In the successive bursts of light, he saw events unfold in clips, each distinct but altogether still too fast to give him time to react.

In the first flash, there was an outline of a figure against the far alley wall, left of where he was aiming.

In the second flash, that figure had halved the distance between them, its pale hands outstretched towards him.

In the final flash, the figure was on him, its furious blue eyes inches from his own.

In the darkness that followed, Jonas felt a frigid hand at his throat, a dull thud on the back of his head, and then those shadows washed over him in a cold wave, dousing the lights of his consciousness.

TWENTY-THREE

Lita slapped Jonas across the face. Hard.

Groaning, he opened first one eye, then the other. "Ow. Seriously? A hot cup of black would have worked just as well."

"Sorry," Lita said, "It looks like you're fresh out."

Jonas blinked a couple of times and looked around to find himself in the middle of his own inn room. "How did you..." Lita tapped herself just above her right breast. Jonas scoffed. "Of course." After his terrible handgun marksmanship, Jonas' memory was his worst quality as an assassin. He wasn't forgetful, per se, but he constantly questioned what he remembered. As often as he was set up in different inns for jobs, he couldn't get past the worry that he wouldn't be able to find his way back on foot. Thus, despite the fact that Cleric would maim him if he knew, he always kept the name of his current accommodations written on a card in the breast pocket of his coat.

Lita couldn't blame him for the fear any more than she could blame herself for avoiding fire or physical contact. Getting lost as a boy had put him on the path to becoming the man he now was.

"So...to what do I owe the pleasure of your company,

dear Lita?" Jonas asked with a self-confident smile. She knew full well that he was feeling out his bonds.

"Well, you were always trying to get me back to your room with you."

"True. Never thought you'd want to tie me up though. Seems like a scrubber trick. That's not how you're making ends meet these days, is it?" He had known immediately that he was sitting in the wooden chair from the room's corner desk. His palms were pressed together behind his back, each finger secured to its counterpart with what felt like medical tape. More tape encircled his hands and wrists, and he thought there might even be fabric tied about them as well. The same bed linen, perhaps, that had been torn into strips and was holding his legs to the chair's just below his knees and was also wrapped tightly around his chest below the sternum.

Lita smirked, but also pointed a warning finger at him. She didn't take kindly to being called a whore. "Even if I was, you couldn't pay me enough. Anyway, I'm not particularly in the mood, darling. Just came to talk."

"Seems like a bit of overkill for a conversation. I could just promise not to run off again," Jonas replied.

"I said I'm not in the mood. I didn't say he's not." Lita nodded towards Rain as he approached from behind Jonas carrying the room's small bedside table. The lamp was still atop, its sickly glow giving Rain's features a deathly appearance. He set the table down on Jonas' right, the lamp's curiously long cord still offering plenty of slack to the wall outlet.

Lita had to admit, when Cleric put them up, he did so in decent style. It wasn't that the room was extravagant or even large, but it had electricity and heated running water. That was a pretty big deal. Furthermore, he always threw in a bit extra to ensure that the innkeeper didn't ask any questions. It came in handy when you waltzed in armed to the teeth, spattered with blood, or just dragging an unconscious man and asking which room was his. The portly man at the desk had simply glanced up from his book, muttered "217," and gone back to reading. Keepers and tenders went to the same tight-lipped finishing school.

"So I take it he plans to torture me?" Jonas asked coolly, looking over his shoulder. He watched as Rain walked to the bed and picked up his collapsed staff and a roll of medical tape from where they were lying next to his neatly folded coat. He returned and set the items on the table, then began rolling up his sleeves.

Lita shrugged. "I guess so. He hasn't really said much."

"Did you tell him Cleric trained us to resist torture?"

"Sure did, but he seems pretty determined. Plus, a few centuries of practice? I'd bet he knows some stuff Cleric didn't teach us. I'm actually a little excited to see what he's got in mind," Lita said with a wry smile.

"I thought you weren't in the mood," Jonas replied. His feigned good temper was fading.

"Maybe he's just better at getting me there than you are."

Jonas' smile disappeared completely. "Partners for eight years and you end up getting juiced over a bloodrat. Figures."

"I'd be careful saying things like that. He doesn't really like it."

As if to confirm Lita's warning, Rain picked up his staff and moved it close to Jonas' chest. With a twist of his hand, its blade ejected, locking into place less than an inch from Jonas' throat. Jonas, unflinching, just glanced down and then back up again.

Not uttering a sound, Rain took hold of Jonas' shirt collar and carefully sliced the knife in a straight downward motion, slitting the fabric until he reached the bonds encircling Jonas' chest. Lita was astonished at how sharp the blade must be. He didn't saw at the shirt, and the fabric made little more than a whisper as it parted.

"Hey!" Jonas said. "I liked this shirt!"

Rain ignored him and continued, making two more incisions perpendicular from the bottom of his first, creating an upside-down T. He then laid open the two sections of shirt, putting Jonas' chest on display, completely bare save for a small pendant necklace. It looked like a triangular shard of junk metal attached to a short silver chain. When Rain stepped away, Lita tilted her head curiously. Jonas wasn't the type to wear jewelry.

Catching her gaze, Jonas put back on the smirking mask that he seemed to think would get him through this intact. "Like what you see? I've been lifting a lot in my spare time."

"His is better," she said, turning her eyes to follow Rain as he headed across the room. Jonas' mask fell again.

The room had French doors that opened to a small balcony overlooking the street two floors below. Rain stepped out long enough to pick up the potted fig tree there, then carried it to the bathroom. Lita and Jonas both watched him quizzically as he yanked the tree—root ball and all—from its pot and placed it carefully in the toilet. He disappeared from view then as he took the pot over to the bathtub.

"I'm going to have to pay for whatever mess he makes, goddammit," Jonas muttered. He heard the shower come on, followed by the hollow drumming of water spraying inside the ceramic pot. Then there was a swirling and a splash. Rinse and repeat.

"I think that's the least of your worries," Lita said. "You'd do best to just start talking now, before he finishes whatever he's doing."

"I don't know what you want me to tell you."

"Sure you do. I asked you plain as day in the bar, so stop wasting time…especially yours, which might be pretty fucking short." Lita kept her eyes on the bathroom. Rain reappeared, snatched a towel off the wall, and carefully dried the clean pot. He then took the lone glass from the basin sink, filled it with water, and returned to the center of the bedroom. He set the glass of water on the side table and knelt in front of Jonas with the pot.

"I should have ordered more than water at the bar," Jonas mused. Lita nodded in agreement.

Rain removed Jonas' shoes and set them aside, then did away with his socks as well. Jonas leaned forward as best he could, trying to see what Rain was doing. Using the blade of his staff, Rain carefully cut off Jonas' pants below the knee, turning them into shorts. Jonas didn't protest about his clothes this time. His breathing got heavier by the minute, and he could feel the hair on his neck growing damp with sweat. He watched as Rain lifted his legs just enough to slip his feet inside the pot and set it down on the floor. Then he stood.

Jonas wiggled his toes, feeling the cold, rough ceramic beneath them. He turned his eyes to Rain who just stood by the side table, looking down at him. Jonas wanted to shrink away from that gaze, and he felt his throat grow suddenly dry and tight.

Rain stayed that way for what seemed like ages, just staring at Jonas, staring into him. Jonas' breath grew ragged at the sight of those unwavering dark blue eyes. Even Lita shifted from one foot to the other, her stomach knotting with anticipation.

Then, moving suddenly, Rain grabbed the lamp's cord and yanked it from the base. The bulb immediately went black, and though the ceiling lamps above and in the bathroom still gave plenty of light, to Jonas the room seemed much darker.

Rain held up the lamp cord—parallel sheathed wires splitting off at frayed copper ends—and slowly peeled the two wires apart until he had a few feet of give between them. Then, leaning forward, he held those wires out towards Jonas' face. Jonas squinted and leaned back as best he could. Still staring at Jonas with that emotionless intensity, Rain touched the two exposed wires together briefly. There was a pop and sparks showered over Jonas' chest. He flinched this time as the room was momentarily bathed in stark white light and long, stretching shadows. Shadows that appeared to loom over him in a wide circle, waiting like vulturous wraiths for his pain to begin.

Lita took a step back and thought that Rain had better remember what she said about killing Jonas. She told herself that she was pretty sure she could trust him, and was immediately startled by how certain she really was. She might have explored the notion further, but her train of thought was interrupted by the acrid smell of burning metal. She wrinkled her nose and waved a hand in front of her face.

Rain had picked up the roll of medical tape and knelt by Jonas' feet. Jonas didn't watch. He didn't want to. His stomach was already turning. Lita did watch, however, and with keen interest as Rain taped the end of one of the wires to the inside wall of the pot, a couple inches above Jonas' bare feet. He then stood back up, put down the tape, grabbed the glass of water, and unceremoniously threw its contents in Jonas' face.

Jonas coughed and sputtered, shaking his head in attempt to clear his eyes. He felt something touching his chest, but by the time his vision had cleared it was already finished. He coughed one last time and looked down to see the other wire taped to his sternum.

When Jonas looked back up, Rain was standing before him, rolling that staff back and forth between his palms. Occasionally, the blade would catch the light and shimmer. Lita had retreated a few paces. She stood near the bathroom door now, her arms crossed, watching silently.

"Hello, Jonas," Rain said calmly.

"Hi," Jonas croaked, then cleared his throat.

"Jonas, we are going to have a very simple conversation in which you are going to answer some questions. If at any time I feel you are avoiding that conversation, there will be a consequence. Am I at all unclear?"

"I don't know anything you want to know," Jonas replied.

Without a word, Rain knelt down, reached behind Jonas' left leg, and drew the blade quickly across his calf. Jonas hissed in a sharp breath and felt wetness begin to course down his leg.

Rain stood once again. "It was a simple yes or no question, Jonas. I haven't time for circles. As soon as you answer my questions, you will be set free and we will be on our way. Lita has asked me not to kill you, and so long as I learn what I need to know, I can fulfill her request. But if you keep trying to give me the runaround, eventually your blood is going to hit that wire and our conversation will be over. Now, are you going to answer my questions?"

Jonas took a deep breath and tried to shut out the pain in his leg as he considered how to answer. After a moment, he said, "That depends on what they are."

Rain frowned, then nodded. "Fair. First, where did Cleric take Alex and Amelie?"

"Alex is the blond kid that was with you, right?" Jonas asked. Rain started kneeling down again. "Hey, it's a fair question! I need to know who I'm telling you to find, right?"

Rain paused and looked up at Jonas. "Do you have any reason to believe I'd be talking about anyone else?"

"No," Jonas replied. Rain cut a slit in the other leg. Jonas cried out this time. Lita shifted her stance uncomfortably. This wasn't her style.

"I don't like repeating myself. Answer the question." Rain warned.

"You don't understand," Jonas said, "You don't know what you'd be walking into if you…"

Rain was already reaching for his legs again.

"Rain, wait. Let him finish," Lita said, stepping forward. "If he knows something that we need to prepare for, we should—" she clenched her teeth as Rain carved another tally into Jonas' calf. A trickling sound started coming from the pot as blood began to pool around Jonas' feet.

"Please," Jonas said, his voice cracking, "Listen to me. If you go down there, you'll both die, and they'll still be just as dead. There's no way you can—" his words broke off in a sharp cry as Rain opened a fourth gash in his flesh.

Lita was on them then, moving quickly. She grabbed Rain by the elbow, tugging on his arm to pull him away. "Stop it, Rain! We can't find out anything if you don't let him talk!"

Rain turned on her in a flash. Bolting to his feet, he took up a fistful of her shirt and pushed her across the room, shoving her against the wall by the front door. He slammed the blunt end of his staff against the wall inches from her ear, and his eyes flickered violet as he came nose-to-nose with her. "I will bleed him dry if that's what it takes," he growled.

"Hey! Let her the fuck go!" Jonas yelled with renewed strength as he struggled futilely against his bonds.

Lita's initial shock was quickly replaced by rage. She delivered a sharp jab to Rain's sternum, then grabbed his shirt and turned with him, slamming his back against the wall. "That is the second time you have pinned me against a fucking wall! There will *not* be a third!"

Rain's eyes shifted instantly back to blue, and though dizziness made his head swim momentarily, a small smirk appeared on his face. "That *was* the third, by my count," he said quietly.

Lita's cheeks flushed a deep red, but she held her

ground, glaring at him. A tense moment passed, and then Rain whispered, "Dance with me."

She squinted at him, confused, but let him go and took a step back. He gestured to Jonas and she nodded, then turned to head back to their subject. As soon as her back was to him, Rain grabbed her ponytail in a tight fist, yanked her head back, and put his blade to her throat.

"What the fuck are you doing?" Lita cried in a strained voice. All at once, that newly discovered trust in this man, which had seemed so profound only moments before, was suddenly transformed into a tenuous dike trying hold back the flood of over a decade's worth of honed survival instincts. It didn't matter that her rational mind knew this was all an act (*is it? what if it isn't?*), she was already planning the head butt, elbow jab, wrist break, and gun draw that would get her out of this. It didn't matter that she was pretty sure he meant her no harm (*how sure? sure enough? he's a fucking vampire, Lita, and he's got a fucking knife to your…*), she was already calculating how long she could remain conscious and able to fight if he nicked her artery. So with all her strength, she began to struggle…not against Rain, but against all the forged fibers of her being that were screaming at her to (*kill that motherfucker before he can touch you again*) actually fight back.

"Let her go you piece of shit!" Jonas hollered. He started thrashing harder, and the chair began to rock.

"I wouldn't do that," Rain said calmly. "If you splash blood on that wire, you won't be saving anybody. Now, do I have your attention?"

"Let her go!" Jonas screamed.

"Then answer my question. You say we'll die if we go. You don't care if I die, so what you mean is *she'll* die. So if I just kill her right now, then you don't have anything to worry about." Rain moved the blade slightly, drawing a small trickle of blood from Lita's neck.

Her muscles flared with burning intent, the surging waves of instinct battering that little dam, causing it to creak and groan against the onslaught. Her hands went to Rain's forearm and his own blood sprang forth as she dug her nails into his flesh so hard her knuckles turned ghostly white.

"No!" Jonas cried, seeing the blood run down Lita's neck. "Stop doing that!"

"Then answer my question. Hell, she probably won't even go with me after this, and if she still does she at least stands a chance. You keep your mouth shut and she dies for sure. Last chance, Jonas. Where is my brother?"

Jonas blinked. "Your..." he paused briefly, then said, "The Blacklands. They're in the Blacklands."

Rain released Lita and she shoved him away with her elbow, then spun around to glare at him as she put a hand to her neck. His expression was pained, regretful, and he began to mouth an apology but she turned away. Just looking at him was keeping her tempestuous rage thrashing against the weakened dike. She stormed over to her bag, dug out her vodka and a small medical kit, then headed to the bathroom, intent on assessing her wound and dampening her almost irresistible urge to throw Rain over the balcony.

"Nobody goes there," she hollered out at Jonas as she surveyed her neck in the bathroom mirror. She wasn't about to sideline herself from a conversation she had just bled for. "Why the fuck would they?"

"What is Michael planning?" Rain added.

Jonas sighed and looked down, shaking his head.

"Don't screw around, Jonas," Lita said, appearing in the doorway, a washrag against her neck in one hand, open bottle in the other. "I know you know. Cleric thought we never knew his plans, but you've been peeking at his logbooks since I was still on cleanup. Tell us what's happening." She took a strong swig and checked the rag for blood volume.

"He's going to kill them all," Jonas said quietly, his eyes not moving from his lap.

"Kill whom?" Rain asked.

"The Gifted," Jonas whispered.

Rain and Lita exchanged a look. "How?" Lita asked.

Jonas took a deep breath and raised his head. "Michael has this glove, like the kind a knight would wear. A...gauntlet, that's the word. I don't know where the hell he got it, but I know what it can do. It's a weapon. When he wears it, he can create this ball of energy and cast it at a person, and if they're in any way not human, it burns them up from the inside." He shuddered. "I've seen it done to a vampire. Even for a bloodrat, that's no way to die." He paid Rain a glance, and Rain nodded.

"How does he intend to kill all the Gifted with it?" Rain pressed.

"He and Cleric had this big construct built—down in the Blacklands where nobody would find it—and it's supposed to take the glove's energy and set it off like a bomb. They say it'll cover the Earth, leaving only pure humans left alive."

"That would kill you, dumbshit," Lita said. "Why would you go along with that?"

Jonas nodded down toward his odd necklace. "This is a piece of the glove. It'll protect me from the blast. Michael wasn't happy about it, but Cleric insisted."

Rain leaned forward and reached out to inspect the necklace, but as soon as he touched it there was a sizzling sound and he hissed, snatching his hand away. A thin puff of smoke rose from his fingertips.

"It's a blessed artifact. Didn't I mention that?" Jonas said with a smirk.

Rain glared at him. "What's my brother got to do with this? Why did they take him?"

Jonas had become acutely aware that his legs were

starting to throb. "Would you mind unplugging me? I can't tell if I'm still filling this pot and—"

"Answer my question or you'll be getting some fresh cuts," Rain warned.

Jonas leaned forward, trying to see his feet, then looked to Lita. She nodded reassuringly and gestured for him to continue, so he sighed and went on. "I have no idea why they took him; I wasn't there and I came straight here after locking you two up back at the cemetery. Maybe they wanted him as insurance in case you two came after them, or maybe he knew something they wanted to know, or…" he paused, his brow furrowing, "…no. Could he?" he said, mostly to himself.

"Could he what?" Lita asked.

"Well, for Michael's plan to work, he needed more than just the glove and that building. Cleric said they were looking for something called the Catalyst. It's the thing that concentrates the glove's energy and then detonates it. Trouble was, they didn't know what form it was in. Could be a jewel, a shrub, anything. Cleric once said it might even be a person. If Alex is it, and the Visgaer saw him—"

"The what?" Rain asked. He glanced back at Lita, but she shrugged.

Jonas sighed, annoyed and antsy to get out of this chair. "You want the long version or the short one?"

"Short," Rain said.

"Six-and-a-half-foot-tall demon hunting hound. Monster. Claws, fangs, the whole package. Psychic, telekinetic, deadly. Ugly as a bag of smashed assholes. Good?"

Rain nodded.

"Anyway, Cleric was expecting it to find the Catalyst today, even with all this shit going on. If your brother is the key, it'd explain why they took him alive."

"Why would it be my brother?"

"No clue. All I know is that it was supposed to be special

in some way. It was pre…pre…"

"Predestined?" Lita offered.

"That's the one," Jonas said.

Rain shook his head. "That doesn't make any sense. Alex isn't out of the ordinary. He's not a Gifted, he doesn't even have our familial power. He—"

"Came back from the dead," Lita said. Rain looked at her. "I'd call that pretty fucking out of the ordinary."

"Do you think that's it?" Rain asked.

She shrugged. "No clue, but it also doesn't matter. Obviously this thing hasn't gone down yet because you're still standing, so why don't we just focus on finding them and worry about the rest later?" She turned her attention to Jonas. "How do we get to the Construct and what kind of forces does Cleric have down there?"

"There's a map in my bag by the door and you'll have Cleric, the Visgaer, that Michael creep, and at least ten vampires. Maybe a dozen. Although, they may not be all that loyal to Cleric. He had them build the Construct, but they didn't exactly do it willingly."

Lita nodded. Vampire slave labor was, surprisingly, not unheard of. They were strong, didn't have to sleep, and could be controlled with the right exploitation of weaknesses. But no matter their loyalty, that still stood to make for some pretty ugly odds for her and Rain. "Alright, last question and then you're off the hook. When's this supposed to go down?"

"At the height of the lunar eclipse today. It's right at at dawn, which gives you…"

"Less than five hours," Rain finished.

"Better hurry. It's almost a four-hour drive just to get down there."

"Why the eclipse?" Lita asked.

"I thought I was off the hook," Jonas said.

"Humor me."

"Who knows? Maybe Michael was busy for brunch. Does it matter?"

"I guess not," Lita said. She grabbed the lamp cord and yanked it out of the wall outlet. Jonas had only a moment to breathe a sigh of relief before Lita grabbed his shoulder and tipped him over backwards in the chair. He landed with a thud and a groan, feeling his full weight land on his hands and forearms. Lita knelt and freed his chest and legs from their bonds, then retied the strips of fabric around his upper calves, just tight enough to slow his bleeding some. Then she rose to her feet and looked down at him. "I'm sure you can get out of the rest yourself, but I'd wait a while until your legs stop bleeding." She turned to pack up her things.

Having found the map in Jonas' bag, Rain pocketed it and walked over to him. He placed one heavy boot on the center of Jonas' chest and leaned down, his eyes furious. "You are only alive because Lita requested it, but you helped plan a genocide. If I see you again, she will not stop me from spending days killing you."

In approval of Rain's threat, Lita returned and knelt down once more to yank away Jonas' necklace, sending bits of the chain flying this way and that. "And if we don't make it in time, you get to reap what you've sown."

With that, Lita stepped over her old partner and walked away, Rain following right behind. Jonas didn't say a word. He couldn't think of words. It wasn't until after they were gone that tears filled his eyes and he whispered, "Goodbye, Killer."

As soon as they were out in the hallway, Lita spun around and cracked Rain across the jaw with a hard left hook. He took it well, only stumbling back a step.

"Putting a knife to my throat is not my idea of dancing, and if you ever want to find out what is, you will never threaten me again. Am I clear?"

"Perfectly," Rain replied as he rubbed his jaw. "One question though."

"What?"

"Do we get to have sex every time you hit me?"

"Oh my fucking god!" Lita exclaimed, then turned around and pounded down the stairs.

TWENTY-FOUR

I

As they neared the southern outskirts of Maple City, Rain shifted gears and lit a cigarette while Lita ran her hands over the flawless leather upholstery by her legs.

"How have you kept this car in such good shape?" she asked.

"Alex helped a lot," Rain replied. "I had plenty of knowledge of vehicle maintenance and construction stored away in my head, and with his knack for practical application we were able to work wonders."

"So you spent some time reading up on cars?"

"Not just cars. Everything. In one of the countries that existed before the Last War, there was a library that stored a copy of nearly every book in existence. When it was abandoned after the war, I lived in it for a few years before coming to Ayenee. I'd spend most of every day working through the stacks."

"And you remember every word?" She still couldn't wrap her mind around the seemingly endless amount of knowledge he had managed to amass.

"Everything I read, yes. I was able to reproduce

schematics and Alex made them work."

"So you can just look at something once and it's there, sealed in forever?" Rain nodded. "Even faces? If you closed your eyes—don't, your driving is shit enough as it is—but if you did, you could describe every detail about me?"

"I could do that without perfect memory," Rain replied, paying her a glance as he took a pull off his cigarette.

Lita smirked. "That's a good line. You read that in one of your books?"

"Yep. *How to Pick Up Hard-Nosed Killers.* I was saving it for just this occasion."

Lita scoffed. "Figures. But don't call me that. I don't like it any more than you like being called a vampire."

They exchanged a look and Rain nodded.

There was silence for a time, and then Lita went on. "But I guess there's no denying it, huh? I mean, hell, five years of tending bar and I jump back on the horse at the first sniff of a contract like no time has gone by. Sneaking into that palace felt normal as breathing. I didn't want to be doing it, but goddammit if for the first time in years I didn't feel like...like me, you know?" She sighed and slouched in her seat, trying to ignore the urge to reach for her bottle.

"You're a predator, just like me," Rain said. Lita shot him a look, but he held up a hand, then took a long drag off his cigarette before going on. "I've spent a long time being something I don't want to be, and it took me years to realize that the only way to live with that is to come to terms with it. A predator is what you are, and nothing you can do will change that. But being a killer is a choice you make. That's the dilemma of free will. You can't change your nature, but you can decide how to act on it."

"Five years, and I'm still making the wrong decisions," Lita said, looking back down.

"I don't see any fresh blood on your hands."

She stared at them hard, opening and closing her fists.

Then she looked back at Rain, her eyes shimmering with a glassy sheen.

"Your nature brought you to that girl," Rain went on, "but you made the choice to help her. You probably saved her life, and if everything Jonas said is true, we stand to save countless more before this night is over."

"You honestly think I can change?" Lita asked, her voice unsure—not of his faith in her, but of her own faith in herself.

"I think you've already started," Rain replied. "You just still have a long road ahead."

"A lonely one," Lita sighed, looking out ahead of them.

"It doesn't have to be," Rain said. Their eyes met for a moment and Lita couldn't help mirroring the tender smile that he offered her. They each had been alone on their own roads for so long that they hardly knew what to do with another by their side. But whether they meant to or not, they had already begun to press on together.

Rain finished his cigarette and pitched it, then rolled the window up. Quiet fell in the car once more. But this one was not uncomfortable. In it, they rode for some time, each mentally preparing for what might come when they reached their destination. At least, that's what they told themselves they were doing. Really, a deeper part of their minds was mulling over what might come ahead between them. As they made their way along the seemingly endless dirt road, trees whipping by them in the dead of night, they stole brief glances at one another. Taking turns, each would look to the other for just a little bit, then dart their eyes away right before the other did the same. They both nearly convinced themselves that they were the only one doing it, but some remaining part knew that the other was as well. It knew, and it made them feel special in a way neither of them had felt in a long time, if they ever had at all.

It made them feel wanted.

Lita looked at Rain's hands—pale, slender, and unmarred by the years they'd spent building things and turning pages. Rain looked at Lita's hair—wavy and vibrant in the beauty that she tried to ignore. She saw his coat—wondering where he'd gotten it. He saw her cheek—wondering how warm it was. Both of them pondered what the other's hand might feel like in their own, but they could not bring themselves to make it a reality. Not yet. Just a little more time.

II

Coming around a wide curve in the road, Rain eased the car to a stop and leaned forward, peering intently out where the headlights cut though the black of the forest.

"You need to see the map again?" Lita asked, reaching for where it sat folded by the gearshift. Rain gave her a sidelong glance. "No, I guess you wouldn't," she said, then unfolded it to look for herself.

"It should be a bit farther up on the right," he said, his eyes scanning the stretch of road that looked no different than what they'd been on for hours.

"I don't see where we're at," she said as she eyed the rudimentary, hand-drawn map.

"It's upside down," Rain said, not moving his eyes from the road. Lita scoffed sheepishly and turned it around. "Okay, that still doesn't help—" Rain reached over and tapped a spot on the map, still without looking. "Oh, alright. Now I've got it."

"Good, now help me look," Rain said. He started driving again, but kept it at about ten miles per hour.

"What am I looking for?"

"Disturbed vegetation. They may have tried to cover the entrance to the path, but it will likely still appear unnatural. I'm watching the grooves in the road, looking for any sign that they turned—"

"Or it could just be that turnoff right there," Lita said, pointing.

Rain blinked and brought the car to a stop once more. "Cleric must have felt very sure we wouldn't follow him."

"He had no reason not to. Jonas has never defied a direct order before. Hell, even I'm surprised."

Rain nodded and pulled off the main road, onto a narrow path that amounted to little more than a pair of ruts winding off into the forest. Once clear of the road, he gunned it, tearing through the woods at speeds no human would dare on a path like this.

Given Rain's sharp senses and his love for this car, Lita knew she was probably in safe hands, but still felt nervous at the speed they were travelling. Averting her eyes from the road, she looked to Rain and initiated conversation to keep her tension at bay.

"What was the world like before the Last War?" She wasn't sure why she chose that question in particular. It was standard primary school knowledge that she could easily read about in the Maple City Library. Thinking of that place, she suddenly found herself also thinking of snow, and she had no idea why. Regardless, it wasn't textbook knowledge she was after. She wanted to know more about Rain and the things he'd seen.

He chuckled ruefully at the question, and then answered with the first explanation that came to mind. "There were a lot more people."

"Oh?"

"Yes. More than nine billion," he paused for a beat, "but I guess that doesn't really put it into context. Tell me this: if you wanted to go a week without seeing another human being, how hard would it be?"

Lita shrugged. "Not at all. There's lots of places I could go with no one around."

"Exactly. You couldn't before. Humans crammed

themselves into cities ten times the size of Chicane. They lived in rows of houses as far as the eye could see. If you wanted to be alone—truly alone—you had to go to the desert, the middle of the forest, or the top of a tall mountain. Even then, you'd often run into somebody else looking for the same thing."

"That sounds fucking terrible. I hate people."

"So did they. So much so that they just plugged themselves into televisions and computers and music players so that they could pretend no one else was around them."

Lita nodded. She understood what he was saying, but those pieces of technology were abstract concepts to her. She had read enough to know that motion pictures and music had been streamed into every corner of every household, and she had seen computers and monitor screens during her tenure at the Maple City Hospital, but the notion of these things being a part of everyday life was completely foreign to her.

"Well, after the war, none of that stuff went anywhere, right? I mean, we still salvage a lot of it now. So why didn't people rebuild it like it was, the way Amelie said Michael seems to want?"

"Numbers had a lot to do with it," Rain said, then lit a cigarette. "There just aren't enough people around to keep the whole machine running like it used to. But I think there's another reason too. It's my own theory, if you care to hear it."

"May as well. Seems like you'd have as good of an idea as anybody, what with having seen it firsthand."

"Survival," Rain said, then cracked his window and flicked some ash out of it. "Before the war, humans were at the top of the food chain. Most of them never really had to question their own survival. They had no reason to fear that someone or something would drag them off and kill them in the night. Without that fear to give their lives focus, they were left to their own devices and created a world full of things they didn't need. It's different now. Knowing you could die at any time puts things into perspective."

"So you're saying that my need to sleep with a gun under my pillow means I'm not wasting my life?" Lita asked skeptically.

"I'm saying that before the Last War, people romanticized a life like yours. They wrote books and made films about it. That's how boring and meaningless their lives were."

"That's..." Lita grimaced "...ugh. Forget I asked."

"Look at it this way," he said, "at least you—"

Without warning, Rain suddenly grabbed the hand brake and yanked. It made a decisive click. Lita felt every muscle in her body tense. One hand grabbed the dashboard and the other hit the ceiling as the car began to skid, spinning to the right. She felt a yelp escape her when it bumped violently over the raised center between the ruts in the road, then once more when it happened again. The car continued its forward motion as it spun, finally stopping its revolutions at two-hundred seventy degrees, leaving Rain's door facing back the way they had come. It continued to slide sideways along the those ruts for a moment longer, but Rain was already out of the car before it stopped, leaving his door wide open as he sprinted down the road, his long coat billowing out behind him. His half-smoked cigarette threw up a shower of embers where he dropped it on the ground.

Lita's breath came in short, ragged heaves. It took her nearly thirty seconds to withdraw her hands from their locked positions and to finally convince herself that they had stopped moving and were not, in fact, dying in a fiery wreck. With that realization came her trusty rage, and the only thing that kept her from screaming at him as she climbed out of the car was the knowledge that they may be nearing enemy territory.

She had to squeeze to get around the back side of the car, it was so close to the trees and bushes bordering the road. Breaking into a jog, she hurried to where Rain was crouched in the road nearly fifty yards away. "Are you fucking insane?" she asked as she reached him. Dropping her hands to her knees, she bent forward and looked over his shoulder to where he appeared to be rubbing a pinch of dirt between his fingers. "You want to tell me what the fuck that was all about?"

Rain smelled his fingers and then held them up for her to see. "This is Alex's blood. It stretches back almost a mile."

Lita's stomach dropped and the color drained from her face. "Is he…"

"No," Rain said. "There's not enough here. I think he did this on purpose."

"He knew you'd find it?"

Rain nodded and stood, starting back towards the car. "We're close."

"You know," Lita said, following him, "I'd have to be a goddamned idiot to get back in that car with you."

Rain didn't say anything, and Lita knew he didn't have to. He could have wrecked the car and she still would have gone the rest of the way with him on foot.

Back in his seat, Rain dropped the emergency brake and slammed the gearshift into reverse.

"You're really close to the trees," Lita warned as she buckled her seatbelt. "You're going to want to—"

Rain revved the car backwards and it stopped abruptly with a loud crunch. Lita grunted, but he barely seemed to notice. He shifted into first, yanked the wheel hard to the right, and peeled out back onto their path.

"That works too," Lita said, wincing at the thought of what the back bumper must look like.

They drove in silence after that. A cold resolution began to wash over both of them. Each knew the lengths they might have to go to when they arrived, the vows they would have to break. They knew, and they could live with it. Damnation wasn't a foreign concept to either of them, and if it meant saving Alex and Amelie, whatever they did that night would be just another drop in the bucket.

III

Then, as though somebody had pulled back a curtain, Maplewood Forest was no more. Rain brought the car to a stop, killing the headlights, and they both stepped out to survey what lay before them. Lita let out a low whistle and even Rain, with his centuries of experience, was awestruck by what he saw.

Fifty feet past the tree line, the earth dropped away in a sheer hundred-foot cliff. Below and ahead of them, as far as Lita could see, was utter wasteland. The Blacklands extended out twenty-five miles from where they stood until it reached the Atlantic Ocean. Its dead, calloused surface stretched over three hundred miles of Ayenee's southeastern coastline. Seventy-five hundred square miles where nothing lived, the scar left behind from the great world war over who would get to call this young continent their own.

Lita opened her mouth to ask the obvious question, but Rain pointed to the answer before she did. To their right, the ground slopped down more gradually from the edge of the cliff. There, a slender road snaked its way back and forth in tight, hairpin turns until it reached the basin of the Blacklands.

"The Construct is about ten miles out," Rain said, peering out over the cliff once more. "I can see its fires burning." From here, he could even smell the salt of the ocean beyond that.

"So we know where we're headed," Lita said, then eyed the way down cautiously. "And we get to go by the lovely scenic route. Who says you don't take me anywhere?"

Rain smirked in spite of himself. "We'll have to do it with no headlights. We can't risk them seeing us coming. You won't be able to see where we're going, but I promise you, I can make it down."

"I trust you," Lita said, and looked at him with startling earnestness. The truth was, she really did. It was terrifying.

It took Rain a moment to gather words after that, but he finally said carefully, "I can get us down, but you have to know that there's no guarantee we'll make it out of this. If we don't, or if one of us doesn't, I need you to know that I—"

Lita held up a hand. "Whatever it is, Rain, it can wait until after. We're going in, and we're coming back out. I'm in a spin over you enough as it is. Don't fog things up more for me now. Not until we're clear of this."

Rain looked taken aback, even hurt. In that moment, Lita felt something give inside her. Something that had remained barricaded and hard her whole remembered life finally sighed and collapsed under the weight of everything that had happened over the last few days. She approached him and laid a hand gently on his arm, rose up on her toes, and planted a soft kiss on his cool lips.

"If it's what I think it is," she said, her emerald gaze swimming in the blue sea of his eyes, "I never wanted to hear it until today. Now, I'd kill for it. Let me use it to get us through this. Let me look forward to it."

Rain managed a small smile and a nod. Lita nodded as well and then turned to head back to the car. Suddenly, Rain took hold of her arm and pulled her in for a fierce hug. She tensed for a moment, her hand instinctively moving towards her gun. But with a shaky sigh, she relaxed against him, then slipped her arms around his waist and rested her head on his shoulder. If she had ever been hugged before, she had no memory of it. It was a strange feeling, but one she thought that maybe she could get used to. It was certainly better than the empty feeling that followed when they finally released each other and reluctantly returned to the car.

Lita got in and buckled up, starting to mentally prepare herself for the harrowing drive and all that was to come after it. Rain stayed a moment longer to gaze out over the scorched earth before them. It brought to mind a quote from a book he had read lifetimes ago.

"This inhuman place makes human monsters."

He slipped back into his seat, shifted gears, and locked eyes with the woman at his side before they started rolling. With fiery hearts and icy resolves, they began their dark descent into the Blacklands.

TWENTY-FIVE

Rain and Lita quietly approached the Construct on foot, having parked the car behind a sizeable outcrop of rock nearly a mile away. As they neared the coliseum, Rain whispered, "Are you ready for this?"

Lita adjusted the shoulder strap of the rifle she'd taken off Henrik and checked her handgun silencer for tightness. "Sure am. But I don't like it. Something about this is too easy. Why the fuck aren't there any guards posted?"

"I'm guessing the two palace guards from the cemetery were supposed to be here. Without them, all Cleric has is vampires he probably can't trust out of his sight and that Visgaer thing. He must be relying on the remote location to keep them safe."

"Maybe," Lita whispered, "but I'd just as soon run into neither a monster nor a horde of vampires, so let's watch our asses."

"I can handle myself," Rain said as he drew his collapsed staff from inside his coat.

"I'd still feel a lot better if you carried a gun."

"You'd be surprised how many bullets I can take and stay standing."

"Yeah, well, Cleric carries a sawed-off twelve-gauge in

his coat. One shot from that will blast you in half, so like I said, watch your ass."

Rain nodded and started moving close to the side of the coliseum. Lita was right behind him.

"The way this is built, it looks like there's an inner and an outer wall," Rain whispered as they made their way carefully around the large building. "I doubt the inner door is across from the outer one, so we'll probably have to make our way through a hallway. You watch out behind us, I'll take the front."

"You got it," Lita replied. "How are we on time?"

Rain glanced out at the horizon, which was growing lighter blue with each passing moment, then up at the moon, which only had about a quarter-crescent of white left on the edge of the red shadow spilling over it. "Maybe twenty-five minutes."

Lita grimaced. "I hate working on a fucking deadline. And you should have brought your sun gear."

"This'll be over well before the sun crests the coliseum wall, one way or the other," Rain said.

About a quarter of the way around the coliseum, they came upon a small open doorway. Dim, flickering light spilled out from it, illuminating the cracked, uneven earth at their feet. Rain pressed his back against the outside wall, gripped his staff tightly, and carefully peered around the corner, first to the left, then to the right. Both directions looked the same: bare, stone hallway curving around to disappear, illuminated by a torch in a wall sconce every dozen feet or so.

"Take your pick," Rain whispered, nodding to the doorway. Lita dashed across it, backed against the wall on the other side, and took a look for herself.

"Fuck, I dunno. Left, I guess."

Rain nodded and proceeded inside. Lita took up the rear, walking backwards, keeping her gun drawn and aimed at the empty hallway as they moved, quickly but quietly. The corridor had no floor, making it fairly easy to silence their footfalls on the bare dirt.

After they'd been walking a while, Rain came to an abrupt halt and Lita backed into him with a grunt. Looking over her shoulder and past his arm, she saw why he had stopped and turned to face the obstacle herself. Just ahead, the hallway ended at a single door. It was a simple thing, wooden planks thrown together with a pair of cross boards, held up by barrel hinges. It didn't even have a knob, just a hole to grab it by.

Rain's nostrils flared and he gritted his teeth.

"What is it?" Lita asked, sensing his tension.

"Vampires," he replied. Together, they advanced on the door.

Slowly reaching for the door, Rain felt a familiar tightening in his stomach. Something about being at the end of a long, dim hallway, opening a mysterious door with the knowledge that danger could creep up behind him at any time. He forced himself to stop breathing, collect himself, and just open the damned thing.

He did so very carefully to be sure he didn't make a sound. When he saw what was inside, his jaw clenched, and he heard Lita take in a sharp breath.

The room was a worker bunkroom. It had no windows, just six pairs of stacked beds, three per wall to the left and right. Each bed held a ratty military-grade blanket and a pillow without a case. Unlike most such rooms, this one did not smell of masculinity and body odor. It reeked of hollow, decrepit death.

Rain's quick eyes counted the piles of dust almost instantly. Three of the lower beds were covered with it, and possibly some of the higher ones as well. They were the first to go, killed before they could even rise. There were four in various spots on the floor. Those had been kicked around and stepped through, their remains disturbed by the ensuing fight. He couldn't quite tell how many vampires there had been to begin with, but he knew there was only one left intact.

And he wouldn't be much longer.

The Visgaer had its curved back turned towards Rain and Lita, the well-defined spurs of its scraggly spine jutting out as it stood hunched over its final victim. They could not see what it was doing to the vampire, but they could see the vampire's arms, held splayed out at his sides by some invisible force. His hands were shaking uncontrollably, blood pouring off his fingertips. He was emitting a wet, guttural, choking sound.

Rain reached out and placed his hand on Lita's chest, just above her breasts. He pushed softly and glanced at her, nodding as he began to slowly back away from the open doorway. She moved with him. They had retreated a full three steps—were about to turn away, in fact—when the Visgaer suddenly whipped its head around to face them, its bandage-covered eye sockets seeming to stare straight into them. When it turned, they could see the vampire in its grasp. Lita's stomach turned when she realized that not only had the vampire been eviscerated, but the Visgaer's long claws were plunged up under his chin and all the way through the roof of his mouth. His lips hung open, blood pouring out over them. His eyes were rolled into the back of his head, his eyelids twitching. Lita was astonished that something could still be moving after all of that, undead or not.

The Visgaer took in a breath, its thin grey skin pulling even more taut against its emaciated ribs before it released a horrifying screech and used its free hand to tear the vampire's head clean off with a moist ripping sound. Both pieces of the tortured creature immediately crumbled to dust.

"Go," Rain whispered forcefully. "Now!"

"Fuck that. I'm not leaving you alone with—"

Rain shot her a quick look, keeping the Visgaer in his periphery. It didn't make a move for them, only tilted its head slowly to the side like a curious bird, as though it was interested in their conversation.

"That thing just tore apart a room full of vampires. I'll be lucky if I can slow it down. Get to Alex and Amelie," Rain hissed.

"Oh, I'll fucking slow it down," Lita said as she pushed Rain's hand away. She quickly raised her handgun and fired three shots, each one making a *pop* as it left the barrel.

Even Rain's eyes weren't fast enough to watch the bullets' movements clearly, but they could make out a blurred path. He couldn't be positive, but as he saw the three black lines extend across the room, he could have sworn that they curved away shortly before reaching the Visgaer. The first hit the stone wall to its right, kicking back a cloud of dust. The second went to its left, emitting the same. The third actually arced downward and buried itself in the dirt.

"No. Fucking. Way," Lita whispered hoarsely.

"Go!" Rain ordered, pushing her back once more, this time with far greater force. She stumbled backwards a few steps and would have fallen had she not caught herself on the hallway wall.

Without waiting for an argument, Rain stepped into the bunkroom and slammed the door. He then drew one of his daggers and buried it almost hilt-deep just below one of the hinges, jamming the door so it couldn't be opened from the outside.

When he turned around, the Visgaer was looking at him again. Its mouth was open, its long, sharp fangs dripping viscous fluid, its thick black tongue writhing.

Rain raised his staff, gripping it tightly in both hands. His eyes turned down into a glare and his lips turned up into a smirk. "Shall we?"

The Visgaer lunged at him.

TWENTY-SIX

"It's time," Michael said. He was standing near the center of the Construct's arena, staring up at the almost eclipsed moon.

"Looks like you're on, kid." Cleric said as he approached Alex. He and Amelie were still bound to their post, gagged as promised. Between them, their fingers were intertwined, and when Cleric reached down to untie the young man, Amelie squeezed his hands tightly and started to yell indistinctly around her gag. Alex, however, simply sat still and remained silent, watching Cleric work.

"This will all be over soon, Amelie, I promise," Michael called.

After releasing Alex's ankles, Cleric made quick work of the bonds tying his hands, making sure Amelie's remained secure in the process. He then removed Alex's gag and tossed it aside. "Glad you've decided to face this like a man," Cleric said, gesturing for him to stand.

Alex spat a bit of blood at his captor's feet. Cleric only chuckled and motioned to him again. When Alex stood, Cleric moved behind him and took tight hold of his upper arms, then began leading the young man towards the center of the arena.

They had advanced maybe ten feet before Alex suddenly bent at the knees and jumped, throwing his head back as he did. He felt the crown of his skull connect with Cleric's chin and heard the man grunt as he released his hold. Alex quickly dashed away from him and stooped down to snatch up two grapefruit-sized stones from the ground. Turning to face a slightly dazed Cleric, he took a few steps back and lowered himself into a defensive position, gripping a stone in each hand.

"I'll show you how I face things like a man," Alex said, his lips curling back from his teeth in a snarl.

Cleric rubbed his jaw and grinned broadly. "You just don't give up, do you kid? I'm almost ready to start rooting for you. Under different circumstances, you might have made a good hitter."

"Come see for yourself," Alex replied, tightening his grip on his makeshift weapons.

"You really want to play this game?" Cleric asked. "Just because I can't kill you, that doesn't mean I can't make you bleed."

Alex said nothing.

"Alright, kid. Let's play," Cleric said and began to advance on Alex.

"There will be no games!" Michael yelled. Both men looked to see him standing by Amelie, his sword drawn, the tip pointed at her throat. "Drop the stones and stop trying to resist your role in this, or I will be forced to make her die slowly. Neither of us wants that, I think."

"Michael…" Cleric warned in a low tone, his large hands balling into fists.

"You're going to kill her no matter what I do," Alex spat.

"Unfortunately, yes," Michael replied, "but the other way she will go along with you, and quickly. This way, she suffers, and you will be forced to watch."

Cleric looked to Alex, whose eyes moved from Michael

to Amelie. She shook her head vehemently, her own eyes wide. Giving her a regretful look, he sighed and released his hold on the stones. As they landed on the bare earth with a thud, he dropped his hands to his sides, defeated.

Michael sheathed his sword and Cleric approached Alex. "That was impressive. So much so that I'm not even going to hit you in the head," he said, almost admiringly, before grabbing the young man's shoulders and ramming a knee into his stomach. Alex released a strangled cry and dropped to his knees, holding himself.

Not about to give Alex time to recover, Cleric grabbed him by his underarms and dragged him to the center of the arena. There, the two long chains Cleric had been carrying earlier were dangling from opposing pillars of the altar, and at the end of each was a large iron cuff. Cleric yanked Alex to his feet and locked up each of his wrists, then stepped back to survey his work. The young man was chained so that his arms formed a Y and his feet barely held enough purchase on the ground to support him.

"Is that what you had in mind?" Cleric asked, looking to Michael.

"Yes, that will do," Michael said absently, his attention elsewhere. He was standing at a waist-high, unmarked stone slab near one of the rune-inscribed pillars. Upon that slab sat the wooden chest he had kept hidden in his bedchamber study, and he was staring down at it pensively.

"Are you planning to put that thing on at some point?" Cleric asked.

Michael almost seemed to flinch at the question, his wide eyes jolting up towards Cleric. For just an instant, he looked like a startled fawn. Then, in a blink, his countenance became one of annoyance. "Of *course* I am. I already told you, the gauntlet and its power take a heavy toll on the body. There is no reason for me to needlessly waste energy by putting it on before it is necessary to do so."

Just then, everyone in the arena looked to one of the coliseum doors as the Visgaer's loud screeched echoed through it.

Michael shuddered. "Cleric, while I take no quarrel with your pet killing off our wretched workforce, does it really have to—"

"That was a warning cry," Cleric interjected, throwing open his coat and drawing his shotgun. He took several steps backward, positioning himself such that he could keep an eye on both coliseum doors.

"Are you saying that someone followed us here?" Michael asked, alarmed.

"If they did, it doesn't matter. The Visgaer has them now. And even if they somehow manage to get past him, I'll be ready." He waved a hand at Michael. "You just focus on your job. Start as soon as you can."

"Of course," Michael said. He pulled off his rosary and looked down to the key hanging from it. "The time is close now…"

TWENTY-SEVEN

As the Visgaer moved towards him, its claws and teeth bared, Rain willed himself not to move until the last possible second. Finally, just as it was bearing down on him, he ducked and sidestepped simultaneously, lunging forward with his staff out to the side. He felt it connect hard with something near the Visgaer's midsection just as its talons hissed past his ear, but as he spun around and took two steps back, he cursed silently, realizing he had only hit a telekinetic buffer guarding the creature's flesh. He wasn't sure how he was going to get past the defenses of a creature that could reroute bullets, but he hoped that it was not unlike blocking with a limb, and that perhaps he could still hit flesh he moved faster than the creature could defend. His attacks would have to be quick and surprising, and—worse—delivered from a very close range.

As he dropped into a ready stance once more, the Visgaer pivoted around and lunged at him. Again, Rain waited until the last second and swung his staff down in a hard arc at the top of its head. He was not nearly fast enough. The Visgaer shot its hand up, stopping the staff inches away from its palm. It lashed out with its other hand, flaying open Rain's shirt and cutting three deep gashes in his midsection. Rain groaned, but barely had time to truly feel the wound before the Visgaer tightened its telekinetic grip on his staff and whipped both it and him across the room, slamming him hard against the door. It creaked loudly and Rain sank to the floor, his head swimming.

As he sat there slumped, unmoving, his mind not seizing on anything more than the dancing white orbs in his brief semi-consciousness, he found himself just cognizant enough to notice something interesting. For a moment, the Visgaer looked confused. It turned its head to the left and right, seeming to be looking for something. Then, as Rain moved to stand, it turned immediately and looked straight at him, hissing loudly.

Rain suddenly formed a theory, and he knew just how to test it. He moved again into a ready position and the Visgaer came for him a third time. This time, just before it attacked, Rain sidestepped smoothly but made no move to counter. Instead, he slipped between the nearest bunk bed and the wall and pushed himself back into the corner. He realized immediately that if he was wrong, he might have just gotten himself killed. However, he forced that and every other thought out of his head as he stood perfectly still.

Emptying his mind was easy for him. Because he never truly slept, at least not the way living creatures do, he had long ago trained himself to shut off his thoughts every day when he lay down in his bed. Like his forced breathing, it gave his existence a semblance of human normalcy. There were times when his demons haunted him so fiercely that he was unable to achieve this state no matter how hard he tried. But somehow, in the midst of this battle, he slipped into it seamlessly.

And it worked. The Visgaer stood up straight and suddenly began whipping its head back and forth, looking around like a frantic predator who had just lost sight of its prey. Rain was right. If he remained perfectly still, in mind and body, the Visgaer could not see him. It made perfect sense, really. Its sight relied on perception of movement and thought. Without those, it was blind. He wondered briefly how the thing didn't run into inanimate objects, but when the Visgaer turned on him and hissed, he decided now was not the time to ponder such things.

Though he had given away his position, Rain had still startled the Visgaer, and he seized the opportunity. Bursting from his hiding place, he thrust his staff out hard, connecting with the creature's sternum. It cried out, reeling backwards as Rain rocketed the end of the staff up to crack it under the jaw. The second hit felt softer, more buffered. The Visgaer had blocked it somewhat, but still not completely. It fell on its haunches in the space between the opposite bunk and the wall.

Rain's first instinct was to attack the cornered creature, but he quickly realized that would be a mistake. Its psychic defenses would be back up once again, so now was not the moment to get in close. Instead, he pulled back and dashed to the far end of the room, where he crouched and waited.

He remained still and watched as the Visgaer reached up and wrapped its bony fingers around the corner pole of the bunk bed, then pulled itself back to its feet. It stepped back in line with him, directly in front of the door, and began scanning the room, first to the left, then to the right. It opened and closed its jaw, jagged teeth tapping together and an annoyed clicking sound emanating from its throat.

It looked over the room once more and then suddenly slashed its claws from left to right in a blind swing. Its reach was incredible, probably close to five feet with those talons. It took a step forward and swung at the empty air again with the other hand, hissing angrily when it failed to harm anything but a top bunk mattress, its stuffing popping out and drifting to the floor. Not breathing, not moving, not thinking, Rain remained crouched and waiting.

The Visgaer advanced, one step and one swing at a time.

Step.

Swing.

Step.

Swing.

Still, Rain did not move. He waited with the patience of centuries until the Visgaer was right on top of him, its sharp knees inches from his face. Above him, he heard the swing of the creature's arm and felt dust from its scratch across the wall fall on the back of his coat. Before it had time to let out a screech of anger, Rain swung his staff around at the back of its knees, connecting beautifully. The Visgaer stumbled backwards and fell on its back with a thud. Jumping to his feet, Rain raised his staff high and brought it down as hard as he could towards the creature's face.

It stopped mere millimeters shy of hitting its mark, and in that instant, Rain knew he wouldn't get another shot.

Gripping the end of the staff tightly in one hand, the Visgaer suddenly thrust its other palm upwards, and Rain felt a searing tightness in his chest. He struggled to release a cry, but nothing would come out, and a split second later the Visgaer was on its feet and slamming Rain's back against the wall. Every muscle in his body went simultaneously taut against his will, forced rigid by the creature's telekinetic hold.

The Visgaer moved in close, its blind, bandaged eye sockets coming within inches of Rain's fixed gaze. Its impossibly wide mouth somehow grew wider, turning up into a fanged grin as it hissed in Rain's face, its acrid breath curling around him with the stench of carrion and decay.

He felt it working over his body with its mind. Every single muscle wrenched and turned, burning under the creature's psychic manipulations. He wanted to scream, but he couldn't. No function in his body was under his control. And then, just when he thought the pain was too much to bear, he felt some invisible force begin to bore into his mind.

Rain closed his eyes and felt the world fall away around him. He was still aware of the pain that the Visgaer was inflicting on his body—all too aware—but in his mind he was suddenly transported someplace completely different.

He was back in his own living room, in the house he had built with his bare hands. All the furniture was gone, and the lights were out. The curtains had been thrown open and bright moonlight filtered in, illuminating the room more than enough for him to take stock of the carnage that lay piled at his feet.

Bodies. Scores of them heaped on top of one another all around him. They lined every inch of the floor and were stacked three deep all the way up the staircase. He recognized every one of them. The gutted Catholic bishop. The dissected elderly couple. The skinned pair of twin toddlers. This place and this vision weren't real, but every one of these people had been...and every one had died by his hand.

As he slowly turned and looked downwards, his eyes filling with tears at the sight of every unspeakable thing he had ever done, he issued a small cry when he noticed his freshest victims at the top of the pile.

There was Alex, his side slashed open with a dagger, his dead eyes wide open and staring at Rain in a final pained look that seemed to condemn him for his betrayal.

And there was Lita, her throat torn out, her lovely blonde hair matted with blood, her face a twisted vision of pain and suffering.

Then reality rushed back in around Rain, and when his eyes opened, they glowed deep, furious violet.

The Visgaer's grin disappeared as it felt its grip loosening. Straining every muscle in his body, Rain focused all his will on his hands, forcing them to move despite the crushing strength of the Visgaer's hold on him. Those hands were still wrapped firmly around his staff, and inch by inch he took them back into his own power, just enough to move the tip of the staff under the Visgaer's chin.

In the last second, the Visgaer must have sensed Rain's intentions, as its hollow eyes seemed to widen just before Rain twisted his hands and the staff's blade jutted up into the creature's skull.

Rain sighed as he felt the monster's psychic hold fall away just as hot blood poured over his hands. With a grimace, he tossed the scrawny thing aside. It slid off his staff and fell to the floor in a heap. Rain snatched a blanket from one of the beds and quickly wiped off his hands and staff, then headed for the door.

In the hallway, he pocketed his dagger retrieved from the door, but kept his staff at the ready as he broke into a quick jog, intent on catching up to Lita and putting an end to this whole thing.

TWENTY-EIGHT

I

Lita grumbled to herself as she strode down the hallway. She wondered just what the fuck he was thinking, locking himself in a room with that fucking thing. Even after he had pushed her out, she had tried to go back in, but the door wouldn't budge. She had stood outside that door for nearly a minute before forcing herself to move in the other direction. Waiting around wouldn't do either of them any good, and she had to guess, hope, or believe that Rain hadn't survived such a ridiculously long time by getting himself into situations he wasn't sure he could get out of.

Still, she was frantic with worry about him, and she didn't like that sensation one goddamn bit.

She had passed the door they'd entered through a little ways back, and with every step she took around the curvature of this corridor, she was more and more sure she'd come upon the doorway to the inner arena. She hadn't actually been walking that long—a minute at the most—but the repetition of the torches on the wall was driving her insane.

Finally, Lita saw dim moonlight illuminating the hallway

362

up ahead. She stepped more quietly but kept up a steady jog until she came around the bend to find a wide doorway that led into the Construct's arena. Five feet away, she slowed her pace and crept up to the edge of that doorway, seeming to feel every pebble under her boots as she walked. She pressed her shoulder against the wall, brushed her hair out of her eyes, and tightened her grip on her handgun as she slowly peered around the corner.

She only peeked out for a fraction of a second, then quickly drew back. It was more than enough to get a feel for what she was up against. Cleric was the first thing she noticed, standing a few feet from the center of the arena with shotgun in hand, apparently monitoring her entrance and the one across the way simultaneously. She didn't see Amelie anywhere, and she didn't get a look at the moon, but she knew time must be running short. Alex looked like a sacrificial lamb strung up crucifixion-style with who she assumed must be Michael standing just a few feet away from him. She couldn't tell if he had been wearing any gauntlet, but she knew she had to act fast. If he got a chance to use it, she'd be the only one left alive.

She wished Rain was there. Not that he'd be much help. He didn't even have a gun, the fucker. Still, she wished he was there. But she didn't have time to wait for him.

She slipped her handgun into the back of her belt and pulled the automatic rifle from her shoulder. It only had twelve rounds in it—she had checked hours ago—but it was something. Closing her eyes, she released a soft sigh through her nose as she tried to steady her nerves. She thought of all the things she was going to get after this was done. A hot meal, a tall drink, and a nice, long shower…possibly with some company. Her cheeks burned at the thought. That would be just fine by her.

Her eyes snapped back open.

Time to work.

She pushed off the wall, stepped into the doorway, and started shooting. She kept the spread of her fire tight as the rifle blew through rounds in a series of explosions which seemed to overlap as they bounded off the corridor walls. So sudden was her attack that Cleric didn't even budge until the second bullet had left the gun, but then he didn't dawdle. He dove for cover behind one of the altar's tall stone slabs, squeezing off a near-blind blast from his shotgun just before disappearing from sight. The boom of the shot echoed loudly across the arena and chunks of rock rained down in front of Lita from where the slug hit just above the doorway. Michael took even longer to react, but once he realized what was happening, he scrambled behind the pillar to Cleric's right.

"Hoo, fuck!" Lita said excitedly to herself after she dashed the rest of the way across the doorway. She pulled the rifle clip briefly, then reinserted it with a click. Four rounds left. She waited for a moment, listening for any signs of movement.

She couldn't help but smile when the next thing she heard was Alex's voice calling, "Lita, is that you?"

"You fucking know it, kid! You okay?" she hollered back.

"I'm fine, but watch out! You hit Cleric in the leg, but he's not hurt badly. He has that gun, but Michael only has a sword and a dag—*aagh*!"

Lita felt her stomach drop. "Alex?"

"I'm okay. Cleric threw a rock at me."

"Don't sweat it, kid. I'll kill him for you here in just a minute."

"Is that so, young lady?" Cleric's voice boomed.

"You're goddamn right, old man! You're outgunned. So long as I stay back here, you'll never tag me with that shotgun!"

Cleric let out a bellow of laughter. "You're forgetting my

lessons! Never get in a standoff unless you have time to kill! I can sit here all night, but your little friends only have about ten minutes to live!"

Lita clenched her jaw as her mind raced. He was right. She didn't have time for this. "I guess I'll just have to kill the kid!"

Alex and Cleric's voices both came in unison, "What?"

"Alex, listen to me! If Michael goes through with this thing, it won't just kill you, but also every nonhuman and Gifted on Earth, including Rain and Amelie. If I kill you, it'll save them and thousands of other people! Do you understand?"

"You have to stop her," Michael hissed. Cleric waved for him to shut up.

There was a pause. "Y-Yes," Alex said, barely loud enough for Lita to hear him.

"I'm sorry, kid! I wish there was another way!"

"It's okay," Alex yelled shakily. "It's not your fault. Just tell Rain…"

"I will, kid! And don't worry, I'll make it quick!"

"Okay."

"Are you ready?"

Another pause. "Yes."

"Cleric!" Michael urged.

"Lita, stop!" Cleric yelled.

"I'm a little busy here, Cleric!"

"Come now, young lady! Surely you're not too busy to talk business! Michael here has—"

"Save your breath, Cleric! You couldn't offer me enough!"

"What about the fight you really want?"

Lita smirked. It was working. "Go on!"

"We both throw our guns away and you come out and face me! If you win, the children are yours!"

"What are you doing?" Michael whispered.

"Shut your mouth," Cleric shot back. "This is the only way to buy you enough time to do what you need to do."

"How do you know she's not bluffing?"

"She doesn't bluff. I trained her better than that."

"You've got a deal, Cleric!" Lita yelled. "You first!" Leaning over, she peeked around the corner just long enough to assess Cleric's hiding place. A moment later, his shotgun came flying out from behind the pillar, landing in the dirt several feet away.

Lita stepped out into the arena then, rifle still drawn. "Now give me one good reason why I should drop mine!"

"What have you done?" Michael whispered.

"Michael, do us all a favor and shut the fuck up," Cleric replied. "Oh, you'll toss it away, Lita, because I've still got a knife in my hand, and you know good and well I can kill the boy with it and not have to step foot out from behind this stone! You may be willing to kill him, but I know you won't pass up a chance to save him!"

Lita lowered her eyes and considered this for a moment, then stood up straight and tossed the rifle, followed by her trusty handgun. "So how do you want to do this?" She glanced up at the moon. Only a tiny sliver of white was still visible against the creeping red shadow. She was going to have to make this fast.

II

Cleric rose from his hiding spot and rounded the stone pillar to face Lita from about thirty yards away. Even from here she could see that malicious grin on his fucking face. "Why don't you decide, young lady? Your years of service have earned you a proper severance. How would you like to die? Hand to hand?"

"Ha!" Lita laughed. "You wish. You're as big as a fucking truck, you asshole." She retrieved a combat knife from her boot. "We'll settle this like we're in a Maple City alley."

Cleric chuckled and held up his large buck knife. It was almost twice the size of Lita's blade. She didn't give a fuck.

"Ready when you are, teacher."

"Then by all means, come to the front of the class."

Lita broke into a dead sprint, rushing for Cleric. She reached the altar in seconds and passed within feet of Alex as she closed in on her old mentor. But she wasn't stupid. She knew there was no way she could take him head on. Just a few feet away, she dropped into a slide on the bare earth, and her blade slit a clean six-inch gash in his calf as she passed by. She finished off the slide in a roll and quickly bounded to her feet, turning on her opponent and hopping back to put some distance between them.

It was a good thing she did, too. As soon as she got Cleric back in her sights, he was rushing at her, bellowing with rage, seemingly unaware of the wound she had just given him. He swung his knife towards her neck, and she ducked and sidestepped, moving her own blade in an arc towards his side. She felt it connect, but knew she had done little more than flay open his coat.

As they turned to face each other again, Lita was grinning from ear to ear. Cleric didn't look nearly so happy. "I'd almost forgotten how fast you are," he growled. "There's a reason you were always my favorite."

"Well then, who better to finish you off than your best student?"

Cleric snarled and rushed at her again.

III

As the two of them went at it, Michael emerged from his own hiding place. Once he was sure the woman was completely distracted, he hurried over to the wooden chest, fumbling to get hold of the key on his rosary.

"She's going to kill him and then come over and do the same to you, you know," Alex said calmly.

"Shut your mouth," Michael muttered without looking up.

"I think she's almost done. You should probably hurry," Alex said.

"I said shut up!" Michael screamed, turning towards him this time. "Just shut your mouth, demon! In just a few seconds, I will—"

Michael cried out in fright as something hit the wooden box and knocked it right off the pedestal. It fell to the ground, and he looked down to see that there was a small knife sticking out of it. Looking back up, his eyes widened at the sight of Rain sprinting straight for him.

Moving with surprising fluidity, Michael drew his rapier and raised it for a high block, stopping Rain's staff mid swing as he tried to bring it down on the young man. Sidestepping, Michael dashed back a couple of steps and dropped into an *en garde* stance.

Rain actually looked somewhat impressed. "You've done this before."

"I've been the Chicane Academy champion since I was nine years old," Michael said. "It's only fair that you know."

Lowering into a fighting position himself, Rain raised his staff. "Ever done it with a real sword?"

Michael swallowed, but his gaze did not waver. "It's no different."

"We'll see," Rain said, and then lunged forth, aiming his blade straight for Michael's midsection.

IV

"You look like you're getting tired, old man," Lita said with a chuckle. As Rain entered the arena and began facing off with Michael, Cleric was looking a bit worse for the wear. While Lita had sustained a flesh wound across her upper arm, she had delivered a much deeper gash to Cleric's hip in the process. He was presently favoring his right leg and breathing heavily.

"Just getting started," Cleric growled.

"You sure? You don't look so good. Tell you what, the door's right over there. Throw your knife down and I'll let you walk out of it. I won't kill you as soon as you turn around or anything, assassin's honor." She was grinning broadly, enjoying this more than a little bit.

"You little bitch," Cleric spat. "I made you what you are. I can unmake you just the same."

"By all means, show me," Lita said. He was already moving by the time she was halfway through her sentence, but she wasn't the least bit surprised. As he thrust his knife out in a straight shot for her throat, Lita sidestepped, grabbed his forearm with her right hand, and plunged her knife into his armpit with her left.

Cleric dropped his knife and let out a loud bellow of pain, but as Lita moved to retrieve her knife, she found he had grasped her hand tight, squeezing it painfully around the handle of her blade. She tried to pull away, but as soon as she did, he moved with her and yanked the knife from himself with a grunt, then abruptly twisted her arm downward. She felt a tearing flash of pain in her wrist, but it was immediately dwarfed as Cleric forced her to bury her own knife hilt-deep in her inner thigh, just below her crotch.

V

True to his word, Michael was proving himself to be an expert swordsman. Rain's speed and experience were to his advantage, but Michael's form was nearly flawless, and his weapon was far better designed for the contest. Though

Rain could block most any attack with the long staff, only the end of it could easily deal a lethal blow. Michael had over three feet of blade to work with.

But when Rain heard Lita's scream of agony and looked over to see her collapse to the ground and Cleric stumbling away, he tried to break away from Michael and rush to her aid. The young man was quick, and he sidestepped in front of Rain, intent on finishing the contest.

"I don't have time for this," Rain snarled, and as Michael thrust forward, Rain actually moved into the attack, allowing the length of the blade to penetrate straight through his shoulder, all the way to the hand guard.

Michael just blinked. "That's cheating..." he said quietly. Confused, he released his sword, leaving it embedded in Rain's shoulder as he stumbled backwards. Doing so, he felt Rain's own blade slide out of his chest. He looked down and touched his wound, utterly perplexed by the sight of his own blood. In that moment, Rain thought how Michael looked like little more than a child and realized that he must have never once thought it could possibly come to this. Michael dropped to his knees and said wistfully, "...I was supposed...supposed to be..." and then he fell to his side, the life already gone from his eyes before his head hit the ground.

Rain yanked the sword from his shoulder with a grunt as he ran across the arena towards Lita. Dropping both weapons, he knelt down next to her. She was crying, grasping for the knife, but he grabbed her hands to stop her. "Do not pull it out, it might be keeping you alive. Just put pressure on it and stay put." He pulled off his coat as he glanced over to see Cleric moving towards the center of the altar, stumbling like a drunk. "I'll deal with him."

"Yes, please kill that motherfucker!" Lita groaned through gritted teeth.

"I intend to," Rain said, already on his feet and headed

that way.

VI

Thinking that Cleric was heading for Alex, Rain swung wide in his approach so as to put himself between the two. By the time he realized his mistake, it was already too late. Cleric had Michael's wooden box under his arm and was breaking it open with Rain's own knife. Rain started towards him, but froze in his tracks as Cleric pulled the gauntlet from the box and tugged it on.

"Oh, God," Cleric gasped as the runes on the glove began to glow bright white. He shoved Rain's throwing knife into his belt and marveled at the sensations flowing through his body. Suddenly, all of his wounds had stopped hurting. Standing up straight, he glared at Rain and backed a few steps away. "That kid wasn't kidding when he said this thing gave you power."

Rain said nothing, only held his ground. He was acutely aware that they had reached dawn, and while there was still some time until he was in any real danger of direct exposure, he could already feel the ambient light beginning to slow his body and dull his senses. That was the last thing he needed right now.

"I no longer have any reason to fight any of you," Cleric said. "Allow me to walk out of here and this ends now."

Rain gave him a short nod. "I'd advise against ever crossing paths with us again."

Cleric chuckled and continued backing away, unwilling to turn his back on his opponents even until the last. However, about halfway to the coliseum door, he stopped in his tracks and suddenly took on a thoughtful look. He glanced up at the lightening sky where the red veil had just begun to recede from the moon's pale face. "Lita…"

"What?" She said in a strained voice from her place on

the ground.

"Tell me, what did I always teach you about loose ends?"

Her eyes widened. "Cleric don't!"

Even as she said it, Cleric was already raising his arm. Michael had told him that using the gauntlet was purely instinctual once you put it on, and he was surprised at how true that really was. Suddenly, its runes flared up almost blinding white and a burst of energy erupted forth from its palm—and headed straight for Alex.

Alex saw the deadly energy coming towards him. He felt his heart lurch in his chest and his stomach turn into a terrified knot, despite everything his brother had taught him about fearlessness in the face of danger. He was still, after all, only a boy. In that final instant, he could only close his eyes and wait for what was coming.

A moment later, through his closed eyelids, Alex saw a burst of white light. But he felt nothing. When he opened his eyes, all he saw was Rain's face, so close to his own. Time seemed to stand still as he took in his brother's pale skin, perfect but for the deep red scar he had earned killing the man who had tormented them both. He saw in the sea of Rain's blue eyes, filled with centuries of knowledge, an endless swell of brotherly love…and incredible, unbearable pain. Barely above a whisper, Rain said, "I love you, big brother."

And then he fell to the ground.

"No!" Alex screamed, but there was nothing he could do. The gauntlet's energy was already starting to take over Rain's body. An ember appeared on his chest, burning through from his back, and began to spread in an expanding ring, leaving nothing behind but ash. No words could describe his pain. All he could do was turn his head to gaze at Lita, so near, yet just out of his reach.

Lita's eyes filled with fresh tears as she realized what Rain had done for his brother. Everything made her want to curl into a ball, to close her eyes, to pretend this wasn't happening. She wanted to awaken in Moonshadow Manor to the smell of cooking breakfast. She wanted to open the door knowing he was standing just outside in the hallway. She wanted to let him finish what he had to say on the bluffs over the Blacklands.

But she couldn't go back, she couldn't go to sleep. She could only stare into his eyes from the closest she would ever get to him again and softly say, "I see what kind of man you are."

Even through all the pain that was blocking out everything else, Rain heard her. He heard her, and his lips turned up into a smile that didn't disappear until his body burned up completely and everything he was fell away.

And Rain was gone.

VII

Halfway across the arena, Amelie, who had been forced to helplessly watch all of this play out, sat bound to that post, tears streaming down her face.

Lita's mind was blank except for a swelling rage telling her to get her hands on a weapon, any weapon. She was about ten seconds from pulling this knife from her own leg and going after Cleric with it.

Cleric, meanwhile, looked down at the gauntlet to find that all the light had gone out of it. His brow furrowing, he shook it, but nothing happened. "I guess I'll have to finish the rest of you the old-fashioned way." He scanned his eyes about until they landed on his shotgun, and he started that way.

But he stopped after only two steps and blinked at what was suddenly happening all around him.

There was a low noise coming from seemingly everywhere at once, so deep that it was just barely audible. It was as though something was slowly stirring the very air inside the arena. Loose stones that littered the ground here and there began to tremble. Just a little at first, then more noticeably. Then, some of the smallest rocks actually began to levitate a few inches off the ground. The air grew dry, ionized. Cleric looked down and saw the fine hairs on his forearm begin standing on end.

Then, the very light around them seemed to somehow dim, as if the low morning sun had slipped behind a fog bank. But as Cleric turned around he saw that there, in the middle of it all, Alex had begun to glow. A radiant violet aura appeared all around him, and in it he was hanging there, eyes clenched shut, chest heaving wildly.

As the others looked on in frozen awe, Alex opened his eyes. They burned such a brilliant violet that his whole face was illuminated, making him appear otherworldly—and completely out of his mind. Then he took in a single deep breath, and with an enraged scream, let loose all of that building energy.

The shockwave crossed the arena in less than a second, creating a deafening explosion. Dust and rocks flew up in every direction. Lita rolled to her side, throwing her arms up to shield her face. Cleric stumbled and fell to the ground. The post Amelie was tied to actually ripped free of the ground and came back down on its side, splintering. She smacked her head on the ground, but she also felt her hands come loose of their bonds.

The Construct took the brunt of the blast. Two of its pillars cracked, collapsing. Two others fell over with booms like giant dominos, one of them mere feet from Lita. And there in the center, the cuffs around Alex's wrists suddenly shattered, and he dropped to his feet, fiery eyes set on Cleric.

Lita uncovered her eyes in time to see Alex sprint across the arena. She had never seen a human being move so fast.

When Alex reached him, Cleric was trying to get back to his feet, but he had no time to do anything other than throw up his hands in a weak defense.

Alex grabbed the gauntlet with one hand and crushed it with ease, the metal crumpling and shattering nearly every bone in Cleric's hand. He screamed, but the sound was cut off by Alex's fist barreling into his mouth, knocking out four of his teeth and sending him sprawling in the dirt. Alex pulled the destroyed gauntlet free from Cleric's hand as he fell and threw it aside.

But he didn't stop there. Still fueled by incomprehensible rage, he advanced on Cleric again. Grabbing him by the collar of his coat, Alex began pummeling him, punching him in the face over and over. Cleric coughed, beginning to choke on his own blood.

Finally, Alex yanked the man who was better than twice his size off his feet like he was nothing and glared up at him with eyes that seemed to have traded in all traces of sanity for pure, unbridled fury. Drawing back his fist, he prepared to deliver a final blow. But before he could, Cleric pulled Rain's knife from his belt and swung it at Alex's side.

Alex had seen that move before. He had thought about it dozens of times while falling asleep at night, asking himself what he could have done differently. It had become so ingrained that when the opportunity came once more, he acted completely on instinct. Dropping his arm, he moved it into the path of the dagger. The blade sank deep into his forearm, stopping it before it hit his side.

Oblivious to the pain in his cloud of anger, Alex dropped Cleric, yanked the knife free from his own arm, and buried it in the man's stomach.

Cleric gasped, his jaw opening and closing twice. He fell to his knees, clutching at his abdomen. Alex took a step back then, and, as quickly as it had come on, the rage and all its energy fell away from him. His world began to spin.

Amelie, finally having wriggled loose from her bonds, was running across the arena towards Lita. When she arrived, Lita pointed to Cleric's shotgun some ten feet away. She knew it wasn't over until Cleric was dead. "Go. Get the gun," she ordered.

Though Cleric had dropped to his knees, he hadn't fallen completely. He was doubled over, his back rising and falling heavily. Alex stumbled backwards and his feet caught each other, bringing him down hard on his rear. He stared at Cleric, waiting for the large man to topple over.

But like some nightmare beast that could not be vanquished, Cleric refused to stop. Turning bloodshot eyes up towards Alex, he grabbed the knife protruding from his stomach, yanked it out with a grunt, and began crawling towards the young man.

Alex gasped, trying to push himself away. But his limbs were so shaky he could barely move. He tried to scoot himself backwards, but his head was spinning so bad that he could hardly keep his eyes on Cleric, let alone regain a sense of direction. And the man was getting closer. From behind the long strands of silver hair partially obscuring his face, Alex saw his mouth turn up into a wide, murderous grin. Blood poured over what remained of his teeth and soaked the handkerchief under his chin. He was getting closer and closer, his eyes wide and utterly mad, knife grasped tightly in his hand. He was nearly at Alex's feet now. In a raspy voice, he croaked, "I can...still...kill...you..."

Amelie had just reached the shotgun and snatched it up. When she turned around, her eyes darted between Lita and Alex.

Lita was waiting with outstretched hand and yelled, "Amelie!"

Gripping the gun tightly, Amelie prepared to throw it. Just before she let it fly, something inside her told her what to do. She screamed, "Alex!" and tossed the gun straight at him.

Somehow in spite of his dizziness, Alex reached up on instinct and caught the shotgun just as Cleric was raising the dagger over his stomach. Without thinking, he shoved the barrel of the gun in Cleric's face and pulled the trigger.

The blast rang in Alex's ears and he felt a shock of pain in his shoulder followed by a crushing weight as Cleric's headless corpse fell on top of him. He groaned and struggled to slide out from under the large body. It took him a moment, but when he finally wriggled free he shakily climbed to his feet and stumbled over to where Amelie had knelt down next to Lita.

"We did it," Amelie said quietly.

"Yeah, we did," Lita said. "Nice shooting, kid." It was all she could think to say.

"Huh?" Alex said, then looked dazedly to the shotgun still in his hand. "Oh…yeah." He held it out to Lita, but she waved dismissively.

"It's yours now," she said.

"I…I've never shot a gun before," Alex said.

"It's the easiest thing in the world," Lita replied.

Alex nodded, then blinked and looked around slowly, as if waking up from a dream. His eyes began to fill with tears, and they trembled as he looked over to the spot where his brother had disappeared. His whole body began to shake. He dropped the shotgun and whispered, "Rain…" before collapsing in a heap next to Lita.

TWENTY-NINE

"Alex!" Amelie gasped worriedly, rushing to his side.

"He'll be alright," Lita said hoarsely. "He's just taken a beating. We need to get the hell out of here so we can get patched up."

"Let me see what I can do to help first," Amelie said. "Lie back."

Lita eyed her warily.

"I'll leave your scars, just let me keep you from bleeding to death, okay?" Amelie said. "I don't want all of my friends dying tonight."

Lita blinked, then nodded and obeyed. "Friends?"

"Well, what else should I call you?" Amelie asked as she moved over by Lita's legs and untied the last remnants of rope from her own wrists.

"I dunno," Lita replied, "I've just never had much in the way of friends, especially not royal ones."

"Don't worry, it'll have its perks. I'll see that you two receive the best possible care at the Chicane Hospital. Now be quiet for a moment, I need to concentrate." As she spoke, Amelie tore open the fabric on Lita's pants, exposing the knife still buried in her leg. Gingerly placing one hand around the spot that the blade was penetrating, she grabbed the hilt of the knife with the other, and then closed her eyes.

Turning her head to the side, Lita looked over to the empty spot where Rain had departed. As she did, her vision began to shimmer at the edges. There was nothing left. Nothing to bury, nothing to mourn. She was just...

"...alone," Lita whispered.

"What?" Amelie said absently as she opened her eyes and watched the white glow begin to flow from her hand and around the blade of the knife. Very slowly, she started to pull the knife out as she closed the wound around it.

"He left me alone," Lita said in a cracked voice.

Amelie's brow furrowed as she forced herself to go deeper and push harder than she ever had. She'd never attempted to heal a wound this severe. Finally, she was able to pull the knife free, eliciting a gasp from Lita. She quickly tossed it aside and covered the wound with both hands. Beneath them, the ragged flesh started to slowly close. Lita sighed as the pain gradually began to subside.

Then, suddenly, the energy disappeared back inside Amelie's hands and she fell backwards, her chest heaving, her eyes wide. "Oh God..." she whispered.

Sitting up, Lita said, "What? Oh God what?" She looked down. Though her leg was not completely healed, it was far better off than it had been two minutes ago. It would still need some serious medical attention, but she would probably be able to stand. She looked back to Amelie, confused. "What is it?"

"You..." Amelie gasped, "You're not alone."

Lita gave her a perplexed look. "What are you talking ab—"

Then Alex coughed and moaned, rolling onto his side and curling into a ball, cradling his heavily bleeding arm against his chest. They both looked at him worriedly.

"You got anything left in you for him?" Lita asked.

"I think so, yes," Amelie replied.

"Good, go to it," Lita said, then groaned as she pushed herself to her feet. She limped over to Rain's staff a few feet away and picked it up, collapsed it, and slid it into her belt. She then looked around, searching for something.

There it was, a dozen feet away. It had blown away in Alex's outburst and nearly been covered by dirt. Moving as quickly as her aching leg would allow, she walked over to Rain's coat and picked it up. She brushed the dirt off it as best she could, then brought its collar to her face and inhaled deeply. She felt her chest tighten, and fresh tears sprung up in her eyes. With a sigh, she turned around and headed back towards Alex and Amelie.

"Is he ready to go?" Lita asked.

"As ready as he can be," Amelie replied. "I couldn't do as much as with you, but he should be okay until we reach a hospital."

Lita nodded. She knelt down, slipped her arms under Alex, and groaned as she hoisted him up, cradling him against her as she stood.

"Be careful," Amelie warned. "Your leg could still tear open. Do you want me to help you?"

"I've got him."

"At least let me take that coat."

"No. I've got it. Just grab the shotgun there and my handgun by the door and let's get out of here." Amelie nodded and did as she was told, walking next to Lita in case she needed any support.

On their way out, Amelie paid the arena one last look. "I'll send people down here to make sure this whole thing is demolished." Lita nodded in agreement.

It took them a while, Lita having to stop to catch her breath a few times, but they finally made it out of the coliseum. She laid Alex on the ground and had Amelie stay with him while she commandeered Cleric's car to get her out to where they had parked Rain's—if it even was Rain's car anymore. But who else's would it be?

When Lita returned, Amelie helped her place Alex in the back seat.

"I'll sit in the back and watch over him," Amelie said as she headed around to the other side.

"Good call," Lita replied, and watched as she climbed in the back seat and placed Alex's head in her lap. Lita shook her head, amazed at how much Amelie had grown between the two times she'd tried to kill her. Now, despite all that had happened, Lita was fortunate enough to count her as an ally or even, as she had put it, a friend. It almost felt like atonement.

Almost.

Settling into the driver's seat, Lita placed Rain's coat on the passenger side and got the car rolling. She sighed, feeling the weight of the last few days trying to settle in on her shoulders but knowing there was no way she could really let it all come down. Not yet. Not here. She had to get Alex somewhere to be seen; she maybe even had to be seen herself. Then, sometime after that, when she was alone and maybe halfway through a good bottle of vodka, she could let it loose. She could open the floodgates. And oh God would those waters flow.

Behind her, she heard Alex stir and groan.

"We're alive," he said weakly.

"Yeah, kid. We're alive," Lita replied.

"But...but Rain..." Alex whispered.

"He saved your life," Amelie said.

"But if I hadn't..." Alex said.

"No," Lita said firmly. She grabbed the rearview mirror and tilted it so she could see him. "Don't do that. You didn't do anything wrong. Today, yesterday, or a year ago. None of this was your fault."

Tears were streaming down Alex's cheeks, cutting clean lines in the dust that covered his face. He sniffled. "But I'm alone. I've never been alone."

Amelie looked up to Lita, who stared back at them for a long moment, then turned her gaze down to Rain's coat. Reaching out, she placed her hand on it softly, feeling its aged, battered leather against her palm.

"You're not alone," Lita said. "You've got me, kid. I'm not going anywhere."

And the truth was, she wasn't. For longer than she could remember, Lita had never known exactly where she was going. Always uncertain of the next job, the next meal, or the next place to sleep—she hadn't stopped moving for more than half her life. Now she had a home to go to. She had friends to be with there. So many things in her life were still unsure, unclear. But for the first time, she felt certain about one thing. She was where she was supposed to be.

FIFTH INTERLUDE

Close thine eyes now, my sweet love

Thou art watched by stars above

In moonlight shadow, troubles cease

Come morrow's dawn, thou shall find peace

Centuries had passed since his death, and he saw everything.

In this place, no mortal constraints held sway. He never aged past his young eleven years. His blue eyes never tired. His blond hair never grew. He never yearned for food or drink. He was never cold. He was never bored. He was never in pain.

But he could still feel, and sadness pervaded his entire existence.

He had been reminded countless times that he could have anything his heart desired if only he left the Room of Attachment. There were limitless feasts of every food imaginable. Vast oceans to swim in that never grew stormy nor saw the chill of winter. There were infinite trees to climb, endless days of eternal summer to bask in, and whatever else he could possibly dream of.

But he would not leave this room.

He had been told the room was different for everyone. Some were comfortably furnished with luxurious sofas and the action played out on a stage. Some were simple grass huts with bare walls and dirt floors, and the images came in a fire burning at their center. Some had no room at all, and the watchers just floated above everything they saw.

In his, the only things that remained static were him, sitting cross-legged, and the large circular pool before him. Everything was displayed in its shimmering surface. Around him, the walls constantly shifted in shape and color. Sometimes they swirled furious shades of red. Occasionally they were streaked with stark, hopeful beams of white. But more often than not, they slowly dripped black and rippled deep, dark blue. Those were the colors of his grief.

Today, those dark shades were everywhere. His eyes almost never left the pool any time, but on this day he was utterly transfixed. He didn't even look up when his guide entered.

"I'm not leaving."

"You say that to me every time I come to you," his guide replied, "but for the first time, you are wrong."

The deviation from established routine was enough to cause the boy to break his gaze. He turned his eyes towards his guide and blinked in surprise. For countless years the guide had come to him monthly and only ever displayed casual acceptance of his determination to stay.

"What did you say?" the boy asked. Though he was intrigued, his eyes moved back to the pool before he had even finished his question.

Smiling, the guide approached the boy and sat down next to him. They were nearly the same height, for they had been nearly the same age when they had died. As the boy sat staring intently at the pool, the guide sat staring intently at the boy.

"How is he today?" the guide asked, nodding towards the pool. The boy shook his head sadly.

"Not well. I think he means to kill himself."

"You can see into his mind. Is that what he is thinking about?"

"Yes, but he's thought about that more times than I can count. This time it looks like he might actually do it."

The guide followed the boy's gaze, and together they looked at their view of the world below. There, sitting on the edge of a cliff overlooking a vast forest, was the boy's brother. His black hair hung over eyes rimmed with glassy tears. As they watched, one of those tears fell down the path of the scar that marred the man's left eye. He was gazing at a horizon that was gradually shifting from black to blue. Before long, the sun would rise, and the man believed it would set him free from the pain he had felt and his brother had witnessed for lifetimes.

All around them, the walls began to swirl as trickles of white slipped in amidst the folds of darkness. The guide observed this, then looked back to the boy.

"Tell me what you're thinking," the guide said.

"I want to save him," the boy replied.

"You know we're not allowed to intervene."

"Not from here," the boy said, then looked to his guide firmly. "I want to go back."

The guide frowned, but not in disapproval. It was a look of concern. "Are you aware of what that entails?"

"I know the rules," the boy said. Eagerness was beginning to creep into his voice, and the walls were starting to swirl faster, more and more white pouring into them. "After two hundred years, any person who wishes to return may do so. I've been here a lot longer than that."

"That is not all there is to it," the guide said.

"What else is there?" the boy inquired. He kept glancing at the pool, but he was gradually allowing the guide to have more and more of his attention.

"Two centuries is the time requirement, yes, but the rule is meant to go hand-in-hand with the Room of Attachment. You have not fulfilled the purpose of this place."

"How is that?" the boy asked, his brow furrowing. "I've spent more time here than anyone ever has."

"That is exactly my point," the guide replied. "The room is meant to give you a place in which to let go of everything that ties you to the world. The time spent here is different for everyone. I have seen people tarry less than an hour, and I have seen some linger long enough to watch their great-grandchildren grow old and die. But yours is a singular case. No one has ever remained here longer than a century and a half, let alone so long past the required term of stay. No one has ever held a connection to something that long."

"That gives me a better reason than anyone to go back."

"Quite the opposite. You have not seen what this place has to offer beyond this room. You cannot fathom what you would be giving up."

"I don't have a choice," the boy said, nodding towards the pool. "He's my brother. I can't turn a blind eye to him. I can go back, I can help him. Then, someday, he and I can both take the grand tour together."

"No, you cannot," the guide said slowly.

The boy looked at him and blinked. "What do you mean?"

"If you leave this place and continue your mortal life from the moment you left off, someday you will die once again. When that happens, you will not be allowed to return here."

"Then…where will I go?"

"I do not have the answer to that question." It was the first time the guide had ever said that to the boy, so he felt compelled to elaborate. "Just as only those who have been here can comprehend what it is, only those who have been elsewhere can comprehend that."

"I don't think I understand," the boy said.

"Is this place at all like you dreamed it would be when you were alive?" the guide asked.

The boy looked around for a moment, as if he were somehow unfamiliar with the room he had been sitting in for centuries. "No, I guess not."

"Then whatever other place—or places—await those who do not come here cannot be imagined any more accurately."

"But...now I know what this place is. If I go back, I can tell him. I can give him something to be hopeful for. A reason to try to come here, even if I can't."

The guide shook his head. "The living are incapable of bearing knowledge of this place. Upon your return, you will forget every moment you spent here. To you, it will seem as though only an instant has passed since your death."

The boy looked down at the pool thoughtfully. "That'll be confusing."

"I imagine so," the guide replied. "But upon your second death, you will remember once more. You will remember, and you will exist forever elsewhere, knowing what you gave up. Would you sentence yourself to an uncertain eternity for him?"

"He's my brother," the boy repeated. "I gave my life for him. What more is an eternity?"

"Quite a lot, actually."

The boy looked up suddenly, youthful curiosity filling his eyes. A splash of green danced across the walls. "How do you know so much more than I do? I've been here longer than you."

The guide smiled. "In the Room of Attachment, time flows as it does in life. Outside these walls, it moves differently. I've had millennia to learn everything this place can teach. You cannot imagine what awaits you if you step out of this room with me."

It was the boy's turn to smile. "You're going to try to persuade me right until the last moment, aren't you?"

"'Warn' would be a more appropriate word."

"Warn? Warn me of what? You don't think he'd hurt me, do you? I mean, I know what he did to you, but after that he…"

The guide held up a hand and shook his head. "No. I am well aware of the change my death brought about in him. In fact, if you go back, I know exactly how far he will go to protect you…as well as everything that will happen as a result."

"Are…are you saying you can see what will happen to him if I go back? You can see whether or not I help him?"

"I can."

"Can you show me?"

The guide was silent for some time. When he finally spoke again, he sounded almost fearful. "If God spoke to you one day and told you that when the final battle comes, it will not be a war between demons and angels, but rather a single fight between two humans…two children with warring hearts of light and dark…would you believe him?"

"I…I don't understand…" the boy said.

The guide rose to his feet. "Stand with me and close your eyes." The boy looked at the pool apprehensively. "I assure you, he will not die in the time it takes for you to see this. You can trust me."

"I know I can," the boy said then looked up. "You've been the only person I've known for so long." he paused briefly "But it hasn't always been you, has it? Before you arrived, I was…"

"Alone," the guide finished. "Only what you allow can exist in this room, and before your brother's heart changed, your turmoil was so great that you would not let anyone near you. Only once I arrived did you begin to feel hope. It is why I was chosen to be your guide."

"And that was all leading up to this?"

"Yes, as this will lead to everything I am about to show you. Now stand and close your eyes."

The boy paid one last glance to the pool, then nodded and did as he was told. At first, there was nothing but blackness. Then, he felt his guide's fingertips touch him lightly on the forehead.

In an instant, he saw everything that was to come.

He gasped sharply, his eyes shot open, and he stumbled backwards, falling onto his rear. He began to tremble. All around them, the walls erupted in a violent riptide of deep purple.

"That's what will happen?" the boy cried. "That's what will happen if I go back?"

The guide nodded.

The boy scrambled to his feet. "Then show me what will happen if I don't go! I need to know if it would be better if I didn't!"

"I cannot," the guide said calmly.

"What? Why?" the boy demanded.

"I can only see futures that are possible, and there are none in which you do not return."

"That doesn't make any sense! If I was going to go anyway, and I'm just going to forget, why did you show me?"

"Because it was not meant to dissuade you."

"Then what was it for?"

"To make you resolute. Because you believe you can change what I've shown you, and nothing I say will alter that belief."

The boy's eyes dropped and moved slowly over to the pool. Below, his brother sat awaiting death, completely unaware of what was about to begin.

"Are you ready?" the guide asked.

"Almost…" the boy said.

"You have a final question."

He did, and even though he knew he wouldn't recall the answer after leaving this place, he couldn't depart without asking.

"What does my brother have to do to atone for everything he's done?"

The guide looked down and shook his head. "Out of everything I've learned in this place, the answer to that question is the most bitter irony I have ever known."

The boy gave his guide a puzzled look. "What do you mean?"

"Your brother believes he must answer for thousands of deaths, including my own. However, one cannot sin without free will. All the atrocities committed by your brother were the work of a monster inside him. He is not responsible for those acts."

"Are you saying his conscience is clean?"

"No," the guide replied, looking back up slowly. "He committed one murder of his own volition, and it is the only one he will never ask forgiveness for."

The boy's eyes widened and he raised a trembling hand to cover his mouth. But before he could say anything, the guide approached him, placed a hand on his chest, and whispered something to him so profound that, in the instant before he was sent away, the boy almost asked to stay.

It was not like falling. There was darkness and pain and then, suddenly, a blinding burst of light.

And there he was. Trembling, naked, lying on the scorched earth and unaware of how he had gotten there. As the world came into focus around him, the final remnants of where he had been slipped away from him like a splintered dream. He tried to grasp them, but to no avail. As he turned his eyes up to meet the startled, disbelieving gaze of his brother, the last thing his guide had said to him drifted through his mind one final time.

"She's coming. God help you all."